Difficult Husbands

A Christmas tale of family, friends
and new beginnings

'The perfect
Christmas treat'
TRISHA ASHLEY

Mary de Laszlo

Bookouture

Published by Bookouture
An imprint of StoryFire Ltd.
23 Sussex Road, Ickenham, UB10 8PN
United Kingdom
www.bookouture.com

ISBN: 9781909490734
eBook ISBN: 9781909490727

ACKNOWLEDGEMENTS

With many thanks to my agent Judith Murdoch and my editor Claire Bord.

To my family and friends - love always.

PROLOGUE
Christmas in Summer

'Reset.' The director, his hair tied carelessly back in a ponytail, called out, and for the umpteenth time Lorna knocked on the fake front door, complete with Christmas wreath, while an underling, with the rosy face of a mischievous cherub, scattered fake snow at her from above. This tickled her nose and made her sneeze and the director sigh, call 'cut' and the whole take started again.

Christmas, anxiety gripped her, Christmas in summer. If only it was over when this shoot was. Even though it was months away she was dreading the real thing; her first Christmas without Stephen, without even her parents to escape to.

'Reset.' This time it went better. She opened the door and the camera focused on the 'room' conjured up in this stark warehouse. She counted to five while she pretended to be amazed by the magic she saw before her; blazing logs in the fake fireplace, cards hung in streamers among sparkling decorations. There was a show of Christmas fare laid out before her – at least she hadn't had to cook it, the thought scudded through her mind – then the camera wheeled away to groups of happy, happy people toasting each other with pretend champagne. There were some spotless, tidy children behaving so nicely and quietly – a dream Christmas, when in reality it was often hell.

A small girl – pretty in pink – ruined this cheerful scene by tearing the paper off a 'present' only to find a block of polystyrene concealed under the glitzy paper. She howled in disappointment.

Poor little thing, Lorna thought, as her mother scuttled onto the set to retrieve her sobbing child, that is life though, disappointment often lurks under the glitz. She caught the eye of one of the 'happy' people, a woman whose face held remnants of beauty, who'd confided in her before they started shooting that she hated Christmas, her memories of a houseful of cheerful, noisy family celebrations taunting her, now she was alone.

At last it was over, 'a wrap'. Thankfully, Lorna took off her winter clothes, handing them back to the wardrobe girl. She signed her chit, waved goodbye to the others and left, going back into the sunny day, probably the best one of the summer and she'd missed it while she acted out Christmas inside. Being an extra or 'supporting cast' as it was now called, was just another, rather unpredictable way – a fun way, if you didn't count the early starts – of earning money.

It was a strange world of unreality; the commercial she'd just worked on portrayed only the pleasure of Christmas. There was no sign of it being a religious feast, or of unhappiness from a fractured family. It peddled dreams and perhaps spawned resentment in people, most people she'd have thought, especially in these hard times, who'd never achieve such a spectacle.

What would her Christmas be like this year? She could hardly bear to think of it. All those years of special, magical times with her parents and siblings, and continuing it all with her own children. Even when her parents died she had never confronted the fact that there could come a time when she could be alone for Christmas.

Lorna got into her car, hoping she wouldn't get lost going home. These studios were usually stuck out somewhere on an industrial estate and were difficult to find, even sometimes for the Sat Nav. She always headed off hours early for if you were late on set you were sacked – that was it. 'End of,' as her children would say.

Her children, the thought of their pain when Stephen left them brought tears. Marcus said he'd probably go away for Christmas, not able to bear it without his father there, the father as he used to be. Flora slammed a few doors, muttering the same threats. This Christmas she could easily be alone, for the first time in her life, and it terrified her.

CHAPTER ONE
Dumped For An Inferior Model

Lorna's stomach churned like an out of control washing machine as she hovered outside the door to her ex-husband's love nest. There was no make believe here, no fake door opening to reveal a Christmas wonderland as there had been in the publicity shoot she'd done way back in the summer. Christmas now swamped the shops and cluttered up the media, filling her with dread as how it would be this year, the first one without Stephen.

She jabbed at the bell quickly before she lost her nerve, before the ache of her broken heart overwhelmed her. Footsteps clacked on a wooden floor, hesitated, continued, and the door was cautiously opened. A girl stared fearfully at her.

Faced with her in the pallid flesh, Lorna was surprised. This was hardly the sexy siren she'd imagined. 'Hello,' she greeted her sourly. 'I'm Stephen's ex-wife. The horrible woman, who never loved him, never bought up his children or kept the house and his life in order.'

Stephen's 'sex toy', as Lorna thought of her – the only way she could deal with this frightening change in her once kind and dependable husband – was 'bottle blonde' with dark roots and a doughy complexion. She jumped back into the flat as if she were about to be lynched. Lorna crossed the hall in a couple of strides into the living room, tossing the envelope containing Stephen's mail onto a table by the door. The girl followed her, shooting nervous glances at Stephen. He stood rigidly at attention by the pseudo-marble fireplace, his expression like that of a schoolboy caught out with a porn magazine by his mother.

He looked old – and he was – and, sour joke, he had left her for a 'younger' woman, when she, his wife, was far younger than he was in the first place.

'You may not notice the age gap now, darling, but you will in a few years,' her mother warned her, though her eyes had lit up at Stephen's lean and athletic looks. Stephen had weathered well, like an old piece of furniture. He had been much cherished by her, she reminded herself, and it hurt to look at him; so familiar, so loved and yet now so different.

He'd been her boss; they'd been drawn to each other at once, a *coup de foudre*, no less. Early on in their marriage, in her insecure moments, she'd wondered if he might leave her for someone more mature, not so ditzy, who couldn't remember the aftermath of the war, ration books and a young Cliff Richard, because they hadn't been born yet. But to her and everyone's surprise and the children's utter horror, he'd upped and left with someone who could in fact, she glanced at the girl, be not much younger than her, though there was a kind of waif-like look about her that might appeal to a man who seemed to have lost his self-esteem and sense of identity.

Why on earth was she putting herself through this agony? Lorna asked herself. There was no need; until now the post office had presumably re-delivered Stephen's mail successfully, but she'd been hit with a sort of defiance, sick of bundling up his letters and sending them on, letters that had come home when he had not.

Even now, standing here in this drab love nest, its drabness exacerbated by the autumn colours of the trees outside, glided by the October sun, she realised that she still harboured a faint hope that this trauma was just a mad moment, an old age crisis, a nightmare she would wake from, and that he would come back to her. She'd have found him waiting here, the man he used to be, before the shock of losing his job had lured him into the clutches of a dubious shrink and this waif. Seeing he was not, she felt unbalanced and alone. Now she understood why some women, like her dearest friends Gloria and Rosalind, would rather carry on living with the devils they knew, than be alone.

Once they'd been so happy, so madly in love. She *must* not cry; must not stand here snivelling while this new woman in his life looked on. They were divorced, only just but divorced all the same. She still had not come to terms with it or the guilt she felt that she might have been able to prevent it, if she hadn't been so occupied with her new cake business at the time, or questioned more thoroughly his furtive absences from home.

She'd trusted him too much – or some might say taken him for granted – to suspect anything as monumental as this.

To steady her nerves, Lorna concentrated on the room. It was a rented flat in Earl's Court, with coffee-coloured walls, a beige and brown carpet and upholstery; the colour of shit, really. Dull and safe to suit all tastes, except for hers. She wondered what the bedroom was like, and the word stabbed her like a knife.

Stephen didn't look well, hardly a good advertisement for a rampant sex life. Perhaps it wasn't rampant, surely he was past rampant, he had been with her, anyway. Their lovemaking had become cosy, sporadic. She, wondering if he was afraid of impotence, and dared not mention it. She knew from friends that one mention of the dreaded 'I' word was a sure way of seizing up their hydraulic system.

'This is not doing you any good, Lorna.' Even his voice, once so rich and vibrant, sounded tired, and despite everything, it tore at her heart. Perhaps he was stricken by some mortal illness added to whatever happy, solve-everything pills his bloody doctor had prescribed. The man she had loved had been spirited away by a drug pusher hidden under the guise of a sleek, fashionable shrink, although, and this hurt her most of all, he had started to see this girl *before* his mind had been addled by the shrink. He'd met her in a club he'd been taken to by some of his colleagues to cheer him up, on the evening he'd been made redundant. It hurt her to think that this woman possessed something Stephen thought he needed that she, his wife, did not.

'I'm off now. I don't know why I came, perhaps to remind myself that our marriage is really over.' Lorna said, scrutinizing the round face of the girl, whose slightly bulbous eyes reminded her of a Pekinese. All she needed was a squashed nose then she could be entered for Crufts, she thought bitchily. She couldn't remember the girl's name, if she'd ever known it. When Stephen told her he was leaving – pacing round their living room not meeting her eyes – he'd said, 'I've found someone else, she's had a difficult life and needs to be looked after'.

'*I* need to be looked after,' she'd wailed. 'Have you forgotten you promised at the altar that you'd look after me until death us do part?'

'You're different, you're strong and you're so busy now with the shop and … you're never here, always out doing things.' He'd gone on to tell her about this girl's sad life, on and on as if he couldn't help himself and he expected her to understand. It was 'she' this and 'she' that. Perhaps he didn't know her name either, but just felt macho and wanted by someone more vulnerable than himself and, guess what? She needed a visa. Looking at her now, Lorna thought the only thing in this girl's favour was her youth and that was wasted on her.

'None of this is helpful,' Stephen's voice held desperation.

'Helpful to who? Or is it 'whom'?' Lorna challenged him, pain making her harsh. 'It is hardly helpful to your wife and children to walk out on them just to help a complete stranger. Why can't you work for a charity if you want to help people in trouble?'

The girl gasped, her hand clawed in Stephen's direction, as if afraid Lorna might turn her over to some homeless organisation, or contact Immigration and shop her for being illegal, if she was.

'Why did you come, Lorna? You could have sent on my mail, you have before.' He fixed his eyes on some point over her head.

It was the approach of Christmas that had made her wobble, come to 'suss things out' as Marcus would have put it, coupled with a foolish hope that once Stephen had seen her in this dreary flat beside that dreary girl, he would have realised his mistake and been mortified at his out of character behaviour, and, despite their recent divorce, come back home. But she'd been wrong. He seemed devoid of emotion, for her, or the girl. No doubt the happy pills had wiped them out; if you feel nothing, then life is possible.

She would not see Stephen and this girl again, he'd made his choice and it wasn't with her. She had failed him in some way she couldn't fathom but she must accept it and move on. Was there, she wondered, in this competitive society, some sort of kudos at finding your other half enamoured with a glamorous 'sleb' or even royalty, instead of a plain, nondescript person like this one?

Lorna charged down the two flights of stairs to the front door of the block of flats. It smelt stale, of lost hopes, adding to her misery. She hurried out into the street, gulping in the chilly air. How could Stephen have given up their comfortable home life for this? Had he chosen to return here because he remembered that time from his youth when Earl's Court was thought exotic; studded with flats and bed sits, humming with a hotchpotch of races and creeds, all bringing their own rhythm and vitality with them? He'd lived in a huge, draughty flat not far from here and she'd blissfully given her virginity to him there one winter's afternoon. The memory smote her now, bringing the tears that were never far away.

She'd thought that their marriage would only end in death, probably his, as he was so much older than her, twenty and three quarter years, to be exact. Had she been too smug, pulling up the drawbridge on the outside world, not seeing the storm approaching? She was convinced that his early retirement had brought this destruction. Stephen's firm had been taken over and those near retirement made redundant, and he'd never seen it coming, imagining his job was safe. It was a sudden and savage end to his career. Stephen was sixty-three, with two, possibly three more years to go before retirement. Losing his responsible, well-paid job shattered him; he had, as the experts loved to say, 'lost his identity.'

It had been a shock to her too; she had never envisaged such a brutal end to his employment. She'd tried hard to be supportive, to keep her own fears – of less money, and of finding something to keep him occupied – to herself. It hadn't helped that just before he'd lost his job, when life was stable, she'd used most of the money her mother had left her to buy a share in the cake shop with her friend, Martha. It was sod's law that as Stephen lost his job and needed her there to lean on while he adjusted to this massive change in his life, she had become frantically occupied in getting this business off the ground.

At first Lorna was pleased he was there with time to help her to make sense of all the figures and rules and regulations, but he'd become dictatorial. This had upset Martha, who had put in most of the capital, so Lorna had felt she must stop asking for his advice. Perhaps this had made him feel even more unwanted, emasculated even, until he took up with this needy girl and, later, got into the clutches of the Harley Street drug pusher. It was like a bereavement; the man she'd known and loved, and who'd loved her, had gone. His body was still there, he still looked the same, but he was not. She'd heard people describe losing members of their family to dementia in the same way.

She turned into the Earl's Court Road, the smell of a kebab shop reminding her she was hungry. She'd hardly had any breakfast, the thought of seeing Stephen and his new set up had taken away her appetite. But she'd done it, faced it once and for all and must now, difficult though it was, accept that she was a divorced – no, an *independent* –woman again.

She reached the tube station, she had a busy day ahead and travelling on the tube would save her the most time. Inside it felt warm and fetid, taking off the edge of her feelings of isolation. She joined the stream of people passing through; a Rastafarian in a woollen hat, two giggly school girls, a Muslim woman holding tightly to a small boy, preoccupied men in suits, all together, yet not together, all intent on their own lives.

She got out at Sloane Square and, not seeing a bus, walked down the King's Road to the Chelsea Town Hall. There was a pre-Christmas Fair held in aid of Cancer Research, and she was sharing a stall with Gloria, who sold cashmere jerseys and scarves. Lorna, now with more time on her hands, had taken up a previous interest in making jewellery. They were casual pieces with unusual beads and buttons she bought on the Internet; twisted rope bracelets which looked great with jerseys and day clothes. She'd also put in a couple of boxes of her homemade cakes advertising the shop she had with Martha, hoping they might draw people in to buy them.

The first stall she encountered was a table laden with pâtés and cheeses, with a large half-cut ham in pride of place in the middle. The smell of the ham brought back memories of her childhood, her mother had cooked one every Christmas, and the aroma of tangy marmalade and Bourbon whisky mingled with the cooking meat wafted round the house for days.

This memory enclosed her like a security blanket from the past. Her mother would have stood no nonsense from that girl; she'd behave as if Stephen couldn't possibly have left his wife and family for such a person, making him see how foolish he was being. She smiled in spite of her pain. Oh, Mum, I wish you were here, she thought, still sore from her death two years ago.

'Could I have a slice of ham, please,' she addressed the man wielding a knife on the other side of the table.

'Just *one* slice?' He frowned at her, two furrows biting into his forehead. His brown hair fell in unruly locks over his eyes. He kept looping it back behind his ears with his free hand and Lorna expected the imminent arrival of some Health and Safety inspector who'd decree that he imprison his curls in a hat to avoid germs polluting the food. He wore a navy and white striped apron over his clothes.

'Yes, please.' She felt a flush of embarrassment. Why ever should she explain? But seeing Stephen had unhinged her and she was overcome with this tiresome feeling that she had to justify herself.

'Samples are there.' The man gestured towards a green plate that held slivers cut from the edges of the ham. Before she could ask him again for her *one* slice, a gushing woman pushed herself in beside her and began to scoop up armfuls of pâtés, cheeses and chutneys in their festive wrappings and hand them to him. Once he'd taken the first load from her she picked up some more with little trills of excitement. 'How lovely, beetroot and blueberry, and this homemade marmalade, such a treat, bought stuff is so jammy.'

The man beamed – no frowning eyes at her – as he added up her purchases, packing them into smart blue bags. Lorna picked up a sliver of ham from the plate of samples and put it into her mouth. It was so succulent, with a richness of orange coupled with muscovado sugar, and a hint of brandy in the glaze. She took some more and then, as the man was still dealing with his extravagant shopper, found she'd emptied the plate. She must hurry now or Gloria would wonder where she was and she must wash her hands before working on the stall. She turned to go and find a washroom.

'I thought you were going to buy a slice, not scoff all my samples,' the man called after her.

'I'm sorry, but you were busy and I couldn't resist it. It's wonderful ham. I've got to rush now and go and help my friend. I'll buy some for supper on the way out.' She fled, washed her hands in the dank washroom and then, keeping well away from the food stall, went in search of Gloria, who was, to her relief, on the other side of the room from the man with the ham,

'There you are! Was it ghastly?' Gloria hugged her.

She nodded, Gloria's concern flooding her eyes with tears. 'Been busy?' she managed, sniffing madly, taking off her coat, rolling it up and storing it and her handbag under the table.

Gloria laid a jewelled hand on her arm in a gesture of comfort. 'Not bad, cakes are almost gone and I sold two of your bracelets and quite a few of your button brooches, they love them with the jerseys.'

'Good, I must make some more.' Lorna's tears were mercifully halted in their tracks by the same woman who'd bought all those chutneys and pâtés and was now scooping up armfuls of cashmere and throwing in some rope bracelets. Whose money was she spending, she wondered idly as she packed them up, her husband's, her lover's or her own?

Gloria was a friend from childhood who had also married an older man, a friend of Stephen's. Adrian was an alcoholic, an amusing cheery man when well, and utter hell when not. Gloria did all sorts of jobs to make ends meet; threw him out, took him back in, and some of their friends remarked, perhaps unfairly, that she saw her role in life as his saviour. Their only child, Justin, found his father's behaviour intolerable and rarely came home, much to Gloria's distress. But every time Adrian lapsed and Gloria was called upon to come and collect him yet again out of the gutter or from some sordid club, she stoically went. 'I'm used to him,' she'd say, as if he were an old coat she could not bear to part with. 'Besides we had such good times together. I cannot leave him now.'

Lorna respected Gloria for that and had, in the bleak loneliness of the night, even envied her for still having him, though she feared that her care for him was destroying her. No one ever asked how Adrian was, they knew just by looking at Gloria. She looked fine now; her long blonde hair tied back, her face less strained than usual, yet Lorna, who knew her like a sister, could see the pain deep in her eyes.

The jerseys were selling well. They were well cut with a good selection of colours – they were every man or woman's cashmere, not the best stuff. Lorna was going to buy one at cost price when she had a moment. She dithered between a raspberry pink and a pistachio green.

A male hand appeared among the colours, picking up the last raspberry pink jersey and thrusting it at her.

'Seeing there are no samples I shall pay for this,' he said, and she saw it was the man from the ham stall. He was about her age; his skin tanned more from being outside in the fresh air than sunning himself in some foreign sun. He gave her a weary smile; his face strained with exhaustion.

'Are you sure you want this one?' Lorna said, bossily. Perhaps she could persuade him to take that china blue or the primrose instead. It was, no doubt, for the woman in his life and *she* wanted it. It was on the tip of her tongue to say it was not for sale.

'I am quite capable of knowing which colour I like. *This* is the one I want,' he said. He pulled out his wallet and thrust some money at her.

'Fine.' Lorna cursed herself for saying anything; if she'd wanted it so much she should have taken it sooner. She took his money, frantically working out the change in her head. He'd given her two fifty pound notes, which she could easily cope with, but somehow by standing there so close to her, his eyes homing in on her face, he flustered her.

'Twenty-five pounds change,' he said with a laugh, as if he knew she was hopeless at maths.

'I know,' she said, though she was relieved that he'd confirmed it. Maths eluded her – that was another reason she missed Stephen. He was a wizard at figures, so she hadn't bothered to try and improve herself; even the children laughed at her incompetence. She handed the man his change and with a last stroke of farewell, she slipped the pink jersey into a bag for him. She saw now, with a little unwelcome jolt, that he wore a wedding ring and wondered if her own smashed-up marriage would sour her towards all married men, imagining them cheating on their wives, trading them in for peculiar women who perhaps knew some bedroom tricks their wives did not. She wondered too if his wife or maybe his lover – he might have both – would look better in the jersey than she would.

'Thank you.' He took the bag from her. 'If you still want your slice of ham I'll keep you a piece. It's almost time to pack up, thank goodness; it's been a long day. Oh,' He caught sight of the last cake in the box with its swirl of dark chocolate icing studded with nuts, 'can I trade this in for the ham?' He picked it up with a smile and disappeared before she could say anything.

An elderly lady approached the stall slowly as if mesmerised by the bright colours. She took a long time to make her choice, so by the time everything was packed back in the large, plastic zip up bags Gloria kept them in, Lorna assumed she would be too late for the ham. The room, before so festive like an Aladdin's cave of tempting presents; luscious silk wraps and jackets, bright painted toys, shimmering jewellery and lots more was now half-empty; the stalls bare, boxes and bags piled up on the floor making the place appear tawdry and bleak.

She passed the ham stall; it had all been packed away. The cheap wood of the table now exposed was stained with years of pinpricks and ink. She felt a tinge of disappointment and turned away.

'There you are.' He appeared from another room, a small bag in his hand. 'Don't forget your ham. One slice.' He smiled the weary smile of someone who wanted to be on his way.

Was he sorry for her for having no one else to share it with? She must curb this ridiculous self-pity she scolded herself, there were so many people worse off than her and anyway, why should he think of her at all?

He held out the navy bag and she took it from him. 'Thank you so much, what do I owe you?' He'd helped himself to her cake as a trade in but she felt she ought to ask.

'Have it on the house as I had your cake, which, by the way, was delicious.' he said with a tired smile. 'But I've packed everything away now and it is rather an end piece.'

She wanted to say that she wished for a nice piece, a succulent piece from the middle with a thick layer of the glaze, but she did not; perhaps he'd sold it all and it was the last piece left.

'Goodbye,' he turned away and walked out of the room, making her feel she'd offended him somehow. She really must stop being so sensitive; she'd never see him again. He'd go back home to his wife; she may even be here having helped him on the stall. He would give her the raspberry pink jersey and perhaps grumble to her about this mad woman who'd eaten all his ham samples as if she hadn't had a square meal in days.

She peered into the bag and saw on top of the waxed paper wrapping the 'end piece', a cream card written in dark blue lettering. 'Nathan Harwood, Victualler', it read with an address in Sussex.

CHAPTER TWO
Another Difficult Husband

Gloria Russell dropped Lorna at her house in Putney on her way home to Wimbledon. It had been a long day at the Fair; her back and legs ached and she longed to get home, throw off her shoes and flop down in front of what was left of the seven o'clock news, but when Lorna suggested, her eyes slightly pleading, that she come in for a drink, she accepted.

She knew only too well the empty, panicky pain of being alone waiting for one's husband to return; far worse for Lorna suffering the loneliness of waiting for Stephen who wouldn't come home again.

She still had Adrian, though she rarely knew where he was or what he was up to. It terrified her that one day he, like Stephen, would not come back. He'd be found dead in a gutter or go off with one of the women he'd sometimes been found with, women that wanted his money – or anyway someone that assumed he had money. His body had conked out as far as sex was concerned. He could no longer perform with her, which hurt her deeply.

Even though her head knew that impotence was common among older men, especially alcoholic ones, her heart ached with the fear that he no longer loved or desired her. A warm cuddle in bed at night would have been reassuring and she'd tried to say this, holding him close and explaining that full, frantic sex was not necessary to show that two people loved each other. But he'd clammed up and moved to the further edge of the bed, protesting he was too tired. Many a night she cried herself to sleep, stifling her sobs, as she could not bear to provoke any more reasons for him to want to leave her. Any moment she expected him to make some tawdry excuse and move into the spare room.

She was being pathetic, she thought now, as she followed Lorna into her empty house. She'd seen how hard it was for Lorna to be on her own and she couldn't do it. She'd rather live with Adrian as a hopeless drunk with occasional bursts of contrite gratitude and vague affection than be abandoned and live alone.

Lorna walked ahead of her, scrabbling in her bag for her keys, mildly grumbling that they needed more street lighting, as she couldn't see what she was looking for in the muddle of her handbag. She looked so much better now than she had a few months ago when Stephen had left her. Gloria hoped that Lorna's trip to see him and his sluttish-sounding girl, would, with luck, mark the start of her new life without him, and open the possibility of finding someone new.

The break-up of Lorna and Stephen's marriage had unsettled her; it had unsettled all of them, but especially her and their younger friend, Rosalind, who had married Ivan, one of Stephen's friends, as his second wife. All three husbands, now in their sixties, were playing up, though only Stephen had actually left home, upsetting the balance of their long friendship.

Lorna unlocked the door and went in, dumping her bags on the floor. 'Thanks for coming in, Gloria; I still find it difficult since Stephen left. An empty house has a sort of lost, barren feeling doesn't it? Waiting for people who never come – though the children do, of course when they're home from Uni.'

'I know love, perhaps you should have some music switching on the minute you open the door, give it some life, or get a cat or something.' Gloria said, though she didn't think either much of a good substitute for a loving husband.

Stephen would not come home again. He had rung her, sounding like a stranger, defensive; as if he expected her displeasure, but didn't deserve it. She had not told Lorna about his call, it would hurt her too much. She felt guilty that'd he'd called her at all and said such dreadful things about his wife – her friend. She felt tarnished by it. She'd always liked Stephen, fancied him a little in the early days, but it seemed that he'd changed dramatically from the kind and friendly man he used to be.

'I feel stifled by my marriage,' he'd begun, belligerent and defiant as if he had no control over his emotions, which perhaps in the circumstances he did not, though Gloria thought he was not on the mind-changing drugs then. 'I've met this person and she's given me a new lease in life, shown me a new freedom. I'll never go back to my dead marriage now.'

For a moment she'd been stunned by him ringing her at all. She'd just come home after spending most of the day with Lorna who'd been distraught; incoherent with grief at his desertion. He'd gone on. 'Lorna expected too much of me, she was suffocating me.'

'Oh, rubbish, Stephen, you had a good marriage, better than most,' she'd scolded him wondering – as they all did – if the shock of his sudden redundancy had brought this on. But when he'd gone on about their love life being almost non-existent she'd said with fury – fury directed at Adrian too – 'Just because some tarty bitch can turn you on with some clever tricks you want to exchange all the wonderful, precious things in your long marriage for a bit of grubby sex.' And she'd slammed the phone down, shaking with misery and indignation.

She went to the loo while Lorna opened a bottle of wine. She wondered which was worse, knowing your marriage was really over and you must move on as best you could, or exist in the sort of limbo she lived. Adrian did come back, or was more often brought back, always the worse for drink. Perhaps he too felt suffocated and was frantic to leave her, only because he was often so comatose with booze he never made it.

'You've got more courage than me,' she said to Lorna as she dropped down on the sofa, letting her large handbag clunk onto the floor beside her. She watched Lorna coming towards her, carrying a bottle of wine and two glasses. She'd lost weight since Stephen had left her and it made her look younger; her grey eyes larger, and her features finer. She'd had new streaks put in her hair, making it lighter, and it suited her. She'd never admit it but she bet she'd had it done to impress Stephen, perhaps hope she'd find the man he used to be waiting to come home.

'Courage, whatever do you mean?' Lorna laughed as she poured Gloria a glass of wine and put it on the table beside her.

'Letting Stephen go, striking out and going it alone.'

'You make it sound as if I'm leaving civilization and going out into the wilderness.' Lorna curled up in a chair facing her, cradling her wine glass in her hands.

'You are, in a way. Marriage is so many things. It's still a sort of protection, even today. You can use a husband as an excuse to get out of things, know you've always someone to go home with. Well, perhaps not always.' Gloria took a large gulp of wine. Adrian had been known to slope off without her to go on one of his benders.

'I had no choice. He left me, remember.' Lorna said. 'Even I, who strongly believe in marriage and doing all you can to make it work couldn't stay when I was so obviously not wanted. I sort of hoped the effect of the drugs might wear off and he'd come back, just as he used to be, but seeing him and that girl today ... and knowing that he'd started seeing her ... or someone like her ... before he was put on the drugs ...' Her voice tailed off.

'I'm so sorry, love. I still find it hard to believe that this happened to Stephen, of all people. He always seemed so sane and predicable, but then, you never really know someone, do you? How they'll react if their stability is snatched away.' She sighed.

'I ought to leave Adrian. How many more nights can I go on waiting and wondering if he is alive or dead?' Lorna may have had no choice but she'd done it, cut off her rotten marriage like a diseased branch. 'It's a dreadful thing to say, but it might be better if he died, then I could mourn him in peace and smother his grave with flowers.'

'Oh, Glory, I know how you feel. I've thought that about Stephen. Dead people are so much easier to live with,' she smiled ruefully, 'if you see what I mean.'

'Perhaps we three; you, me and Rosalind, were wrong to marry them,' Gloria said, remembering her parents warning her that marrying a man so much older than she was could mean that they might spend their best years as carers for them. But she couldn't see it then; Adrian was so alive, so amusing and so loved her. She and Lorna, buoyed up with the optimism of youth, were convinced that they could cope with whatever life threw at them. These older men had adored them – it was a powerful aphrodisiac. They'd been kind and caring husbands but now, for whatever reason, had flipped back into outrageous adolescence.

'We had many happy years and, most importantly, the children,' Lorna said. 'They are worth any amount of pain now, though I hope,' she looked troubled, 'it won't cloud any romantic relationships they might have.'

'You're right.' Gloria's heart ached. Children. She'd had so many miscarriages, so many deaths of potential hopes, but she had Justin, he was her world. Sometimes she wondered if all those miscarriages hurt Adrian more than she knew and he'd drunk too much to hide his pain, and now, after all these years of heavy drinking, his body couldn't cope with it as well as it used to.

'I just hope I'm not wasting my life, wasting Justin's life, by being so caught up with Adrian.'

'No, you're not, Glory. Are people, like you, who devote their lives to people who have incurable conditions wasting their lives? What if Adrian suffered from one of those frightening neurological diseases or was paralyzed from an accident? Would you look after him then?'

'Yes, I would, or I hope I would,' Gloria said. 'But that wouldn't be his fault. I know some people think alcoholism is a disease but I can't help blaming him for not admitting he has a problem and getting help.'

She'd said so many times to Adrian, making him angry. He'd responded by telling her she was a nag so it was no wonder he kept away from home. The pain bit deep and to block these thoughts, made worse by being so exhausted after the long day working at the Fair, she said, 'Your cakes all went, you should bring more next time.'

'Yes, there was one left and the man who had a food stall came and traded it for a slice of his ham.' Lorna got up and fetched the navy blue bag she'd left in the hall. 'I should put this in the fridge – or we could eat it now. I could make a risotto or a sandwich. There's only one piece and he said that it was an end one.'

'But he only took one cake. Perhaps if you'd given him a whole box he'd have given you a ham.' Gloria said with a laugh. 'I wish I'd bought some goodies from Nathan, what else did you buy?'

'Just the ham, or as I said we – or rather, he snitched my cake and said he'd give me a slice of ham instead. Do you know him?'

'Yes … sort of. He's often at these fairs, you'll get to know him if you come to more of them, he has his own business in the country.' Gloria watched Lorna; Nathan was a very attractive man. There was a sort of gleam in her eyes – the gleam that people had when talking of someone sexy and famous, but surely it was just because he was a more welcome topic than their dysfunctional husbands?

'Sussex.' Lorna flushed a little.

'Yes,' she regarded her keenly. 'He's one of those foodies who prefer to go back to the old country skills instead of the cut and thrust of the board room. He might be persuaded to sell your cakes, they look so smart in their dark red boxes, you could always ask if you see him again and he wasn't poisoned by the one he stole!' Gloria joked, 'I could ask him if you like.'

It was tempting to stay here and eat the ham but she must go home now or she'd fall asleep. She struggled up and made for the door. Adrian might be there, probably having lost his key and wondering where she was. She ignored the icy fingers of fear that she would wait and worry all night, imagining the most terrifying scenarios that now plagued her life.

CHAPTER THREE
More Complications

It was fortunate that they had 'downsized' just before Stephen left her – perhaps another reason he'd become so peculiar. For most of their marriage they'd lived in a large, Edwardian house in Hammersmith but they decided to sell it and get something smaller, now the children were on the brink of leaving home, and buy a holiday house in Italy with what was left. This plan had tempered her sorrow of leaving the family home where they'd been so happy, but having made the move, the happiness had not followed them and though, to her relief, she could keep this house, there was obviously no question of buying somewhere abroad.

The house was at the end of a terrace in a nice street, and had just enough room for her and Stephen (if he'd stayed) and two occasional children. But today, after seeing her ex and that dreary girl, her fear of the future without him gripped tighter and she was glad when Gloria came in with her; she brought life into the house for a while. The nights were always the worst, especially now, as it got dark so early.

At least she knew that Stephen had gone, left for good and would not be lurching back here in the dead of night. She worried about Gloria sitting waiting for Adrian, wondering if he would come home this evening and in what state. She often threatened to leave him but Lorna wondered if she ever would.

Gloria was twenty-one, and Adrian recently back from a long stint in Canada when Stephen brought him to a party. Adrian soon fell for Gloria's warm, bubbly personality and they married. He'd been such fun. He was always the one to think up amusing things for them all to do together; a chocolate trip to Bruges, the wine festivals along the Rhine, arranging walks round obscure parts of London. He was flattering and flirtatious in the nicest way. Occasionally – just enough to give them hope that all would be well – he became his old self again, amusing and generous, but when he was drunk, his clothes stained, often with his own wee and vomit, it was hard to imagine he was the same man.

'Do you think I'm wasting my life?' Gloria often asked this question and people usually said yes, she was. Adrian had made the choice to drink himself senseless so she should leave him, start a new life for herself. In fact if she left him it may shock him enough to make him pull himself together. Some of their friends thought, and indeed said, that her kindness in picking him up and bringing him home was almost like colluding with his behaviour, and that what he needed was the sharp shock of being abandoned in the gutter. But Gloria, perhaps exhausted by her struggle to keep the whole show on the road – finding money to pay the bills, running after Justin, her adored son – rarely listened to any advice that didn't suit her.

Letting go after making a home and having children together was very hard to do. If, despite everything, Stephen came back, told her he loved her and was sorry for his despicable behaviour, she'd take him back, wouldn't she? Love, she thought wryly, took a long time dying.

Lorna remembered how attractive and glamorous these older men had seemed then compared to the callow youths their own age, and they had been happy, it was only when their husbands hit their sixties that things seemed to fall apart.

She was hungry; she'd eat that ham for supper. She got up and took the bag into the kitchen. She'd told Gloria that Nathan had bought one of her jerseys and just stopped herself saying 'for his wife'. Gloria, who loved romance, real or imagined, would jump on her remark about his wife, and worry it like a terrier with a rabbit until she'd convinced herself that Lorna found Nathan attractive or something equally far-fetched.

'Oh, did he? That's kind of him, but then he is kind. Sexy, too,' she'd giggled. 'Next time Adrian short-changes me in the bed department I wouldn't mind a romp with Nathan. Have someone my own age for a change.' And she'd scooped up her large bag and left, decidedly happier than when she'd first come in.

Alone in the silent house, Lorna thought of Nathan. He was an attractive man and she'd been warmed by his smile and was ridiculously grateful that tired though he was, he'd remembered her slice of ham, Perversely, she felt irritated that Gloria fancied Nathan too. He was married and wore a wedding ring so was out of bounds. Anyway for her, she'd hate to put another woman through the agony Stephen had inflicted on the family. She sighed, being dumped like she had been made her in grave danger of turning into a crabby old witch. Why on earth shouldn't he have a wife? No doubt she was very pretty and very, very nice; someone everyone adored.

Lorna unwrapped the one piece of ham. It was a thick piece with a large chunk of the glaze and just the smell of it made her mouth water. She could not resist cutting off a piece and eating it. She explored the fridge and corralled some rather tired vegetables together. She would stir-fry them to accompany the ham. By the time she'd done this, though, she'd eaten most of it.

She glanced at Nathan's card, running her finger over the embossed writing. She'd propped it up against the jam pot she and Stephen had bought on a holiday in Brittany some years ago. She was surrounded by memories of their life together, everything from jam pots to pieces of furniture; which made up their home and told a story of a happy family life. Apart from his clothes and quite personal things, he'd left most of the rest behind. To distract herself, she picked up Nathan's card. She'd order some ham for Christmas; she did so hope the children would be here, it wouldn't be Christmas without them. It made her ill, thinking that they may not be, unable to cope with their father's absence or, worse still, if he suddenly turned up with that girl.

Afraid of being alone for Christmas, she'd asked her older sister Felicity and Jonathan, her banker husband, for the day. They were spending their first Christmas without their eldest daughter, Becky, who was somewhere far away on her Gap year.

Felicity, her bossy older sister, was a Cordon Bleu cook, and somewhat difficult to feed, which made her a tiresome guest. Nathan's stall had pâtés, cheese and chutneys and probably other things she hadn't paid attention to. They would add a 'certain something' to her meal. Perhaps he had a catalogue? She could ring and find out.

Without thinking, she dialled Nathan's number and before she realised what she'd done and put down the receiver, the call was answered by a cheerful, female voice. 'Thank you for ringing Nathan Harwood. Our hours are nine to six every day but Sundays. Please leave a message and we will call you back.' There was a ping, followed by a silence waiting for her message. She blurted obediently, 'Ham – no, sorry, a catalogue please.' She dropped the receiver as if it were red hot, realising then that she hadn't given her details. He wouldn't know it was her, anyway, no doubt his wife picked up the messages. He'd be too busy cooking hams.

The phone rang almost the moment she'd put it down. Nathan must have recognised her voice and dialled ring-back. She stared at it a moment, flushed with embarrassment, before gingerly picking it up, bracing herself for his sarcasm.

'Hello.' She hoped she sounded strong and forceful.

'Mum, it's me. Are you sitting down?'

'Flora, darling, no I'm not sitting down; I'm in the kitchen, having supper. It's good to hear you.' She laughed with pleasure at hearing her daughter's voice. 'Why should I be sitting down?'

'I just want you to in case you fall over.'

'Why should I fall over? I'm not drunk.' Did her children imagine her hitting the bottle alone, every evening? Another instinct kicked in, something was wrong. She moved from the kitchen into the dining area and sat down on one of the chairs. 'What's happened?' She hoped she sounded calm. Perhaps Stephen had died, or had some sort of attack, his aged limbs contorted and intertwined with that girl's.

Flora responded defensively. 'Why do you always think the worst?'

Because recently it usually has been, she thought, saying instead, 'I don't, but when people tell you to sit down it's often because they are about to break some bad news.'

'I only said it because *you* might think it is bad news, but it isn't really.'

'Just tell me, then I can decide.' If only Flora was not so defensive. Unlike Marcus, her younger brother, Flora seemed to find life such hard work. She took after Stephen, always feeling she had to do better than anyone else as if someone important was watching and judging her every move. Though Stephen must have forgotten this trait judging by his current behaviour.

'I'm having a baby.' Flora blurted.

'A baby?' Lorna said numbly. She'd heard the words yet she hadn't really registered them. Flora was twenty, studying at a college on the outskirts of Oxford, and had no money or job prospects.

'Yes … Mum … I'm … sorry, I know it's a shock … it was for me, but …' she tailed off, then said, slightly frantically, 'It's only a baby – not *cancer.*'

'You're sure darling?' Lorna struggled to make sense of it. Being a single mother at her age would curtail the life and opportunities Flora should be having now. Jamie must be the father, which was a disaster, for he was far too lazy to take on any responsibilities. But he obviously had not been too lazy to father a child.

'Yes. I'll come home at the weekend and we'll discuss it.' Flora said in a small voice. 'I'd tell Dad, only I don't want to speak to that slut. Perhaps he'll come home if he knows he's going to be a grandfather.' Her voice was wistful, and Lorna's heart went out to her.

'How pregnant are you? And you … you're really are certain that you are? You know you're not that regular.' Lorna prayed that Flora was mistaken. She remembered a few heart-stopping times herself with Stephen that had turned out to be false alarms.

'Yes. I've done the test … three times in fact.' Flora said, gulping back tears.

Perhaps making practical plans would ease her churning emotions. She should be offering advice, as her own parents would have done, but today's parents were discouraged from delving into their children's lives or being 'judgemental'. No wonder there were so many dysfunctional children since the parents' role had been so undermined. 'So, how pregnant are you?' Lorna asked, still unable to grasp it.

'I don't know, two months, possibly three.'

'Have you seen a doctor?'

'Yes, I'm booked in for a scan.' Flora sounded scared, adding to her anxiety. There was no mention of marriage, but Jamie was far too immature for that. Her baby was having a baby, without the support and comfort of a loving, sensible man. Stephen should be here, sharing the problem with the family. She longed for him – the man he used to be.

'What does Jamie think about it?'

There was a long silence and then Flora said, as if she was owning up to some crime, 'Oh, it's not his, we broke up … we broke up ages ago.'

'I didn't know that.' She'd only seen Flora a few weeks ago and she hadn't said anything about her condition, or her love life, but she obviously hadn't known then.

'He's hopeless; just lies about drinking,' Flora sounded defensive.

Lorna took a deep breath, struggling to calm her growing panic. 'So whose is it, then? I didn't know you were seeing anyone new.' Please don't let it be some random man Flora succumbed to during a drunken party, she prayed, her heart racing.

'You don't know the father,' Flora said slowly, 'but you'll like him. The only trouble is,' she paused, then rushed on, 'he's married.'

'Married? Oh, Flora. How old is he?' Images of Stephen fathering more babies sprung up to torment her.

'He's over sixteen, so what does it matter?' Flora was crying now.

'Oh, Flora, darling!' It was getting worse and worse. If only she could be with her daughter, it seemed so cold to be talking about this over the phone. 'Is he still married? Has he other children? Is he one of your tutors?' Panic rose in her, she was bordering on hysteria, but she couldn't stop the words pouring out like molten lava.

'If you're going to be difficult, I'm going to ring off,' Flora said, desperately, perhaps facing for the first time the severity of her situation.

Lorna forced herself to sound calmer. If only she could hold Flora in her arms while they talked it through.

'I'm sorry, darling, but it's such a shock, I can't quite grasp it. I've had a difficult day seeing Dad and my replacement.'

'Oh, Mum, sorry, I forgot you were going to see him today. Is she dreadful, a blood-sucker?'

'Yes, all that, but let's talk about you. I wish I were with you. Why didn't you tell me all this when you came home?'

'I didn't know, and anyway it's easier like this. I don't want to see your face looking sad and cross.' Flora pushed on quickly, sniffing back her tears. 'He's thirty... well thirty, five, and his wife can't have children. He thought he couldn't, either, so we didn't always take care, but it seems he can.' She sighed heavily, 'I don't know what to do, Mum. Just my luck to be caught out by an infertile man.' Flora laughed sourly, but Lorna could feel her anguish.

She wished now that the baby were Jamie's. At least she knew him; and his parents, after their initial shock, would have been supportive in the situation, but a married man and one so much older, though she could hardly criticise Flora for that. Guiltily, she remembered her own parents' anxiety at her marrying a man not much younger than they were. She had accused them of overreacting. Now she knew what they felt like.

She and Stephen should be facing this together as a unit, strong against the world, protecting their child, and the thought hit her – their *grandchild*. But instead of her, he'd discuss it with that girl. He might even make her pregnant too, giving Flora a half-brother or sister younger than her baby. No, it was too macabre; she must not allow her mind to imagine such scenarios. Her life was complicated enough as it was, and without Stephen at her side, however would she cope with it all?

CHAPTER FOUR
An Unexpected Legacy

Lorna was tortured with hideous dreams of Stephen brandishing a baby, demanding that she look after it. She woke with a start, her body fizzing with anxiety. Unconsciously, she thrust out her arm to touch him for reassurance, but his side of the bed was empty, as it had been for months. Whenever would she get used to it.

What if Stephen and that girl did have a baby together? It was shocking, disgusting even, and she lay there, ridged in her tangled sheets, her mind fighting to dismiss this new nightmare.

It was Flora who was having the baby, not Stephen, who was now almost sixty-six but possibly could still father a child? What if he wanted one to show off to his OAP contemporaries that he was still potent? Or that girl wanted one to secure him and his money? Foolishly, she'd not thought of this scenario, assuming that Stephen was not virile enough to make babies. Certainly, thinking of his last attempts to make love to her, he was not, but perhaps Viagra and this girl had turned him into a stud again.

The thought that Stephen could make love to other women, but not to her, brought a rush of tears. She must not allow him to dominate her life like this. All her energies were needed to keep going; to earn more money and be there for the children, and now Flora had added to her problems by getting pregnant! And worse, with someone else's husband.

She switched on Radio Four, welcoming the familiar voices of the presenters while she picked at breakfast; numerous cups of freshly ground coffee, toast and a rather dry orange. She ate it while she wiped round the granite surfaces in the kitchen, at first mechanically, then with more energy, whirling the cloth back and forth as if she were a dervish dancing into exhaustion. She stopped, feeling slightly foolish as if she was being watched, but her blood was singing, and she felt better for it.

She'd go into the cake shop in Wandsworth today. She didn't need to, as Martha's sister Jenny was working there now, but she wanted to be among people, throwing gossip about like bread to ducks, shunting her own anxieties aside.

'Cake Box' was a sliver of a shop off the common which sold decorative and delicious cupcakes for all occasions. The cakes could be boxed up, decorated as the client wanted, or bought singly as a small, pretty treat to lighten someone's day. The business was plodding along in these dire times; it badly needed some sort of publicity that wasn't too expensive.

Flora was coming home this weekend, Lorna had mixed feelings, longing to see her and hold her close yet full of anxiety over how to deal with this problem. It upset her that the coming child would cause so much heartache instead of joy.

She'd told Marcus about the baby when he rang her later that evening. He hadn't been fazed by the news. No doubt he assumed, as with their guinea pigs and hamsters, that she'd take over when they grew tired of their responsibilities. She could almost hear Marcus saying to Flora, 'A baby will give Mum's life some meaning, now that Dad's gone.'

She'd been happily down that road with Stephen. Did she want it all again, full-time for all those years? No, she did not, and not in this way. Besides, and the thought was scary, in the unlikely event that she might find love again she was just about capable of having another baby herself. This made her laugh, trust her to overreact! Scarily, though, it was possible for three new babies to be born in this mixed-up family – but that really would be going over the top.

The telephone rang, scattering her thoughts.

'Is that Mrs Sanderson?' The female voice at the other end was hesitant.

'Yes, speaking.'

'It's Clara, Mr Barnes' housekeeper. I'm afraid I have some bad news. H- he's very ill, sinking fast … he … I think you ought to come … if you can.'

'Oh . . .' her mind fought to absorb this. 'I'm so sorry Clara, yes…I will…. I'll leave at once.' This was yet another shock, but not altogether unexpected. Fergus Barnes was her godfather; he'd been unwell for a long time since a hunting accident. Adultery, an impending birth and now an approaching death; all crucial events of life; all assaulting her at once, she thought.

Fergus had been a recluse these last years, waiting impatiently for death. He'd instructed his solicitor on his funeral plans some years before and, until recently, he'd enjoyed taking them out and re-arranging the hymns and readings.

'He doesn't want me to worry you, Lorna, and he left his solicitor a list of people to contact when he went, but if you could come I think he'd like it … There's no one else left he cares for now.'

'I should be with you in just over an hour, Clara. It is a shock, it's hard for you, you've been with him so long.' She suspected Clara was in love with Fergus; she had looked after him devotedly since his accident some years before.

Clara's voice was thick with tears; 'I can't expect him to go on as he is, with no real quality of life, especially for someone who was so active.'

Lorna was seized now with purpose, overshadowing her other anxieties. She scurried round finding her bag and getting her coat, taking a map in case a road was blocked or something and she had to take a different route to the one she was used to. She hadn't been to Ravenscourt, Fergus's house in Sussex, for ages, as he'd hidden himself away refusing to see anyone.

Fergus had been her father's best friend. They'd got up to all sorts of escapades together at university. Dad eventually settled down to marriage – though her mother always kept a wary eye on him – while Fergus continued to party, having a highly chequered love life. He'd married twice; neither marriage worked, owing to his numerous infidelities.

'I thought it exceedingly bad manners to refuse a pretty girl,' he told her when she'd met him for lunch at the Ritz to celebrate her engagement to Stephen. 'Trouble is, it upset my wives; they didn't realise it meant little in the scale of my love for them. So, my dear, take some god-fatherly advice: love is all, lust just a passing whim, and an affair is usually no more important than indulging in too much chocolate or booze.'

The traffic was bad; Lorna crawled through Roehampton to the A3. She felt very close to Fergus, as if he were hovering just out of sight. She remembered that lunch at the Ritz, and how she'd giggled at his remark, thinking it sophisticated. She'd been in love; so sure that Stephen, who adored her, would never stray. She'd dismissed Fergus's advice with the arrogance of youth.

Ravenscourt was the perfect house for a recluse. It was hidden in a dip in the Sussex countryside, at the end of a long drive lined with old, knarled oak trees, known as 'Sussex weeds' as they were so prolific in the county. The house could only be seen from the air and even then in the summer it was difficult to see it through the trees.

When he'd bought Ravenscourt, over forty years ago, Fergus was very rich. His family were well-known biscuit makers. Fergus sold his shares in the company, and lived cheerfully and disgracefully on the income, until his accident confined him to a wheelchair. She'd often visited him, sometimes taking the children. Marcus would charge him round the garden in his wheelchair, pretending it was a chariot, which Fergus thought highly entertaining, urging him on ever faster. But over these last years, as his body slowly shut down, he refused to see anyone but Clara, his housekeeper.

Ravenscourt had been such a sumptuous house. Originally Georgian, it had been re-vamped, especially inside, into a mainly Victorian concoction. As Fergus's fortune had dwindled with his life in the fast lane, furniture and pictures were sold to pay bills and after his accident, the house fell into disrepair. Lorna hadn't seen him for over three years. She'd telephoned him and tried to insist that she come and visit, but he'd told her, often through Clara, that he was too old and decrepit and he didn't want her to see him like this.

'He's a vain man and used to women throwing themselves at him and now all that's gone he wants to hide away. You must respect that,' Clara explained to her. So Lorna contented herself with writing to him, sending him books and music CDs she hoped would amuse him.

As Lorna turned through the gates leading to the house, she was overcome by grief. It was dreadful to think of Fergus living out his last years alone and disabled here, and yet he'd led a riotous life, some might say a selfish life, and his end was only what he'd brought upon himself. Clara had faithfully cared for him, so he'd not been left alone.

The house had an imposing porch flanked by four pillars, and long, lean windows running each side. It was half smothered by creepers and some of the windows were blanketed by ivy that had thrust through the more exotic climbers that used to clothe the outside with such charm. Lorna wondered if the tenacious grip of the ivy held up the house, eating into the ancient brickwork while holding it together with its little sucker feet.

As Lorna pulled up outside the house, crunching on the gravel, Clara darted from a side door to greet her. She was a slim, tidy woman, her eyes and nose swollen with weeping. She was dressed in grey with a dark purple scarf tucked in at her neck. Her short, grey hair was so neat it could have been sprayed on her head. Poor Clara, thought Lorna, but it pleased her that the old roué, ill and decrepit though he was, was loved to the end.

'The doctor is here. I thought it best and Fergus doesn't seem to mind … he's peaceful now, drifting a bit.' She wiped away a tear. 'I told him you're on your way.'

Lorna pulled out her handkerchief, a large Irish linen one of Stephen's that she used for funerals. She mopped at her eyes, remembering her father's death. Clara patted her arm in comfort and led the way to Fergus's bedroom, which, since his accident, was on the ground floor.

For a moment she hovered on the threshold, dreading seeing him so near the end. A young man sitting on a chair beside the bed got up when she came in and smiled at her.

'He's very peaceful,' he said quietly. 'Come closer so he knows you arc here.'

Lorna crept forward, afraid of what she would see. The room was still, as if time was suspended. She reached the bed and forced herself to look down at Fergus. He looked so old, knarled like an ancient tree. She took his hand and bent down to be close to him.

'Fergus, it's Lorna, come to see you.'

For a moment she thought he hadn't heard her. His breathing was harsh and laboured. He opened his eyes. 'Lorna,' he said, trying to focus on her face as if to be certain it was her. 'Ravenscourt ...' His voice faltered as if it was too much effort to speak. 'Ravenscourt,' he repeated, 'is for you.'

'What, Fergus? What do you mean?' she leant closer to him, kneeling down on the floor, He closed his eyes and though she waited with him for over an hour, he did not speak again, and slipped away from them with barely a sound.

'I shouldn't be sad,' Clara said later, as they sat in the kitchen over a cup of coffee and a plate of cheese sandwiches. 'He'll be glad he's gone; he was always grumbling about how he was left on this earth too long in his state.'

'A recluse was the last thing you'd imagine him becoming. I always felt that he needed people around him to play to all the time,' Lorna said. Her mind kept running snippets of times spent with him like trailers of past films. He used to come and stay with her parents, with whatever wife or girlfriend was in residence at the time. He brought with him such an air of carnival that when he left, the house, which buzzed with plenty of family life of its own, seemed lacking in excitement.

Her father died before Fergus became a recluse, for he would have visited him; crashed through whatever barriers Fergus put up. But now they were all gone. She did so hope they had met up again in some carefree paradise.

Clara busied herself making more coffee, pouring boiling water over the grounds from an ancient kettle into an equally ancient coffee percolator that gurgled and spluttered while it burped up the grounds.

'The indignities of old age infuriated him. It was cruel of fate to leave him so and he didn't want anyone he loved to see him that way. Oh, he'll be glad he's gone at last,' Clara repeated, blowing her nose fiercely.

The doctor made the arrangements for Fergus to be taken away by the undertakers. As they tearfully watched him go, Lorna remembered his last words, 'Ravenscourt is for you,' had she heard him right? If so it was a monumental bequest.

She tried to dismiss her last sight of him, remembering instead how vital he'd been, charging through life, grabbing it up in handfuls like a spoilt child. He had been so full of charm and generosity that he was always forgiven. Though would he have amused her if she were his wife, or even his daughter? Her own husband had behaved badly, and it had broken her heart.

'He's left you the house,' Clara said. 'You realise that, don't you?'

'I haven't really take it in but I thought that's what he said. ...' Lorna glanced round the huge, bleak kitchen with the tall, narrow cupboards, the cream paint worn off around some of the door handles after years of use, revealing the pine beneath.

She could see how much the house had deteriorated since she was last here. It was rackety and enormous; even now the wind was shaking it as if picking it up in a huge hand, making the windows rattle. It would need a fortune spent on it just to make it comfortable, let alone wind and water proof.

Fergus had given Clara a cottage in the grounds, but when he'd become too infirm, she'd moved into a room off the kitchen to be near him. He'd turned a sitting room on the ground floor into his bedroom. The large dining room and the drawing room were icy, the radiators having rusted up long ago. The vast fireplaces probably hadn't been swept for years. The two floors above had been left to their own devices. They contained bedrooms and a few cold and damp bathrooms and attics, and were probably home by now to bats, mice, moths and goodness knows what else.

'You're the closest to him left,' Clara explained quietly, 'Ralph, his only child, died childless, as you know and he hated his other relatives. They all live abroad anyway. He adored your father and often spoke of him and thought you very like him. He said you could come here with your children for a bit of country air.'

'But my children are grown up and at university.' Fergus must have imagined that they were still small children, bursting with energy that would profit from dashing about in acres of land.

Clara poured out more coffee. 'Anyway it's yours, though perhaps it is rather a white elephant. Sad though it is to say, it probably needs pulling down and starting again. I'll be happy to retire to my cosy cottage. I'm going to be a granny soon. Gina is having a baby in the spring.'

'Oh, congratulations, that will be nice for you.' Gina was married and she and her husband had saved for five years before they'd thought of having children. Now one was on the way and it was something for Clara to look forward to, unlike her situation with Flora's baby, whose birth was surely going to cause painful complications, adding to her concern for its wellbeing.

Any minute Clara would ask after her children. Lorna dreaded having to admit that she too would soon be a granny, but to an illegitimate child whose father was married to somebody else.

To her relief, Clara seemed more preoccupied with Fergus and Ravenscourt. She went through his deteriorating health before progressing back to the house. 'It's been neglected for too long. The wiring and plumbing should have been seen to years ago. He meant well to leave it to you, but he didn't realise how much needs to be done to it. '

'I can't remember if I told you I'm divorced.' Lorna hated telling people. She cringed at the words of horror and comfort that sometimes gushed from them, or the more prurient questions about the cause of it.

Clara was shocked, for she'd liked Stephen the few times she'd met him. The news now conjured up memories of when she had been deserted by Gina's father. She described this in morbid detail and it was quite some time before Lorna could steer her back to discussing the house.

It was sad going about the bleak rooms. The damp cold pervaded everywhere, clinging like a mist, the larger rooms echoing with neglect. Once, long ago, there had been herds of staff to care for it, and many guests with their sparkling wit, flirtations and gossip; vibrant life that coursed like blood through the house. All was gone and nature had taken over, rotting the beams and staining the fine plaster work. Dust to dust. Lorna was glad to return to the warm kitchen, shabby though it was.

She trailed back on the motorway towards London cocooned in her small metal box. It was dark now, the wind whipping the trees into a frenzy, like huge brooms brushing the sky. A stream of headlights dazzled her coming the other way. Her mind was spinning with this new surprise of owning Ravenscourt.

She was hit with a nerve-wracking thought; could Stephen demand a share in it? He was so different now to the man she'd known and trusted that she had no idea how this unexpected legacy would affect him. She didn't dare even discuss it with him; not knowing what his reaction would be. Fergus had left her his beloved Ravenscourt, with the best intentions. She'd do all she could for it. Even if she had to sell it, as was likely, she would not have its fate compromised by the man who no longer loved her.

CHAPTER FIVE
Dreading Christmas

Gloria wiped her eyes on a piece of kitchen towel and forced herself to re-check her pile of cashmeres for the Fair she was going to in the morning. She used to love Christmas, look forward to it like a child even though it was such hard work. She'd enjoyed the ritual of it. She made the cake and the pudding in September, feeding them with brandy as though they were alive; pets to be nurtured. But these last couple of years it had been a minefield, spent wondering what state Adrian would be in. Now, what she had dreaded had happened. Her boy, her beloved only child, had just telephoned her from Bristol where he was supposed to be studying and told her that he may not be coming home for Christmas this year.

His plans were vague; he might go to a skiing resort and try and get a job there, or go to Cornwall with friends, Scotland with others. 'Can't you go after Christmas? Boxing Day, even?' she'd asked, hoping he couldn't hear the plea in her voice and feel he had to come back just for her.

'I'll see how it works out, Mum. I'll come home before, come and see you soon. Dad there?' he added in a rush and she knew that what he really wanted to say was, 'I'll come when he's not there, I can't bear to see him like he is now, his behaviour is so embarrassing.'

'No, he's not back yet.' She made it sound as if Adrian was still at work, or somewhere normal and important. Not drinking himself into a stupor somewhere, pissing himself, lying in the gutter.

'Drunk somewhere, I suppose.' Justin's voice was harsh with pain and disgust. 'I'll see you, Mum,' and he'd rung off, leaving her to cry alone.

Adrian used to be such an amusing father, one who got down on his knees to play with Justin and took him out on 'boy's jaunts'. He even took him to the pub for his 'first drink', and taught him about the quality of fine wines; the grapes, the vineyards, their history. She remembered him talking about the ancient skills of wine-making as if it were a religion, which perhaps it was, to passionate growers.

When had the joyful *bon viveur* turned into the monster? She couldn't quite remember. She'd noticed he seemed a little more affected by the amount he drank at dinner parties and curtailed her own drinking, so that she could drive them home. The first time he had staggered home legless she'd been annoyed, really because she didn't want him to set Justin a bad example. Then, one night, when he was sixteen, Justin had rolled home the worse for wear after a party. She put him to bed rehearsing what she would say to him when he'd sobered up. She would explain that getting drunk was stupid and could put one in danger, of being mugged, run over – she was going to add rape to the list, as she'd read of boys being raped by men. But she'd decided not to; he was young and not used to alcohol and a thudding headache in the morning might hopefully deter him from doing it again. She had expected Adrian to back her up. Only he hadn't. The memory of that night haunted her still.

A friend almost as inebriated as himself had brought Justin home. It was after midnight and Adrian was asleep in bed. She'd put Justin to bed and then Adrian had woken and demanded to know what was going on. She'd made a slight joke of it, saying that coming home drunk was part of growing up, and that they would both speak to him in the morning.

'We'll speak now.' And before she could stop him, Adrian had charged into Justin's room and dragged him from his bed, shouting at him for being drunk; saying how disgusting it was and that he wouldn't have it, and that if Justin did it again, he'd chuck him out. She'd been horrified, terrified too, for she had never seen him so angry, and angry about something that really was not that serious, not this once. Anyway, hadn't he too drunk too much recently?

Justin had walked, or rather staggered, out – though she had begged him to stay, holding on to him until he promised he'd go to his friend in the next street. She'd followed him, creeping behind in the dark, itching to catch him as he swayed and once almost fell over the curb, to make sure he was safe. But that episode woke her up, forced her to stop making excuses and realise that Adrian was no longer the amusing drunk, but had a serious problem. He had apologised, tried to make it up to Justin, but the warmth and joy they'd shared as a family had gone. Now it looked as if Christmas would be ruined, with just her and Adrian sitting forlornly together.

She blew her nose firmly. She must get on, or she'd be late. She packed up the cashmeres in one of the large, squashy bags she used to transport them to the fairs, checking she had enough of each size and colour. She wondered if Nathan would be there. She planned to buy a lot of his produce this Christmas, having neither the energy nor the heart to make her own things. She had taken on many more fairs this year as money was getting tight. But was it worth buying anything if Justin was not coming? Adrian wouldn't appreciate it any more and if Justin wasn't there, what was the point of making any effort just for an old soak?

The thought of her lonely Christmas made her want to cry again, but then her eyes would be red and her face blotchy and she hadn't time to re-do her make-up, so she firmly switched her mind to Nathan. She hadn't really noticed how attractive he was before and she felt her body warming thinking of him. She hoped he would be there tomorrow, then she could buy the goodies she wanted straight away and save on the postage.

She wished she had an attractive, loving man in her life; someone fun who'd make her laugh, hold her in his arms and love her like Adrian used to do. She sighed. The thought of an affair crossed her mind. That's what I need; a passionate, sexy affair.

That would wake Adrian up! Perhaps make him see what he's missing. She smiled to herself; she'd never had an affair before so perhaps it was high time she had one while all her bits were still fairly presentable.

CHAPTER SIX
Hint Of A Mad Idea

The traffic was snarled up all the way from Piccadilly to Knightsbridge, where Lorna was to meet Gloria and Rosalind for lunch, so she was late. Gloria poured a glass of wine, 'I really don't know if he'll be there or not and... Adrian doesn't take in a thing I say about his drinking.'

Lorna took off her coat and settled down on a chair. She was starving; she'd only had a cup of coffee for breakfast. She picked up a piece of bread, dipping it in the dish of green olive oil in front of her and popping it into her mouth, savouring the taste.

Poor Gloria. Lorna guessed she was going through another of her bad times with Adrian. The Christmas season was a difficult time for her, for them all. Adrian had ruined last Christmas, appearing drunk at lunch time, embarrassing Justin their son, who'd stormed out with the girlfriend he'd invited. She'd dumped him soon after. Gloria had cried for days. Lorna shuddered, what would Christmas be like this year?

As if she had guessed her thoughts, Gloria turned to her, her eyes bright with tears. 'Justin might not be here this Christmas.'

She tried to sound as if it were no big deal, he was, at nineteen, grown up, after all, and could make his own plans.

'What's he going to do?' Lorna asked, squeezing her hand in sympathy. All their children were special, but Gloria had suffered many miscarriages before Justin was born. She felt the tension grip her too, what if *her* children decided to opt out of Christmas this year? Marcus had threatened it and now that Flora was pregnant, she might go and spend it with the father of this child.

'I'm not sure, his plans are vague. He might go to a skiing resort, persuade some chalet girl to let him camp on the floor of the chalet she's working in, or go to Cornwall with another friend. Anything but suffer a re-run of last year's fiasco,' she said desperately. 'He can't bear to see his father in such a state. They used to be so close, I used to feel left out,' she laughed bitterly, 'but now?' She lifted her hands in a hopeless gesture. 'But enough,' she smiled bravely. 'Let's enjoy our lunch together. What are you going to eat?'

They ordered their food and Rosalind, who was a few years younger than them, said, 'It will be hard for you this year, Lorna'. She pressed her shoulder sympathetically 'Your first one since the divorce.'

Lorna gulped at her wine, not wanting to think about it.

'I can't afford to divorce, though if I did leave Adrian it might force him into rehab,' Gloria said despairingly. 'Getting the value of half our house would hardly leave me with enough to buy a hut on some far off moor. That's the trouble with this 'no fault' divorce; cutting everything in two often leaves not much for either person. Also, I just hate being alone,' she said. 'Feeble, I know, but I've never lived alone in my life – coming from such a large family, not to mention various hangers-on.'

'I doubt you'd be alone for long, Glory,' Lorna said, certain she'd rather be alone than put up with the worry of not knowing where and what state her husband was in.

'I wouldn't want someone just for the sake of it,' Gloria sighed. 'I just want Adrian really, but not drunk and dirty of course. Deep down I'm furious with him for not making an effort to get help.'

The topic of conversation was one that had preoccupied the three of them since their older husbands had started playing up so alarmingly. Lorna's divorce had shaken them, especially when they found that, unless you spent a fortune fighting it, the law decreed that as the 'partnership of marriage' had broken down, their money and possessions should be divided fifty- fifty. Divorce was brutal; the cold, calculated murder of a dying marriage

Lorna had had to make a list of all she possessed, even down to the five Premium Bonds she'd been given for her Christening, and had forgotten about. It was hard, and in a sense ridiculous, not to be able to ask Stephen how much she needed to live on. He was the one person who knew all the answers to their finances; insurance, pensions and all the things she had relied upon him to cope with, which he'd done with great efficiency before being befuddled by the 'happy pills'. She'd achieved it with the help of her family and friends. It was over now but she could understand why Gloria and Rosalind battled on with such difficult husbands.

It was good being here with these friends, whose once-decent husbands seemed to be struck down with some insidious form of self-destruction, threatening to drag the whole family down in its wake.

Rosalind too was going through a difficult time with her husband Ivan, who having retired had developed a penchant for social workers connected with the voluntary work he was engaged in. This was not made any easier by her 'princess' type stepdaughter Polly, who hated having to share her father with another woman and was jealous of her younger stepsisters.

They were eating in a bustling Italian restaurant. Rosalind had the dark looks of her Italian grandmother and enjoyed showing off this heritage becoming quite excitable; her hands swooping like birds as she ordered *tagliolini con asparagi*. Lorna and Gloria humoured her as they always did when they ate at an Italian restaurant, amused when often the waiter stared at her exclaiming, 'Yer what?' pizza being the only Italian word in his vocabulary.

'Ivan has hurt and humiliated me more than I can say with all this womanizing, even bringing one home last Christmas.' Rosalind's face was tight with pain. She poured out more wine, finishing the bottle. '*Per favore,*' she waved the empty bottle at the waiter as he approached the table. 'It's not as if we didn't have a sex life together, or slept in separate rooms, or I had constant headaches – in fact *he's* the one with headaches.'

'Impotence,' Gloria said. 'We all know that men worship their willies, would rather lose the use of their legs than that.' She smiled pityingly at the waiter before ordering another bottle of wine, in English, 'And I suppose now they look old and we, being so much younger, do not. In fact I think we look very good, and many career girls, still single at our age, are making frantic clucking noises to settle down and make babies, while we've done it.'

'Not every man behaves like that,' Lorna chipped in, thinking of some of their other older male friends, who seemed perfectly happy to potter about in their sheds, or bury themselves in their books while still being good to their wives.

'True, but perhaps the fact that we are still young and energetic, especially you, Rosalind, has panicked them, made them behave like geriatric adolescents. If we were nearer their age we could moan about our saggy and aching bits together.' Gloria leant back as a plate of steaming pasta was put before her. 'Ivan and Adrian are sixty-five, born in the same month and Stephen …?' Gloria turned to her.

'Just sixty-six.' Lorna said.

'And we are hovering round forty. I felt so secure with Ivan when we first started going out, even though he was going through hell at home. He so enjoyed being with me, it made him feel wanted. As I've told you, I wasn't very happy growing up … it was heaven.' Rosalind's dark eyes glazed a moment before flooding with tears. She sniffed madly.

'Even after I met Polly and suffered her spoilt princess behaviour, we were happy. Then we had our two, but now they've hit adolescence and things seem to get more tricky every day. Ivan seems to have opted out of being a father, as if he can't go through any more teenage behaviour, at least with Emma and

Chloe. He seems more interested in the teenagers coming in on work experience where he works.'

Lorna smiled sympathetically, worrying how Stephen would take the news of his daughter's surprise pregnancy.

'It's the constant worry of wondering where Adrian is and what state he's in that gets to me,' Gloria said. 'Even if we did split up, it wouldn't stop me worrying about him. You can't just cut off all feelings for someone you've loved and lived with for years and who's given you a child. It's not like pruning a plant.'

'I suppose that's what they bank on,' Rosalind said. 'They know we don't want to break up the family we've given so much time to and struggle with less money, a smaller home, being alone, and all the rest of it, so every so often they are nice to us, just to lull us into a false security and make us hold on.' She turned to Lorna. 'You've been through the horror of Stephen leaving you, you are braver than us, and though I know it is hard, you're doing marvellously. Sometimes I envy you.'

'You needn't,' Lorna wondered if she really would rather have Stephen as he was now than be alone, especially facing Flora's bombshell.

Lorna was itching to tell them about Flora, but she felt that, until she'd seen her, she should not release her news about becoming a grandmother. *A grandmother* – that aged her, a mad state of affairs when perhaps *she* could still have another child herself. She told them instead about Fergus's death and the house he had left her.

'A house in the country! What fun!' Gloria perked up. 'You can do it up, use it for weekends and holidays, even sell your London house and move in.'

'Sadly the house is far too big and needs so much doing to it. Anyway the last thing I want now is to be stuck alone deep in the depth of the country.' She went on to describe Ravenscourt.

'Sounds like Colditz,' Rosalind said. 'I wish I could rent it off you to put Ivan in until he comes to his senses and remembers he still has a lot of years fathering to do.'

Gloria laughed. 'What a good idea! Adrian can join him, then at least we would know where they were.'

'We could find their old school matron or someone like that to keep them in order,' Lorna giggled, having a sudden picture of the three men there, all reminiscing and ragging each other as they had in childhood.

'They'd love it. It seems they have regressed into their teenage years anyway, they'd think they were back at boarding school or university together,' Gloria added.

Their laugher froze: they were all struck with the same ludicrous thought.

'We couldn't.' Rosalind was the first to speak.

'It would never work, they'd escape.'

'We'd be arrested for kidnap or something. Think how they'd love that; they would get everything and we'd be out of the way.' Lorna felt suddenly flat. When she and Gloria were children at school, they'd come up with mad ideas to alleviate the boredom of boarding school, each topping the other with ever-wilder ideas. Now, together like this and perhaps a little drunk, they'd succumbed to that old habit of thinking up mad schemes perhaps as a sort of antidote, or light relief, because each of them was going through a hellish patch, dreading Christmas with their difficult husbands.

'It might work if they enjoyed being there,' Gloria sounded hopeful. 'If they thought it was their own idea. They are all retired, or consult occasionally, like Ivan with his investment advice, which he does along with his charity work with the work experience scheme so they could take time off without much difficulty.'

'Short of bringing in dancing girls and unlimited amounts of booze and porn, we'd never keep them there,' Rosalind said, in her sensible voice. 'And since it appears they have all that already they won't be drawn in, especially if it is cold and miserable.'

'Sad it won't work; think what a relief it would be for us to have a few days respite, even just for Christmas,' Gloria said wistfully.

'Especially for Christmas,' Rosalind jumped in. 'It would take away that awful anxiety of not knowing what mood they'll be in on Christmas Day. If Ivan has someone from his charity work that he feels sorry for, or wants to impress, I'm never sure which, he insists they come for the day and spends most of the morning fetching them. If I make a fuss he makes me feel mean, saying the woman – they're always female – is alone and all that. You dread what they are going to be like and how everyone else will behave with them, or worse still how Ivan behaves with us all, as he brings in a stranger and makes a fuss of them while his own children feel left out.'

'He's not …well, he's not sleeping with them is he?' Lorna asked in horror, having visions of an older man grooming adolescent girls. 'Surely your daughters and Polly, if she's there, complain, even if it is only to him later?'

'Not the young women, no, he doesn't sleep with them,' Rosalind said quickly. 'It's the slightly older women – social workers, I suppose they are – who run the work experience scheme.'

'The bastard,' Gloria exclaimed.

'It's as if he has convinced himself that I have invited them, even though he … well, with the older ones, he often wants me to think he is going to bed with them … as a sort of … punishment,' Rosalind finished in a rush, fiddling with a piece of bread, scattering the crust over the tablecloth.

Lorna and Gloria exchanged furtive glances. Gloria said gently, 'Punishing you for what, Ros?'

Rosalind looked embarrassed; a blush crept over her face. 'He . . . well, he can't get it up any more, so he blames me. Says he can with other women so …' she shrugged sadly, biting her lip against tears.

'That is nonsense,' Lorna touched her restless hands as they picked savagely at the bread. 'It is a well-known mechanical failure that can occur in any man, especially older ones. Stephen was the same with me…'

'And Adrian with me, love. Short circuit doesn't always fire, so they blame us. You know that cruel joke about doctors telling heart patients only to make love with their wives as anything more exciting will kill them!' Gloria laughed hoarsely. 'So Ivan is flaunting other women in front of you to punish you because *he* is suffering from reptile, no,' she giggled, 'I mean *erectile* dysfunction.'

Rosalind giggled through her tears. 'Reptile dysfunction – that's a classic, it will make me laugh next time it happens. I'll think of crocodiles.'

'I've tried to talk to Adrian about it, telling him it's the drink that does it – and truthfully,' Gloria glanced at the two of them, ' I do feel it's a bit much to have to give up on sex myself at my age.'

'So do I,' Rosalind said, 'and *we* don't go rushing off with younger, randy men, but perhaps we should. I don't feel I'm wanted by my own husband any more and it makes me feel as if I have lost all my sex appeal.'

Gloria turned to Lorna. 'Perhaps Lorna is the only lucky one. I know you're going through hell now, love, but at least you've got away while you're still young. We all want our old husbands back, as they used to be, but as they've seemed to have metamorphosed into monsters, we may be better off without them.'

Lorna didn't like to admit that she would take Stephen back tomorrow if he came back as the man he used to be. Instead, to relieve the tension, she said, 'Shutting them in Ravenscourt so they'd be away from temptation might make them come to their senses and realise what they might lose, or, in Stephen's case, what they've already lost. Pity it wouldn't come off.'

'We could say we all wanted to stay somewhere different for Christmas, get them to Ravenscourt then leave them.' Gloria said. 'Decorate it to look like a wonderful country house; greenery, tree, Christmas fare and all and when we've got them there, we somehow lock them in.'

'But even if we got them there, could we keep them there? We can hardly drug them and lock them in; if we disconnected the telephone they'd call for help on their mobiles. The house is isolated but not that isolated, and if we took their cars they could walk up the drive to the road and flag down a passing car.' Lorna laughed at the madness of the idea.

'I know it sounds far-fetched but even if it was only for Christmas Day it would be enough. Like you two, I'm so afraid my girls will refuse to spend Christmas at home. A family at their school sort of asked them to stay during the holidays. They were mortified by Ivan's behaviour last year, I can't tell you how embarrassing it was.' Rosalind said in despair.

A draught of loneliness settled in Lorna. However badly Stephen had behaved, this Christmas, this first Christmas without him would be very hard. Why do we all have such an illusion of happy family Christmases? she thought. Families and friends all gathered round the laden table together, beaming with love and good will towards each other when, nine times out of ten, over-tired, overfed and drunk people pecked and squabbled with each other like agitated chickens in a confined space.

Lorna felt sorry for Rosalind, who was one of the kindest women she knew, who in most circumstances would welcome someone who was alone for Christmas, but Ivan's 'guests' were different. He boasted to anyone who'd listen about his ability to help some of the teenagers who came to his office, but in truth he was more interested in the people who helped them, social workers or minders of some sort who he liked to parade at home, perhaps to impress them or even to show Rosalind how they were impressed by him. Lorna and Gloria suspected that the sex bit was just Ivan's wishful thinking, though it hurt Rosalind dreadfully. She came from a broken family herself with a father who'd deserted them, and had looked on Ivan as her saviour.

Another of Lorna's fears was that, for the children's sakes, she could be forced to have Stephen for lunch, because if she didn't they would feel sorry for him and might even spend it with him, leaving her to the mercy of her sister and her 'religious counselling'.

A young couple came into the restaurant. Their hair was tangled by the wind, their faces pinched with the cold, and yet they had a glow about them; their limbs forever touching, their eyes sending out messages of love and desire as they sat down close together. The man unwound the scarf from his girlfriend's neck with a gentle intimacy that proclaimed how much they were part of each other. The three women looked away, close to tears. Once they had been like that, the loves of their husbands' lives. Would they ever be loved like that again?

'Well,' Lorna said, briskly, to chase away their melancholy, 'you must come and inspect Ravenscourt. You could give me your advice on what to do with it. I just hope,' she attempted a laugh, 'that Stephen won't try and muscle in somehow.'

'Why should he? The divorce is over. Did you know your godfather would leave the house to you?' Gloria said.

'No, it came as a complete surprise, but perhaps he could make a case against me for a share of it, I don't know. We did have to divide everything we owned between us after all.'

'Ask your lawyer if you're worried, but knowing him, he will probably have some ideas about what to do with it.' Rosalind frowned.

'Let's go and see this house . . . Ravenscourt,' Gloria said, seeing that Rosalind's words were spooking Lorna. 'You said it's in Sussex, where?'

'Near Chichester, deep in the countryside.'

'That's great. Nathan lives near there and I want to buy various goodies from him for Christmas. I want to make it as tempting as possible so Justin will come. He's being a cagey about it and I know it's because he can't bear to see his father in such a state.' Gloria gulped down the dregs of her wine.

'Nathan?' Lorna said, an unwelcome flush suffusing her body.

'Yes, you know, that man who sells hams and other things. We could go to him, buy some stuff and see your house on the same trip,' Gloria said. 'You both might want to get some things from him too; he has quite the best Stilton. He goes and picks them out from whoever makes them and watches them mature until they are perfect. He has really good pâtés too, and smoked duck breast, and salmon. I'm sure you'd both find something you wanted, but if it's a bore I'll go down in my own car.'

'Sounds great,' Rosalind said. 'I'm always open for good food places. When shall we go?'

After a short discussion it was settled that they would all go to Ravenscourt together the following week. Lorna did not want to go to Nathan's but Rosalind was keen, questioning Gloria about his cooking skills. If she protested too much they'd quiz her and turn a foolish feeling she felt for him – 'spinning', she'd heard it called, when a person – her in this instance – exaggerated friendliness from a casual acquaintance of the opposite sex, into a deeper, more meaningful relationship.

'Where exactly does he live?' She hoped she sounded as if she didn't care, but to her annoyance she was feeling quite flustered at the thought of seeing him again. With luck he lived too far away and they would not be able to fit in both visits.

'Are you all right?' Gloria regarded her sharply.

'Of course, why wouldn't I be?' Lorna wiped her mouth on her napkin. What on earth was the matter with her? She was behaving like a love-crazed adolescent at the very mention of a grumpy, untidy man whose wife was surely wearing the raspberry pink, cashmere jumper she wanted for herself? Was she turning into one of those ridiculous women she so despised that went all giggly and silly whenever an even passable man was mentioned? She did so hope not.

CHAPTER SEVEN
Warring Grandparents

'*Who is this dirty old man who has seduced my daughter? I'll take him to court, I'll....*' Lorna put the telephone down on the table so Stephen could rant to the air while she finished opening her letters. She dreaded telling him anything now, for she had no idea how he would react. He'd have been furious and upset in the past at such news, but he'd have been practical and thought of how best to deal with it.

Anyway what right had Stephen, who was now playing the role of a dirty old man himself, to be so angry with his daughter? Perhaps it was his guilt talking but he obviously didn't feel guilty enough to dump the girl and come back to support his family.

Had he forgotten that he'd seduced her? Lorna was tormented by a sudden flashback from all those years ago; his tenderness as he showed her the delights of lovemaking, her first, her only lover. Though, unlike Flora's situation, Stephen had not been married and they had not had children until they were.

She struggled to compose herself, reminding herself that the loveable man he'd been then had gone; that she must accept that and stop hoping he'd turn back into the man she'd married. She picked up the telephone receiver again, determined to hang up, but all she could hear was his heavy breathing. Was he having a heart attack? Should she call an ambulance? Would it be murder if she did not and he died? He gasped and gathered strength for another tirade, before becoming breathless again. She said quietly,

'Thirty-five is hardly old, nor do I suppose is he dirty, but you at sixty-six shagging a girl not yet thirty are, so you have no right to criticise Flora.' She heard him sputter and protest but she went on, 'I hope you are past getting a girl pregnant for if *you* do, that will be the most shocking and disgusting thing.' She rang off and burst into tears.

If only she were more like her mother, who thought all men were difficult so was never disappointed. She must move on from her shattered marriage, find a new life for herself, though it seemed like a new life had found her, thanks to Flora's slip up.

Flora had returned home last night, pale and exhausted.

'Hi Mum.' Her voice was upbeat, a touch defiant, but when she hugged her she sagged against her and wept. Lorna was reminded of the times when Flora had been little and she or Stephen were able to solve her dramas: small things; an unfair teacher, a friend letting her down, events which may have seemed petty to them but which Flora, drama queen *célèbre*, made much of. But this was a serious, grownup problem and Stephen was not here to support them. This pregnancy, whatever the outcome, would affect their lives forever.

They'd sat down on the sofa together, arms still round each other. Since Flora had told her the news Lorna had had time – too much time – to think about it.

'Have you told your father?' Lorna asked, having not yet suffered Stephen's onslaught.

'Yes.' Flora eyes swam with tears. 'He thought it was disgusting, but he's doing something far worse, with a bit of trash. Ben is not like that, he's decent and honest and we didn't think it would happen.' Her voice was raw with pain, a child abandoned by her beloved father. Lorna suffered with her. Eventually she bundled her to bed with a mug of hot chocolate and words of comfort. The real discussion was yet to come.

It came after lunch and after Stephen's telephone call, of which she'd said nothing to Flora. The bright morning became dark and the wind threw torrents of rain against the windows.

There was reluctance on both their sides to discuss the pregnancy, each of them knowing how vulnerable the other was, and hoping to avoid a row. At last, Lorna felt she must make the first move, and said, 'Well, darling, we must talk about this. What are you going to do?'

Flora was sitting on the floor in the living room, leaning against the sofa, her long legs outstretched over the brightly coloured rug they'd chosen together on a family holiday to Morocco. Her hands curved round a mug of peppermint tea.

'Have it of course,' she said. 'Ben's so happy about it.' Joy flared in her face for an instant, before fading. 'He's got to tell his wife and that's going to be terrible. I mean,' she clenched her lips and didn't look at her mother, 'she can't have children. They have been trying with IVF, but nothing's happened.'

'That is tragic.' Lorna was hit with sympathy for this unknown woman; yet another woman betrayed by her husband. What made it worse was that it was *her* daughter he'd betrayed her with. Another thought barged into her head. What if this woman and her husband adopted this baby – her grandchild? Took it away from Flora? She didn't want Flora to be pregnant at this time in her life, and certainly not with a married man, but she was suddenly overwhelmed by a surge of possessiveness. Since seeing Flora she'd almost got used to the idea of this baby, and she didn't want to lose it.

'Tell me the story from the beginning. At first I thought you and Jamie were an item and that it was his.'

'No, he's hopeless. I met Ben by chance. I was coming back from my drawing class when my bag broke and my things fell into the road. He helped me pick them up; my drawings were blowing into puddles.' She paused, stared into her mug, Lorna waited.

'He was so kind, so caring. Other people, well, anyway, Jamie, would have just left them in the dirt. He took me into a flat he'd just come out of … he was looking after it for a friend and he laid my drawings out on a towel on the floor and put books on them to keep them flat. It sounds stupid …' Flora flicked a look at her, 'but it was his kindness that drew me to him. With Dad and all I'd been feeling sort of lost … We met a few times more and he was sad too, about his wife, and somehow that made us close.'

'But Flora he is married and quite a bit older than you, old enough to know better,' she said wildly, her stomach knotting with the anxiety of having to cope with this, add a baby into their now broken family. 'What about his wife? She must be devastated.'

Flora looked guilty. 'We didn't mean to hurt her. He asked for my email so he could tell me when my pictures were dry. We met up when I collected them, he emailed me some more ...just little things. We kept seeing each other, by chance at first; he works near my college and we passed each other most days. Then we started to look out for each other, sometimes we had a coffee or walked back together and talked ... It was so special to talk. I was upset about Dad and breaking up with Jamie, and Ben was upset about his wife not getting pregnant. Then one weekend she was away and it happened.'

'But it shouldn't have done, Flora. Doesn't he care for his wife? Shouldn't he show some compassion and do all he can to support her through this difficult time?' Anger burned in her – anger with Stephen for going off with that girl, and with his shrink for overdosing him; anger with this man who'd cheated on his wife and made her daughter pregnant.

'I can't explain it, Mum,' Flora retorted, awkward with shame for a moment. 'It was nothing to do with her; it was just us at that moment. I felt so close to him, wanted to be part of him.'

'So it only happened once?'

Flora squirmed a little in embarrassment. 'No, quite a few times actually. We care for each other, we do, and we need each other.' She finished defiantly.

Lorna's imagination went wild, seeing Ben as a Svengali kind of figure controlling Flora, perhaps even making her pregnant so his wife could have a child – hurriedly she dismissed this overdramatic scenario. She must not allow herself to overreact to the situation. 'Why didn't you take precautions?' She said bossily.

'I was on the pill but I stopped it when Jamie and I broke up. Ben and I used condoms but as he said he couldn't have children, we didn't always bother.'

'Oh Flora, you have had sex education thrust at you since were too young to understand. Surely you know how easy it is to get pregnant, even Jamie knew that.'

'Ben's so different from Jamie. He's grown up, he takes care of me, he's there for me, unlike Jamie who *I* had to look after. Jamie's hopeless; he loses his money, can't remember his pin number, he's such a baby.' She said this as if it were reason enough to have got into this mess.

'So now you're left with another kind of baby.' The words came out before she could stop herself but she felt panicky now, thinking of the complications Flora's condition would cause.

Flora glared at her, her blue eyes cold as glass. 'That's completely different.'

'Yes, it is.' Lorna said sharply, swirling with panic at having to cope with this. She swallowed; she must not allow her terror of this new situation to act like a blowtorch and scorch her words, turning Flora away from her. She was painfully conscious that she was her only parent now.

'So Mum, will you help me or not?' Flora asked defiantly, her eyes hard upon her. 'You know Nicola says being a granny is the greatest thing as now she has time for her grandchildren as she never did as a mother.'

'Nicola is the same age as Dad and she has a lovely husband and not much else to do.' Lorna felt near tears, she went on, 'I don't think you realise the magnitude of this.' Lorna was cowed by it herself. 'This baby will be your and its father's responsibility forever and you're going to have to give up a lot to bring it up. I'd hoped…' She felt far too young and not ready to be a grandmother, and how would Stephen react when it was born? He was so unpredictable now. Would he insist on helping out, having it to stay in his dreary flat with that Pekinese woman? She swallowed, struggled on, 'I'd hoped that in a few years' time, you'd marry someone lovely, like your father used to be, have children then.'

'But that didn't work in the end, did it?' Flora's voice was raw with pain.

'No, but it did for all your childhood.' She felt defeated, fearful of what was to come. She got off the sofa, sat down on the floor beside Flora and put her arms round her.

'We're all upset after Dad going off like that, but you know I'll help you, darling, when I can. And Dad still loves you somewhere in his addled brain, but the bottom line is it is your and … Ben's responsibility.' It was no good being sentimental, she told herself firmly. Flora and Ben were the parents of this child, and both were old enough to care for it. 'Babies … children are hard work and a great responsibility, you must know that and that falls squarely on the parents.'

But even as she said this she knew she'd be there with them too, for love was crafty, it bound you in, and you never quite escaped. Even if your husband no longer loved you and had left you for someone else, and your children were grown, invisible strings still held you, never letting you go.

CHAPTER EIGHT
Plans For Ravenscourt

Gloria, Lorna and Rosalind drove down to Ravenscourt together. The sun glowed with a syrupy, golden light, intensifying the colours of the changing leaves. There was a carefree atmosphere among them, a feeling of playing truant from their usual routine.

Lorna was the most subdued of the three. Last time she'd done this drive, it was to Fergus's funeral. It was a sad occasion but she was glad she'd been there at his end. She understood how he must have hated being so infirm and hoped he was now at peace. She wished she had someone to go with her. The children were at university, her elder sister Felicity was in America with her husband, and her brother Andrew, who lived near Inverness, was snowed under with work. None of her friends knew him.

'I haven't seen him for years,' her brother said, 'anyway he was your godfather and has left you that great house.' He sounded envious. 'If you don't want it, you can give it to me. Stella's always grumbling we haven't enough room now the boys are bigger.'

Lorna assured him that Stella would hate the house and it would bankrupt him to put it right. Her sister in law was obsessively tidy, fighting a daily, losing battle with three boys who scattered their belongings around as if determined to mark their territory.

She did not tell Stephen of Fergus's death, he hadn't seen him for some time and the last thing she wanted was him coming with her. He was so unpredictable now, possibly he would even bring the girl and even if he didn't she'd be there in spirit, as large as a blow-up sex toy sitting between them.

The sombre hearse waited outside the church, the coffin still in it, before being carried in. There were a few stiffly wired flower arrangements stacked by the path. She'd been hit with grief at the sight of the props that represented that final leave-taking. She grieved for Fergus as he used to be; so full of life that he seemed immortal. This grief spilled over to the loss of her parents, both gone within a year of each other, and the death of her marriage. Stephen should be here beside her, her soul mate, kind and supportive, as he used to be. A surge of anger and sorrow at his absence surprised and slightly unnerved her, mourning the loss of the man he used to be. She was going to have to get used to going to such events alone.

Clara's face was pale and pinched in her black coat. She'd loved Fergus and now he'd gone he'd taken so much of her life with him. Lorna blew her nose and wished she'd brought her dark glasses with her. She went over to Clara and hugged her, putting her own feelings on hold; Clara was the one who needed comfort now.

'So, what plans have we made?' Gloria, who was driving them all to Ravenscourt in her battle-worn Volvo, glanced at Lorna who was sitting beside her.

'Go to Ravenscourt, have lunch at a pub. Clara says she's there all day, she offered to cook us lunch but she's got enough to do and a pub's more fun.'

'We've also got to go to Nathan, remember, he's not far away. I've looked it all up on the internet. He's there all day too and about five miles further on from Ravenscourt. Shall we do him first or last?'

Christmas was six weeks away and Lorna remarked that surely it was too early to buy fresh stuff, but she'd been persuaded by Gloria's explanations that Nathan sold many things that would keep until Christmas and they could put in their orders for ham and pâtés.

Lorna hoped that Gloria would go off the idea of visiting Nathan after spending time at Ravenscourt with her and Rosalind, all vying with each other over ideas of what to do with the house, followed by a long lunch at a nearby pub, where she could tell them about Flora's baby. She was not sure why she was reluctant to see him. He'd been in her thoughts recently, perhaps because Gloria occasionally mentioned him if she'd seen him at a fair or was praising his food. There'd been something about him that stirred her heart, something tangible she couldn't explain. But her heart had been upset enough by Stephen not to mention the prospect of becoming a grandmother to an unfortunate baby whose arrival would cause such havoc. Anyway, by then it would be dark and surely Gloria would want to get home in case Adrian needed her.

'Let's do Nathan first. Chores first, fun later,' Rosalind said cheerfully. 'Once we've been to him we can go on and enjoy ourselves without watching the clock.'

'Good idea,' Gloria said, 'OK with you, Lorna?'

'Fine,' she said, though it wasn't.

Nathan's house was near Climping. It was a farmhouse, smaller than Lorna had envisaged, having imagined fields and barns and even stables scattered over the Downs. Its name, Mulberry Farm, was on a painted plaque beside the gate.

'That sign's new,' Gloria remarked as she swept in, coming to a sudden halt, spraying the gravel about. 'I suppose people kept getting lost coming to see him.'

Beside the square, flint house with its yellow front door and window frames, was a huge barn also flint, with a tiled roof, part of which had been hastily patched. It was here that Gloria led her troops.

'Nathan, it's us, are you there?' Gloria called out as she approached the slightly open barn door. A woman with short curly hair and a flustered expression conveying that she had so much to do she hardly had a moment to see to anything else, came out to greet them.

'Hi, Gloria, good to see you.' She greeted her with a vague kiss somewhere in the air near Gloria's left ear.

Was she Nathan's wife? Lorna studied her with interest, ignoring the curdled ooze of jealousy in the pit of her stomach. She was younger than them, slim and pretty, and no doubt a canonized saint as well. What a relief she was not wearing the raspberry pink jersey. It would look marvellous on her with that dark hair and slightly tanned skin, and make Lorna feel a fool to have ever thought of buying it for herself.

'This is Beth; Lorna and Rosalind.' Gloria gestured at them. 'How's his lordship?' she laughed, following Beth into the barn.

'Pretty frantic,' Beth said.

Inside, the barn was buzzing. Vast ovens stood at one end and a young man was basting a load of hams, the sweet, tangy aroma of their glaze escaping from the air filters into the room. A young woman whose hair was covered with a white cap, was ladling red chutney into jars and another older woman with crisp white hair, no cap, full make-up and chunky gold earrings was labelling them, her hands encrusted with rings. She wore the same overall as the other workers but it was pulled on anyhow as if she was only wearing it under sufferance. She glanced up as they entered.

'Gloria, thank goodness you've come and I can stop putting on these pesky labels. One of the helpers is ill so I've had to step in.' She sounded like someone who had never seen a jam jar and who, if she ate chutney at all, kept it in a silver pot.

'I'm sure you're enjoying it really, Sonia.' Gloria laughed. 'This is Rosalind Copeland and Lorna Sanderson. Sonia Harwood, Nathan's mother.'

His *mother*. Now that Lorna studied her, she did see a resemblance to Nathan in her strong lean face and those large topaz-flecked eyes.

'Don't let us stop you! You must have so much to do.' Gloria picked up one of the labelled jars. 'Mmm, spiced cranberry and orange relish, sounds delicious.'

'I never eat them; seeing them and smelling them day after day,' 'We must go now 'but now you are here, I'll stop and have a rest. Come into the house and have some coffee.'

Gloria, quickly refused, knowing that having coffee with Sonia would eat up the whole morning. 'No thanks, Sonia; we've a lot to do today. We've come down to see Ravenscourt, the house Lorna has inherited, it's not far from here.'

'Ravenscourt?' Sonia regarded Gloria as if a description of the place was written on her face. 'Who lived there? Do I know them?'

'Fergus Barnes, he was Lorna's godfather.'

Sonia began to interrogate Lorna as if it were of vital importance to know every detail about Fergus and his family. It would not have surprised Lorna if she'd asked what school he'd been to – or, knowing Fergus – probably expelled from.

'Was he that man who lived rather a shocking life, had girls all over the place? Not that I was shocked of course, but people in the country can have very prim ideas.' A glow of excitement sparkled in Sonia's eyes. 'He was very rich wasn't he? Made his money in food.' Sonia was in danger of sneering until she remembered that her son, her only son, made his living the same way.

'Chocolate bars, crisps or something,' she finished lamely making it sound as if Fergus's food was vastly inferior to Nathan's.

'Biscuits, the Barnes Company,' Lorna turned away, pretending to be interested in some jars of pâtè. She was not going into the fact that Fergus had sold his share in the business, spent the money on a riotous life and had ended up virtually broke.

'Where's Nathan? We want to order some things,' Gloria broke in. 'If he's not here I'm sure Beth can do it.' She smiled at Beth who was busy counting the filled jars. 'After all,' she went on, 'you know as much about the business as he does, even more, probably.'

'He's in the office, we've had a crisis. We were going to do a publicity shoot for next year's Christmas brochure. You know, country house, log fires, swathes of greenery, the whole works, to show off our produce, but the place we were going to use has been flooded. Burst boiler, I think.' Beth sighed, underlining something on her clipboard with fierce, decisive strokes.

'How dreadful,' Gloria answered mechanically, her mind on the food she wanted to order.

'Of course we could do it later in the year, well next year really, but he'd rather do it now, because we don't need to pay for expensive effects as it is the right season – it is planned to come out next Christmas, not this one, and we're cooking all the Christmas food anyway. We're trying some new lines; sweet chestnut vacherins, Christmas puddings with a crystallized orange in the centre, things we've been working flat out on to get ready for the shoot and produce for next year.'

'Can't you use this house?' Rosalind asked.

'No, we need a house with period rooms, sort of sumptuous,' Beth said quietly, as if she didn't want to offend anyone by implying that Mulberry Farm's house was less than sumptuous.

'Oh, Gloria, you came.' Nathan strode into the barn looking grim and harassed. He glanced rather impatiently at them, as if they were the last people he needed to deal with. Lorna turned away and pretended to read some leaflets listing his produce. She felt strangely agitated. She prayed he wouldn't remember her and say something derogatory about her eating all his ham samples, expecting her to be on the scrounge again. She wished she'd brought a box of her cakes as a sweetener.

'Sorry, I'm rather tied up,' he continued. 'Would you mind if Beth dealt with your orders? I wasn't expecting you so early.'

'That's fine.' Gloria appeared disappointed but she smiled bravely. 'Is there anything we can do to help?'

'No, I doubt it.' He looked despairing, 'unless you have a county house you could lend me for our publicity shoot.'

'You can borrow our house in Wimbledon, though it's hardly grand enough,' Gloria offered. 'What bad luck, what happened?'

He sighed. 'It's far worse for the people who own the house, I mustn't lose sight of that, but I was going to borrow a friend's house and avoid having to pay the huge rent these places charge. I'd pay for the decorations, tree, food and everything and photograph it as a country house with wonderful ambiance all enhanced by our Christmas produce. It may sound old fashioned but it still stirs something deep in people; an illusion of old-time Christmas cheer, with everyone happy and sharing delicious food.'

Lorna knew exactly what he meant. She didn't say she'd been part of such a shoot herself, but done in the middle of summer with fake snow and possibly fake food. She had a feeling it would irritate him if she mentioned it.

He smiled ruefully. 'Simon rang me in a panic last night, they'd been away and came back to a leaking water tank; water gushing everywhere flooding the place, bringing down part of the ceiling. We can't possibly use it now.'

'Sounds horrendous,' Gloria said.

'So, if you'll excuse me I'm going to see what else we can come up with, though I think I've exhausted all avenues now. It's all I need when we are so overstretched here.' He waved his hand at the lines of filled jars and the empty ones waiting their turn. There were rows of Christmas puddings waiting to be packed, fruitcakes waiting to be iced . . . Perhaps, Lorna wondered, she could persuade him to take some of Martha's Christmas cup-cakes. She'd made some delicious spicy ones decorated with sugar robins and Santas, on white, red or holly green icing, but perhaps now was not the time to launch into a sales pitch.

Suddenly Gloria shrieked, her eyes shining with excitement. 'I know, Lorna's house! That's a big country house isn't it, with massive rooms? Nathan can borrow that, can't he Lorna? You said it's empty and no one but the housekeeper is living there?'

Nathan spun round and studied Lorna, his expression half-hopeful, half-incredulous. She saw that he recognised her but she suspected he was racking his brains to try and recall where he'd seen her before.

'The slice of ham and the chocolate cake,' he said musingly, as if a person who only wanted one slice of ham, even though it was traded for a rather good cake, couldn't own a country house worth using for his upmarket food brochure.

Lorna, taken aback by Gloria's preposterous idea, managed to say at the same time, 'No, I'm afraid it wouldn't do at all Gloria. Most of it hasn't been lived in for ages and it's in a very bad state ...' Looking round, she saw them all staring at her with such interest, Beth and Sonia almost open-mouthed with astonishment that she owned such a house. She felt fiercely protective of Fergus, she couldn't bear them to sneer at it, blame him for letting it get in such a state.

Gloria, on a roll with her idea, was unstoppable. 'But you described Ravenscourt as a large, period house set in rural land, so surely it would be perfect ... you must see that, Lorna. Surely we can drape decorations around and just photograph the good bits?' She had a tendency to take charge, no doubt admirable in some situations, but not in this one.

'It is quite unsuitable, however many glittery trees and garlands draped around – it won't hide the bad bits,' Lorna felt cornered by them all. She'd been so upset by Fergus's death the last time she'd been there she hadn't really taken it all in, though she couldn't forget the ravages of damp and decay.

She caught sight of Nathan's face. It had been taut with strain when they'd first seen him; Gloria's suggestion had lifted it, making his eyes shine, a half-smile of relief on his face. Now it had fallen again and, to her annoyance, she felt as if *she* had let him down, was even perhaps, in some sinister way, responsible for the flood in the house he'd been planning to use. If only she could deal with him on his own without Sonia and Beth and even Gloria with her sometimes extravagant ideas, they might get it to work. She felt a glimmer of excitement; she'd been in enough photo shoots to see how bleak, soulless places could be transformed into places of beauty... surely there was no harm in him seeing it? She was about to suggest this when Beth jumped in.

'I know Ravenscourt. I went to an art exhibition there – years ago. The rooms were lovely, great proportions, wonderful fireplaces – everything a dream country house should be. I'm sure we could do something with it, even if it is run down.' She turned eagerly to everyone, describing various tricks used to transform a place; camera angles, lighting and suchlike. She talked as if it had already been decided and that she, and she alone, could make it possible by her skills and so was the obvious person to be in charge of it all.

Lorna decided that she had taken an instant dislike to Beth, which had nothing at all to do with being jealous that she was married to Nathan and that the raspberry pink cashmere was tucked neatly away in a drawer somewhere in her bedroom.

Rosalind, always the peacemaker, added her bit. 'We haven't seen the house yet and Lorna has said that nothing's been done to the main rooms for years. It may be completely derelict; creeping damp, ceilings down.' She caught Lorna's grateful glance. 'Bats, rats ...' she embellished further.

'How can we know until we've seen it?' Beth said bossily. Having got her teeth into this, she was determined not to let go.

They were all looking at Lorna expectantly and she felt too outnumbered to think up any more excuses as to why she didn't want them there, picking over the remnants of a once sumptuous house like scavengers. Nathan was watching her, his eyes gentle on her face and she felt a spark of warmth, wishing it were just him who would come to Ravenscourt. Surely he would understand her feelings of protecting Fergus's memory from their scorn. She felt overwhelmed by being the owner of such a house, cowed by the impact it seemed to be having on her life and her friends. Gloria, without even consulting her was handing it to Nathan as a backdrop for his Christmas brochure and worse, what about that crazy idea to put their errant husbands there for Christmas?

She hoped that Gloria, who was now bursting to speak again, would not embarrass them by mentioning that.

Nathan raked his fingers through his hair as if he might pull it out in handfuls.

Seeing this, Beth began to describe again how she would disguise the house with decorations and special lighting, until Lorna felt she'd scream. Nathan put up his hand to staunch Beth's outpouring, saying, 'I'm sorry that this was thrown at you, Lorna. Gloria is so impulsive,' he threw her a smile, lightening her heart. 'It just seems that you have an empty country house and we've just been let down with the one we were going to use. Your imagination is probably running riot imagining all sorts of horrors. Maybe if I explain exactly what we'll do…'

'I've explained but I'll go through it again, more slowly,' Beth interrupted him, turning to Lorna with a patient smile as if she was about to explain something of the utmost simplicity to an idiot.

'I know exactly what it would entail,' Lorna said wearily. 'I happen to have been in a Christmas advertisement, though it was done in the summer, months before Christmas, and I know that Ravenscourt will not do.'

'My dear, are you an actress? Someone we ought to know?' Sonia exclaimed as if Lorna might be in line for an Oscar.

Before she could answer, Nathan said, 'I prefer to do my brochures at Christmas time, this one will be for next Christmas. We have all the food and the shots taken outside – and I'd like a few of those – look better in the proper season. The house may not do but please could we at least see it?' His voice dropped an octave, soft and rich, tugging at her heart in the most annoying way. She was a fool; just because she so craved the kindness of a nice man she was going to lie down and roll over and become his slave.

Beth began again to boast about how she could transform anywhere into a magical setting, however dank. Lorna wondered why these exceptional skills could not turn this barn into the cosy, country house setting they envisaged.

Nathan came over to her and said quietly, 'Look Lorna, I know it's a dreadful imposition, especially as it seems you've only recently inherited it but if it's at all possible I'd love to see it. I'm sorry I can't pay you, I've got cash flow problems just now, but I'd give you a whole ham.' He smiled, his eyes tender as he regarded her. Her heart lifted and for a moment she felt close to him as if they were the only two people in the barn.

'All right … you can come and see it, but don't expect too much,' she said and feeling hemmed in by all the others congratulating her and throwing out their ideas as if her consent had given them carte blanche for any other crazy plans, she slipped away out of the barn for a moment of peace to think it through.

A wind had got up, whipping round her like a knife, but it was a relief to get out in the fresh air away from the warm, almost suffocating smell of the cooking hams and chutneys. She pounded over grass, which was like a green carpet thrown over the ridges of the roots of the tress that lined it. Ahead she saw a copse of fir trees and she went towards it, wanting to escape all this and be alone to digest the bizarre events Ravenscourt had suddenly spawned.

CHAPTER NINE
Divided Loyalties

Perhaps she had been too bossy. Gloria felt a twinge of guilt but really, someone had to take charge and it was hardly poor Lorna's fault that she was so indecisive at the moment, valiantly struggling to adapt to her new life of being single again. Of their three husbands she'd have thought Stephen was the most reliable, the one least likely to do a runner on his family, but then, did you ever really know anyone? Perhaps he'd been so used to life going his way, and the kudos of having a top job in his company, that suddenly being made redundant at an age when finding another well-paid job was difficult had pushed him off the rails.

Adrian had always drunk too much, although what was too much? There had always been a good selection of bottles on show whenever she'd visited him in the legal firm where he worked – very tempting for someone with a taste for it. The consumption of alcohol had become a sort of flag of honour these days with people boasting that they'd been legless, listing the amount they'd drunk as if it were something to be proud of. In fact, in some circles, if someone didn't drink they were thought of as wimps, 'not one of the team'. She'd heard of people being turned down for jobs or missing promotion because they didn't join in these drinking sessions. This strange 'bonding' seemingly could only take place if everyone was drunk.

Ravenscourt was now the main topic of their conversation as they all stood round in the barn, discussing whether or not it would do as a backdrop for Nathan's brochure. Beth dominated the discussion with her ideas and Gloria could see that this irritated Lorna. There was a sort of hunted look about her eyes and she was about to pitch in and stop it by saying they must be on their way when she saw Nathan talking intently to Lorna. After a moment, everyone looked their way and she saw Nathan smile, touch Lorna's arm and thank her, and she felt relieved that she must have agreed to let him see the house. Everyone else realised it too, and began to throw about their ideas as if they were there already and had taken the house over. She moved to congratulate Lorna, when she saw her slip round the back of them and go outside. She was about to follow her when Nathan came up to her and said with relief, 'She's agreed I can see the house, I understand her reluctance, as it was rather thrown at her and I feel bad at jumping at it, but after being let down with the one we were going to use, I felt quite desperate to find somewhere else in time, while we have all the food and stuff. You haven't seen the house, yet, have you? So you've no idea if it will do or not?'

'No, we're on our way to see it now, we came to you first as you are the furthest away. Lorna wasn't expecting to inherit it at all, so she's still stunned by it, and faced with your request

... well, she ... none of us were expecting it and also she ...'
She paused, wondering if she should she tell him about Lorna's
predicament?

'Go on ... she what?' Nathan questioned her.

'She's going through a very tough time. Her husband was ff'ed
up by some shrink and has careered off with some visa-seeking
nymphet.'

His expression deepened with concern, 'I'm sorry. If I'd
known, I wouldn't have burdened her with this.' He glanced towards the barn door as if he would go after her and tell her not to
worry, that he wouldn't go to Ravenscourt after all.

'I'm sure she'll be fine about you seeing it. It might not be
right for your posh brochure at all,' she laughed.

He smiled and touched her shoulder and it sent a little frisson
of desire down her body.

He said, 'I'll go and find her, having gone through all that, it's
hardly surprising she's reluctant to let us loose there.'

Beth, overhearing the tail end of his remark, said rather
scathingly, 'Lorna changed her mind?' Her face was creased with
impatience. 'Where is she? I'll explain *again* exactly what we
want to do.'

'Leave it Beth, I'll go and talk to her.' Nathan moved towards
the door.

Lorna was quite subdued today. Stephen's departure had shattered her and Gloria knew she was determined to pick up a new
life, though the pain of losing the old one could creep up and
pull you down when you were least expecting it, as she knew only

too well with Adrian. She should have held her tongue and not started this fiasco.

'Don't worry, I'll deal with it,' she smiled, laying her hand on Nathan's arm, resisting an urge to stroke him, her feelings torn between doing right by Lorna and getting Nathan what he wanted and gaining his gratitude.

She left the barn, looking round for Lorna and saw her just about to disappear into the clump of trees in the corner of the lawn. She called to her to wait and ran across the lawn, the wet earth sticking to her thin, leather boots. Lorna waited for her, but she was scowling.

'Oh, Glory, why did you come out with it without asking me first? I'm sorry for Nathan losing the house he was going to use and I don't mind him seeing it but it's the others. Well, Beth, really, she's so forceful and I can't bear it if she and Sonia sneer over its sad decline. I thought we'd have a good time exploring it just the three of us, and now if they come, it will spoil it.'

'I'm really sorry, Lorna but Nathan looked so fraught I couldn't help myself. And the house can't be that bad. Beth will transform it, or corners of it, so they can take their photographs.'

'That's what I'm afraid of, I don't want it transformed.'

'But remember our plan to house the boys there. If they make it Christmassy we'll ask them to leave the decorations up, even add some food and we could pretend it was a hotel we are all staying in for Christmas and then somehow . . .' She must convince her, she couldn't bear to lose Justin, thinking of it tore at her heart. 'We'll find a way to persuade them to stay while we go home and have a peaceful time with our children.'

'Not that idea again, Glory. It was a joke, a mad idea like we'd have thought up when we were children. It will never come off,' Lorna said gently, almost laughing about it. 'Remember they'll have their mobiles and their cars with them.'

'We'll see,' Gloria squeezed her arm, thinking it better to leave their plan out of it just now. 'Let them come over later to see the house when we've had a bit of time there, just the three of us as we planned.'

CHAPTER TEN
First Impressions

It didn't take them long to get to Ravenscourt. They drove through the wrought iron gates, long tethered open by grass and weeds. The fields either side of the drive had been rented out to a local farmer and some wind-blown sheep huddled into a shelter under the trees.

Lorna was silent on the journey, anxiety ploughing through her. She wished they hadn't gone to Mulberry Farm before seeing Ravenscourt, or better still, not gone there at all. She'd seen the palaver of a shoot, all those cameras and cables and people milling round and she didn't want that for Ravenscourt. She felt sorry for Clara and wished she'd thought of her before she'd agreed to this. How would she feel having various strangers poking about the house, perhaps making derogatory remarks about the state of it? She knew that, although she had no cause to, Clara felt guilty that the house had fallen into such a sad state. Yet it was far beyond a good hovering and a flick of a duster.

She'd wanted to make it clear that they couldn't all come, that Nathan could slip in – on his own – for a few minutes. When he'd seen how bad it was, that would be the end of it and he would have to find somewhere else.

She geared herself up to say this when she reached the barn but was infuriated when she heard Beth saying she'd go to the house, photograph it and show the pictures to Nathan later.

She'd read too much into Nathan's manner; his kindness had led her to imagine that he cared for her. She had quite lost sight of the fact that he had a company to run and needed a house, Ravenscourt, for his brochure. Emotions didn't come into it, this was business, and she must learn from it. Why not try and get her cupcakes in on the act too?

She was about to barge in and say there could be no photographs when Nathan broke away from the group and came to her. 'Thank you so much, Lorna, for letting me come and see Ravenscourt. I feel I've rather pushed you into it, but it could just be perfect for my publicity shoot.'

'You will be coming yourself, I hope.' she said, her heart lifting, hoping he would understand her feelings for Fergus. She'd tried to explain them if he came.

'Yes, I'll be there.' She felt relieved, and wanted to say, 'Come on your own,' but she did not, afraid it would sound unbusinesslike. Anyway, Sonia and Beth were already determinedly coming towards them.

'Here we are,' Lorna said, as Gloria pulled up in front of the house.

'Wow, some house!' Rosalind exclaimed in awe.

Clara appeared out of the kitchen entrance to greet them, obviously impatient for their company. Lorna introduced them.

'It's quite grand,' Gloria said. 'Imagine sweeping up to that front door in some classy car. I suppose in the past a butler opened the door and a little maid came and unpacked your suitcase? Is that what happened when you arrived in the old days when there was staff, Lorna?'

'We didn't have a classy car. There were staff, but I can't remember if my case was unpacked for me. The house was beautiful when I came as a child, almost magical, I used to think the passages led to secret rooms as it's all so topsy turvy upstairs, especially the top floor. Funny little rooms tucked in here and there. Then gradually it grew more shabby, it is so sad to see how much it has deteriorated.'

'So Stephen knows it?' Gloria asked.

'He came once or twice when the children were small. I brought them down for the day sometimes without him in the holidays. He may not remember it now. I hope not, I haven't told him about it yet and don't know what his reaction will be.'

'It's surely nothing to do with him now you are divorced,' Gloria said firmly.

'Must have been lovely in its heyday,' Rosalind said, to change the subject. 'Sad that no one can afford to live in these huge houses now. Except Russians and 'slebs' of course.'

'Come in and have some coffee to warm you up.' Clara led the way through the side door into the kitchen. Lorna, now seeing it through her friends' eyes, thought how old-fashioned and drab it seemed with its tall pine cupboards and deep china sink. It appeared worse as they went round the rest of the house. The creeping plants that blocked the windows cloaked the rooms with an eerie, green hue. The hall was large and icy cold with a stone flagged floor. A brass chandelier, festooned in cobwebs and dull with age, hung from the ceiling.

The drawing room seemed even bleaker, with a large water stain resembling a group of islands running down from the corner of the ceiling and over half the wall, bubbling up the faded wallpaper. Part of the moulding from the ceiling had crumbled and fallen like lumps of icing sugar onto the floor.

Clara said apologetically, 'I know it looks a mess, but it's so hard to keep clean. There was so much to do in the rooms he used and looking after him. We used to have more help but…'

'Of course you couldn't keep up with it. It's far too much for one person. These places need a fleet of staff.' Gloria smiled at her. 'It is lovely though. Well, it would be if it was all put back the way it was.'

'It's the damp,' Rosalind shivered, 'that's what kills it. You need roaring fires and I must say the fireplaces are magnificent, so enormous and ornate they'd be shocking anywhere else with all those inlays of different coloured marble, but here in these huge rooms they look fantastic.'

'Beth will be mad about those,' Gloria said, then, seeing Lorna's face, went on, 'sorry love, I took over. But you must admit it is beautiful even if it does need a complete makeover.'

'I just wanted to get used to it being mine before other people intrude with their ideas of what to do with it.' Lorna said. Being here again and seeing the sad state of it wrung her heart. There was so much to be done. The task was too daunting to contemplate just now.

She opened the door to the dining room, leading the way in. It was colder than being outside in the garden. There were hunting prints on the walls, and holly green velvet curtains held back by faded green tassels. Here and there Lorna noticed little bald patches where mice or moths had made a meal of them. It was warmer in the smaller rooms where Fergus had lived. His bedroom, with its French style double bed, was comfortably done up in duck egg blue and fawn. It opened into a modern, rather austere bathroom made more cheerful by a red carpet.

'I made him buy that to brighten it up a bit and warm his feet too,' Clara said. 'He sat in here, his study.' She opened another door into a good-sized room, the walls lined with reams of books on smart wooden shelves. A large mahogany desk stood near the window overlooking the garden and there were a couple of comfy chairs by the fire, but somehow the thought of the two of them, sitting forlornly there day after day, with no other visitors, was unbearable to Lorna. But Fergus had refused to let her come until his last breath and she must accept that.

'He must have been very lonely?' she said to Clara, hit with the reality of it.

'He was lonely for the life he'd lost and all the people who'd died before him. He would talk of them for hours, of the war and his friends who'd been killed. He felt guilty sometimes that he hadn't died with them. Whatever life they all lived after that war, it never left them, and at the end all his memories of it crowded back.'

'And yet he lived such a glamorous life after that, though it seemed he could never settle down with one woman,' Lorna reminded her.

Rosalind shivered, clasped her arms round herself. 'It is a sad house being so neglected; it will cost a fortune to restore it, Lorna. You know how these old houses are.' She spoke from experience, having done up a wreck of a house herself. 'You start on one thing and uncover a multitude of other things that need urgent attention. I'm sure he meant well, but being confined to these few rooms, he probably didn't realise how much needed doing to the rest of it.'

'I know, I'll have to think what to do with it.' Lorna sighed, knowing the answer but feeling as if she were letting the house down.

Unconsciously Rosalind rubbed it in. 'Poor house, but even as it is now, you can feel its character.'

'Like an aging great beauty without make up,' Gloria said. 'Well, I don't know about you all but I am freezing. We'd better go and have lunch and be back for Nathan.'

Lorna explained to Clara about Nathan coming over later as he wanted to see if it was suitable for his photo shoot. She finished, 'I'm sure it won't do, he has very high standards and will not think it smart enough for his posh food.'

'It won't do for our other idea either,' Rosalind laughed, 'though I must say it is secluded enough.'

'What was your other idea?' Clara asked, as they scurried back into the comfort of the warm kitchen.

'Oh, it's mad.' Lorna wished it hadn't been mentioned, it sounded so crazy. 'Just dumping our husbands here while we enjoyed a drama-free Christmas without them spoiling it for us . . . well, namely the children, as they have in past years.'

Gloria said, 'you see, Clara, we married men far older that we are. They were lovely people but since hitting their sixties, they have all become difficult husbands. Mine drinks, Rosalind's Ivan would rather help disadvantaged teenagers than give time to his own . . . oh, not that *they* are disadvantaged,' she said quickly, though she might have added, 'but they could be soon if he doesn't become a better father to them.' She went on, '. . . and he seems to be attracted to their social workers and often brings them home for Christmas, and poor Lorna, well, she may have told you about her husband.'

Clara nodded sympathetically. 'But you want them to come and stay at Ravenscourt? How would you get them here?'

'I'm afraid we let our imaginations run away with ourselves. We didn't realise how derelict this house is. We thought, well, not seriously,' Gloria looked embarrassed now at admitting to such a scheme, 'that we could get them here, give them some sort of Christmas for themselves and leave them here, out of our and our children's hair, until it's over. But of course they'd escape, ring out for help on their mobiles. It's a mad idea, born out of desperation.' She laughed rather hollowly, but Clara looked serious.

'Mobiles don't work just here, you have to go up to the top of the hill. Once we were stuck in here. A huge tree fell down over the drive; we had to walk right round through the woods to the road, quite a way. It would be near impossible to go that way now, as the woods are thick with brambles. They used to be so well kept, but there it is, soon as you turn your back, nature takes over.'

'Still wouldn't work,' Lorna said. 'We'd need someone to look after them, make sure they stayed put.'

Clara said, 'I know just the person, Jane Purdy. She lives in the village. Spent her whole working life as a school matron in a boys' public school. She had to leave when the school closed down and she didn't feel like starting somewhere new. She's past seventy, but you wouldn't know it. I could cook for them.'

A flicker of excitement shivered through the three women but then as quickly died.

'It's a tempting thought,' Gloria said with a sigh, 'but it would be too complicated and really the house is far too cold and uncomfortable, though how I wish it were possible so that we could, just once, give our children a stress-free Christmas

CHAPTER ELEVEN
The Great Inspection

'So when is Flora's baby due?' Rosalind turned towards Lorna, her face a study of horrified compassion. The three of them were in a local pub. The bar was festooned with Christmas streamers and polystyrene robins and reindeers lurking in any spare spaces, filling the three women with panic instead of goodwill.

'About April I think.' Lorna said. 'Having a grandchild, even years before I envisaged having one, should be a time for rejoicing, but with Stephen gone, Flora so young and the baby's father married, it's a mess. A sad story instead of a happy one.'

'You don't think she did it as a cry for help, hoping to get Stephen back? Or got involved with an older man because she's missing her father?' Rosalind laughed awkwardly. 'You know the sort of psychobabble spewed out today. We are all meant to be crying out for help, aren't we? Though I bet if *we* cried out, we'd be shut up in a darkened room, or put on Prozac.'

'I did wonder if subconsciously she got pregnant to shock Stephen into returning, but I think she was careless because Ben said he couldn't have children.' Lorna had sieved through every scenario in the loneliness of the night.

'In our day, they used to say they were infertile if they hadn't got a condom, remember,' Gloria chipped in.

'Yes, but we didn't fall for it, we were so terrified we'd get pregnant.' Lorna said, thinking with a pang of Stephen and his tender lovemaking. 'I also,' she went on, firmly pushing that image from her mind, 'wondered if the man is a control freak and used her to give him the baby his wife couldn't.' It was a relief to be able to confess her innermost fears, extreme though they may be, to these friends without experiencing ridicule.

'I did hear once of someone using a surrogate mother, only the husband fell in love with her and left his wife.' Gloria wondered if this had happened to someone she knew or if she'd seen it on television or read it in a novel.

Their discussion became intense and occasionally far-fetched, but slowly, soothed by their concern, Lorna began to feel better. Gloria and Rosalind were both trusted friends and she could rely on their support. But even as she felt this, she was seized in a sickening vice of grief. She missed Stephen as he used to be, not the man who'd been struck by this adolescent sex-fest before impotence – at least with her – grounded him.

Gloria seeing her distress squeezed her arm saying, 'It will all work out; no one cares today if you have a baby without a husband. We'll all love it, be its surrogate grannies.'

'But what if Stephen has a baby with that girl? If she had his child she could stay in this country, couldn't she?' Lorna blurted, pinioned in the grip of the fear of it. Would Stephen, though he had two children already, feel he must prove his potency again?

Rosalind poured a drop of milk into her coffee, watching the colour change and then adding a tiny bit more as if she was choosing paint and it had to be an exact shade of beige. 'That would be a bloody nightmare, but I'm sure he won't – can't, by the sound of him. Ivan could do the same,' her face tightened, 'come home with a baby under his arm, or a pregnant social worker he expects me to look after.' She shivered with the horror of it. 'But I'm sure this latent sex craze is a front, a last fly of the flag, because they are virtually impotent anyway,' she added hopefully.

'If you've already had children you know what hard work they are. All those sleepless nights at the beginning. Surely an old man wouldn't want to go through that again.' Gloria said.

'Ivan certainly wouldn't, he wasn't too bad when the girls were born but now they've reached their teens he loses patience very quickly.' Rosalind said. 'I don't think he was very good with Polly either, he felt guilty about his marriage not working and spoilt her, giving her presents instead of time and discipline, and as you know, she's still desperate to get her own way.'

'Stephen might have forgotten, or pay for a nanny.' Lorna fought to curb her rising panic. She could hear her mother saying in that singsong way she had when handing out advice – as though by putting on a jokey voice it did not sound judgemental – 'Don't worry, it may never happen'. How that voice had irritated her then, but how she longed for it now.

This fearful thought brought more frantic discussion until they suddenly realised that Nathan, if he hadn't changed his mind, would be arriving at Ravenscourt any moment.

He arrived just before they did, in an ancient sports car that looked as if it could have been made from a kit. Sonia was with him. They were both standing outside staring at the house. The day was closing in, the dying sun touching the old house with one last burst of gold. There was a hint of melancholy in the air that seemed to add to the desolation of a past life, a house now forgotten.

'In a few feet of snow it will look very romantic,' Sonia greeted them.

Surreptitiously Lorna studied Nathan's reaction. She wanted him to like Ravenscourt; it was Beth she couldn't take. But if Nathan liked it, Beth would take over, bossing about, making her feel ashamed for having such a house and letting it get in such a state even though it was not her fault at all. She would criticise Fergus's taste, and then hers if she made any suggestions.

She was sick of criticism. In low moments she imagined Stephen chanting all sorts of personal insults to justify him leaving a perfectly good marriage, perhaps telling his Pekinese woman that his ex-wife could castrate a man just by her expression. Her sister Felicity, safe in her own marriage, had advised her to pray more, do the Christian thing of turning the other cheek. 'Which cheek?' she'd retorted, 'Both, all four if you count my bottom, have been metaphorically slapped hard.' No, the whole episode of letting strangers into the house would be fraught with drama she hadn't the strength to cope with, added to the ones she was going through already.

Clara appeared flushed and star struck at this invasion and ushered them into the kitchen, saying apologetically that it was the only warm room in the house. Gloria started gushing to Nathan about the old cupboards and the ancient stove, pointing them out as if he could not see them for himself, opening the door to the larder with its brick floor and scrubbed, pine shelves holding a few empty jars and extra cooking pots, exclaiming how she wished she had a larder to fill with homemade jams and bottled fruit, igniting Nathan's interest as if he could picture it filled with his tempting produce.

Feeling tired and dejected, Lorna could not see anything good about the place. She wondered how much its on-going deterioration was costing her every moment as more damp seeped in somewhere, window sills rotted and the winter wind pierced through the loose windows to ice up the water pipes and crack more of the plasterwork. She must sell it and fast, finding someone with the resources to bring it back to its former glory. She ought to go to the nearest estate agent and ask them to take it off her hands as soon as possible.

'I remember that make of stove; we had one when I first married. Very simple and it works beautifully, just fill it up with fuel and the room is as warm as toast.' Sonia said admiringly.

'We also have a modern stove,' Clara gestured towards an alcove near the pantry door that housed something that could have been called modern in the sixties.

Nathan turned to Lorna, his face impassive. 'Mind if I just walk around on my own, just the downstairs rooms?'

'Go ahead, Fergus only lived in a couple of rooms in the last years of his life,' she repeated, feeling she had to stand up for him.

It was important to her that Nathan would not think badly of Fergus for allowing the place to fall into such ruin.

'That's OK,' he said quietly, as if he understood. He went down the passage that led from the kitchen to the hall.

Sonia sat down on a chair and undid her coat. 'I'll leave him to it.' She smiled round at them. 'He's like his father, quite incapable of making up his mind if he's disturbed by other people. He hates people coming at him with their views and ideas until he's sure of his own.'

Lorna wondered if Sonia's eyes slightly strayed in Gloria's direction, but she may have been mistaken. But if this trait in him was true, how on earth did he get on with Beth?

'It so sad that it needs so much doing to it and I haven't the sort of mega bucks such an operation would need. I suppose the best idea is to put it on the market, or at least get it surveyed. Do you know of a reliable estate agent locally, who could be left to get on with it?' she asked Sonia.

'Yes, Carson's, Sonia said. 'Henry Carson, old boyfriend of mine. It's his firm and his son runs it now, though Henry still works some days.' She rummaged in her large handbag, pulling out a pink, leather diary. 'If I can borrow your phone I'll ring him for you. I don't have a mobile – they give you cancer.'

'It hasn't been proved.' Rosalind, who got withdrawal symptoms if she didn't have hers on her, and could not be in constant touch with her daughters, broke in.

Sonia shrugged and took the walkabout phone Clara bought to her.

'You are surely not going to put the house on the market before Christmas, are you?' Gloria asked her pointedly.

'I don't know, I hadn't realised how bad it really was. I'd like to get an estate agent to see it, just to hear what they say,' Lorna said. She didn't want to sell it but what other option had she? 'I know I can't afford to live here, or do it up, even superficially.' Nor would I want to be somewhere so isolated, she said to herself, smiling at Clara, hoping she hadn't hurt her feelings. 'It was darling of Fergus to leave it to me but he couldn't have known how much attention it needed. Far better it goes soon before any more bits drop off and I get too attached to it.'

'But our plan,' Gloria reminded her. Lorna pretended not to hear.

Sonia dialled a number. 'Ah, Henry darling, you are working. I hoped you were, I've got this marvellous house for you to sell. So much atmosphere, so grand, needs a lot of TLC but people like that, don't they? Would make a lovely bijoux hotel, or a Russian or one of those footballers might like it as a country house. It's certainly secluded enough.'

She prattled on, outlining her ideas to improve the house, leaving Lorna feeling superfluous; furious that the Harwood family seemed to assume they could take charge of everyone and everything. She left the room before she lost her temper. When they'd gone she would ask Clara for the name of a different estate agent and not allow Sonia's 'admirer' anywhere near Ravenscourt. She had momentarily forgotten Nathan and almost fell over him in a dark corner in the hall.

'This is wonderful,' he said. 'With a roaring fire in that grate and garlands of greenery and a table laid up with silver and glass, and lots of food, it will be perfect. If you agree, Lorna, I'd like to use the drawing room as well, with its spectacular moulding, get in lots of people as if there is a party. Photograph the side that isn't damp.'

'I'm selling it,' Lorna said irritably. 'In fact your mother has probably sold it already. I expect the builders to arrive almost as we speak.' She was trembling with fury. Was she so insignificant that people – namely Stephen, now joined by the Harwoods – could just walk over her and snatch what they wanted without a care for her feelings?

Nathan sighed. 'Oh damn, she can get out of hand. I suppose she's rung one of her admirers. If you want something, a good doctor, plumber, whatever, ask my mother. She has an admirer in almost every profession, useful if you want one.'

'She's on to an estate agent now but I did say I wanted to sell it as soon as possible.'

'But you'll let me borrow it first? Please, Lorna.' His voice was soft, melting her ill humour.

It was dusk now and the strange green light that had struggled through the creepers had been replaced by a muddy yellow glow coming from a few still live, but dusty bulbs in the chandelier. She imagined she could feel his charm oozing into her. It was warm and comforting and she wanted to bask in it, like a cat stretching out to be stroked. She took a step towards him. Gloria, striding through from the kitchen and calling for her, saved her from any foolishness. She did not see Nathan in the shadows and she said in a frantic whisper.

'You can't sell it before Christmas, remember our plan. I'm sure we could pull it off if we set our minds to it.' Gloria stood, feet firmly planted, one hand on the curve of the banister like a general disciplining her troops.

'What plan?' Nathan stepped out into the light. 'Are you going to stay here for Christmas? It would be lovely and if you get the fires going it won't be too cold.'

'No, not really,' Gloria backtracked, looking embarrassed. 'But how do you like it Nathan, will it do?'

'Absolutely. Fires, masses of greenery, people,' he laughed. 'We'll bring in all our friends, provide food and wine and have a party, take some pictures and we've done it.'

Sonia came through to join them. 'There you are,' she said smugly. 'Henry is coming over almost at once. He has a client already, one of those city types who've come from nowhere and made millions and now want a lifestyle to match.'

'But you never asked me first,' Lorna burst out, quite forgetting that moments before she'd wanted to put the house on the market before it bankrupted her.

Nathan scowled at Sonia. 'Ring him back and put him off. Lorna will decide when she wants to put it on the market.' He turned to her. 'Ravenscourt would be perfect for our brochure if you'd allow it. If we make it nice, even though it will just be cosmetic, you may get a better price for it when it does go on the market. What do you say?' He looked so eager, his smile lighting up his face, that she had to turn away. She was tempted to say, 'No. You, your mother and your wife in the pink jersey that *I* wanted, must get out of my life, you disturb me too much.' But true to form, Gloria burst in.

'That will be perfect. If you make it look Christmassy, warm and inviting, everyone will want it.' She threw a meaningful glance at Lorna. 'If you think you can transform the place, Nathan, then do it.'

Rosalind joined them, appraising the place, mentally designing her own transformation. 'It could be made wonderful. There's so much scope here.'

'You're right,' Nathan said. 'Thank you so much, Lorna. I'll ring Beth.' He snatched out his mobile.

Clara was the most excited of them all. With everyone chattering away about creating a Christmas scene, she had got confused and appeared to think that Nathan was a film director and that Ravenscourt would soon be occupied by such lovelies as Colin Firth and Kate Winslet, or even some of the older heartthrobs she used to lust over in her youth.

'It's so exciting, how I wish Fergus were here to see it all.'

'It will only be Nathan and his friends dressed up in their party clothes, no one exciting. It's for his brochure on Christmas food.' Lorna felt mean as she saw Clara's face fall, but it was only fair to tell her the truth. 'It's not a film, Clara, and anyway I don't know if I can agree to it. There are bound to be dozens of health and safety regulations in case the house falls down on top of everyone – which it looks like doing imminently, and I'm sued for millions.'

'Oh, I see,' Clara drooped with disappointment, before shaking herself out of her despondency. She added, 'but it would be exciting all the same, wouldn't it? Bring some life to the old house again.'

Nathan came over to her, smiling. 'We can make this marvellous, thank you so much. I'll leave you enough food for an amazing Christmas. A whole ham,' he laughed, 'then you won't need to eat all my samples.' He grabbed her hands. His face was flushed with enthusiasm; his eyes glowed warmly at her. 'We'll take such care of it, I promise.' He dropped her hands and went back into the icy dining room.

Gloria, hovering beside her, said quietly, 'You'll be glad you've let him do it. He'll take some lovely photographs, and perhaps make it possible to carry out our plan to send the men here for Christmas.'

'That idea was mad, Glory, just a joke,' Lorna reminded her. 'However can we get them here? And even if we did, they'd escape. Adrian might be persuaded if he was drunk but I doubt Ivan would come, or that I'd get Stephen here. He knows Ravenscourt and always thought it too secluded, and *if* he did come he'd bring that girl.'

'We only want to keep them here a few days so we can have a relaxing Christmas.' Gloria said. 'Three days, even two would be heaven. I've had so many Christmases spoilt by Adrian. I want a good Christmas this year – if I don't,' her voice wobbled, 'Justin won't come home. He can't bear it you see; his father drunk, looking so dirty and smelly, and everyone on tenterhooks wondering what he'll do or say next. Justin used to ask his friends over but he doesn't any more and I find that sad.'

Lorna put her arm round Gloria's shoulders. This would happen to her too. Their children were mortified at their father's behaviour and had threatened to do their own thing for Christmas this year, dreading a re-run of last years' traumatic one when Stephen kept disappearing on mysterious errands and returned late for lunch looking bedraggled. When Dan, her cousin, asked what he'd been up to, Stephen mumbled something about seeing to some work and that the car had played up, delaying him.

'More likely *you've* played up,' Dan retorted. The memory of the shame and pain of it and the horror on the children's faces burnt her still. Would Stephen think it was his divine right to come for Christmas this year? Would he want to bring the girl, making up some story to prick her conscience, as Ivan did for Rosalind with his social workers, about being kind to someone who had nowhere else to go?

Flora could easily choose to spend Christmas with Ben, the father of her coming baby and his mother, who longed for a grandchild. Ben's wife might leave him and Flora marry him and their life together might not include her. Rosalind felt the same about her children, who were too young to leave home just yet, though there was a possibility that they could be invited to go skiing with a family they knew from school. Normally they would have hated to be away for Christmas but now, feeling moody and unloved by a father who seemingly preferred to be with other adolescents and their social workers than them, the idea of being away in the snow for Christmas seemed enticing.

Ravenscourt had thrown up a sort of mad solution, but the choice was clear: it was between putting up with their husbands or losing their children, and she knew which all of them would sacrifice. Why stay with a difficult husband who no longer cared enough to treat them properly, when you could lose your children and possibly future grandchildren too?

'It won't work, Gloria, but how I wish it would. I'll agree to let Nathan use the house for his shoot, if he can get out some insurance in case there is a dreadful accident.'

'You're a star,' Gloria kissed her. 'We'll make our Christmas plan work, you'll see. It might give the men a fright and bring them to their senses.' She went off happily to find Nathan and tell him the good news.

Clara produced some tea and they all sat round the kitchen table discussing Nathan's brochure. Clara gave him her telephone number saying she'd be available any time to let people in and do anything he required.

Nathan sat down next to Lorna. He'd made some notes and he asked her what she thought of them. 'The hall could be made to look like a dining room, don't you think? I know the staircase is there and that in itself is amazing, sort of Arts and Crafts, so ornate with all those twisting vines and lilies, we might use it in another shot as part of the scene.'

They sat close together at one end of the kitchen table and every so often his fingers would brush against hers as he turned over the pages of his pad of paper, or leant close, his hand skimming over the paper as he drew a sketch of how he wanted the scene to be. Her body glowed as if it were lit from inside. How good it was to be close to such an attractive man again. She caught Sonia's eyes on her and pretended indifference. Trust a mother to suss her out; she expected that any minute, Sonia would remind Nathan that he was married. But these moments with him were harmless. She was surely too wise to read anything romantic into his gratitude at lending him Ravenscourt. It was just good manners for him to tell her his ideas, and ask her own, and hadn't she only a short time before been complaining to herself that she felt left out?

It was dark now; the lights in the kitchen dim from lack of working bulbs – the lights were set so high it would be quite an exercise to clamber up a ladder to change them. The dusk pressed in through the windows; the scratch of branches against the glass coupled with the half-light added to the feeling of intimacy. Lorna's leg was against Nathan's and he did not move his away, not that there was much room to move it to. What if he put his arm round her, leant his face close to hers, his lips caressing her cheeks, her own lips ... The thought flowed into her and she let it grow in her imagination, warming her body. I can dream, can't I, she told herself, my life's so tough just now, what harm is there in escaping into a fantasy world for a moment?

'It's dark, we'd better get back.' Rosalind broke the spell. Gloria agreed, getting up sharply, the leg of her chair whining against the stone floor.

'Well thank you so much again, Lorna,' Nathan smiled at her. 'I'll give these notes to Beth and see what she makes of them. I hope you'll come down for the shoot and keep an eye on us.'

It was as if a cork had been pulled from her and all her foolish dreams and happiness ran out, dispersing into the gloomy room. Beth would be the one to take charge of everything that might have made her happy. But how foolish she was being. Just because her leg had sat cosily against Nathan's leg, it didn't herald undying love – or even love at all.

CHAPTER TWELVE
The Father of the Child

It was Saturday and Flora was bringing Ben to lunch to meet her. Lorna was dreading it. It was one thing accepting that her daughter was pregnant and a baby would soon be here, quite another to accept its father, a man she disapproved of for cheating on his wife, but it had to be done.

Lorna cooked one of her famous fish pies, followed by Flora's favourite pudding – if she didn't feel too nauseous to eat it – homemade cinnamon ice cream and pears poached in red wine. She'd made a batch of cupcakes too to try out for the shop, Victoria sponge mixture with a dollop of fresh fruit curd hidden inside. She had made three different kinds; passion fruit, orange and lime. Marcus was supposed to be here too, though Lorna now wished that he wasn't coming. She hadn't arranged it, thinking it better to tackle this first meeting with the errant husband alone, but he'd rung her last night to announce that he was coming home for a night or so. He had some revision to do and he might as well do it in comfort.

'I'll give him the once over,' he'd said. 'Flora's mad to get knocked up like that.'

If only Marcus were older and would take this situation seriously, but then, he was only eighteen and took life as it came without much thought of the consequences.

She heard the scrape of Flora's key in the lock, the sound of the door opening, Flora calling out, 'Mum, it's us!' and the door close behind her.

Her heart was racing, if only she could escape, but it had to be faced. Pinning a tight smile on her face she went into the hall to greet them.

Flora kissed her and turned to the man behind her. 'Mum, this is Ben.' She threw his name at her with an air of defiance, as if daring Lorna to dislike him.

'Hello, Ben.' Lorna regarded him carefully; the man who'd fathered her grandchild, and was surprised. His brown hair had begun to recede quite sharply; his face was square, ordinary-looking but pleasant. He was wearing dark trousers, a blue shirt and a grey corduroy jacket, clothes that looked stiff with newness as if he'd bought them especially for the occasion. He was quite different from the man she had created in her mind.

Flora steered him into the living room, making Lorna think of rounding up a confused sheep. They all sat down awkwardly.

'Flora's brother is coming for lunch.' Lorna broke the tense silence, addressing Ben who sat on the edge of his chair as if poised for flight. 'He only rang last night,' she explained to Flora, in case she was annoyed at having to share this meeting with him.

'I know, I asked him to come.' Flora's face was tight and sulky and it tore at her heart. Her hair hung loose around her face and she looked very young and pretty. She went on, 'as Dad's not here, I thought Marcus should be. We should be as near a family as we can be.'

Lorna got up to offer drinks to hide the sudden tears in her eyes. There was beer and wine. 'Are you still drinking, darling, or does it make you feel ill?'

'Alcohol tastes like metal, hope I'll be able to drink after it all,' Flora said. 'I'll have water, no, tea; I'll go and make some tea. I drink a lot of that at the moment, I used to hate it before. What will you have Ben? Beer? Wine for you, Mum?' Flora went to the door to go to the kitchen.

'Tea, please.' Ben half-rose to follow her, his face anguished.

'I'll do it,' Lorna said.

Flora called back over her shoulder, 'No, talk to Ben, get to know him.' She disappeared. Ben, swallowing nervously, slumped back in his chair and bowed his head as though waiting for her verdict.

Was she really as terrifying as all that? Lorna rather despised him. She'd imagined a dashing man; perhaps a bit of a rogue who was amazingly attractive to women and seduced her daughter, been so persuasive that Flora couldn't help herself, like Stephen when she'd first known him. Ben didn't look as if he had the guts or the charm or whatever it was, to dare to be unfaithful to his wife. She'd have to tackle this but she was reluctant to start, not knowing what to say.

She took a deep breath and began hesitatingly, 'B … Ben, this is a difficult situation. Is it not? Flora is so young and …babies need a lot of time and care, not to mention money.'

'I know.' He looked miserable.

'How did it happen?' She blushed, 'I ... I mean your relationship. I understand you are married – or are you separated?'

'I ... I'm married, and Flora is so kind, so understanding,' he mumbled.

'That is no reason to make her pregnant, or even sleep with her.' He flinched at her tone of voice. Her irritation made her sound sharp, but she felt sharp. She'd not been expecting such a mouse of a man. Would he be any support at all in the situation? She didn't want to take full charge of this baby. It may be the sweetest thing and she'd love it but it was its parents who should take the most responsibility for it. She needed to be independent, make a new life for herself now she was on her own and not allow herself to be tempted back into the safety of the nursery.

The front door opened and slammed and Marcus charged in, dumping a large, squashy bag, no doubt full of dirty laundry, in the corner of the room. 'Hi, Mum.' He seemed even taller and skinner than when she'd last seen him. He bent over to kiss her, his over-long hair flopping into her face. Then he turned to inspect Ben. 'I'm Marcus.' He thrust out his hand, and she could see from his expression that he was as surprised as she was.

'Hi,' Flora appeared, a glass of wine in one hand, a mug of tea in the other. She put these down near Lorna and Ben and turned back towards the kitchen.

Marcus glanced at her stomach as if expecting to see the baby through her clothes. 'How's things?' He threw himself down on the sofa. 'Get me a beer, while you're there, please.' He addressed his sister. Turning to Ben, he said 'Beer, mate?'

Ben shook his head. 'No thank you, not just now.'

Flora returned with Marcus's beer and a glass. He pulled open the tab, licking off the white foam that crept round the opening of the tin before pouring the rest into his glass. 'So I'm going to be an uncle. It's a bit grown up.'

Lorna sighed; she didn't feel grown up enough to be a granny.

'You might all be pleased,' Flora said grumpily.

Lorna remembered the fish pie in the oven. Flora was sitting down again but it needed to be checked. What could she say about this situation anyway? Sermons on babies needing stable, two parent families like they had had, would be wasted. The young didn't seem to think like that any more. If a baby came along it was just like another friend, or worse still, a pet they'd acquired. Flora would love it, she would love it, perhaps Ben would love it, and Marcus would play with it and Stephen... what would Stephen do? So far he'd just ranted like a Victorian father. But that was not the same as having a proper home, a routine, she remembered her mother saying. People didn't have routines today, not if they interrupted their lives.

'It's a difficult situation,' Lorna said. 'But let's have lunch, we can discuss it later.' She got up quickly and went into the kitchen with the large alcove that doubled as a dining room, and led into a small garden. She'd laid the table nicely, an arrangement of fresh flowers in the centre and the creamy, linen napkins that used to belong to her mother. She'd decided she would make an effort for Ben – the Ben she had imagined.

'I'll help, Mum.' Marcus followed her into the kitchen. 'Mmm fish pie, my favourite.' The pie was perfect; crispy potato and sweet potato, topping fish in a creamy sauce. There were carrots and beans to go with it.

'He's a bit of a nerd,' Marcus whispered as he nipped off a piece of crusty potato and popped it in his mouth, 'not at all what I imagined.'

'I thought that too,' she said, and then, feeling disloyal to Flora, added, 'I'm sure he's very nice.'

'Hidden depths,' Marcus laughed. 'Let's help ourselves in here, I'm starving.' He called to the other two to come and get their meal.

Marcus kept them going through lunch, telling them about his goings on at college. It was a wonder that he found time to study, though Lorna didn't say anything; why should she spoil his fun, just because she didn't have any? He came to the end of his stories and there was a long silence. He'd been so animated a moment before and now, his face strained as if fearful of her answer, he blurted, 'So, Christmas. Mum, what are we doing?'

Panic whirled through her, were they both now going to say they had other plans, abandon this new, one parent family? She said as cheerfully as she could, 'Aunt Felicity and family are coming, perhaps the Elliots, and you both I hope and . . .' she glanced at Ben. 'You are of course welcome, if you have no other plans.' Then she thought the way she had said it sounded a bit unfriendly, but what was she meant to say? And what about his wife?

'What about Dad?' Marcus clenched his jaw as though the question hurt him.

She swallowed, picturing images of happier Christmases: Stephen carving the turkey, paper hat on his head, reading out the silly jokes from the crackers, often in his Peter Sellars voice, drinking champagne while they opened their presents. 'No,' she said, 'he won't be coming. Remember we are divorced.'

'He is our father,' Marcus said.

'I know and you … both of you …' She picked her words warily as if she were walking through a minefield, 'must see him whenever you want to. I just can't, that's all.'

Flora said, 'I think he's disgusting going off with such a young girl. She's only after his money; he's such a fool. You don't think he'll marry her, do you, Mum?' Her face was anguished.

If only Ben wasn't here, studying his plate as though the pattern on it was a code that needed breaking. But obviously it was awkward for him, thrust into the middle of a wounded family as well as being inspected as the father of Flora's child. They must talk of something else and Lorna racked her brain to think of another topic to discuss.

'He might just turn up and we can't turn him away at *Christmas*. Other divorced people have to do it, get together for family things. You are both our parents after all and if we get married, or at our graduation and things like that, you both ought to be there,' Marcus said defiantly.

'We simply can't have that girl here,' Flora said, her mouth curling, her eyes anxious. 'I wouldn't talk to him anyway, but it is Christmas and I bet she can't cook, not as well as you can anyway Mum, and you know how Dad loves his food and always said Christmas lunch is his favourite meal of the year.'

She felt tortured, they were Stephen's children and no doubt under their pain and confusion they still loved him, she could not expect them to turn him away. They might not understand, or want to understand, what hell it would be for her. Perhaps they both harboured a hope that he would snap out of the stranger the drugs had created and be the loving father they were used to. Even if they asked him, he wouldn't come without that girl and she couldn't cope with that. They were divorced, their marriage severed in two. That was it; simple, yet fraught with complications. If only Gloria's idea of shutting them all in Ravenscourt could be made to work.

To change the subject, Lorna began to talk about Ravenscourt, reminding them of the times they'd gone down there as small children.

'Why don't we go live and there?' Marcus said, 'Sounds great for parties.'

She explained about the sad state of the house, trying to include Ben in the discussion. She told them about Nathan's project of using parts of it – heavily decorated – for his Christmas brochure.

'Why don't *we* have Christmas there? I could ask loads of friends, it sounds just the place.' Marcus said excitedly. 'It's quite big, isn't it? We could have Dad, put him in the west wing or something, keep him out of your way most of the time.' He regarded her intently, looking so like his father, willing her to agree.

'No.' She thought again of Gloria's idea. 'It wouldn't work; it's damp and cold for a start. We'll have Christmas here as usual.' If Stephen asked to come she'd tell him he couldn't, but then she was probably panicking over nothing, he'd want to be with that girl, he wouldn't want to be with her. Unless, and the thought was like a stab wound, he asked the children to go over to him, or took them skiing, or out somewhere glamorous and exciting, leaving her without them.

As they cleared the table and she made some coffee, the idea of putting the three men in Ravenscourt gripped her like a rabid dog. There must be a way to get them there; she'd ring Gloria this evening.

The meal and a beer had relaxed Ben a little, but she could see that Flora was the dominant one in the relationship. The more Lorna covetously watched them, the more she realised that her 'little girl' had obviously not been seduced by an experienced older man. In fact Lorna was very much afraid it was Flora who had done the seducing. Dull though Ben appeared to be, there was a cosiness about him reminiscent of a comfortable teddy bear, which had probably appealed to Flora in her present state of mind, feeling lost with the painful departure of her beloved father.

Lorna felt a lecture on the dishonesty of sleeping with a married man come upon her. She could not say anything about that now, though she hated to think that Flora had broken up another woman's marriage, just as Stephen's Pekinese woman had broken hers.

Ben spoke slowly as if he was unwrapping and inspecting each word before he uttered it. 'We've been going through a difficult time, Tess …. that's my wife, and me. I met Flora and we got talking, she was unhappy and so was I.' He stopped speaking, looked round at them with anxious confusion as if that was all there was to it – and perhaps it was, two unhappy people going to bed together for solace, but ending up with a baby.

Lorna wondered if Ben knew that Flora had told her that he and his wife could not have children together. She wondered if it was true at all or whether he had just fabricated the story to gain her sympathy. But if it were true, this seemed like the worst betrayal of all.

CHAPTER THIRTEEN
It Must Be Made To Work

Lorna felt as if the whole country in its build up for Christmas was conspiring against her. Catalogues offering festive cards, decorations and lavish presents, not to mention Christmas food littered her house. The shops now glittered with magic and glamour, adding to the pain of those not able to have the perfect family celebration. 'The empty chair,' a friend of her mother's had remarked sorrowfully, at their first Christmas after her father had died. But it was Stephen's fault that his chair was empty this Christmas, as it was he who had chosen to leave them for the Pekinese woman, and she was damned if he would try and sneak back into it, probably towing her behind.

Ben and Flora left after tea to go back to Oxford, leaving Lorna feeling that the situation was far worse that she'd imagined. Flora had not helped matters by flouncing upstairs 'for a rest' leaving the three of them together. Lorna, Marcus and Ben had sat there over yet more cups of coffee in a state of awkwardness. She'd offered her cakes, hoping to sweeten the atmosphere, but only Marcus took one, eating it quickly, saying it was 'all right', which didn't help her decide if they were a good idea or not. She'd take the rest to Martha tomorrow, and see what she thought.

At last, Ben shyly announced that he needed some fresh air and would like to walk along the towpath by the Thames, as he knew the area. Neither Marcus nor Lorna offered to accompany him, so he sloped off alone, returning barely an hour later announcing his presence with a timid ring on the doorbell.

Marcus, apart from raising his eyes heavenwards and emitting an exaggerated sigh, did not want to discuss the affair and besides, they were both afraid that Flora would overhear something that would induce one of her tantrums. He watched sport on television while Lorna cleared the lunch, refusing his halfhearted offer to help. She wanted to be alone, struggling to find something positive about the situation and failing miserably.

When they left, Flora was still sulky and off-hand with them, leaving Lorna tormented with guilt that she had not handled the meeting well. Neither Ben nor Flora seemed to her to have grasped the enormity of their predicament. They hadn't even discussed how it would affect Ben's infertile wife. She realised that she was almost more anxious about this unfortunate woman than she was about Flora.

Marcus stayed on that evening, flopping down in a chair facing the television; the sports pages of the newspaper, beer cans and crumpled bags of crisps around him. This mess that spawned from him usually annoyed her but she let it go, pleased to have him here relieving the loneliness of an evening spent on her own, tormented by her problems. She would have liked to discuss the day's events with him but he was immersed in Sky Sports and she knew all she'd get from him was a succession of irritated grunts. When at last he'd tired of watching, he called out, 'What's for supper, Mum?'

'Pasta,' she fell back on that old standby.

'I always eat pasta,' he said, getting up and then throwing himself down again beside her on the sofa. 'I feel like a steak, a great, big juicy steak. Can I go and get one? I'll cook it.'

'If you want, but don't get one for me, I've had too much lunch.' She reached for her bag, handed him twenty pounds and in a sudden burst of generosity, suggested he bought more beer and anything else he wanted to eat.

'Thanks, Mum.' He leapt up, hovered a moment as if he'd kiss her, before making for the door. 'Great to be home again,' he said, as he disappeared into the hall.

That's what's really important, she thought, the love of one's children; making them a home they are always happy to return to. She leant back on the sofa, savouring the warm feeling his words left in her. A moment later the doorbell went. She smiled indulgently and got up. Marcus must have forgotten something, probably his mobile, his security blanket. No doubt he'd left his key behind, too. She opened the door. Gloria stumbled into the house; her face streaked with tears, her hair in disarray, and collapsed on to the sofa.

Adrian is dead, was Lorna's first thought. He'd been run over or fallen down somewhere while drunk and smashed his head in, or someone else had done it for him.

Taking a deep, shuddering breath Gloria said, 'So sorry to barge in like this but I couldn't bear to be alone. Adrian's been found in the bed of some girl. He didn't come home last night and I've been worried sick.'

'Oh, love,' Lorna sat down beside her and took her in her arms. This was not the first time it had happened but he'd sworn he would never do it again. That Adrian was probably too drunk to know what he was doing or be any sort of a lover was no comfort. Whatever the state of these men's minds, you could not help but be furious and hurt at their betrayal.

'I can't go on like this, I really can't,' Gloria gasped; closing her eyes as the tears ran down her face. She'd been like this before and rallied for the next battle, but each episode chipped away at her strength and surely there would come a time when she'd had too much and left him. No one would blame her. Most thought she should have chucked him out ages ago. Everyone liked Adrian, but most had tired of this fatal flaw in him.

Lorna listened to the sad and sordid story, punctuated by tears. It was one she had heard so many times before. Adrian's brother had gone looking for him and found him in some lap dancer's bed and he was now sleeping it off at his house. 'Fortunately Zoë is away, she won't have him in the house when he's like that and I don't blame her.' Gloria finished, blowing her nose furiously.

They talked around the problem as they always did, getting nowhere, and were interrupted by Marcus coming back, laden with enough food for a dinner party. He knew the sorry tale about Adrian's alcoholism and Lorna thought she detected a note of irritation in his expression when he saw Gloria, his godmother, rumpled and tear-stained, slumped on the sofa. But he put down his shopping, kissed her and said how good it was to see her.

'I'm sorry for you to find me here like this, Marcus.' Gloria moved half-heartedly to get up, 'I'll go now. You'll want to spend time together.'

Lorna was torn between wanting to enjoy being with Marcus and talking through her fears about Flora and Ben with him, while knowing that Gloria needed her too.

Marcus said. 'Don't go. I've got some work to do. Stay and gossip with Mum.' He sat down in a chair beside them, obviously in no hurry to go into his room to tackle his work.

Gloria asked him about his life at Uni and Marcus answered her dutifully but Lorna had a feeling that he was keeping something from her. Had he been sent down? Got into some dreadful trouble? Every so often he glanced towards her with anxiety as if afraid she too might collapse into pieces like Gloria. At last he blurted out. 'Dad rang just now on my mobile.'

Her stomach contracted. Marcus studied his feet in their blue and once white trainers as if they were of immense interest. 'He says . . .' he paused, 'well, Odile ...'

'Odile, is that her name?' Lorna spat it out as if it were snake venom.

He shrugged. 'I suppose so. She's got to go home for Christmas. She booked her ticket ages ago and her parents are very religious and Dad can't go.'

'I hate religious people who act as if they are holier than thou, they're always the ones you have to watch, destroying other people's marriages.' Lorna exclaimed.

Marcus frowned, a little fearful at her fury. 'Anyway Mum, he's alone for Christmas and thought we could all be together.' He said it quickly, watching her warily as if she would suddenly explode and maim them all.

'No,' Lorna said. 'He cannot come here. He can be alone. I'm alone. Night after night I'm alone while he's with this … this religious tart. He's chosen to be with her instead of me so he can get on with it.'

Marcus's face creased with anxiety. 'But it is Christmas, Mum. And you never know, she may not come back and he'll be sorry and …'

'No, Marcus, it won't be like that. It's too late, our marriage is over. It's hard to accept, I know. It's hard for me to accept he was seeing this woman before that shrink destroyed his mind, but it's happened and I … we, have all been hurt and humiliated far too much to go back to the way it was before.' There had been too much pain and anger between them. Being left alone together here in this house would be worse than anything she could imagine. There was no going back.

Gloria leant over and laid her hand on Marcus's shoulder. 'Look, love,' she said, 'I know how hard this is for you and Flora. Justin feels the same over his father's shameful behaviour. Stephen is your father and a child's love is stronger for a parent than a wife's for a husband – at least if their father has been as good a one as yours was before this nonsense. But what he's done to your mother and to you children is inexcusable. It is far too soon to expect your mother to have him here as though nothing has happened. You must see that.'

'But it is Christmas,' Marcus repeated miserably.

'A family time, which makes it worse if things are so smashed up.' Gloria said. 'Your father's behaved in the most disgraceful, hurtful way. He chose to do this and he must take the consequences. If this woman does not come back and he does not go off with someone else, in time things just might… resolve themselves… though I doubt it,' she added quickly, seeing Lorna's face, 'and not now, not at Christmas.'

'So where will he go?' Marcus demanded, and Lorna could see him weighing up which parent needed him most. What would Flora think? She'd always adored her father before he'd turned into this stranger. Stephen would find it easy to manipulate them into doing what he wanted. If she was not careful she might well end up the loser and she would be alone for longer than Christmas.

Lorna and Gloria flashed a glance between them, before Gloria spoke. She seemed hesitant at first, thinking through what she should say. She knew what she *wanted* to say but she mustn't forget that Stephen was Marcus's father, however badly he'd behaved.

'As I expect you know Marcus, I … and perhaps more so, Justin, have a difficult time with Adrian and his drinking. Rosalind and her girls have troubles with Ivan, too, different ones, but just as difficult, and your father …' she paused, watching him, curled up on the chair, arms round his knees as if he were holding himself together, and her heart went out to him. How could these men cause such hurt to their children? She went on, curbing her anger, '… for whatever reason your father seems to have chosen a different lifestyle, which is very hurtful … We're so afraid their behaviour will spoil Christmas, we had a mad idea, Rosalind, your mother and I, to have the three men spend a lovely Christmas together in that house your mother has just inherited.'

'What, Ravenscourt?' Marcus's glance spun back to Lorna. 'I suggested we all go there, but you said it was far too cold and bleak.'

'It's a bit different now. You know that a … a friend of ours is using it as a backdrop for his food brochure – he's shooting it now in readiness for next year. After all, Christmas seems to start in August, with all the festive catalogues and such.' She knew she was waffling but she must convince him and she felt she was losing him.

'So there'll be enough warm rooms for them, but not for all of us as well,' she ploughed on. 'Plenty of food too, and we thought if we could get them there they'd have such fun being all men … old friends, together and we could all have a peaceful Christmas on our own. You know…' she went on more frantically, as he tried to protest, '…how these men can ruin Christmas with their embarrassing behaviour… in front of your friends, and we just want to give you all a happy Christmas without them spoiling it. Surely you can understand that, Marcus?'

'It sounds crazy,' Marcus looked from one to the other as if they were some strange species that was alien to him. His father had gone mad, now it seemed his mother and Gloria had too. Perhaps he'd go back to Uni tonight after all.

Guessing his thoughts, Lorna chipped in, telling him how the three men had been friends for a long time; how they would enjoy themselves together, drinking and smoking cigars without their families to interfere. She got rather carried away, building up a picture of a wonderful country weekend with bracing walks over the countryside, good books to read and visits to the pub, and Marcus began to believe her.

'Sounds great! Perhaps I'll join them, better than having Flora puking all over the place and Aunt Felicity preaching to us.'

'No, it's better it's just the three of them.' Gloria said quickly. 'The only thing is, and maybe you have some ideas on this, how do we get them there?' She smiled sweetly at him.

'I'd have thought it will be easy if it's going to be such fun,' Marcus said enviously

'It is disgusting, shaming too, what Dad has done. I suppose I hoped if he came for Christmas things would resolve themselves, but I see they won't and it would be difficult after knowing what he has done. But I don't want him to be alone.' He appealed to Lorna.

'He won't be; he'll be with two of his oldest friends.' Gloria said.

'OK, then,' Marcus got up and went to his room, exhausted with it all.

'So it seems it is on,' Gloria said.

'Hardly. We still don't know how to get them there or make them stay when they are there.'

'I can get hold of Adrian's mobile, he's always leaving it about. And we'll ask Clara and that friend she mentioned to look after them. We'll pay them to do it, it will be worth it. Somehow we'll have to immobilize their cars, but if the weather is bad and there's enough booze and good food … and don't forget, they're getting on now, and inclined to be lazy …' Gloria said with a strangled laugh.

'But getting them there in the first place is the difficult thing,' Lorna said, wondering if they would ever pull it off.

'We'll have to pretend we are all going to be down there,' Gloria said. 'I'm pretty sure Adrian will do anything for me now after this sordid venture … until the next time.' Her face sagged with despair. 'I don't know about Ivan, but Rosalind must think of something. I'll ring Nathan; find out when he is doing his shoot. We don't want the green garlands to be dead when they arrive. They'll have to think it is a house party all waiting for them.'

'But even if we sabotage their cars they could walk up the drive to the road or telephone from the house. Maybe Clara could disconnect the phone.'

'It is feasible,' Gloria looked much happier than when she had arrived. 'We simply must pull it off. Let's ring Rosalind and see what ideas she's got.'

'I'll drug him, dump him and possibly castrate him too, while I'm at it,' Rosalind almost spat down the phone, clearly furious with Ivan. Chloe, one of their daughters, was in trouble at school and they'd been called in to discuss her behaviour with her headmistress. Ivan hadn't turned up, despite having promised he would. He still hadn't come home and she'd been trying his mobile for ages but he'd switched it off, as he was apt to do if he didn't want to be contacted. 'I bet he's cosying up to those social workers, helping out with their teenagers while his own daughter is threatened with expulsion.' She finished, near tears.

'Less than four weeks to go until Christmas, we've simply got to make it work,' Gloria said. 'We'll tell Nathan to leave up his decorations as we're having a house party; there's no need for him to know the guest list. Once he's taken the photographs for his brochure he won't go to Ravenscourt again.

CHAPTER FOURTEEN
Difficult Husbands

It was dusk and the cars crawled up the Fulham Road with their headlights glowing like saucer eyes. Lorna and Rosalind were having tea at Maison Blanc and barely noticed, being deep in conversation. Lorna had spent the day in her cake shop. She and Martha had spent the weekend experimenting with 'non-fattening' cakes, if there were such things, cutting down on the refined sugar and using sweet vegetables, apples, dried apricots and lots of spices instead. They'd sold quite a few, some people saying they were perfect for a breakfast on the way to work.

She was especially pleased with the window display – eat your heart out, Beth, she'd said to herself as she and Martha admired it. Spirals of cupcakes resembling Christmas trees, each with a whirl of dark green, red or white icing sprinkled with glitter and tiny Christmas themes arranged in silvery, snow. It was clearly lit and attracted quite a crowd, especially from children on the way home from school, which made for more sales. The cakes were selling quite well but they needed more publicity and she wondered if she might sneak in a few among Nathan's produce, and persuade him, as a sort of return favour, to order some and include them in his brochure. They were Christmassy after all, in the dark red boxes and wrappings. The miniature fruitcakes; ginger and orange, or apple and cinnamon and other 'winter spices', each one decorated like a small work of art were all perfect for the festive period.

'Let's hope people remember that sad Christmas chunk of cake left in a tin until Easter and buy our smaller and more fun cakes instead,' Martha said. They made an unusual present, packed into a festive box.

Now she and Rosalind were talking about Ravenscourt, it seemed all three of them talked of little else when they were together.

'But surely you want to be there to keep an eye on things. It is your house after all.' Rosalind said, as they sat together over tea and pretty pastries, enjoying the comforting fragrance of hot chocolate and coffee, though having been surrounded by sugar all day, Lorna wondered if it was possible to put on weight by osmosis.

'I've so much to do; work at the cake shop, make more jewellery for Gloria's stalls, finish repairing books for presents, and all the Christmas preparations.' She was not going to admit to herself, let alone Rosalind, that she wanted to see Nathan again. She remembered how close she'd felt to him in the kitchen at Ravenscourt while he showed her his plans for the shoot. If only it could be just the two of them working on it, without the hustle and bustle of the others all jockeying with each other to be in on the action.

'But you only need go down for a day. I want to go, so does Gloria. You must want to see what's going on? After all, it is not as if strangers are poking about your own, personal home.' Rosalind said in her jolly, no- nonsense voice.

'You know . . .' she paused, examining her immaculate nails, 'we just want to see if getting the men there for Christmas is at all feasible.' Rosalind's expression tightened with strain. 'I can't take another Christmas with Ivan sloping in with that cocky way he has, as if he has pulled a fast one on me. Last Sunday he came home smelling sort of musky. He said it was incense as he'd just popped into the Brompton Oratory to listen to the sung Mass. Goodness knows, I've been drenched in enough incense at school to know it wasn't that; it was cheap scent.' She wrinkled her nose in disgust. 'Anyway, my mother might be coming to stay this year if she doesn't get a better invitation, and you know what she's like. She'll give me a hard time over it; say she told me so for marrying such an older man and one who couldn't make his first marriage work either.'

Lorna cradled her cup of tea in her hands. Would she have hung on, pretending things were not as bad as they were had Stephen not actually upped and left her, set up in that shit coloured flat with that girl and filed for divorce? It was scary being alone after being in what had been a loving relationship for so long. She was sure it felt worse to be dumped than widowed.

'You know you're afraid Stephen will turn up on Christmas morning and persuade your children – if they do spend Christmas with you, and you know that's not certain – to let him in. All our children do still love their fathers, or at least the fathers they used to be, and they naively hope that things might get better again.' Rosalind went on.

Her words cut deeply. She'd not dared ask Marcus and Flora outright if they were coming for Christmas. In the past she could count on it, now she could not.

'I couldn't face having Stephen for lunch and us all pretending we can get on, as we are now,' she said, remembering Marcus torn between the two of them, imagining that if his father came for Christmas all would settle down as it used to be.

Her children's bewilderment at the change in their once loving and dependable father wrenched Lorna's heart. Some bossy person had told her she must stop taking responsibility for her children's emotions; that they had grown up and would be buffeted by joys and hurts like everyone else. But she found watching their suffering was almost worse than coping with her own.

'Gloria is determined our plan will work. Adrian's latest obsession is lap . . .' Rosalind giggled, 'I keep calling them laptop clubs, which I know is not right but I'm sure the girls end up on the men's laps anyway.'

Lorna smiled, 'Poor Gloria . . . poor *us*, we never thought it would end this way, did we? They used to love us so.'

Rosalind's eyes glazed with tears. 'It's so humiliating. You know my father deserted us when I was twelve, upped and left for the US and we've never heard from him since. Now I feel deserted all over again. I can't bear my girls having to go through what I did, I'm sure it's affecting Chloe's behaviour at school.' She sighed, 'But Gloria sets great store by Clara. She's convinced that somehow we can get them there and they'll stay those few days. Even one day, Christmas Day, would be a bonus.' Rosalind said with feeling. 'Gloria says Nathan's going to spend a couple of days getting the house ready, and do the brochure there on Saturday. He's told you that too, hasn't he?'

Lorna nodded, 'He emailed me, apologised for not ringing, but it was the middle of the night.'

'Apparently he told Gloria . . . I'm beginning to wonder if there isn't something going on there,' Rosalind joked, 'do you think there is? He's frightfully attractive.'

'I don't know.' Lorna felt sick at heart, 'I don't know what Beth would think of it.'

'Beth?' Rosalind looked surprised, 'What's Beth to do with it?'

'I thought she was his wife.'

'Whatever made you think that? Though I bet she wishes she were. They might sleep together, for all I know, he is divorced. I don't know the ins and outs of it but he's not married, anyway,' she went on. Lorna digested this. He was not married to Beth, or to anyone, though strangely he still wore a wedding ring, but that didn't mean he was free.

'He told Gloria,' Rosalind continued, 'that we must be in the party scenes. It might be fun. Thank goodness you'll know what to do, as you've done the real thing in your film extra-ing.'

'At least there won't be fake snow and blazing sun outside.' Lorna said, 'Though I suppose most companies do it then to catch that year's Christmas. Nathan's doing it for next year as he plans to have more things to sell then.'

'And also,' Rosalind paused, regarding her as if she wondered whether to go on...

'Also what?' Lorna's stomach clamped with anxiety of what she was going to say.

'Well, it's only an idea, Gloria's actually, but it appears that Nathan is looking for somewhere to move, he can't go on living with his mother and he wants to expand his business so Gloria thought that Ravenscourt...'

'Why does Gloria always want to take over?' Lorna wailed, 'I've no idea what I am going to do with it yet, I've barely had it five minutes, why should Nathan have it? He hasn't any money for a start, remember he told me he had cash flow problems which is usually a euphemism for being broke and he paid me in food for the shoot, surely she doesn't expect me to *give* it to him?' She was furious, how dare Gloria suggest such a thing without even informing her first?

'It's not like that,' Rosalind laid her hand over hers, 'she's said nothing to him, it was just an idea. I mean you have said you can't afford to keep it and perhaps he'll have money after Christmas or could buy it in instalments or something...but no forget it, I shouldn't have told you, it's only one of Gloria's ideas to help you solve how to do the best for Ravenscourt and for you.' Rosalind looked distraught at her disclosures, but it left Lorna feeling even more stressed than before. Much though she valued her friends she wished they wouldn't stick their noses into her affairs.

Lorna sighed, she supposed inheriting such a house was bound to cause excitement and Gloria and Rosalind meant well but now it was only two weeks to Christmas and something had to be done urgently if they really were going to try to get their men there. Would the decorations last that long even if they were garlands of evergreens and the place like a deep freeze?

She half wanted to go to Ravenscourt for the shoot. She must be there to safeguard it and see that the photographs taken did it justice. Though Beth would take over, shine as the capable girl with 'wonderful' taste, while she'd be side-lined. Somehow she'd didn't mind Beth so much now she'd found out that she wasn't married to Nathan, though that didn't mean there was nothing between them ... but she wasn't going to think about it. She would go to Ravenscourt and they would do their utmost to get the men there safe and out of the way for their children's sakes so they could have a drama-free Christmas.

'All right,' she said, 'I'll ring Clara.'

'Don't tell me you're getting cold feet?' Rosalind eyed Lorna sharply. 'You voiced some concerns over insurance claims if anything went wrong with Nathan's shoot, but our men, if angry and drunk, may be far more dangerous.'

That remark did worry her, but she said, 'if we ever get them there, I'm sure Clara and her friend Jane – who after all is used to adolescent boys – should be able to deal with them.' 'I can't believe we're doing this,' Rosalind went on. 'Men make such fools of themselves over sex.'

Lorna agreed, 'and what pain and destruction they leave behind. I'm afraid that that poor wife of Flora's man will be devastated when she finds out about Flora and the baby.'

'With luck *they* can't make babies any more,' Rosalind shuddered. 'It's not as if Ivan's social workers are very pretty, but I suppose they are grateful to be taken out. I'm sure their jobs can be very dispiriting, but it doesn't mean they should go after other people's husbands,' she said sadly.

'Are you sure he sleeps with them and isn't pretending to, to get your attention, Ros?' Lorna asked her. 'You don't think he's jealous of the time you spend with your girls ... his girls too, of course, and he should be there alongside you with them, but if you don't mind me saying, he doesn't seem a very hands-on father.'

'No, he's not. Remember, he didn't really want any more children, and who can blame him after Polly? As you know she did her best to sabotage our marriage – egged on, I suspect, by her mother.'

'The stepdaughter from hell,' Lorna said. 'Though I suppose it was difficult for her, as she didn't know about you until you were almost married. I suppose she felt she was losing her father again to you, a glamorous young woman.'

'I know, I did try though,' Rosalind sighed. 'Things got better when she went to Uni, and he agreed, quite reluctantly, to have a child, and then,' she smiled, 'I was a bit lax with the pill after having Emma, and Chloe was born. He loves them, there's no doubt about that, he just gets so impatient with them if they don't behave exactly how he wants them to. And he doesn't give them enough of his time. He prefers to be with his male friends playing golf and all, or doing his so-called "charity work".'

'But surely some of the teenagers he helps with work experience have problems and must need an awful lot of patience.' Lorna said.

'Of course, but it's not so personal then, not your own kids.'

'He sounds so selfish, Ros, I can't bear it for you,' Lorna said with feeling. She remembered how much in love the two of them used to be; perhaps it was hardly surprising that his daughter was so jealous. 'What does Polly think of it all? Or doesn't she know about it?'

'She knows about it all right, might even encourage it. She often pops in when he's working and goes out to lunch with him, but then she's grown up, and can do what she likes, while her stepsisters are only thirteen and fourteen.'

'It's hard. I suppose Polly yearns for his attention as much as you and your girls do. He should understand that and share his time with all of you; it's not as if he's tied to office hours or a gruelling profession any more.' Ivan lived on his looks – he was dark and sultry – but Lorna had always found him a little too self-centred, though he had suffered badly in his first marriage and she'd been delighted when he'd met and married Rosalind.

'Ivan is good company as long as I don't mention his behaviour.' She sighed. 'We were so happy together once. He loved me; was relieved to be with me after his tricky first marriage. We were soul mates.' She looked sad. 'Perhaps it's *marriage* he's not happy with, and he prefers the excitement and the secrecy of an affair.'

'I'm sure it's not that, Ros. I just feel it's something to do with their time of life; all of them were successful in their careers and suddenly – at least in Stephen's case – it was snatched away. And instead of having a wife the same age sitting waiting to entertain them at home they have us, twenty years younger, still with busy lives.'

'I suppose that's true. As the children grew up we all took on other interests, more work or whatever as they were often away on business trips and we had more time for ourselves. That would have been fine if we'd been closer in age, so I suppose that's one of the drawbacks of marrying much older men,' Rosalind said. 'But all the same, I'd hate to be alone. I know how hard it is for you after all those years you were married, but you're so brave, Lorna; you're struggling on regardless.'

'I've discovered something since I've been on my own.' Lorna said, 'though it may just be me being sensitive, but you know that psychologically people who think you're still married, invite you to things, even if your husband can't come, well I've found that some wives ... I'd been told this but didn't take much notice of it, really are suspicious of divorced women, imagining, I suppose that we are frantic to get our hands on another man. There've been a few things I was always asked to but haven't been since my divorce, so I assume this must show that they too, are feeling insecure about their husbands.'

'S'pose that's true, and it depends on the women. I know you're not like that but some we know. .. like Sophie Alcot, for instance, certainly do seem to be on the prowl again, even before their divorce is through,' Rosalind said.

Lorna expected to feel envious of Rosalind, still having her husband's support, but she did not. She didn't want to be with a man who treated her so badly. She'd been Stephen's wife, was the mother of his children, and she deserved better. She felt quite bullish after this revelation. Times were different now and being an independent woman had many advantages.

'Stephen's woman has gone to whatever country she came from, and may not come back, or be allowed into the country again for all I know, but our marriage was over the moment he chose to be with her rather than me. I'd rather be alone for Christmas than know that he is only with me as he has nowhere else to go.'

'But you won't be alone for Christmas if he's at Ravenscourt and your children are with you,' Rosalind said. 'I know Felicity and her family are going to be there, but admit it, without your children that won't be enough.'

'You're right.' Lorna admitted. 'Felicity means well, but she has a knack of making me feel rather feeble and that I could have done more to save my marriage.'

Rosalind took her hand, held it tight. 'We're doing this for our children, Lorna, to keep our families together as much as we can – and the families our children might have in the future.

'I know. We'll do all we can to get them there.'

Rosalind paid the bill after a minor squabble over it, and they left the café, walking out into the Fulham road. It was dark now; the lights in the shops turning each one into a magical stage set. Everything hinted – some screamed out – 'Christmas'. Shining garlands were laced over clothes; glittering snow decorated a selection of food in the Italian shop; gold fir cones were arranged on an antique table; dark leaves and red ribbon wound round a chandelier. The coming festive season was inescapable. She used to welcome it, but this year it seemed to Lorna that it was taunting them.

The two women said goodbye; quick kisses and a touch of a hand sending out messages of support. Rosalind lived in Kensington in a smart, white house with pillars by the door. The house had been derelict when they had bought it years ago and they had lived with builders' squalor for ages until it had emerged comfortable and beautiful from the ruins. Rosalind's lifeblood ran through that house, which had started her passion for interior decorating. She now worked part-time in a firm doing up flats on short lets for foreign business people.

Lorna rang Clara that evening and was miffed when she discovered that Gloria had already been in touch and seemed to be quite involved in the plans for the Christmas brochure. As she'd guessed, Beth had taken over and she had to curb her tongue as Clara enthused, 'Beth has some good ideas. It's quite like the old days, people coming and going. If only Fergus were still here, he'd have loved it.'

Lorna cut through Clara's descriptions of Beth's genius and told her about the three of them coming down to Ravenscourt on the Saturday.

'You could come on the Friday. I could get some beds made up. It's much warmer now the big fires have been lit. Nathan thought it best to try them out first. We had a sweep in, who had lovely time. He said it quite brought back the old times when chimneys were chimneys.' Clara said.

'I'll ask the others, let you know, but time is quite tight and I doubt we will stay the night.' Lorna thought staying too complicated … and far too cold.

'Gloria discussed your plan with me about your husbands, so you can decide where the men are to sleep and see what we can do to keep them here. I've talked it over with Jane – you know, my friend who's coming to help out, and I'm pretty sure we can pull it off between us.'

Lorna could detect a hint of excitement in Clara's voice. She sighed; it seemed that their mad idea was on.

CHAPTER FIFTEEN
The Other Wronged Wife

Lorna was sitting at the kitchen table, carefully sticking a paper hinge into the hollow spine of a damaged book. It was a fiddly job and she was annoyed when the doorbell rang. She thought it might be Gloria, who had said she'd pop in on her way back from yet another fair. It was quite early for her, just after lunch, but maybe she'd sold out, or had enough.

Lorna had trained to do book conservation before she married and had worked in a geographical library before the children were born but then she'd gone freelance so she could do most of the work at home. It was spasmodic work, but it suited her.

She finished lining up the paper in the gap in the book's spine with the tweezers, so she covered it with non-stick paper, bandaged it up and put it aside to dry. The bell went again, more stridently this time. She went to the door and opened it, expecting to see Gloria, a joke on her lips, but stopped abruptly

A young woman eyed her nervously. She wore a navy knitted hat with a matching crocheted flower on one side, a navy skirt and a pale blue, wool jacket. She was pretty in a faded sort of way, but she appeared dispirited, as if life had ground her down.

She could be a Jehovah's Witness but they usually travelled in pairs and she couldn't see anyone else. Perhaps she'd mistaken the house. Lorna smiled and asked who she was looking for.

'You, I think,' the woman said. 'Mrs Sanderson?'

'I'm Mrs Sanderson. What can I do for you?' Perhaps she'd brought some books for repair, but she didn't remember meeting her before, and she wasn't carrying anything other than a small handbag.

'Could I come in?' The woman stepped forward with determination, her hands clenched round the handle of her bag. Lorna felt a tinge of disquiet. Was she something to do with Stephen? Some other woman he had got involved with, who now wanted to tell her some grievance she had? She moved in front of her, blocking her entry.

'Please tell me who you are and why you want to see me.' She hoped she sounded firm.

'I'm Tess . . . Ben's wife,' the woman admitted, almost apologetically.

For a moment Lorna didn't click; then it hit her. The wife of Flora's boyfriend who'd fathered her grandchild.

'Oh God, d- do come in.' What could she say? Was this woman dangerous, come to wreak havoc in revenge for her daughter's crime of stealing her husband, and carrying the child she could not?

Once inside the narrow hall with the front door shut behind her, Tess's courage seeped away. Nervously she looked round as if she were trapped. She glanced furtively back at the closed door as if wondering whether to make a run for it.

'Can I get you something, coffee, tea?' Lorna asked, realising that they were both afraid of each other's reactions. If only Gloria would turn up, help her out.

'No nothing. I just want to talk . . . See you.' Close to, she appeared much older, mature, more like Ben's mother than his wife. Perhaps she was past childbearing and would never conceive. Perhaps Ben had left her for Flora because she was younger and could give him a baby. Her mind spun with complicated scenarios as she led the way into the living room,

'Come and sit down, talk all you want. I don't know if I can help you, but I'll try.' Did Tess even know about the pregnancy? She didn't want to be the person to tell her. It was for Ben to do that, not her.

Tess stumbled forward into the room, came to a halt, whipped round and blurted as if she was afraid she'd lose the courage to say it, 'My husband is having an affair with your daughter. I want him to stop. I want you to tell her she can't have him. He's married and he won't leave me.' Her voice was edged with desperation, and despite feeling a pang of sympathy for her, Lorna wanted to say, 'They do leave us, even the most loving husband can change and leave us.'

Instead, she steered her to a chair and Tess slumped down on it as if her legs could no longer support her. 'I am so sorry about it. I know it's not right; they shouldn't have done it. Have you asked him to give her up?' Lorna felt cowed by the situation. It must have taken a lot of courage for Tess to come and confront her over her husband's infidelity.

'It's not his fault,' Tess cried out. 'She seduced him. I'm sorry to tell you this, but she stole him away from me. She doesn't want him, not like I do. She's young and pretty, she'll chop and change over her choice of boyfriends, but I can't bear to lose him.'

Tess's distress brought tears to Lorna's eyes. She couldn't bear to lose Stephen, but she had, at least she had his children. This poor woman didn't have any. Even if Flora did give up Ben, the coming child would always link them together. Whatever could she say to comfort her?

'Have you discussed it together?' Lorna sat down on the sofa beside Tess's chair. 'I didn't know Flora had broken up with her previous boyfriend. I didn't know anything about … Ben….until recently.' She added, feeling it best to admit knowing about it.

'He won't discuss it. He just stays silent.'

'Is he still living with you?' She didn't even know that. Flora had told her about the baby and about Ben, but she knew nothing about their living arrangements. Now she recalled there had been a flat belonging to a friend where Ben had dried Flora's muddy drawings. Did they live there together, or just meet there, or had the friend returned?

'Yes, he is, but he visits her, I know he visits her.' Tess looked down at her hands twisting in her lap, as if they were alien to her. She seemed almost embarrassed, as if she were at fault for not stopping these visits.

'But you must talk to him. It will be hard at first, but once it's all out in the open you will know what you are dealing with.' How painful it was to hear the truth, face up to it, but at least then Tess would know where she stood and would no longer be left hanging in hope.

'But couldn't you . . .' Tess's voice was pleading, desperate. 'Please, couldn't you tell your daughter to let him go?'

Lorna leant forward and put her hand over Tess's. If only life were so easy.

'She's twenty, with a mind of her own and as you know, away from home. I have talked to her, pointed out that what she is doing is wrong, but I can't force her to leave him, nor can I make him give her up and, go back to you, and anyway ...' Lorna paused; Tess was gazing at her, her eyes filled with hope that she could solve their problem. 'After this, things between you might be so different to what you hope for. This ... affair . . . this betrayal ...' she wished she could lift the oppressive atmosphere, 'I don't know how you live with that. It might be possible but ...'

'I just want him back,' Tess said tonelessly.

The doorbell rang, making them both jump. Tess's eyes went wide with terror as if it were Ben, who'd somehow tracked her down and would discover her visit. This time it must be Gloria and though minutes before Lorna had longed for her to be here, now she dreaded it. How could she warn her not to say anything about Flora's pregnancy? It was not for them to break such news to this desperate woman. She said, 'That's probably a friend of mine, she said she might pop by.'

'I ... I'd better go.' Tess did not seem to have the strength to move.

The bell went again. Lorna got up. 'I'll just let her in.' She glanced through the spy hole before opening the door, to make sure it was Gloria. Taking her arm she steered her back onto the pavement, away from the door, whispering, 'The wife of Flora's boyfriend and father of the child is here. Please don't mention the baby.'

'God, no…' Gloria looked shocked. 'Shall I go away?'

'No please stay. It's hell for her poor woman, but come in.' She went back into the house, asking her loudly how she had done at the fair.

'Very well, thank goodness, almost sold out so I left early. Look…' She handed her a navy paper bag. 'Special for you, lovely ham. Nathan insisted that I give it to you.' She laughed. 'I said I was going to see you and he said, "Here's a food parcel for her." Perhaps he thinks you're starving, some sort of refugee.'

'Thanks?' she took it, peered inside and the mouth-watering aroma wafted from the packet. She experienced a surge of excitement, Nathan had thought of her. She scolded herself. Of course he'd thought of her; he was keeping her sweet in case she changed her mind about letting him use Ravenscourt for his Christmas brochure.

'Oh, Heavens…' Gloria jumped forward. Tess was standing at the foot of the staircase behind them, holding on to the newel post, her eyes half-closed as if she would faint. The two women rushed to her and led her back to the living room. Lowering her gently on to the sofa, Lorna lifted her legs so she was lying down. Gloria pushed some cushions under her head.

'Would you like some tea?' Gloria said. 'Hot, sweet tea, good for shocks. Or shall I call someone, a doctor even?'

Tess shook her head, her eyes closed, her face ridged with strain. 'No thank you, I shouldn't have come. I just hoped ...' her voice tailed away.

Lorna sat down on the floor beside her. She dared not look at Gloria to voice her fear that Tess, following her out, had overheard her warning not to mention the coming baby. 'I will talk to Flora again,' she said feebly.

It was heartbreaking. What were they to do? Pretend they were talking about someone else, or tell her the truth? Tess would soon find out about Flora's pregnancy, you couldn't keep that hidden. But Ben should have told her. Lorna bit back her anger. He was a weak man, unable to face up to his responsibilities. It was an unpleasant thing to accept that her own daughter had seduced Ben, and through her own carelessness, got pregnant.

'I must go now,' Tess struggled up.

'But do you feel strong enough, would you like some tea?' Lorna said, moving towards the kitchen.

'No...no thank you,' Tess stood up. 'I'm sorry to have disturbed you, only I ... well, I didn't know what else to do.' She bit her lip to stop her tears.

'I'm so sorry,' Lorna said, feeling terrible about the situation.

'I'm afraid life can be pretty bloody,' Gloria said. 'But take it from us, you can get over most things, or anyway learn to live around them. Relationships end, you know, as well as begin.'

Tess said shyly, as if confessing something shameful, 'I love him. I want Flora to leave him alone.'

'I know,' Gloria sighed, catching Lorna's eye, 'and love makes it hurt even more. But sometimes we are mistaken and love the man we thought he was, or even what we want him to be.'

It was a hard thing to accept Lorna thought. The three of them here had been badly let down by the men they'd loved. Charming, loving Adrian had turned into a drunken sot, Stephen, the love of her life, was now an aging lecher and Ben who, no doubt, was loving and charming once, had, through weakness, and, she must admit, Flora, brought this anguish to his wife.

Tess seemed to have found some strength. 'I want you to tell your daughter to let him go,' she said firmly, as if Flora was holding Ben hostage somewhere. She stared at the floor, and lowering her voice, confided, 'Some of it may be my fault. We wanted children and none came so I'd been undergoing IVF. It made me difficult to live with. Then, when it didn't work, I suppose he found it hard being with me, and the disappointment.' She looked up at them both, willing them to understand.

Lorna swallowed a lump in her throat. Flora should be here to see what pain and chaos she'd unwittingly caused.

Gloria said. 'It must have been hell for you, I'm so sorry.'

'But we do have a future together,' Tess said with determination. 'I know we do, but we need a chance. If you could keep your daughter here over Christmas, we could be together. We could start again, talk about adoption.' Her eagerness smote Lorna's heart. Should they now tell her about the child? She could not. She tensed, wondering if Gloria would break it to her, but she stayed silent, looking thoughtful.

'If you could keep her here for Christmas, we'll go away together. My sister has a holiday cottage in Wales she'd lend us.' This idea had suddenly dawned upon Tess, giving her hope. She got up, gathering her things. 'Thank you both so much for listening. Relationships do go through terrible times don't they? Only the strong ones survive them, and I know ours is strong.'

Gloria got up and took her hand. 'Yes,' she said, 'only the strong ones survive.'

The two women did not look at each other as Tess left, though Lorna knew they were both thinking the same thing. Tess was going to need an enormous amount of strength to survive this, and what would she do when the baby was born?

When she'd had gone, Gloria said with feeling, 'Looks like this Christmas is going to be an important turning point for quite a few of us. By this time next year, I wonder which of us will still be standing.'

CHAPTER SIXTEEN
At The End Of Her Tether

Perhaps she was having a nervous breakdown. Gloria massaged her temples. Her head was throbbing; her thoughts skittering all over the place. Her brain had had enough, was opting out, and who could blame it, with all she had to cope with?

After a troubled night waiting and worrying about Adrian, he'd been bought home by 'one of the twilight people', as she called them, who inhabited his world; a fellow drinker or some kind guardian angel, she didn't know. Though his wallet was not with him she was relieved that he was back. Drunk out of his mind, but alive to drink another day, she thought darkly, scolding herself for not being tougher with him. She should be above caring what the neighbours thought of her, but she wasn't or she'd leave him outside slumped on the doorstep for all to see.

He had been found among some dustbins behind the Savoy Hotel. 'At least he chose a more upmarket place this time, well, if he'd been drinking there,' Gloria remarked dryly as she told Lorna when she'd rung, an hour ago, to discuss their trip to Ravenscourt the following morning.

'Oh Glory, I'm so sorry. You sound exhausted. Do you want to come? Will you feel up to the trip? I don't know how long we'll stay down there.'

'I'll come if it's the last thing I do, our plan's got to work, Lorna. I don't care what it takes; he cannot be here for Christmas.' She put the phone down then, overcome with fury.

She'd pulled Adrian into the house and shut the door and he'd collapsed, becoming wedged across their narrow hall. He was a dead weight so she left him there to sleep it off, and went upstairs to bed and tried to sleep. This couldn't go on. She, and indeed their doctor, had tried to make him get help, but it was impossible. Not until something serious happened to him might something be done, and by then it might be too late.

She was woken at dawn by the doorbell. Pulling on her dressing gown, she ran down the stairs. Adrian was still on the floor and she had to clamber over him to open the door. It was a delivery boy who looked about twelve. He peered behind her while she signed for the parcel.

' 'ave yer murdered 'im?' he said ghoulishly, trying to see further into the house.

'I'll murder you,' she muttered, shutting the door and giving Adrian a kick with her bare foot to wake him up.

She'd showered and dressed before Lorna rang with the plans to go to Ravenscourt tomorrow for Nathan's photo shoot and now she sat in the kitchen drinking black coffee, trying to quieten her mind. She'd taken the phone off the hook, knowing Lorna would ring back to try and comfort her. This kindness would be her undoing, make her cry, and once she started she wouldn't be able to stop.

She heard the front door open and close and half rose, thinking that Adrian had revived and escaped to go on another bender.

'Oh Dad, how could you?' She heard Justin say. She tore into the hall to grab him before, disgusted at the sight of his father, he turned tail and fled. Not that she would blame him, but she hadn't seen him for ages and she couldn't bear to have him leave in anger.

'How wonderful to see you, I didn't think you were back until the weekend.'

'Just passing through, thought I'd come and see you,' he said, his face racked with disgust and pain. He tried not to look at his father as he slunk past him in the narrow space between Adrian's now curled-up body and the wall. 'How long has he been like that? Can't we get him to hospital or some drying out place? It's disgusting, Mum.'

He reached her and she hugged him, her skinny, lovely boy. She bit back her tears. She could not lose him; could not bear it if he stopped coming home, afraid of what he would find.

He broke free from her embrace. 'I can't stay long, but any hope of some breakfast? I haven't eaten since yesterday.'

'Of course, let's go into the kitchen. Tell me all you've been doing, it's so lovely to see you. I'm sorry you had to find your father like that, but he'll …' She looked at him and they both knew he would not be all right unless he went for proper help and that would not happen until he admitted he had a problem. 'Why should I join a whole lot of addicts,' he'd said, when they'd tried to insist he went to Alcoholics Anonymous. 'I'm not like them, I can stop any time.'

She scurried about the kitchen, relieved she'd done a shop yesterday. She had bacon, sausages and eggs so she set to, cooking him a huge breakfast, while he slumped in a chair, exhausted from too much socializing.

She told him about Ravenscourt. 'Lorna had a surprise inheritance, though, poor house, it needs so much doing to it,' she said, going on to tell him about the house and Nathan using it to shoot his Christmas brochure.

'Bit late for that, Christmas is any minute,' he said, staring at the floor.

'It's for next Christmas,' she said, prickled by panic, waiting for him to say he was going to be away for it this time.

'Oh…Ok.' He still stared at the floor, frowning a little, and she sensed there was something he wanted to tell her. She didn't want to hear it; couldn't bear him not to be here for Christmas because he wanted to escape from a father who lay like a bundle of dirty washing on the hall floor.

She put a laden plate on the table and poured him out some orange juice and he came over and started to eat it. 'Thanks, Mum, best food in ages,' he said, with a mouth full. She sat down beside him and said, as casually as she could, 'So where are you on your way to now? You said you were just passing through.'

He blushed. A smile hovered on his lips, followed by a look of anxiety. 'I've met a girl…' he started, his eyes shining. 'She lives in Islington, and well… the thing is, Mum,' he burst out, 'I wanted to ask her here for Christmas day. Her family celebrate the night before, so she's with them then, and I thought she could come here, but…' His eyes were agonised. 'I can't if...' He glanced towards the hall.

Here it was. The thing she dreaded. He was in love with a girl and wanted to bring her home but couldn't, because of his drunk of a father. She might lose him and the joy he and his girl might bring.

'Of course you can bring her home,' she said firmly. 'Dad's not going to be here. He's going to be with Stephen Sanderson and Ivan at Ravenscourt.'

Justin looked incredulous. 'You mean that house that Lorna's just inherited? Why there and why just them?'

She told him then, embellishing the state of the house a bit, explaining how Lorna, Rosalind and she were so afraid their children would stop coming home, because their fathers' behaviour upset and embarrassed them so much. They understood that their children didn't want to invite their friends back, and as for a girlfriend… She'd seen that shy joy on his face as he'd talked of her, perhaps it was the first time he'd fallen in love. He was nineteen and love was still new and magical and she would do all she could to nurture it.

'What's her name? Tell me how you met,' she said, her hand on his shoulder. 'Ask her for Christmas, we'll have a lovely day. Uncle Peter, Aunt Liz and your cousins are coming and Dad will be with his best friends at Ravenscourt.'

It will have to happen now, she thought fiercely, even if I have to tie Adrian up and dump him there. I cannot, will not, let Justin down.

CHAPTER SEVENTEEN
Shooting The Brochure

Lorna could not get Tess out of her mind. Having produced her own children so easily, it was difficult to imagine the agonies the poor woman had gone through to try and have a child. That must be bad enough in itself, but what would she feel when she found out that Flora had so carelessly fallen pregnant by her husband?

Pretty, charming Flora. Much though she loved her, Lorna recognised that ruthless streak; the cute baby stamping her foot, screaming until she got her own way. Marcus never bothered to have tantrums; he either took what he wanted, with a steely look of determination in his eyes, or let it go. Was Flora going to be one of those tiresome girls who, grown out of snatching toys, snatched at other women's men instead? It was an uncomfortable truth that children didn't just inherit their relatives' looks; they often inherited their characteristics too.

Stephen's mother had broken up a marriage, grabbing Stephen's father from some perfectly nice woman and breaking her heart. To her relief, Lorna had not seen much of her mother-in-law when she was alive, as she lived in the US, and did not encourage visitors, but perhaps Flora had taken after her.

'You're very quiet, Lorna.' Rosalind broke off from her discussion with Gloria about Christmas at Ravenscourt. Gloria looked exhausted but bullish. Almost as soon as she'd got into the car, she'd said, 'We've got to make our mad plan work. Justin came home unexpectedly and found his father dead drunk, wedged in the hall. He wants to bring a girl he's in love with for Christmas lunch, only he won't if Adrian is there.'

There followed a discussion, mostly between Rosalind and Gloria, on how to do it. Lorna didn't say much, but there was a lot of traffic, and cyclists appearing from nowhere to contend with, which needed extra concentration.

'Are you afraid our plans won't work?' Rosalind said.

'Actually, I was thinking of something else. Did Gloria tell you about Tess coming to see us? Flora's boyfriend's wife.'

'No, how dreadful, what happened?' Rosalind craned forward so as not to miss a word.

Lorna, with embellishments from Gloria, told her the sorry tale. 'I just feel so much for her. She may be almost past childbearing while Flora's at the beginning of it. It seems so wrong somehow.'

'Life is never fair. Maybe Flora will give her the baby to care for while she's at college, if she finds it cramps her life too much. Provided the marriage survives this, of course. How will you cope with that?' Rosalind regarded Lorna keenly in the driving mirror.

'Even though you are shocked at what has happened, you're looking forward to having a grandchild, aren't you?'

'Sort of, though I'd rather have it some years away and when Flora is married and settled. But since meeting Tess, any joy I feel will be overloaded with guilt.'

'Flora is your daughter and, however wrong it all may be, she is the mother of the baby and so can keep it,' Gloria chipped in. 'That's why I'm determined to keep in with Justin. I don't want him disappearing off and marrying or setting up home with a girl I hardly know because he's too hurt and embarrassed by his father's behaviour to bring her home.'

'Why would Tess take the baby? It will just remind her of Ben's infidelity? Once she knows about it, she might leave him anyway. I think I would,' Lorna said. 'I feel very upset that Flora could do such a thing.'

Rosalind said. 'Flora's a sweet girl. I'm sure she didn't mean to get so involved, or hurt his wife. She felt abandoned by her father and here was this man needing comfort too and before they knew it, there was a baby. He's as much to blame as she is, even more so as he's older and married.'

'He may well have concocted some sob story about his wife not caring for him and Flora fell for it,' Gloria said. 'But it couldn't have come at a worse time for you, love, with everything else.' She patted her arm. 'But we're here to support you, all for one!'

'Thank God for good friends,' Lorna agreed, slowing down as they reached the lane leading to Ravenscourt.

They passed through the ornate gates, which still held remnants of black paint, crusted over with rust. Once, these gates had guarded Ravenscourt's privacy; only opened to favoured people by the gate man, who'd lived in a lodge that was no longer there. Now they stood open to all. Lorna drove through the guard of honour of oak trees, and there was the house; muted rose brick and scrambling creeper. The front door was open and there were various cars parked outside.

'I'm dying to see what they've done to it.' Gloria jumped out and made for the open door just as Nathan came out. He was wearing jeans and a dark blue jersey; his hair blown about, his face flushed from the wind. Gloria greeted him effusively with a kiss on each cheek, her hand, like a mark of possession, on his shoulder. Clara followed him. Her eyes were shining. She waved and almost ran towards them in her eagerness to say hello.

Lorna hung back, overcome with a kind of shyness, not knowing how to greet Nathan, embarrassed about the emotions the sight of him evoked in her. He came over to her, smiling.

'Lorna! It's such a wonderful house, thank you so much for letting me use it.' He reached out and she wondered if he was going to grab her, hug her to him, even cover her with kisses in his enthusiasm, but he did not. He just clasped her arm, babbling on like an excited schoolboy about the carved fireplace, the old mouldings and the elaborate staircase.

'We took some shots last night when it was dark. We wanted to achieve the old-fashioned look; you know, log fires, warmth and feasting. Now we're using the daylight. Come and see. I do hope you approve.' His voice was light, yet she detected a touch of defiance, as if to remind her that it was his shoot.

'Sounds good, Nathan. It may be the same old illusion but even if they live in a minimalist box, I think most people still think of Christmas like that, sort of Scrooge and *A Christmas Carol*,' Gloria said. Then, as if she couldn't help the words escaping, she added, 'We've an idea, you see, to have a party here.'

Oh, no! Lorna nudged her. Why couldn't Gloria keep quiet? This hare-brained plan seemed doomed, especially if she told everyone about it. She could imagine Nathan – and especially Beth – shrieking with laughter at their crazy scheme, and the thought made her cringe with embarrassment. All three of them may be under considerable strain with their difficult husbands – in her case ex-husband – but had it made them lose all sense of reason?

Gloria turned to face her. 'It's OK,' she mouthed, though she did look a bit sheepish.

She annoyed Lorna further by moving closer to Nathan, slipping her hand into the crook of his arm and snuggling up to him in the most nauseating way, as she asked him how the shoot was going. Clara, standing beside her, said, 'The house used to be like this in the old days, people coming and going all the time.'

Lorna made some appropriate remark, while wishing she could bundle Gloria back into the car and drive back to London. She was about to remark on it to Rosalind, but she was now walking on Nathan's other side, praising him, though Lorna didn't know what for, as they hadn't seen anything yet. Here they were, three women whose husbands were still causing them

enough pain and upset for them to take a vow of celibacy forever, and at the first sight of another, half-decent man, they were
all jumping round him like adolescent girls hot for a rap star,
craving his attention.

This overexcited group, with Clara close behind, danced up
the few steps, through the front door and into the hall.

Lorna picked up the bag of decorated cupcakes she'd taken
from the shop last night, having spent much of the day making
them. Martha, who was a wizard at cake decorating had iced
them for her. She would arrange them somewhere among his
food. She felt confident that Nathan would agree to include
them; they certainly were very Christmassy.

She went through the front door and into the hall. She had to
admit that it did look wonderful. There was a long table in the
centre laid with silver cutlery and tall wine glasses. Strategically-
placed lighting picked up the soft sheen of the silver and the glass.
In the centre of the table was a cornucopia of fruits, flanked by
large bulbous glasses filled with sugar-covered almonds, Turkish
delight, crystallized fruits and chocolates wrapped in gold foil.
Garlands of evergreens twisted with claret red ribbons and matching glass balls were looped round the walls. Across the mantle-
piece ran a swag of more evergreens; dark glossy leaves and the
softer grey green of lavender wound round Christmas roses and
tiny tangerines. Various people milled around moving lights, setting the scene, carrying cameras. Among them she saw Beth. As
ever, she had a clipboard in her hand and was busy ticking off
things. She looked strained but she threw her a tight smile.

'Hi, Lorna. The house looks wonderful doesn't it? Do you like it?' She added this as if she didn't care if Lorna liked it or not. But she had to admit that it was quite transformed, like a tramp after a makeover and put in evening dress.

'It's wonderful,' she smiled at her, 'it must have taken a lot of work.' Beth nodded, intent on her clipboard.

Nathan appeared beside her and she saw Beth look exasperated, as if she thought her redundant to the scene, and turn away. Nathan said, 'We've got all these garlands and things here, as if it is a dinner party, then in the kitchen we've some sort of still life arrangements of the food we do. Come and see. It was Beth's idea. It looks lovely, reminiscent of an old master picture.' Nathan smiled at her, warming her heart.

'Sounds good. I must say you've done an extraordinary job, all these decorations seemed to have lifted the gloom; raised the spirits of the house.' Lorna said.

'That's what I thought. Surprising what a multitude of decay and destruction these pretty garlands cover, takes your eye away from them. Now come and see how the kitchen's been transformed.' He took her arm and they were about to go down the passage when Beth called to him.

'Oh, Nat, can you spare a moment? What shall we do with the wine bottles?' Beth called after him, darting towards him with a determined expression on her face.

'Don't worry, Nathan, I can find my own way, thanks.' Lorna went on towards the kitchen. Although she'd expected it, she was finding it too much to see that they, or rather Beth, had taken over Ravenscourt; the house that caused her so much anxiety over what to do with it, how to rescue it. Despite her concern over it, it was growing on her and her anxiety was in danger of turning her into a spoilt child wanting to snatch it all up, clutch it tightly to her, and send everyone else away.

She went down the gloomy passage to the kitchen which, to her relief, was empty. The two arrangements on the scrubbed pine table did resemble an old masterpiece. There were hams and a brace of peasants still with their glossy plumage, bright oranges and vegetables tucked around them. There was a pyramid of tiny mince pies, Christmas cakes, and three small Stilton cheeses, all arranged with bunches of herbs and bundles of cinnamon sticks tied together with ribbon, tucked in here and there. Her cupcakes would add a different touch, a kind of modern sweetmeat. She opened the two boxes she'd brought with her and carefully arranged them among the oranges, close to the mince pies. They looked perfect, the coloured icing, with a small scattering of silver stars, blending in with everything else.

The spicy smell of the cakes and pies made her feel hungry. Perhaps she could eat one of those extra mince pies pushed in behind the pyramid? Surely no one would miss it?

She imagined the soft crumbling pastry in her mouth, the burst of sweet fruit, but she couldn't take one, not until the shoot was over. She stood back to admire it again, glad she'd brought her cakes, which she felt completed the tableau.

Beside the triangle of Stilton and just behind the pyramid of mince pies stood an arrangement of Cox's apples. One of them suddenly overbalanced and rolled off its companions. Unconsciously she shot out her hand to catch it. At the same moment she heard someone come in and Nathan say, 'You can't resist my food, can you?' Her hand jerked upwards and the whole pyramid of mince pies collapsed, as the apples, like bowling balls, rolled everywhere, flooding her with horror and mortification.

Before she could explain that she was trying to field the falling apples, they heard Beth coming along the passage calling out to Nathan. When she saw what had happened, she shrieked and dropped her clipboard, her face dark with fury.

'You've sabotaged it, my lovely arrangement! It took me forever to do. How could you?'

Nathan was saying something to her, but Lorna couldn't take it in as Beth's anger hit her. She tried to explain that she hadn't caused it, was trying to save it, but Beth, overwrought, and overtired, threw all her feelings of exhaustion at her.

'You never wanted to lend us this house did you? And now we're here you are determined to ruin it … and what are those hideous things?' she shrieked, pointing to the cupcakes.

Her hysterics alerted the others and they all ran down the passage, crowding into the room, staring at Lorna in horror as if she were guilty of such destruction. She turned and fled through the scullery, out of the back door and into the garden. She would never go back; this was absolutely the end of everything.

She ran along the side of the walled garden, dodging the nettles and brambles that rambled over the path. She reached the gate that led to a patch of woodland, opened it and ran in, hoping it would offer her protection and hide her way of escape. The ground was sludgy with years of discarded leaves; each layer banked down one on top of the other, throwing up a damp, earthy smell as her feet sunk into it. She picked her way through the dense undergrowth and the trees, some fallen, sticking up from the earth like the prows of wrecked ships. Ahead, she saw a fence broken by a stile and she climbed over it into a field laid fallow for the winter. The brown earth, fringed with grass, was stiff like corrugated cardboard. She walked on, keeping to the edges of the field, stumbling a little on the icy knots of grass that clung tenaciously to the earth.

All the humiliations that had been heaped on her over the last months rose up like a tsunami to engulf her. Stephen leaving her and bringing their family and friends such embarrassment and pain; Flora breaking up someone else's marriage and getting pregnant, right in the middle of her studies, with no hope of supporting herself. She could imagine the faces of some of the parents whose children had been to school with Flora, boasting of their own daughters' progress while sneering at her for having a child who had got herself into such a mess. She shouldn't care about what people she didn't like, thought, but she did, and now, Nathan would think her a bitch for destroying that wretched still life Beth had put together so painstakingly.

The wind snatched at her, thrusting through the chinks in her clothes. She was dressed in a cream shirt and jeans, and had left her coat in the car. Perhaps she'd die of cold and they'd find her stiff and still in the ditch and they'd be sorry, she thought with the anguish of a child.

She paused a moment, her legs tired from pounding over the rough earth. She was slightly breathless, the sharp air chafing at her face. She looked out over the Sussex Downs; banks of land falling in gentle folds, clothed in trees that had been there forever. Why did she let the pettiness of life get at her when there was all this beauty? She drank it in and it calmed her raging emotions. What did it matter what Beth thought? She hadn't warmed to her. She minded what Nathan thought, though, and that was foolish enough. Among all this was her growing anxiety over Ravenscourt; how could she save it? It needed a fortune, which she didn't have.

The wind blew again, piercing through her. She'd go back, get in the car and return to London. Gloria and Rosalind could take a train, or Nathan could drive them home. She turned to go back to the car and there was Nathan, standing on the edge of the field, watching her.

Now she would have to walk right round the other side of the field to get back through the trees to the main road and up the drive to avoid him, and get to her car. He walked quickly towards her.

'Lorna, stop. Please listen.'

She went on walking, not wanting to talk to him, have him scold her for trashing Beth's arrangement. It was difficult to go fast; she was tripping in her thin boots on the knotty grass. Nathan's boots were thicker; tough, working boots that coped well with the terrain and he was beside her in a moment.

'Look, it wasn't your fault. After you'd gone, two more apples rolled off the table knocking off the last of the pies. Beth didn't mean the things she said. She's overdone it; she always does when something excites her. She's really sorry.'

Lorna went on walking. He grabbed her arm and pulled her to a halt.

'Please believe me. I don't want this to cause any aggro between us. It was all going so well and the house lends itself perfectly to what I want. We've put those dratted pies back, it's all right, really, it is. And those cakes, Gloria told me you have a business, you should have told me about it, of course we can include them.'

It was heavy-going enough with so many clods of mud on her boots without having to tow Nathan along as well, so Lorna did stop, but she did not look at him. Instead she stared fiercely out at the undulating land, her breath coming fast after her exertions and her heightened emotions.

'Please come back. We were going to have lunch, lots of ham.' She could hear laughter in his voice, but she would not succumb to it. He wanted Ravenscourt for his brochure and would do anything to keep the peace until it was finished to his satisfaction. He'd let her have her cakes in the shot, but would probably airbrush them out later. Even if Beth was not his wife he would stand up for her, she was important to him for the success of the shoot and his business.

She was overcome with a feeling of abandonment. She faced him. His eyes were tender and he was smiling. She felt herself weakening, though Beth's anger still smarted.

'This whole thing has got out of hand. I was so surprised that Fergus left me the house; I never expected it at all. I still can't quite believe it. It may sound ungrateful, but it needs so much doing to it, that, though I hate to say it, it's more of a millstone, really. He probably didn't know the state of it; being too disabled these last years to see to it. Then Gloria, Rosalind and I all got a bit silly with mad plans for Christmas. You've seen it close enough to know how much damage there is under your garlands. I think it's best to contact an estate agent, see what they say, and I might as well do it while I'm here. I'll go into Chichester and find one to take complete charge of it. I'm so tired of everyone else having opinions about it, they… you… all mean well, but it only makes the situation worse.'

'They'll never sell it by Christmas.' Nathan took her arm, walking with her beside the field. 'It's cold and you've no coat. Would you like my jersey? You don't want to add pneumonia to your problems.' Before she could protest, he'd whipped off his jersey, put it over her head and pulled it over her.

It was warm from his body. The scent of him clinging to the soft wool made her dizzy and she stumbled. He caught her by both arms, holding her steady, and she had to shut her eyes to hide her sudden desire from him. How could her body play such foolish tricks? It had been so long since Stephen had held her and she missed that; the feel and the scent of a male body close to hers. She was in grave danger of making a fool of herself, misinterpreting his kindness for tenderness. He wanted to keep her on side until his brochure was done, not start an affair with her, she told herself firmly, moving away from him.

'I know you are going through a bad time.' Nathan took her arm again and led her on as though she was a nervous horse and might start up and bolt off at any moment. 'Gloria told me about your problems with your ex-husband and I'm very sorry. People can become very peculiar in their middle age or at retirement, and it can't be easy for you. It's so good of you to lend us Ravenscourt, I love it; it's a wonderful house. I, and indeed Beth, never wanted to make things difficult for you. She's in tears and I've sent her home to get some rest. She takes things far too seriously.' All the time he was speaking his voice was soft and gentle, soothing her, and for a little while she let herself be soothed, it was such a luxury.

The wind blew again as if mocking them; she felt him shiver as he walked beside her. 'You must be cold in just a shirt, you need your jersey,' she said, but she did nothing to give it back.

'We're nearly there, but perhaps we could walk faster.' He increased his step, looking down at her boots. 'You should have thicker soles, rubber soles. Aren't your feet wet?'

'Yes, they are. I didn't think, I was so...'

'I know.' He slipped his hand from her arm taking her hand in his and squeezed it. Both their hands were cold but she felt a shot of fire go through her as their palms touched. He went on, 'But it's all over now. No one meant any harm by it, and when you see the pictures in the brochure it will be a lovely souvenir for you. I wish...' He stopped abruptly, his face grave. His eyes searched hers and for one mad moment she thought he was going to say he cared for her. He went on with an awkward laugh,

'It's a lovely house but it needs so much tender loving and expensive care, it will need a rich man to buy it.'

'I don't know what it's worth or how much would be needed to restore it.' She was determined he would not guess at her feelings at needing tender, loving but not particularly expensive care herself. 'I would think it would need to pay for itself. I suppose someone could make it into a hotel, one of those small, country house ones, or even a few flats.'

'Carving it up might spoil it. I suppose it could be done well, but…' he smiled. 'There are lots of possibilities. But just now it's a perfect backdrop for my brochure.'

'Have you recently started this business, or been doing it for ages?' She was working up to ask if he'd be interested in taking some of their cakes while she had his attention.

'Mulberry Farm is my mother's house and when my father died I…' he paused and she saw a flash of pain cross his face. He recovered quickly, threw her a quick smile. 'It's a long story, but I had to sort out his affairs and I'd just bought this business so I set it up in the barn, but really it's too cramped and it's too intrusive for her… and me. The business started off as a small thing but suddenly it's taken off. People seem to want to buy traditional, good food; well-cooked real ham instead of that re-constituted pink monstrosity sold in the supermarkets, and Christmas puddings and cakes. I want to branch out into luxury foods that can be eaten throughout the whole year, not just at Christmas. Your cakes…' he added, as an afterthought, as if he could read her mind, 'they look delicious… *are* delicious.

Remember I stole one at that fair? Perhaps we should go into business together.'

His smile made her wonder if he were joking, just saying it to keep her sweet. Wouldn't a more astute businesswoman now throw out some marketing plan? They reached the stile leading into the wood. He jumped over and turned to help her, his hands on her waist as she clambered down to stand beside him. She landed a little awkwardly and for a second he held her close to steady her, she felt his breath on her cheek. How good it would be to lay her face in the crook of his neck, feel his warm skin against her lips, but he moved away abruptly and said, 'Gloria told me you're all coming here for Christmas. Let's hope the house holds up until then,' he laughed. 'You must all come over to us; my mother always gives a large party on Boxing Day.' He let go of her hand and called out to Rosalind, who was coming through the walled garden towards them, looking anxious. 'I'm just saying to Lorna you must all come over to Mulberry Farm for our party on Boxing Day.'

Rosalind darted a look at Lorna and said warily, 'Gloria's told him about our house party.'

'Who is taking my name in vain?' Gloria appeared behind her. 'There you are Lorna! There was no harm done really, Beth just threw a hissy fit over nothing, she says she's very sorry, didn't mean it.' Gloria hugged her. 'Come and pose in their picture, you're a pro at this, Lorna. She's a film extra,' she said to Nathan.

'Oh,' he looked interested, 'then you'll know the ropes, perhaps you ought to direct it.'

'No, I'm sure you can manage,' Lorna said. Beth may have gone home but surely that wouldn't stop Nathan wanting to do it his own way.

'As it seems you are all going to be here for Christmas, you must come over to our party on Boxing Day,' Nathan smiled at Gloria.

'Oh,' Gloria looked awkward. 'Thanks, we'll let you know. We're not quite sure how many we'll be.'

'It's open house. Bring them all, or whoever wants to come.' Nathan said cheerfully. 'Now let's get this shoot done, then we can all have lunch.'

Seeing Rosalind eyeing her in Nathan's jersey, Lorna took it off as nonchalantly as possible. The sudden cold she experienced without it came more from the loss of intimacy she'd felt while wearing it than the biting wind. He took it from her, pulling it on while walking back into the house.

'Gallant of him,' Gloria said dryly.

Lorna said. 'I left my coat in the car. I'm going to put it on now, I'm freezing.'

'Stand next to Nathan and you'll be warm enough,' Gloria said.

'Don't be silly,' Lorna retorted. 'There will be no more complications in my life. I have far more than I can cope with already.'

'You can't stop complications turning up like a string of buses, when there have been none for ages, more's the pity,' Gloria followed Nathan back inside.

'Are you feeling better, Lorna? It was unforgivable of Beth to go off at you like that,' Rosalind said. 'It was only a few mince pies, for goodness sakes, and your cakes looked so pretty among it all. You'd think you had destroyed her whole life by the way she carried on.'

'I'm fine,' Lorna said. 'Let's get on with it.' She went back into the house, feeling suddenly light and happy that Beth had gone home to rest. It would be so much more fun without her.

CHAPTER EIGHTEEN
Telling the Children

'I remember Ravenscourt had great trees to make tree houses,' Marcus said. He'd dropped carelessly down in a chair, one leg hanging over the arm of it, a mug of coffee held precariously in his hand.

'You won't want to build tree houses now,' Lorna said briskly. The children had come back from university for their Christmas break, and, so far, though nothing had been said, it seemed that both of them, to her great relief, would be spending Christmas at home.

After their day at Ravenscourt watching Nathan's photographic shoot, the three women, fiercely driven by Gloria, were determined to go through with their mad idea. 'Aunt Felicity and Uncle Jonathan are coming here on Christmas day with the girls – not Becky of course, as she's in Australia, and Colin and Sue with Toby and Grania.'

'And Dad goes to Ravenscourt?' Marcus frowned. He found Aunt Felicity a pain, with her hectoring code of behaviour. 'I think I'd rather like to go there too, escape Aunt F's religious fervour.'

Lorna's heart sank. Despite Gloria carefully explaining it to him, Marcus obviously didn't realise, or want to face, the reason the three women wanted their husbands to spend Christmas at Ravenscourt. He appeared to think there was a choice as to where each person could spend the holiday; a London Christmas here or a country one at Ravenscourt, though she had to admit that the arrangement did sound rather peculiar.

'I explained that we thought it best if Dad, Adrian and Ivan went to Ravenscourt together, had a sort of male-only Christmas, as their behaviour has been monstrous and sadly, we know from other times, they are bound to ruin our Christmas this year and we've had enough of it,' Lorna said with exasperation.

'It sounds as if you are imprisoning them there.' Marcus exclaimed, as if the men were being shipped off to Guantanamo Bay. 'I think we all ought to go there. There's masses of room, isn't there? We could put them in one part of it and us in another.'

'They deserve it, leave them there until they come back as the people we once loved,' Flora said languidly from her prone position on the sofa.

'It's hardly a prison, it's a lovely place and beautifully decorated, with huge open fires, and wonderful food. Dad will be there with two of his oldest friends.' Lorna went on desperately, ashamed of that dratted guilt that was creeping into her.

'I'd love a Christmas in the country; remember those times with Gran and Gramps? It's more Christmassy somehow, and imagine if it snowed!' Marcus's face became animated. 'Let's all go to Ravenscourt. I'm sure Dad will behave with other people there, and he won't have that silly bitch with him.'

'I don't want to see him ever again unless he changes back into the father he used to be,' Flora said firmly. 'I want to stay here, what's wrong with here? We had a great time last year and I thought it was all organised anyway.'

'That was last year when we were still a family. Dad was here,' Marcus said through clenched teeth. 'It's different now. This is our home and Ravenscourt will be neutral, it would make it easier for everyone.'

Lorna was near tears. This time last year she'd never have guessed how much her life would have changed. Last Christmas had been difficult, though moments of it had been as it used to be. Perhaps she'd pretended that nothing was wrong, for looking back, there were signs that heralded the end of their marriage, but in the bustle of things to do she'd put them on the back burner of her mind. But whatever Stephen had done he was still their father. He'd been a wonderful father before his personality changed so drastically, but there was Gloria and Rosalind to think of too, she couldn't let them down.

On their drive back from Ravenscourt, the three of them had discussed getting the men there for Christmases. The transformation of the desolate house into a festive scene had raised their spirits, making them wonder if their mad idea might be feasible after all.

They all decided to tell their own children the plan today, a week before Christmas. Rosalind's children, Emma and Chloe, were still a bit young to understand it fully, but they were angry and upset with their father for always saying he hadn't time to do things with them while giving his time to other children. He'd tell them when he saw them that the children he spent time with were not as lucky as they were with their nice house, food and new clothes. Polly, hadn't helped by saying she wasn't at all surprised he'd rather stay away from them as they could be such brats, which added to their fear that their father didn't love them. Emma, with Chloe in tow, had recently asked Rosalind if Daddy would have time to come home for Christmas, but said that they didn't want him to come if he turned up with some-one 'who was alone for Christmas' that they, 'who had so much, must be kind to?'

Justin had firmly told Gloria that he would only come home for Christmas if his father were not there. He wanted to invite his girlfriend for lunch but said, 'I can't have Dad drunk all over the place, 'effing it up.'

Lorna had already discussed the plan with her children, and though Marcus had suggested they all go to Ravenscourt, she had not taken his suggestion seriously.

'I'm sorry, but you can't go to Ravenscourt, Marcus. At least,' she added, seeing his face, 'until after Christmas. We've all been very hurt by Dad's behaviour and embarrassed too. He only wants to be with us because he's nowhere else to go. When this… girl comes back he will leave us again and go back to her.'

'He might not. It might be his way of saying sorry,' Marcus said defiantly.

'Too right it is,' Flora burst out. 'I think it's disgusting, my father going off with such a bitch, and so young too. I don't care where he spends Christmas as long as it is not with me.'

The pain in Flora's voice twisted into her. Flora had adored her father and now she hated him for discarding her. She moved to hug her but Marcus broke in,

'You're one to talk! You've gone after an older man, a married man, and are knocked up.'

'That's different,' Flora retorted.

'I don't see why? At least Dad's girl isn't married.'

'But Dad was.'

'Children, please.' Stephen's behaviour was like a hand grenade tossed in among them, causing such tearing injuries. She went upstairs to her bedroom, lay on the bed and sobbed.

The telephone rang, jolting her out of her misery. She dashed away her tears as if whoever was on the other end could see her red, blotched, face. It was Gloria. 'How did it go? Telling them it's on, I mean.'

'Not too well. Marcus wants to go to Ravenscourt too. He thinks it sounds fun . . . more fun than here anyway.' Her voice wobbled.

Gloria said, 'I never thought of that. But don't take it to heart. You probably made it sound too good. I told Justin; or rather I just said that Adrian was going with friends to the country. He didn't even ask where or why. Liz and Peter and their three are coming here too. Justin's coming on Christmas Eve, so I suggest we get them all to Ravenscourt the day before.'

'I don't think it will work,' Lorna said.

'It will; it must. Rosalind has told her girls and warned them not to talk about it with Ivan. He's agreed to go; he thinks it's an impromptu house party you've decided to throw before you put the house on the market. She's afraid he might ask one of his needy women, though she's told him there's no room for anyone extra and that since it is your house, he can't, anyway. We'll drive them down, or I suppose they will drive us. We'll say the children are coming later and once we've got them there Clara and her friend, Jane, will look after them and see they stay there. We'll drive back with the cars. I don't think mobiles work there, Clara will disconnect all the phones and she'll hide one in the kitchen for emergencies.'

Lorna couldn't help but laugh. 'It does sound so mad.'

'Mad things often work because no one thinks they will,' Gloria said. 'Now be strong, think of the peace of mind we're all going to have, with our children happy and relaxed. All come over here for Boxing Day, we'll celebrate, or we could go down to Nathan's.'

'Let's think on that,' Lorna said, wondering if she could take it. She pictured Sonia interrogating her about Ravenscourt and Fergus, and Gloria all over Nathan. Besides, the three husbands might be invited too and there would be a scene and it would all be highly embarrassing, not to mention painful.

Lorna heard the front door slam and went wearily down to the living room to find Flora crying. 'He's such a bastard,' she sobbed, describing her brother. 'I don't want to spend Christmas with him. He can go with Dad and I'll go to Ben.'

Lorna sat down beside her and took her in her arms. She could lose both her children over this. 'Surely Ben will be with his wife?'

'If I asked him, he might stay with me. She's got a huge family, she won't be alone.'

'It's not right, darling,' Lorna said gently, thinking of Tess and her plea to her to keep Flora away from Ben for Christmas so the two of them could be alone. Having met Tess it did not surprise her that her sparky, pretty daughter had seduced her husband, but it was not right that it had happened. But when Flora had come to terms with her father's behaviour – they might even get on again sometime in the future – Lorna doubted she'd stay long with Ben. The best solution to this sorry mess would be if Tess forgave Ben and their marriage worked out and he kept in close contact with the child. He'd shown no sign of ducking out of his responsibility over that. Ben and Tess were far better suited to each other than Ben and Flora.

Flora stopped crying and said sadly, 'It's such a muddle, isn't it Mum? Dad was a bit strange last Christmas but I never thought it would end like this.'

Lorna sighed, stroked Flora's hair. 'Nor me, darling, but look at Adrian and Ivan; they were such decent, good men before something, perhaps the problems of their age, seem to affect them at the same time.' The two of them clung together, weeping over what they'd lost.

Later, Lorna said, 'You ought to know that Tess, Ben's wife, came here.'

'Here, why?' Flora was horrified. 'She's no right to, why did she come?'

'Remember, Flora, she is his wife and she loves him. She wants to stay with him. She wants you to let him go. You can't blame her. I tried to fight for your father, but he is so changed I know it won't work between us any more. Besides, he doesn't want me in this new life he's chosen for himself.' The reality of it wrenched her heart but she went on. 'I think Ben still loves Tess in his way and I'm sorry to say this, but I think you'll get bored of him in time.'

'I won't. And besides, we're having this baby,' Flora said defiantly.

'But, darling, do you love him? Really, really love him?' Lorna watched her carefully when she asked this, waiting for that special glow that thinking or speaking of a lover produced, but she didn't see it in Flora's face. You couldn't help love, that all consuming passion, and though it was wrong to take someone else's husband, love could be like an addiction, and loyalties and reality got trampled on in the rush for it.

'Of course. It's a sort of love,' Flora said uncertainly. 'We found each other when we were both sad.'

'But that is not love, mind-blowing, deep, passionate love.' Lorna had a sudden picture of her and Stephen; the overwhelming need they'd had to touch and speak to each other every minute of the day. She swallowed hard and continued her lecture. 'It's need, I think. Masses of people live together because they need each other and there's nothing wrong in that, provided you don't hurt anyone else.'

Flora looked as if she might cry again. 'I do love him,' she said intensely, as if to convince herself.

'Like you loved Jamie?'

'Oh, Jamie was just a mate. Good in bed, too, when he could be bothered.'

'But that is still not love.' Lorna wondered if Flora had ever fallen in love. Sex could be, often was, confused with love, especially with the young. She went on, 'Tess really loves him; she needs him too. I think she loves and needs him more than you do. But then there is the baby; it needs a father as well as a mother. So that is an enormous complication.'

'He'll be there for it. We are going to live together.' Flora sounded like a frightened little girl, determined not to have to confront the predicament she was in.

'Tess longed for a baby, went through IVF and it didn't work. She feels that the moods she suffered from the procedure – and it must be a horrendous ordeal – turned Ben away from her. Ben should have told her about the baby ages ago. How do you think she will feel when she finds out you are having his child, becoming pregnant through an act of carelessness?' Lorna held Flora close. She wanted her to feel loved and yet she wanted her to face up to things.

Flora went quiet, then burst out, 'I didn't know I'd get pregnant! He told me he couldn't have children and didn't want any, so I let him make love even though we didn't have any condoms that time.'

'You just said Ben doesn't want children?' She pitied this poor baby coming into the world with a rather scatty mother and a disinterested father.

'He does now.' Flora said firmly.

'He owes it to Tess to tell her; he should have done it ages ago. She came here to beg me to ...'

'You didn't tell her about the baby?' Flora exclaimed in horror.

'No, but Gloria came by when she was here and before I let her in I warned her not to say anything and we're afraid Tess overheard the word 'baby'. But I think we managed to steer her away from the truth. She has got to be told this Christmas. Ben must tell her and you must leave them alone while they try and work something out between them.'

'Perhaps I should have an abortion,' Flora said grimly.

'Oh, no, not that, anyway I think it's too late.' Lorna cried out involuntarily. Whatever mess they were in, the thought of the coming child had soothed her pain of losing Stephen. But standing aside from that, it was a new life, a new person, and a gift for them all which would surely bring its own love.

'It seems the best solution, I have been thinking quite a bit about it,' Flora said. 'I'm worried that I won't be able to keep up with my studies and I'll fail my exams. I haven't been able to work as hard as I'd like as I feel so rough all the time. Anyway I've years yet before it's too late for me to have a child. I can always have one later.'

Lorna kept her mouth tightly buttoned although there was so much she wanted to say. She knew she was being a coward for not facing it, but she could not bear to talk of a termination. Instead, she began to discuss the Christmas menu, asking Flora's advice as if she hadn't mentioned the baby at all.

CHAPTER NINETEEN
Getting The Husbands To Ravenscourt

'I understand from Marcus, though he sounded quite vague on the subject, that you've an idea to go to Ravenscourt for Christmas?' Stephen rang Lorna, his voice clipped and business-like, addressing her as if she were his travel agent instead of his once adored wife.

Her chest seemed to freeze up at the sound of his voice. 'Y... yes, Gloria and Rosalind are keen for us all to go.' She said. She wished Marcus hadn't said anything, though perhaps Stephen had shocked him into mentioning it by asking their plans for the day. She had not yet spoken to Stephen about it, putting it off every day, not knowing what to say.

'I could come down for the day ... and perhaps a night, if everyone is going to be there,' he said. She heard the doubt in his voice and she wished things were as they used to be. 'I'll bring some wine.'

It was distressing making plans as though they were still together, even worse that she was lying to him, though had he not lied to her, creeping off to that girl, hiding his infidelity from her? She had to go through with it if he was to be safely delivered to Ravenscourt. Caught up with the plan, she had forgotten his ritual of buying wine for Christmas, how he took such care to choose wines for each course. Last year there had been much discussion over a Californian desert wine made from black Muscat grapes to go with the Christmas pudding. Her heart ached; they would not be drinking together this year – or ever again.

'There's plenty there, Fergus left a good cellar,' she told him. She hadn't seen it but Clara had told her it was there.

'It was very good of the old boy to leave you the house. I seem to remember it was quite large,' he went on. 'You won't want to live in it, will you?'

'I haven't decided.' It struck her that being at Ravenscourt over Christmas might give Stephen time to make plans for it; plans he might plague her with, plans she didn't want. He'd loved doing up their first house together, spending hours into the night drawing up ideas. It was true he'd taken little interest in the smaller house they'd recently moved to, though there wasn't much to do here apart from changing a few colour schemes. But it was too late to change things now.

'So how is Flora? She really shouldn't have been so careless – and what sort of man is he?' His tone of voice implied that he must be some very low species indeed and before she could answer he went on, 'I suppose she expects you to look after the baby so she can get on with her life.'

'Only occasionally, as any granny would.' It was so odd to be talking to him as if everything was normal between them. She felt her guard begin to slip and was tempted from habit to air her concerns for Flora, tell him about her anxiety over the relationship between her and Ben and Ben being married, even ask his advice over Ravenscourt, but she steeled herself against it. He sounded tired and old, hardly a man in the grip of an exciting, sexy affair.

It was tragic that at this time of his life, he had exchanged his family, the only people he could have counted on until the end, for a tacky girl who appeared to be using him as a chance for a visa and a meal ticket. She sensed he was feeling lonely now the girl had gone home for Christmas. Perhaps if he'd sounded contrite, apologised for the dreadful way he had behaved and begged for another chance, she would have weakened. It was Christmas after all, she reminded herself sadly, a time for families, a time to put differences aside.

She was about to say this, thinking that perhaps – for the sake of their children and their coming grandchild – they could try to be friends after all they had shared together when he said brusquely, 'I can't stay for the whole holiday, New Year as well. Odile is due back on the thirtieth.' And all her dreams came tumbling down.

'You are only there for Christmas.' She put down the phone, her heart sore, wishing he wasn't going to be there at all.

Her feelings of sympathy had been set off when Marcus, reported that Odile – just the name of that disagreeable girl made her gag – had already gone back to her family and 'Dad was alone.'

To be fair, Marcus hadn't meant to tell his father about the plan to spend Christmas at Ravenscourt – really because it seemed so crazy he didn't believe it would come off.

'He sounded sad.' Marcus watched her reaction with careful interest, perhaps hoping she would forgive Stephen and so assuage his own guilt, if he had any, about the fact that, owing to his hectic social life, he would not be able to see his father after all during the Christmas period. 'He asked me to have supper with him but I've so many parties if we stay here, I probably can't,' he finished.

'Now he might see what it's like for me,' Lorna retorted.

'You're all right, Mum. You've got all your friends and us. I think he's beginning to regret his behaviour,' Marcus said hopefully, 'and he wants to spend Christmas with us.'

'He is going to Ravenscourt with Adrian and Ivan, and you, if you want to join them.' Lorna bit the bullet and challenged him. She was about to add, 'You'll find it very cold and very dull,' but she stopped herself; her description might make Marcus insist on having Stephen here with them. But luck was on her side. Although Marcus had thought Ravenscourt sounded fun and had almost decided to join the men for part of the time, he'd met a girl he fancied, who was going to be in London over Christmas, so Marcus felt he'd rather stay in London for the whole holiday.

The telephone rang again. Mechanically, she picked it up, then wished she hadn't, for it was Stephen again. 'Is something wrong with your phone? We got cut off,' he said accusingly, and when she didn't answer he went on, 'So when are we going to Ravenscourt?'

'Day before Christmas Eve, about tea time.' No doubt he was girding himself to take over the plans.

There had been much discussion over this. Gloria wanted them to go at the last possible moment so they had less time to escape. Rosalind and Lorna wanted them gone as soon as possible so they could finish their preparations in peace. Lorna was afraid that if Stephen was without his comfort blanket girl too long, he might come and hover round them for company.

Stephen had suggested to Marcus that he and Flora should get to know Odile and they must come round in the New Year.

'No, thanks, Dad,' Marcus refused, but later, suspiciously near tears, he asked Lorna if she thought his father might marry this girl and so make her their stepmother.

Lorna, confronted by the pain etched in Marcus's face, and having already panicked about this, imagining all sorts of lurid scenarios including babies, despaired. Seeing his confusion she hugged him, 'I just don't know darling, but let's not go there until we have to, OK?'

'If he does, I will never see him again.' He broke free of her and stomped upstairs, slamming his bedroom door on his misery.

The plan was to go down late in the day before Christmas Eve. They hoped that the men would not bother to try and escape in the dark, and once bedded down as it were, would become too lazy to try again. They were not after all young any more and all three were plagued with various ailments common to older people; bad knees, hips and backs. These factors, combined with the comfort of lots of good food, drink and cigars – Fergus had been a great smoker of them and there were many good ones left in their special humidified box – and with luck these treats should keep them there.

'You can go down with Gloria and Adrian. I'll go with Rosalind and Ivan.' Lorna told Stephen firmly. She could not bear to be cooped up so close to him in a car, her heart still yearning for the man he used to be while her mind whirled on in overdrive imagining him and Odile sharing the small, daily intimacies that should have been hers. With luck his wonky hip severely curtailed his sexual performance, if he was still able to have one, she thought darkly.

'I'll go down with the children, pick them up whatever time they're ready,' Stephen said firmly. 'I want to talk to Flora. In fact, we'd all better discuss this pregnancy business. I don't like it at all.'

'Pot calling the kettle black.' She retorted.

'What are you on about?' he said impatiently.

She ignored this. 'Better to leave the children to their own devices; they've got parties and things. We can't rely on what time they'll leave, probably the middle of the night.'

'All right.' He sounded unsure. 'I'll drive myself. Remind me of the way. It's near Arundel isn't it?'

Panic gripped her; even now he wanted to take charge. She said firmly, 'We can't take too many cars, there's nowhere to park them, the land's flooded.' She went on desperately, 'Gloria and Adrian want you to go with them, they haven't seen you for ages. Get yourself to them around four. See you there.' She put the phone down, hoping she'd convinced him. Once she'd got him to Ravenscourt, they could leave them there with Clara and Jane Purdy.

Texts and emails – read and deleted – hummed between the three women. Ivan and Adrian had swallowed the story about joining everyone for a Christmas house party and were geared up to go. Ivan, true to form, had asked if there was room for an unfortunate woman he'd met recently who was keen to experience 'a proper English Christmas'.

'She can't experience it with us,' Rosalind answered him sharply. 'It's is not our house. Lorna has invited us and there's no room for anyone else, however needy.'

As Rosalind and Ivan had to pass Lorna's house on the way to the A3, they were going to pick her up. Gloria was leaving from her home in Wimbledon. At ten to four she rang Lorna and whispered, 'Stephen's here with a bag of presents. We've forgotten those and that might make them suspicious.'

'Just say we've left everything there. You've got a suitcase haven't you?'

'Yes. See you there, good luck.' Gloria rang off, leaving Lorna racked with more guilt. Stephen had bought presents, had he one for her? In a weak moment she had bought him the latest crime novel from his favourite author but dithered about giving it to him. She hurriedly wrapped it and pushed it into her bag. The children were both out shopping, leaving their present-buying until the last minute and she would not ask them if they were buying one for their father this year.

Lorna's doorbell rang and Ivan stood on the doorstep, smiling at her. He kissed her. 'Here we are, my dear, shall I come in and help with your bags?'

'I'm fine thanks.' She took a deep breath; this was lift off. She picked up her bag from the hall, she thrown in a few clothes and presents for Clara and Jane, in case someone checked. She put on the alarm, locked up and went out to their car. Rosalind was in the passenger seat trying not to look anxious.

Ivan took her bag. 'Let me put this in the boot. You haven't bought much, nor has Rosalind. Usually whenever we go anywhere she looks as if she's moving in.'

'We've taken most of our things there already, the food and stuff,' Lorna said, getting into the back of the car. It was dusk now and the lights from the street lamps cast a yellowy glow over the row of solid brick houses with their white plaster trims.

Rosalind turned round and whispered, 'All set?'

'Hope so. Gloria rang, she said Stephen had arrived with presents.'

'I've put a few in,' Rosalind said quickly before Ivan got back into the car. 'Thought it might look suspicious if I didn't. I've hidden the rest in my wardrobe, and crackers and things.'

Ivan got into the driving seat and put on his belt, looking at her in the driving mirror. 'OK, we're off. I must say this is exciting, Lorna. You must tell me all about the house. Will you live there now that ... I'm awfully sorry about you and Stephen but it will probably blow over; these things usually do.' He smiled at her, his face strangely contorted in the streetlights.

'It's too late, we're divorced.' Lorna, who had not seen Ivan for some time, thought how fleshy his face had become, his eyes almost lost in the folds of his skin. 'And he's found someone else.'

'I bet he hasn't really. We boys can get a bit naughty sometimes but it means nothing.' His tone was jovial as if she was taking Stephen's affair too seriously and should be more sophisticated about it.

His smug expression sickened her but she didn't remark on it. She must not antagonise him or he may take offence and refuse to come. Glancing at Rosalind's profile she saw, by the set of her jaw, that she too, was fighting to stay calm.

'But Stephen's going to be there, isn't he?' He asked her.

Lorna studied the back of Ivan's head and wondered if he knew that he had a bald patch appearing in the midst of his dark hair like a tonsure on a priest. He'd dyed it too, she realised with amusement. 'Yes, just for Christmas.'

'And the children are coming, aren't they? I haven't seen them for ages. What are they doing now?'

Lorna told him about Marcus and Flora, concentrating on their studies, not mentioning the baby. She wondered if Stephen would discuss it with them and what their reaction would be. Would they be shocked even though, they, notably Stephen and apparently Ivan were playing away themselves with women young enough to get pregnant?

'Will Stephen be there on his own?' Ivan went on. 'I think Christmas is a time – I'm sure you agree Lorna – when we lucky people with a family should invite someone on their own in for Christmas.'

'It depends who that someone is,' Rosalind said sourly.

'He is not bringing the . . . person he is involved with, if that's what you mean,' Lorna broke in quickly. Knowing about Ivan's request to invite some poor unfortunate, she couldn't resist saying, 'If you want to ask someone less fortunate to share Christmas with us I'm sure the local vicar would know of some elderly people who are on their own.'

'Let's see how we go, shall we?' Ivan shut up then until he had to ask her for directions to the house, switching on Classic FM to fill the awkward gaps with music.

To Lorna's great relief she saw that Gloria had already arrived. Then, to her horror, she saw the front door open and Nathan and Sonia, illuminated from the hall lights behind them, come out and hover on the doorstep. 'I thought they'd finished days ago.' She hissed at Rosalind, but Rosalind didn't hear her as she was already out of the car and helping unload the boot.

Gloria came over and hugged her. 'We've done it,' she whispered.

Sonia greeted Lorna and came back with her into the hall. 'So sorry to barge in, Nathan thought you were all arriving tomorrow. He just wanted to take a few more pictures.' Her eyes darted greedily towards each of the men. Stephen and Adrian had now appeared and everyone greeted each other slightly too jovially.

The hall was bright with garlands; a tall Christmas tree decorated with spun glass decorations stood by the stairs, dominating the room. It was the perfect setting for a perfect Christmas.

Adrian kissed Lorna. Once he'd been so attractive but now the drink had coarsened him. She could smell it on him as if it was impregnated into his skin. She nodded towards Stephen, barely looking at him. It hurt her to see him there, an impostor who no longer loved her.

Gloria said, 'Now, this is Clara and her friend, Jane Purdy, who will be looking after you . . . us.'

Lorna went over to talk to them and to meet Jane, a rosy-faced, handsome woman with a twinkle in her eye. But before she could talk to her, Sonia broke into the circle. 'I absolutely insist you all come to my party on Boxing Day.' She smiled over at Stephen, who smiled back. 'You will all promise won't you?'

'Sounds very nice, thank you,' Adrian said.

Stephen was now inspecting the hall intently. The room looked far better than it had when she had first seen it, as many of the cracks and stains were covered up by the decorations. The light was soft, flattering the room with its beautiful moulding and ornate staircase. Lorna wondered how many imperfections would show up in the crueller glare of daylight. A fire was burning in the grate, the flickering flames mirrored in the glass balls wound into the garlands. There was a rich smell of evergreens and spices and roasting meat from the kitchen.

'It looks wonderful, though I can see it needs a lot of work on it. It's sad that it has been let go; I remember it as being very smart.' Stephen came over to Lorna.

'Yes, it was,' she said, wishing he was as he used to be and they could discuss it together. He had good ideas and would have been the perfect person to help her decide what to do with it. Perhaps there'd be some miracle; being here, in a place they'd been together when times were good, it even might bring him back to her as the man he used to be. She turned away, not wanting him to see her tears, and bumped into Nathan.

His face was set and she had the strange idea that he was studying them all as if trying to figure something out. He didn't know about their mad plan and was probably trying to work out who was with whom. She wished she could confide in him, wondering if he'd care if she had a lover or not. His eyes skimmed over her and she turned away, not wanting him to work out that Stephen was her ex-husband and her heart was tortured by his presence. She wondered if Nathan had a woman he loved and was spending Christmas with her.

Lorna watched with irritation as Gloria fluttered up to him, somehow making it appear as if she was asking him something secret and intimate. Nathan must leave, she thought suddenly in alarm, or something will be said and this whole plan will come crashing down.

'This is such a lovely house, Lorna.' Ivan was beside her, he put his arm round her before she could get to Gloria and warn her not to even hint at the situation. 'We are going to have such a good time here.'

Sonia joined them, going on again about her dratted party, but Nathan put his hand under his mother's elbow as if he was arresting her and urged her to the door. 'Time to go,' he said firmly. 'We're intruding on their party.'

'Have a good Christmas,' Lorna said with relief, walking towards them, her arms held out as if she were rounding them up, to guide them through the door.

'Goodbye, sorry we were still here when you arrived,' Nathan said with a smile, 'I'm longing to show you the pictures we took, I haven't really studied them yet but I think we've got some fabulous ones.'

'I'm so glad, look forward to seeing them,' she was warmed by his smile.

'Longing to seeing you all on Boxing Day,' Sonia tried to dart in again but Nathan kept his hand firmly on her arm.

'We'll be there,' Ivan said.

'Let's settle in and see where our rooms are,' Gloria said when the front door had closed behind them.

Lorna went to the window; the two carriage lights, either side of the front door, shone out strongly into the dark. She watched Nathan open the car door for his mother, then go round to his side. He looked up and saw her. He lifted his hand in a kind of salute and she turned away, feeling shy of being caught watching him.

'Follow Clara and Jane, they will show you where things are. We'll get on with the food preparation.' Gloria went on in her jolly, bossy voice.

'Good idea,' Stephen threw Lorna a look as if to say 'Are we sharing a room?' She pretended not to notice, following Gloria and Rosalind to the kitchen, leaving the men ragging each other as they trooped upstairs behind Jane, who treated them as if they were new boys at boarding school, which instantly made them feel at home. Clara bought up the rear.

Once in the kitchen, the three women looked at each other in amazed disbelief. 'We must go now, at once.' Gloria hissed.

'Are you sure? Shouldn't we wait until they've drunk a bit, got stuck in,' Rosalind said.

'No, Clara and Jane know what to do. They are going to say we must not be disturbed as we are sorting out the food and things. I told Adrian we were going to pick up a ham and other goodies from Nathan so with luck they won't miss us for quite a few hours. Oh, before I forget, Nathan left all this for you.' Gloria gestured towards an enormous box of food on the floor.

'For me?' Lorna glanced inside, seeing a whole ham, a cheese, pâtés, a Christmas pudding and jars of exotic chutneys and sauces.

'You do deserve them, lending him your house,' Gloria said. 'Now let's go, I'll help you put this in the car before the men see or they'll wonder why we are going to get some more.' She lifted one end as Lorna struggled with the other.

'I am going over to Mulberry Farm to get some more of his smoked salmon. I stupidly only got one packet and it won't be enough with Justin's friends coming.' Gloria said as they shut the box in the boot of Rosalind's car. 'Do you both want to come?'

Lorna couldn't cope with any more, certainly not seeing Nathan possibly with the woman he loved who might be there, staying for Christmas. It was a great relief when Rosalind said,

'No, if you don't mind, I'd rather go home and get things sorted there. I've hidden things all over the place and I must find them all in time.'

'Me too,' Lorna said. She hugged Gloria. 'Well done, but let's go quickly before they stop us.'

Giggling rather manically the three of them ran out of the side door and made for their cars. A feeling of hysteria took over as if the men would suddenly appear and command them to stay. There was a tricky moment when Rosalind dropped her car keys and they had to hunt for them in the dark. Gloria slipped and fell and lay there too overcome with nervous giggles to get up and she had to be hauled up by the other two, begging her to keep quiet but not able to stop their own desperate laughter. But at last they got in to their cars and drove off down the drive, their headlights picking out the sheep huddled in their shelter, watching them leave.

'I can't help feeling they'll all be back tomorrow and be simply furious with us,' Rosalind said as they hit the road, and turned towards London. Gloria, just behind them, hooted and flashed her headlights before turning off the opposite way towards Mulberry Farm and Nathan.

CHAPTER TWENTY
A Jolly Christmas Day

Lorna got back home after dropping the men at Ravenscourt to find Marcus and Flora decorating the living room. Marcus was up a ladder fixing an arrangement of dark green leaves and tiny gold painted fir cones over the top of a picture and Flora was finishing off the tree Marcus had bought in the market. They turned as she came in, their faces eager with excitement, anxious for her approval.

Memories of other Christmases thudded through her. Small, flushed children enchanted by the magic of the festival growing through to truculent teenagers professing boredom of the whole thing, until some wisp of that past magic touched them and they became caught up in the spirit of it; found pleasure, comfort even, in the familiar traditions. And Stephen, always Stephen there, in relaxed holiday mood making them laugh, making them a family.

'Don't you like it?' Flora demanded accusingly, mistaking her expression of grief for what they'd lost, for one of disapproval.

'No, it's lovely, thank you both so much. I was going to start decorating tomorrow.' She tried to smile and appear cheerful but all she could think about was Stephen's absence, looming like a huge shadow in the room, dwarfing everything else.

When she'd seen him at Ravenscourt she could hardly bear to look at him, hear his voice reminding her of the pain he'd inflicted on them all, but now she was home surrounded by the familiar preparations, she ached for him. Despite everything he'd done, she felt guilty for banishing him to Ravenscourt for Christmas.

'I remember buying these in the Harrods sale when I was small,' Flora said, joyfully unwrapping some spun glass bright birds with elaborate tail feathers.

'You screamed and screamed until Mum bought them,' Marcus said.

'I did not!'

'Did!'

'Please, don't squabble.' Lorna sank down on to a chair, drained by the trauma of the day. Marcus poured her out a glass of wine and handed it to her.

'So, are they all settled in?' Marcus asked quietly.

'Yes.' Lorna was not going to elaborate, spill out her fears of them escaping and Stephen, who sentimentally a moment ago she wanted back, suddenly turning up here and ruining Christmas day for them all.

'Did they guess we didn't want them?' Flora pinned her with a sharp look, fuelling her feelings of guilt.

'We didn't stay to find out, so I don't know how they will react when they realise that none of us are joining them. But I want to forget them, enjoy this time. You won't mention it to Aunt Felicity will you? She wouldn't understand.'

Lorna's elder sister, Felicity, and her husband Jonathan, aspired to live an exemplary life, continuously criticising the mistakes and behaviour of lesser mortals. This was all bound up with their religious beliefs; beliefs that Lorna felt did not encourage forgiveness or the understanding of human frailties. As far as Lorna knew, no great life-changing challenges had ever crossed their smug little path, which meant that life had been easy for them. She was fond of her sister, who, she knew, meant to be kind. She had shown this during the illnesses and subsequent deaths of their parents, but her bossiness could be overwhelming.

'Course not, Mum.' Marcus laughed. 'When will you tell our sainted aunt,' he glanced at his sister, 'about Flora's little surprise?'

'Pig, at least I'm living a life,' Flora retorted. 'Anyway, I don't show that much, do I, Mum?' She turned to her, and Lorna, now she looked, saw a thickening round her waist and the slight shape of a rounded stomach.

'We'll keep off the subject until after Christmas,' Lorna said wearily, wishing now that Felicity was not coming to spend the day with them. When she discovered she was to become a great aunt – the thought made her smile in spite of her anxiety – Felicity would smother her with guidance, both divine and her own, gleaned from various self-help books which she'd suggest she read. It would be like taking an MA in the pitfalls of being a single mother, or more pertinently, a single *grandmother,* and the thought of it exhausted her.

'If she knew what Katie was getting up to at Uni, she'd die,' Marcus said gleefully. He was at the same university as his cousin.

'Really?' Lorna perked up.

'She's quite a goer, must be having escaped from all that sexual repression at home,' Marcus said.

'I hope she's being careful.' Lorna was fond of her nieces.

'Not like me you mean,' Flora said.

'You bet not like you,' Marcus quipped, turning on a quarrel again until Lorna asked him to unpack the box of food she and Rosalind had heaved into the hall. This kept them both happy for a while as they drooled over the contents.

'Did you buy all this?' Marcus asked.

'No, I was given it for lending out Ravenscourt.' She explained about Nathan's shoot.

Marcus eyed her suspiciously. 'All this just for lending the house?'

'Nathan's very generous,' she said, cursing herself for blushing.

Gloria rang soon after supper. 'Did you get back OK?'

'Yes, and you?'

'Justin and I have just had a delicious supper, courtesy of Nathan. His pâtés are so good. He buys them in France from some special place.'

Lorna, who'd made a pact with herself to stop fantasising about Nathan, broke in, 'Have you heard if the men are still at Ravenscourt?'

'No, but I'm sure Clara would let us know if they escape. Isn't she going to ring you from her cottage tomorrow, to tell you how it is going?'

'If she can. I'll ring her there in the morning, though she might not be there if she's cooking their breakfast.'

'It's keeping them there tomorrow that could be difficult,' Gloria went on. 'But it might be the turning point.' Her voice held hope, 'Being banished there might make them come to their senses and make a real effort to become the men they once were.'

'I wouldn't count on it. If they stay it will be because of laziness. After all, there's plenty of food from Nathan and all that booze in Fergus's wine cellar. Checking through the cellar will occupy them for hours so they may not miss us at all. If the weather is bad and they drink enough they won't bother to leave. They'll probably enjoy it without us keeping an eye on them, or bossing them to help in the kitchen,' Lorna said.

'Sonia is insisting on us all going over to Mulberry Farm for her open house on Boxing Day. Naturally I didn't tell her that we're not at Ravenscourt.'

Lorna remembered Sonia's list of 'admirers'. She was obviously a woman who could not let any man who was remotely attractive pass her by without attempting to throw a net over him.

'We've taken the cars, but Clara and Jane could drive them to the party and Nathan...' Gloria paused and Lorna forgot her good intentions at not fantasying about him and sprung on to her remark.

'Nathan was what?'

'He's worn out. It's a difficult time of the year for him, and I suspect he takes on too much because of it, and then he had all that fuss over the brochure. He'd probably far rather shut himself in the house away from the rest of the world and re-appear when it is all over.'

Gloria's remark, 'all that fuss over the brochure,' made her wonder if Gloria was obliquely blaming her for Nathan's exhaustion. Perhaps he had made some bad tempered comments about the house, which was unfair as she'd lent him Ravenscourt and he had professed to love it. She was about to question her further when Gloria suddenly remembered her mince pies were ready to be taken out of the oven, and rang off.

Despite her exhaustion, Lorna slept badly. What did Gloria mean about Christmas being a difficult time for Nathan? Was it just because it was the most frantic time for his business or was there something else? She drifted off and was woken by the telephone. It was Clara.

'They are still in bed so I've slipped across to the cottage to ring you now. I don't dare risk it from the phone in the kitchen in case one of them comes down and catches me at it.'

Cold fingers of dread kneaded her stomach as she braced herself for bad news. The men had insisted on leaving, threatened to call the police, tried to contact friends to rescue them. Clara went on, 'They spent quite a time in the wine cellar choosing wines for the meals. Poor Fergus couldn't drink near the end so I hope the wine is still drinkable. Anyway they drank quite a lot and the room got very warm near the fire and they were so busy talking they didn't notice you were not there for quite a while.'

'I hoped that would happen. They don't have the energy they once had. They just might settle down until Christmas is over,' Lorna said, relief seeping through her.

'We gave them dinner and Ivan asked where you all were. We said you had gone to fetch the children and would arrive later. They accepted it, but they were too far gone to really question it, they were quite tired too. I don't know what they will be like today, though, when we tell them the real story.'

'We'll have to hope they'll have such huge hangovers they'll stay there,' Lorna said. 'What's the weather like?'

'Quite wet, the forecast is for heavy rain all day and there's a nasty, nippy wind, so that might keep them here. We've plenty of food, Nathan left a lot after the shoot and there's the wine cellar. I'll try and ring you later, but Jane has their measure. They seem quite in awe of her but I think they like her too, perhaps they've reverted to their school days.' Clara laughed. 'How Fergus would have loved this.'

Fergus would have taken part in the plan with great enthusiasm and kept them enthralled with his personality. Perhaps he knew about it, and was cheering them on, Lorna thought fondly.

The day passed quickly, as there was so much last minute stuff to do. 'Every year I'm disorganised,' Lorna wailed, but the children seemed to take over. Marcus had slipped into Stephen's role without her realising, and perhaps without knowing it himself. He organised the drink and fetched the turkey, and Flora helped in the kitchen. None of them mentioned Stephen and as the time went on, the three of them getting things done, laughing and joking together, Lorna realised what fun they were having, and how calm it was without Stephen in his new persona.

As the day progressed without any news about the men at Ravenscourt, or indeed from Rosalind or Gloria, Lorna found herself becoming more and more anxious that something would go wrong. She turned off her mobile, wishing she could escape where no one could contact her and spoil the genial mood between them by warning her that Stephen was on his way. She suggested that they go out for supper and then go on to Midnight Mass.

'Don't let's get there too early, it's usually so cold.' Flora was looking tired, her face pinched and drawn. Next year there would be the baby, Lorna realised with a jolt. Next year, what would their lives be like then?

Just before lunch, Clara telephoned. The ring of the phone struck Lorna like a weapon.

'It's me,' Clara whispered as if she was employed in espionage, which in a way she was. 'We had a bit of trouble with them when we told them they were staying here without you for Christmas, but...' She paused. Lorna waited in trepidation, straining for the sound of the doorbell heralding Stephen's arrival. 'They've settled down. Fergus had a huge stack of videos and they're watching those and drinking a lot I'm afraid. Sonia rang to remind them about her party which perked them up, so I think they are quite enjoying being all bachelors together, "not being bossed by their wives" as one of them put it.'

Lorna did not ask which man had said that. Relieved they'd not escaped and were coming hot foot to London, she thanked Clara sincerely, making her laugh and say it was certainly a change for Jane and her and they were enjoying it.

The house was crowded for lunch, with Lorna's sister and brother-in-law and their two daughters, the 'goer' Katie and her youngest sister, Amy; and Colin and Sue Elliot, two of Lorna's oldest friends, and their children, Toby and Grania. Apart from Felicity giving the run-down of their Church attendances – needless to say, they were all in various church choirs – it all passed off well. The turkey was perfect, the stuffing and sauces delicious, and everyone got a spoonful of Christmas pudding before the blue fire of the flaming brandy went out. After lunch the children moved to the corner of the room to play Monopoly, using a tattered old board that they reverted to at Christmas, leaving their parents to their coffee.

Jonathan, who'd drunk a little too much, said jovially, 'Can I ask where my brother-in-law is? I thought he might have played the prodigal, repented and come home for Christmas.'

Sue and Colin Elliot perked up. They knew of, and had witnessed, Stephen's behaviour and Lorna's grief, and were very supportive of her. Colin had tried to knock some sense into Stephen without success, but they were obviously curious to know what he was doing today.

Lorna had been dreading, yet expecting, the question. She said, reluctantly, 'He's in a house party in the country.'

'With friends?' Felicity asked.

'With the girl?' Jonathan asked at the same time.

'Just friends.' Lorna hoped to leave it at that, not mention that they were at Ravenscourt. Both her brother and sister were envious of her inheriting the house. When she'd heard of it, Felicity had asked if they couldn't all share it as a country home. If *she'd* been lucky enough to be left such a house, *she* would have shared her good fortune with her brother and sister.

Lorna did not want her bossy older sister to be yet someone else to muscle in on Ravenscourt's fate, and had explained to her then that the house needed a fortune spent on it, which it did, but she'd exaggerated, describing it as 'virtually derelict'. Before she could change the, subject, Colin said unwittingly,

'Didn't you inherit a large house in Sussex, Lorna?'

'Yes she did, lucky thing. My godparents weren't at all generous to me.' Felicity broke in. 'We must all go down for a weekend when the weather gets warmer. I thought,' she turned to Sue, 'we could share the house for weekends and things. We'd pay our way of course. I don't think Lorna realises how expensive running such a house would be – she'd be grateful for our contribution.'

'Is it very big?' Sue asked Lorna.

If only they'd leave it alone, she didn't want to talk about it. It was bad enough having Beth and Gloria taking over Ravenscourt with their ideas for it, her sister would be far worse. But more crucial than that, she did not want them to know about the three men imprisoned there. She tried to sidetrack them by asking how her niece Becky was getting on in Sydney. This worked for a few moments before Felicity started on about Ravenscourt again, telling Lorna that she was longing to see it and that she could advise her on the best plan for it.

'Perhaps Jonathan could get together a group of friends and buy it and we could lease it out for spiritual study and retreats,' Felicity finished, excitedly. 'Get it to bring in some money for you, and enjoy it at the same time.'

Nathan wanted it for his food enterprise and Felicity for spiritual purposes, how diverse was that?

The children were making quite a noise with their game but there was a sudden silence as Felicity said loudly, 'You must at least let us see Ravenscourt even if it is in a state, Lorna. Dad used to talk about it, remember? Said how lovely it was. Fergus was one of his oldest friends,' she explained to Sue. 'He often stayed there.'

'I'll come with you,' Marcus looked up from the game. 'I loved it when I was little, rushing round the garden and hiding in the attics. We nearly had Christmas there with Dad. Stop, two hundred pounds, please,' he shouted as Toby landed on his space. There was a shocked silence like a shot of icy water between the adults sitting over their coffee.

'Stephen is at Ravenscourt?' Felicity exclaimed, in her most commanding way. 'Lorna, if it so derelict, why is *Stephen* at Ravenscourt?'

'Too late, Flora's thrown the dice,' Toby Elliot announced gleefully.

'But it hadn't hit the board,' Marcus retorted, more interested in getting his rent out of Toby than covering up his mistake in letting slip that his father was at Ravenscourt. Flora kicked him under the table to punish him but he ignored her and he and Toby argued, involving the others over the legality of Toby paying the fine.

'Cool it, children,' Felicity demanded, before turning on Lorna. 'Do you mean to say that Stephen is at Ravenscourt, now, for Christmas?'

Lorna, exhausted by the tension of the last few days and the monumental preparations she'd made for Christmas, nearly wept. It was a struggle not to tell Felicity that it was none of her business, but she knew from past experience that that would bring on one of Felicity's 'caring' moods, which meant that she would put on her soft voice as if dealing with a raving lunatic, make sure she had the others on her side, and try and wheedle what she wanted out of her, until, out of sheer exhaustion, she would give in and tell her anything she wanted to know.

Lorna remembered Gloria's words: 'Above all don't let your sister know about it until it is all over.'

Seeing her distress, Sue said firmly, 'Don't let's spoil this lovely day by talking about Stephen. What's happened is tragic, but I don't think it is fair on Lorna to discuss it now.'

Colin said, 'Yes, come on, let's talk about something else. Tell us how your cake shop is going with Martha. We bought our Christmas cake there and it's almost too pretty to eat.'

Before she could answer him, Felicity said, 'We cannot pretend Stephen does not exist. He's been part of our family life for over twenty years. I would say he looms larger in the room precisely because he is not here. Anyway,' she sounded offended, 'all I wanted to know is why he's at Ravenscourt when Lorna told us it was a ruin.'

'There are some habitable rooms, just not very many,' Lorna said shortly, turning back to Colin to discuss the cake shop.

Jonathan said, in the tone of voice of a doctor breaking bad news, 'So he's there with this… woman then? Of course he couldn't bring her here. I quite understand that.'

Sue and Colin tried to look disapproving at his remark, but Lorna saw they were curious to know whom Stephen was with. She'd found that, while most of her friends had been very supportive of her and shocked and saddened at Stephen's uncharacteristic behaviour, they also longed to know all the juicy details.

'No he's not. I don't want to talk about him or Ravenscourt any more.' Lorna said firmly, getting up and going into the kitchen to make some more coffee, snapping on the kettle and irritably stacking some dirty plates into the dishwasher. It was too much to have hoped that they would get through the whole of today without Stephen being mentioned, or worse still, him turning up, but apart from Felicity's interrogation, the day had gone well and for that she was thankful.

She could hear the young all laughing and ragging each other over their game. It had been a happy day and that was all she cared about. She would not think about how it was going at Ravenscourt, or Flora's pregnancy, or how her sister would react over that. She would save all that for another time when she was alone with her.

To steer everyone away from this fascinating topic, Colin suggested they all go for a walk. Sue agreed, saying she had eaten far too much. Lorna, stressed by this new mood of inquisition, abandoned the coffee, and encouraged the idea. She guessed her sister had drunk too much, which often made her extra bossy; a good, brisk walk would do her good. Felicity leapt up from the sofa and went over to the young, urging them to leave their game and come out for some fresh air.

Flora stretched and yawned, 'I don't feel like it, I'll stay here.'

'Come on Flora, you can't stay cooped up all day,' Felicity insisted, wanting her own girls to go out to stop them being grumpy later and afraid that if Flora refused to come, they would too. 'We must go now, it is almost dark already.'

There was nothing Flora hated more than being treated like a child and made to do something she didn't want to do. 'I'm going to stay, we haven't finished our game,' she said.

'You can come back to it,' Felicity said cheerfully, trying to win them over. 'Come on girls,' she addressed her daughters, 'let's get our coats on.'

Amy her youngest daughter, who was eleven, wandered into the hall to find her coat. Toby and Marcus, now sparring with each other, rushed out of the house, snatching up their coats on the way, their energy urging them out into a larger space. Grania, who rather fancied Marcus, followed them. Katie, who was close in age to Flora, said sulkily, 'Oh Mum, lay off, it's cold outside.'

'Katie and I will stay here, we'll wash up,' Flora said, though she had no intention of tackling all those pans and dishes just now.

'Yes,' Katie said, with a defiant look at her mother. 'We'll stay here.'

Lorna could not help smiling at her niece's stand for independence. There was nothing worse than dragging round a sulky individual who spoilt whatever one was doing by their seething bad humour. Felicity caught this look. Bruised already by not being told about Stephen being at Ravenscourt when she herself had been put off going there, and feeling that Flora had encouraged Katie to disobey her, she spat out, 'Both you girls need an outing. You're putting on weight, Flora. You used to be so thin, you don't want to get fat.'

'I'm pregnant, that's why I'm fat,' Flora said with cool defiance, her eyes glittering with a sudden surge of power on seeing them all staring at her in horror.

'Pregnant!' Felicity turned accusingly towards Lorna.

Lorna said, 'Look, let's all go out, let the girls stay here. I'll tell you about it later.'

'So it is true?' Felicity stared from one to the other in shock.

Colin said hastily, 'On second thoughts, I think it's getting too late for a walk, it gets so cold at this time of the year. If we don't see the children, tell them we've gone home. We had such a lovely lunch Lorna, thank you so much.' He went over to her and kissed her, saying quietly, 'You poor girl, come round and chat any time if you need to.'

'Thanks, I will.' She wished he would stay, people accused Colin of being dull but now she longed for dull. Dull and dependable seemed appealing in her state.

Sue hugged her, 'Thanks so much, love. I'll ring you, chin up.'

Amy came back into the room in her coat, staring at Flora in excited awe. 'A baby,' she said, 'you're going to have a baby?'

'Amy, go out and find the boys,' Felicity said bossily. 'Jonathan, you take her, I'll stay behind and deal with this.'

'No, you won't,' Lorna said firmly. 'I was going to tell you about it Felicity, but not today. Now you know about it we'll talk about it another time.'

'You've had a dreadful time with Stephen, but it seems you've lost control of your family. It's no good Lorna, ignoring things. Stephen should have been forced to get proper medical help and Flora . . .' Felicity glared at her as though she would have locked Flora up in a chastity belt had she been her own daughter, 'should have been given proper guidance on how to behave in sexual matters.'

'I know how to behave, this was an accident,' Flora said. 'And you'd better know it all,' she added with abandon. 'He's married.'

'Married!' Felicity sank down on to the nearest chair.

Jonathan hovered like an ungainly heron. Not knowing how to deal with this new scandal so close to home, he suggested they leave at once, 'and discuss this rationally at a later date.' Preferably, Lorna guessed, one where he was not present.

'All this has happened because Stephen went off,' Felicity said, after reflection. 'No doubt, Flora, you were looking for a father figure in this man. How old is he?'

Lorna, who thought the same thing said, 'Look, let's leave it now. It will work out.' It probably would not, but she didn't want Felicity to know any more about it now.

'How can it possibly work out?' Felicity addressed her. 'Really Lorna, you seem to have completely lost your ability to cope. I shall take charge; get Flora to a doctor at once and see what can be done.'

'You will not,' Flora burst out. 'It is my baby and my problem and it is absolutely nothing to do with you.' And she marched out of the room and upstairs to her bedroom, slamming the door behind her.

'We'd better go.' Jonathan glanced nervously at his daughters as if they too might be tempted to follow Flora's example.

'I see I'll have to take charge,' Felicity repeated with fervour, as if this was to be her new mission in life. 'Stephen's desertion has been a terrible blow to you, Lorna. It's quite unhinged you. I blame myself for not supporting you more. I don't suppose this man will marry her.' She glared at her. 'How can Flora support a child? And what about the man's poor wife, is he still married?'

This was worse than anything Lorna could have imagined. She'd been dreading telling Felicity about the pregnancy, knowing she would have to suffer the third degree over her bad parenting skills.

'She's old enough to have her own child and Ben will stand by her and his child,' she said weakly, but before she could elaborate further the telephone rang; the ring cutting through the atmosphere like a chainsaw. Relieved at the diversion, Lorna went to answer it. It was Gloria, her voice shrill with panic,

'Adrian's fallen down the stairs and is in intensive care. Will you come with me to the hospital? I can't face it on my own.'

CHAPTER TWENTY-ONE
Geriatrics

Gloria and Lorna arrived at the hospital in Sussex, in a state of high anxiety. On the journey Gloria had gone so far as to arrange Adrian's funeral service. She could see herself as the grieving widow, not dressed in black, as she hated it so, imagining the other mourners whispering behind their hands that his death was a mercy in the circumstances. It was all her fault this had happened and she burst out, 'Whatever was I thinking, having him shut up in a deserted house with unlimited booze and his mates to encourage him?'

'How many times has Adrian fallen over and been found comatose in some alleyway while he's been living at home with you?' Lorna said reasonably, 'Maybe it isn't his fault he's an alcoholic, but he could have made some effort to get help to control it.'

'But I was so worried about losing Justin, I left him at Ravenscourt without supervision. I should have asked the others to keep an eye on him.' Gloria was in full crucifixion mode now; she rocked her body forward in her seat as if the movement would add speed to the car to hasten her to his bedside. He'd be dead before she got there and she wanted to say she loved him; despite everything, she loved him, but more importantly, she wanted him to say that he loved her.

Lorna was bitten by anxiety. Felicity's interrogation over Flora and Stephen was bad enough, but Adrian's accident was the last straw. Naturally Gloria was in a state, but Adrian was always causing her grief and she felt irritated with him for being partly responsible for ruining, what had been, all considered, a pleasant Christmas Day. With each moment their anxiety seemed to expand, sparking off from each other, winding deeper, as cars whizzed past her like bullets, their lights flashing at her, some hooting, unnerving her further. She'd surely have a crash, she had to stop. When they got off the motorway to a safer road, she pulled the car over and turned off the engine, causing Gloria to cry out in alarm.

'Stop beating yourself up about this, Gloria,' she said firmly, putting her hand over hers as they twisted in her lap. 'You've done more than you should, trying to look after him. Adrian is a drunk and that is his choice, and if he dies falling down the stairs, it is not your fault. Unless you actually pushed him, of course.' Her tone of voice implied that perhaps it would have been better for everyone if she had pushed him to his death ages ago. Before Gloria could summon up enough energy to respond, she went on, her face animated, driven by her sermon.

'Stop blaming yourself for his behaviour, love. I know I'm doing the same, taking some of the blame for Stephen's involvement with that girl; thinking that I should have taken more notice of him when he was made redundant instead of concentrating on getting the cake shop up and running, but it is them, not us, who have made the wrong choices in their lives. Why should we, their wives, feel so responsible for them? '

Gloria blew her nose, 'I just can't help myself. I'm furious with him for spoiling today. We had such a good time. Justin had his friends over, and this sweet girl, Ellie, he's mad about. Liz and Peter and their kids came, and it was all going so well. Everyone was so relaxed, and even though I missed Adrian sometimes, it was all worth it, seeing Justin and Ellie so happy together. Then Ivan rang.'

'So Ivan rang, not Clara?' After a few deep breaths to calm herself, Lorna eased out into the road again.

'Yes, he sounded drunk too. He was so belligerent, "Have your dumped your husband for good or will you come to his death bed," was what he said.'

'God, what a swine, couldn't he have broken the news in a kinder way?'

'We should never have done it. What if he's dead?'

Lorna tried not to imagine Adrian dead. She was reminded of murder mysteries on television, where bodies were kept in drawers in the mortuary, with a label tied to their big toe. Was this where he was? Ready to be pulled out for Gloria to identify? How foolish they'd been to think it would all work out. The three of them were at the end of their tethers, desperate to give their children a happy Christmas, but it was hardly surprising that despite Jane and Clara's care, putting three dysfunctional men together, with unlimited alcohol, would end in disaster.

They arrived at the hospital. Lorna linked arms with Gloria as they made for the entrance. Lorna wished now that Felicity had come with them; she would have taken charge, towing them along in her wake.

When Gloria had telephoned, Felicity and Jonathan had given up all pretence at not listening to her conversation. Hearing Lorna tell Gloria that she would drive her to the hospital, they waited impatiently for her to tell them what had happened, grouped round her like dogs begging to be taken out.

'A friend's had an accident and been taken to hospital. I must go and support his wife.' Lorna searched for her handbag and keys.

'Who is it? Someone I know?' Felicity said, 'Is it a stroke? They need immediate care if it is, then they have more chance of recovering.' She snapped to attention as if the patient was about to be wheeled into the living room.

Lorna was not going to tell her it was Adrian. Felicity knew about his drinking and would have little sympathy.

'You don't know them,' she said. 'Sorry, I must leave you. Help yourself to anything you want.' She went upstairs to Flora's room and told her what had happened. Flora was curled up on her bed, reading. 'Aunt Felicity *is* leaving isn't she?' she said darkly. 'Wish Katie would stay though, she thinks she might be pregnant too, and we could chat.'

'Oh no, she can't be.' Lorna exclaimed in horror. 'That really would be too much.'

'She's a week late,' Flora said.

'I can't think about that now. I must go to Gloria. I'm sorry I'm deserting you, but it was a lovely day, wasn't it?'

'Great until Aunt Felicity got all bossy,' Flora said.

Lorna kissed her. 'Don't judge poor Felicity too harshly, she means well, though I agree she can be very irritating.'

'Make sure she leaves, Mum,' was Flora's parting shot.

The very atmosphere of the hospital filled both women with dread. Lorna fought to calm her racing emotions and asked at reception where Adrian Russell might be. They were directed to a ward gaily decorated with paper chains. A collection of old men, some barely decent, others mumbling incoherently to themselves, lay in their beds or slumped in chairs. It was an open ward; a wide passage with bays opening off it, each bay holding six beds.

'It's a geriatric ward,' Gloria whispered. 'I thought he was in intensive care.'

'Maybe it is somewhere else on this floor, or he may have come out and there are no beds anywhere else.' Lorna caught sight of Stephen sitting by a bed in the corner. At the same moment a nurse asked who they were looking for. When Gloria gave Adrian's name she pointed to the corner and Stephen.

'How is he?' Gloria steeled herself as she had so many times before for bad news.

'A bit confused and a broken arm, the doctor will talk to you.' The nurse said, whirling away to see to someone else.

Stephen saw them and got up. He appeared awkward and grumpy and pointedly ignored Lorna. He said to Gloria, 'He fell down the stairs, I think he'll be all right. Bore about the arm.'

'Might stop him drinking,' Gloria went over to him, leaving Stephen with Lorna.

They stood there in the main aisle of the ward with relatives and nursing staff walking past them, not looking at each other. What could she say to him? What if it had been him falling down the stairs? Would she have rushed to him, forgiveness in her heart? She waited for the pain to hit her; the grief at losing him, her soul mate, the man she'd loved and had children with. Nothing happened, save the dull ache she was used to. He was standing quite close to her, but he felt like a stranger. The man she'd loved would never return. He said, 'Look, what's happened, leaving us all there in that derelict house, lucky we're not all in here, whatever were you thinking of, Lorna?'

'We had to do it. Anyway, I'm sure Clara and Jane looked after you wonderfully,' she said, not looking at him. 'Don't you ever think how your behaviour is upsetting your children, embarrassing them so they don't want to come home or bring their friends if any of you are there? None of us mothers want to lose our children because our husbands are behaving badly.'

'You always had a tendency to exaggerate,' he said grumpily.

'So us being divorced and you living with an illegal immigrant is *exaggerating* is it?' she snapped, her heart aching, yearning for the man he used to be.

'Yes. She's not illegal and she's had a very difficult life… and you were never at home, always at that shop or doing those films.'

She was so tired; there was no point in arguing with him. She'd always been out and about but as he had always been in the office he hadn't minded. If she'd been the same age as him perhaps she would have been more inclined to stay at home with him when he'd retired. She said, 'I was out working, but that's enough; we're divorced. Let's get on with our own lives. But just think how difficult your children find it, with you as you are.' She turned away and to her relief, saw Ivan and Jane coming into the ward. Ivan looked irritated and tired; Jane all smiles.

'Oh, Lorna, I'm sorry you had to come all this way. Ivan over-reacted. I did say to wait until the doctors had seen him, but maybe Gloria wanted to be here with him.'

'He could have died. We all could have died,' Ivan sounded like a petulant child.

'Nonsense,' Jane said. 'You all had a very good time, you said so yourselves. Enjoyed being all boys together 'without your wives bossing you,' remember you said that?' She winked at Lorna, added quietly to her, 'it could have been any one of them in here. They all indulged too much, but they ate a lot too, so they had some ballast.'

'Thank you so much for coping.' Lorna wondered what would happen now.

Jane's eyes were shining. 'I enjoyed it. It was much more fun than having a solitary meal or just being Clara and I alone, sharing a turkey steak,' she chuckled.

'Do you think Adrian will be in here long? They must be pushed for beds to put him in here.' Lorna looked round at the old men, some who were obviously senile.

'He's not in the wrong ward, dear,' Jane said with a laugh. 'He's counted as geriatric; he's had a fall. Lots of them have here, I shouldn't wonder.'

'Geriatric?' Lorna was appalled. Adrian could not possibly be lumped together with these poor, old men.

Jane guessed at her feelings. 'He's in his mid-sixties isn't he? As are the other two. You may not have noticed the age difference before, but when something like this happens it hits you between the eyes.'

'It sure does.' Lorna glanced at Stephen and Ivan. OAP's be-having badly, she thought, feeling a pang of sympathy for them.

Jane said, 'I understand that they've all recently retired and are finding it difficult to adjust, not that that is any excuse, mind. I can see how much they have hurt you.'

'You are very astute,' Lorna said.

Jane smiled, 'People may wonder what a spinster who's spent most of her life in a boarding school knows about life, but you learn a great deal there about the human condition. Some of the fathers on their second marriages were often mistaken for grand-parents, some were grandfathers and new fathers at the same time.' She frowned. 'This youth culture is no good for anyone, it mocks as all.'

Lorna agreed and followed her to Adrian's bed, feeling the baleful eyes of the other patients watching her suspiciously.

Gloria was sitting beside Adrian, holding the hand of his good arm. Her face was strained, her eyes blank. He lay back on the pillows, pale and unshaven. His appearance shocked her; she'd never seen him at his worst before. He'd been such a good-looking man, now he just looked old and unkempt. She'd not noticed his age so much before, she still thought of him as in his prime, as she had Stephen and Ivan. Now, seeing them all here in this ward, they blended in with the others. Ivan and Stephen were better dressed, their hair brushed, their faces clean-shaven, but they could have been patients about to go home.

Being here was getting to her; she wanted to leave this uncomfortable truth behind, get back to London and the children. Would Gloria want to stay with Adrian until he was discharged? Would Stephen and Ivan insist on coming back with her? Then, anxiety seized her, would Stephen demand to come to the house to see the children? Might he even refuse to budge until his disagreeable girl came back? *If* she were allowed back into the country. Lorna could not cope with that. She wanted to get out of here, get back on the road to London without Stephen knowing she had gone.

Adrian was far from dying. He would put Gloria through this agony again, probably many more times. It was past seven and she dreaded the drive back in the dark. Telling Gloria where she was going, she went downstairs to the main floor to get a coffee to perk her up, and to escape the sad remnants of the male patients who had once been young and vital.

To her surprise, given that it was Christmas Day, there was a stall selling drinks and snacks near the main entrance. Perhaps the woman running it was escaping a lonely Christmas too. She bought a coffee and sat down at one of the tables to drink it, thankful for a few moments peace to collect her thoughts.

'Lorna, there you are. We rang Ravenscourt because I've lost the watch my late husband gave me, it means so much to me. I've searched everywhere at home for it and I just wondered if I'd somehow lost it at Ravenscourt. Clara told us there'd been an accident, so Nathan drove me over to see if there is anything we could do.' Sonia fluttered up, the flowery scent she was wearing masking the smells of the hospital.

Sonia was the last person she expected to see here. Behind her was Nathan, looking decidedly awkward, as if it was entirely her fault that he'd been forced to bring his mother here.

If only she could escape all this! Lorna was exhausted with it all as Jane and Stephen joined the party, Gloria following close behind. Only Adrian, confined to bed with his fellow geriatrics, was absent.

'The doctor will let me know when he can be discharged.' Gloria had not yet realised, as Lorna had, that Adrian was labelled here as a geriatric.

'It's his right arm, of course, and he's going to need weeks of help dressing and washing and everything.' Gloria sank down at one of the tables scattered round the coffee stall. Lorna bought her a coffee to revive her, but Gloria was almost too tired to lift the cup to her lips.

The sight of Gloria's weariness filled Lorna with fury. Why should Gloria kill herself caring for Adrian when, through his own fault, he'd fallen down the stairs? The thought hit her that he might put the blame for his accident on the condition of the stairs at Ravenscourt, though as far as she could remember there was nothing wrong with them. It was unlikely he'd stop drinking now; in fact, being incarcerated at home while his arm mended would probably make him worse. He'd bully Gloria to fetch him a drink until she gave in and then, no doubt, fall over countless more times, expecting her to heave him up so he could start drinking all over again.

All of them would have nursed their husbands if they had been struck down by some accident or illness, but why should they when they had behaved so badly and brought them all so much pain? If she, or Gloria, suffered some catastrophe, would Adrian stop drinking and be there to help his wife? Would Stephen give up that disagreeable girl to care for her? Would they, Hell!

She must get back to London. The drive would take over an hour and she didn't feel up to it, but the alternative was staying at Ravenscourt with the men, which appalled her. Although, she conceded ruefully, it was rough justice in the circumstances. She wondered what Gloria would do.

Nathan's unexpected presence here disturbed her. She hadn't expected to see him and she wished suddenly they could be alone, go off somewhere away from all this and talk. She wondered if he thought one of these men belonged to her, and that he was lurking in the background because he didn't want to intrude. She went up to him and said, 'Did your Christmas day go well? Pity we had to end up here.'

He smiled, 'Yes, thanks; huge lunch, lots of friends and then something else this evening. I must admit, after all that lunch I'd rather stay at home and browse through the books I was given.'

'It's kind of you to come. I think it's all under control.'

'My mother wanted to be sure. As you've probably gathered, she has a rather overdeveloped imagination and she thought it could be something far worse than a broken arm. Anyway, we were on our way out to visit my aunt, who's in a residential home close by. Not that she knows it's Christmas, poor thing, but we like to visit her on the day.'

Sonia came up to them, 'Hello Lorna, sorry about poor Adrian. Hope he'll be up to my party tomorrow.'

The party! She'd forgotten the party. She didn't know if Nathan knew that only the men were staying at Ravenscourt. She smiled, not knowing what to say. Sonia went on, 'We must go now to visit my poor sister-in-law or she'll be in bed. Looking forward to seeing you tomorrow! About six.' She patted her arm and moved towards the exit.

'I'll see you tomorrow, look forward to it. I can show you the photographs of Ravenscourt,' Nathan said, smiling, and following his mother before she could explain that she wouldn't be there.

She went over to sit next to Gloria but before she could sit down, Jane came up to her and said quietly, 'I'm sure there won't be any trouble over Adrian's accident, but if there is, Clara and I will back you up. Adrian was very drunk. The stairs at Ravenscourt are perfectly safe and he only fell down the last three.'

Lorna stared at her in horror. 'What do you mean?'

'It was just that Stephen and Ivan were talking about Health and Safety and, you know … ambulance chasers and said Adrian could probably get some sort of compensation for his accident, if it could be proved the stairs were dangerous.'

'He can't, can he?' She remembered people telling her of dubious firms that offered to fight for compensation for people who'd suffered injuries.

'They may not be serious, just talking about it,' Jane said gently, 'but don't worry. We'll stand by you if there is any trouble.' She went on, louder, to include Gloria; 'Obviously you're not going to drive back to London tonight, so you will stay at Ravenscourt. There's plenty of room, as you know. It will be rather cold, but Clara's doing her best to warm up rooms.'

'No, thank you,' Lorna said. At the same time, Gloria, hearing her remark, said, 'Thanks, I'd love to go to bed right now. I've had it.' She struggled up from her chair, impatient to leave.

Jane, guessing at Lorna's reason for refusal, said quietly, 'It won't be too bad, and really, where else can you go at this time of night, and on Christmas day? Unless, of course, you go to Mulberry Farm? I'm sure Sonia would squeeze you in somewhere, she's very hospitable.'

'Oh no, we'll come to Ravenscourt.' Lorna said hurriedly. She didn't feel up to Sonia drilling her about Fergus and Ravenscourt.

She wondered how early in the morning she could escape back to London. She would try and persuade Gloria to come with her and leave Adrian to social services.

There was a blazing fire in the hall at Ravenscourt to welcome them. If only Stephen and Ivan weren't here, Lorna would have enjoyed spending an evening here with Clara and Jane, listening to their account of Christmas.

'I've made some turkey and chestnut soup,' Clara said. 'I hope you're not sick of turkey already.'

'Anything warm will be lovely.' Gloria rallied a little on the drive here. The men had gone back in Jane's car. Alone with Lorna, she confessed that she did not know how much longer she could go on caring for Adrian; these heart-stopping crises were wearing her down.

'You should at the very least say you will only help him if he gets proper treatment for his drinking. You could leave him in hospital, say you can't cope with him until he's off the booze,' she said firmly.

Gloria didn't answer and Lorna had the feeling that this time she really had had enough. On the drive down to the hospital she'd thought Adrian could be dead, and though distraught, her anguish had been tinged with relief. Having found him very much alive, had she at last come to realise she could not go down this endless road again?

They had supper in the kitchen. Soup and rolls with Nathan's ham and cheese on the side. She would not see him again, Lorna told herself. She would be back in London tomorrow and would miss the party at Mulberry Farm and if she wanted any food from him, she could fill in the order form in his new brochure illustrated with pictures of Ravenscourt.

Stephen was sitting at the other end of the table but they could not help but see each other every time they looked up from their plates. She noticed he was drinking heavily and she made sure to stick to only one glass of wine herself. It was odd and painful sharing a meal with him after so long. She listened to him talk to Ivan and Clara about his life now. He didn't mention the girl, but kept referring to 'meeting up with friends' – though she didn't know who he meant, as most of their mutual friends had stopped seeing him. His discourse made her feel distanced from him as if he were a shadow haunting her from long ago.

After her bowl of soup, Gloria excused herself and went to bed. Lorna followed soon after. Just as she was about to brave it up that icy staircase to her room, Stephen approached her.

'You've had your fun; Ivan and I are leaving here tomorrow. You can give us a lift after Sonia's party. It's only a drinks party so we should be back in London just after nine.' Stephen said, his voice clipped, as if she were a taxi service.

'It might be more than a drinks party, and what about Gloria and Adrian?' She wouldn't tell him she was leaving as soon as it was light.

'She'll have to stay down here with him, of course. Until he is well enough to travel,' Stephen said tersely.

His conviction of Gloria's duty stirred up her anger. 'Maybe she won't. He could stay in hospital, have social services cope with him – as they might well have to cope with you, should you get ill.'

He looked disconcerted, 'But he's broken his arm, he can't do anything for himself.'

'So? He should have thought of that before he got drunk for the umpteenth time. Don't you realise that we've all had enough of you men treating us so badly? You're upsetting the children, making them wanting to escape from it all and not come home. Then you crawl back to us to look after you, when you fall apart.' Lorna went on up the stairs, inwardly fuming and filled with sorrow at how things had turned out between them. She stopped turned and faced him. Her heart was beating fit to burst, but some compulsion urged her on; was it being together in this house, this house that had seen so many lovers come and go? Or even Fergus's spirit urging her to find out the truth once and for all?

'If that woman you left us for doesn't come back, would you, despite our divorce, be sorry and come home again?' she asked him.

For a long moment they stood there together in the barely lit hall; Lorna on the stairs, looking down on him. She felt as if her whole life hung there but she remembered her promise at the altar to stick to her marriage for better or for worse and knew she should try once last time to save her marriage.

'She will come back,' he said quietly at last, turning from her and disappearing into the gloom.

She waited for the pain of his answer to hit her, but to her surprise she just felt relief. Time had moved on and that part of her life was over, she must go forward. She had loved the man he used to be and he had loved her. Now he'd gone and in time she hoped she'd just remember the good parts of their life together.

CHAPTER TWENTY-TWO
A Touch Of Passion

Her room was a small one, stuck on the end of a passage. Lorna remembered sleeping here as a child, when she visited Ravenscourt with her parents. She lay in the narrow bed in one of Clara's winter nightdresses, a stone hot water bottle at her feet and a rubber one on her stomach. What would she have thought all those years ago if she'd known that one day Ravenscourt would be hers? She still could not believe it.

She lay there listening to the sounds of the house, the buffeting wind rattling the windows and whistling down the chimneys; an orchestra of sound. She felt that Fergus's spirit had not quite left Ravenscourt and she wondered if he trusted her to do the best for the neglected house. 'Though *you* didn't do the best for it,' she grumbled to him, as if he could hear her, 'spending your considerable fortune on parties and travel and outrageous behaviour.' No wonder he never stayed married. But she'd loved him, though she'd never had to live with him or rely on him. Their husbands were bad enough, but Fergus was by far the most difficult husband of them all, and yet it was said that his wives never stopped loving him, they just couldn't live with him. At the end, only Clara, his housekeeper, stayed on.

She thought of Stephen in his room down some other passage and how strange it seemed for both of them to be under the same roof, yet alone in their own beds. But he wasn't her husband any more; quite apart from the fact that they were no longer legally married, he had said as much when she'd asked him this evening about his future plans. He'd made it quite clear his life was now playing the part of a dashing lover with a woman he could impress. The end of their marriage was final. Part of her would always love him, the man who'd brought her so much happiness, loved her and given her children, but now he was a stranger and, she realised with relief that it no longer felt odd not to be sharing a room with him.

She lay in bed, the dim light of the bedside lamp leaving the rest of the room in shadow. She clamped her limbs close to her body, away from the icy parts of the bed. She'd loved Ravenscourt as a child and her children had loved it in their turn. It was tragic that it had deteriorated so much. It made her feel as sad, as if it were a much-loved person, crippled by the ravages of time. If only she had the money to restore it, but it would need so much, it was such a large house and so dilapidated. She'd have a surveyor go over it, see what needed to be done, but it would surely be beyond her means.

Tired though she was, she couldn't sleep. Her head whirled with troubled thoughts. She needed a book to distract her; she hated going to sleep without reading, even if she was too sleepy to take anything in. There were no books in the room, and she hadn't expected to stay, so had brought none. She'd go down to Fergus's study, there were plenty to choose from there.

She got out of bed, catching sight of herself in the mirror on the dressing table. Clara's nightdress was enormous; a kind of voluminous tent made of a pink, fluffy material, with long sleeves and a high neck; no doubt a stalwart ally against the icy nights, but a veritable passion killer. She shivered, bitten by a draught, and wrapped herself in the old faded eiderdown from her bed. Having no slippers, she pulled on her black knee-high boots to brave the icy floors. She opened her door and stood listening for any sign of life. Hearing nothing, she crept down the passage and downstairs. All was silent; everyone must be in bed, which was a relief, as she didn't want to be seen in this unflattering get up. The door to the drawing room where they usually sat was half open, the room in darkness, only a few lights were on in the hall.

At the bottom of the stairs was a huge black and gold mirror, its surface blotched by time. She laughed when she saw herself; a cartoon character of a mad woman.

She could hear soft sounds of clattering china far off in the kitchen. Clara and Jane must still be up, she wouldn't disturb them. One of them was sleeping in Clara's cottage, the other in the room Clara had used when nursing Fergus, which was on the other side of the kitchen.

She crossed the hall and went into Fergus's study. The walls were laden with bookcases. He had a good collection of the old Penguin books, the colour of their covers denoting their genre. She was examining these when she heard the door open behind her. Thinking it must be Clara or Jane checking the rooms before they went to bed, she said gaily, 'Can't sleep until I've read something and . . .'

'Neither can I.'

She spun round. Nathan stood there staring at her, obviously trying to suppress his laughter. In her horror at seeing him she let go of the eiderdown, it dropped to the floor, leaving her exposed in the passion killer nightdress.

'Whatever are you doing here?' Her voice was rough in her embarrassment. 'You seem to have taken the place over.'

'I'm sorry to startle you, but Clara knows I'm here.'

The shock at seeing him and her mortification at being caught looking so ridiculous made her grumpy. 'You might have said you were coming here, not just waltz in whenever it suits you.' She could hear the petulance in her voice and knew her remark was unfair, but the suppressed laughter in his eyes and on his mouth at the sight of her was too much. 'Couldn't it have waited until the morning?'

A wind blew through the gaps in the hall windows. She shivered and he closed the door, imprisoning them both in the room. 'I'm sorry to catch you in your nightie but don't worry, you're quite safe from me.' He was having difficulty holding his amusement back and she felt affronted. Of course she was safe in this get up, safe from the most rampant man.

She stood taller, and said imperiously, 'So, are you here to choose a book? Don't you have enough at home?'

He smiled, glancing at the laden bookshelves, 'Yes, I'd love to borrow some. I couldn't resist looking through them when I was here doing the shoot, but no, that's not why I'm here now. You may have heard when we were at the hospital, my mother has lost her watch. I did ask Clara if I could come in and see if I could find it as I pass Ravenscourt on my way back from a party. It was my father's last present to her before he died. He struggled to the jewellers, in great pain, but determined not to let his illness stand in the way of what he wanted to do, and as you can imagine, it means a great deal to her.'

His eyes now gleamed with pain, mortifying her. Events had made her selfish; forget that other people had troubles too.

'I'm sorry,' she said gruffly, looking round the room as if she could see it. 'Have you any idea where it could be?'

'Not really, she could have dropped it anywhere. She came in here to keep warm during the shoot so it could have slipped down the side of one of the chairs.' He went to the nearest chair, which was beside her, and slipped his hand down the soft velvet to the darkness under the seat. Her body stirred, embarrassing her further, and, with as much grace as she muster, she turned back to study the books on the shelf. But she could hardly focus on the titles, she'd just take one and go; scurry upstairs away from his ridicule.

She pulled out one with a green trim, labelling it as a detective novel. Clutching it to her, she made for the door, but Nathan had straightened up and moved closer to the book shelves. She would have to touch him to pass him.

'I'll leave you to it,' she said firmly, taking a step towards him.

'You've chosen a murder mystery. Won't it keep you awake? Especially in this old house, seeped in history and secrets.' He shivered theatrically. 'Great place to hold those murder weekends I've read of, don't you think?'

'No,' she said, 'I don't. I don't feel bad vibes here.'

'Nor do I,' he said smiling, 'I was just teasing you.' He studied the bookcase. 'I like the way the book covers used to be plain. Some covers today are so lurid it puts you off. I especially dislike the ones with a large picture of the so-called heroine; much rather make my own pictures from the writer's description.'

'Do you read a lot of those kind of books?' she asked, having not imagined they would appeal to him.

'No... but my ex-wife used to, she littered the house with them.' His face went tight and then, as if shaking off sad memories, he laughed and said, 'What a nightdress! Do you really go to bed like that? It's the sort of thing a nun would wear in case she met a rapist in the night... and boots too. Very sexy.'

'Don't be silly, it's Clara's,' she said, with as much dignity as she could muster. 'I didn't know I was going to stay here, I was too tired to drive back to London.'

'I've only just heard from Clara that you left your husbands alone here for Christmas and you drove Gloria down when Adrian had his accident. She told me when I rang to ask if I could come in on my way home. I'm so glad you didn't go back to London, I wouldn't have missed this for anything.'

His laugh was gentle but she couldn't bear it, especially as she knew she looked a fright. No doubt Beth looked wonderful in bed – if he shared one with her. But perhaps it was better that she did look like an old frump, it kept her from making a fool of herself. Someone who might reach out and touch him as she passed or worse still, kiss him goodnight. She pushed forward resolutely, intent of going upstairs with as much grace as possible. If this chair wasn't in the way there would be no need to pass so close to him, but it was too cumbersome to move.

He bent down and picked up the eiderdown and handed it to her. 'You've left behind another piece of your armour.'

She took it from him without a word and not looking at him side-stepped past Nathan to get by and escape upstairs. He moved the same way, and they clashed. 'Sorry,' they both muttered, moving the same way again, their faces somehow closer, drawn together and then he was kissing her; his mouth on hers, his hands on her shoulders holding her close and she was kissing him back. Abruptly he released her, and moved away.

'Forgive me,' he said, though he didn't look the slightest bit contrite.

'Of course,' she said, fighting to curb her raging emotions. She told herself his kiss was nothing, people kissed each other – and more – all the time today, it meant no more than a workout at the gym. Now she was single again she must play the game the way it was.

'Goodnight,' she said, 'I hope you find the watch.'

He covered her with the eiderdown, pulling it tightly round her, concentrating on the task and not looking at her 'God, it's cold. You'd better get back to bed or you'll catch your death. And I must get home, it's been a long day.' He said as if they had not shared a passionate kiss a moment before.

'It has been, one way and another, one of the most eventful Christmases I've ever had,' she said hoping she sounded as causal as he did. She must not let her imagination blow the kiss up into the start of a romance.

'Me too.' His voice was soft now creeping into her exciting her senses. Seeing her shiver, he pulled the eiderdown more closely round her, his hands lingering a moment near her face, then as if he was pulling himself back to reality he said, his voice firm, 'This house is seriously cold. That's the first thing that's needed, to dry it out properly and then you can see how bad the condition really is.' He turned away from her towards the door.

'Goodnight.' She turned back to the bookcase, hit with the memory of Gloria's statement that Ravenscourt could be the perfect house for Nathan and his expanding business. Gloria was quite capable, in her 'Lady Bountiful' mood, to suggest something mad like she sell it to him in instalments or pay half its value now and the rest when his business took of, as she was convinced it would. What if she suddenly appeared and found him here, and suggested it?

'I hope you find Sonia's watch, and… safe journey home,' she said, hoping he'd leave before someone found them together and saw her in this unflattering garb.

'Clara said she'd search for it in the morning and with luck you could bring it with you to the party.'

'I won't be coming, I'm leaving at dawn, I want to get home to the children.'

'Oh, I'm sorry,' he looked disappointed, 'but now I know you weren't all staying here, I understand. We must keep in touch, have dinner or something.'

'Yes, that would be fun.' She wanted him gone before they were seen together.

He smiled and left the room. Now she had thought of Gloria and her urge to be kind, she could not help wondering if it was her or Ravenscourt which held the most interest for him.

She listened to his footsteps crossing the hall and fading away before she left the room. Going into the empty hall and up the stairs, her body was singing after their kiss and yet she was close to tears.

CHAPTER TWENTY-THREE
Foot Loose And Fancy Free

The extreme cold woke Lorna at dawn. She curled up tight under the bedclothes trying to get warm. She had not slept well; the memory of Nathan's kiss inflamed her, and yet what did it mean? Was it just a passing thing, a sudden urge that had come upon him as they'd stood so close together? Possibly he was a little drunk after his party? In his right mind he would hardly have been turned on by her voluminous nightie and boots. She cringed with embarrassment, imagining him teasing her about it in front of the others, if they saw each other again. People were always suggesting meeting up with each other again and perhaps they meant it at the time, but so often events took over and they never got round to it, but he had asked her out to dinner, her heart lifted and who's to say he wasn't the kind of person who meant what he said? She must stop feeling that every man would let her down like Stephen had.

She got out of bed, afraid to wake anyone, especially Stephen. Last night he'd made it clear he preferred his life with the Pekinese woman to one with her, so she must accept once and for all that that chapter of her life was over and move on. That kiss – the first passionate kiss she'd given anyone other than Stephen since her marriage – may mean nothing to Nathan, just a sort of reflex action, but to her, it meant that she was free of her marriage, free to perhaps find another love one day in the distant future.

She opened her door carefully. It creaked in protest and she froze, listening. But all was silent. She tiptoed to the other side of the house, where she remembered there was another bathroom. Having removed two huge spiders who lodged in the bath, she filled it with hot water and sank down into it.

Lying in the bath, the steam rising from her into the icy air, she wondered whether to wake Gloria, and see whether she wanted to leave for London at once with her, or would rather stay here until she knew how Adrian was.

She was filled with a sort of fear of seeing Stephen again, afraid of his mood and his reaction to her in the cold light of day. As for their coming grandchild… anxiety gripped her as she remembered that scene with her sister. How would Stephen react to being a grandfather, would it add to his terror of getting old? She pushed that thought to the back of her mind to take out and worry about later, while she allowed herself one more moment to savour the memory of Nathan's kiss.

She crept back to her room and dressed. The early morning light cut through the dusty windows; showing up the damp-stained walls, pinpointing the cracks and chipped paint, the dried out lino on the narrow back stairs. Poor house, it needed so much love and care, she couldn't bear to think of someone else pulling out the guts of it, perhaps transforming it into a series of modern box-like rooms devoid of soul. If only there was a way she could save it, but it needed far more money spent on it that she would ever have. Perhaps she should take up her sister's offer. Jonathan made good money and Felicity's job was quite well paid, perhaps if they restored it little by little and somehow made it pay for itself by hiring it out …. Nathan's murder weekends came to mind. It seemed such a huge undertaking, she wouldn't think of it now, until she'd had a survey, but she'd have to make a decision soon.

She went down the back stairs to the kitchen in search of coffee and found Jane and Clara having breakfast together at the kitchen table.

'We're both early risers and like this quiet time to have a meal together before the day starts,' Jane greeted her. 'The men are never down before ten, so we have plenty of time to have our breakfast and then get theirs.'

'Am I disturbing you? I just got so cold.' She hadn't expected to see them so early. She blushed, did they somehow know of the passionate kiss? She went on quickly, to cover her embarrassment, 'The windows in my room are full of gaps and the draught blows straight through.'

'Of course you are not disturbing us.' Clara got up. 'Coffee or tea? I can do a cooked breakfast if you like, the men enjoy that,' she said cheerfully.

'No thank you, just coffee and toast, please.' Lorna sat down at the table with her back to the stove; the warmth from it enclosing her like a comforting blanket.

After a few remarks about the weather and the difficulty of heating such a house as Ravenscourt the conversation came round to their difficult husbands.

'I'm glad I never married,' Jane put some fresh toast on the breakfast table. 'I've had some heartbreaks in my time but there seem to be many couples about who struggle on miserably together when there is no love, or even respect left for each other.'

'I do know of some very happy marriages still going strong,' Lorna spoke up for some of her friends. She envied them. They may be criticised for not having an exciting relationship, but they appeared to be content, comfortable with each other.

'Then they are blessed,' Clara said. 'My marriage came unstuck early on, but I can't say I've missed having a husband. My daughter was enough for me, we lived all over the place together … and then …' She fumbled for her handkerchief in her sleeve and blew her nose. 'I came here to work for Fergus and it was the happiest time in my life.'

'We may look like a couple of old spinnies, but I'd say we've had a good life. I must say,' Jane regarded Lorna with sympathy. 'I don't envy any of you three ladies with those husbands of yours. Don't get me wrong,' she held up her hand as if Lorna was going to protest, or apologise for their behaviour. 'We got on with them perfectly well, sometimes even glimpsing the men they must have been. Once they realised that...' Jane paused, then went on, 'they were 'dumped here', as they put it, they were very angry, hurt too, I'd say but then... we did tell them that they were here because their behaviour upset their families and you three women were frightened it would chase away your children.'

'We've all told them that, and they didn't seem to take it on board. I hope they took notice of you,' Lorna said.

'Being a school matron all those years taught me to say it straight,' Jane said. 'Adrian and Ivan looked rather sheepish and Stephen said the children were old enough to make their own minds up, but they accepted it in the end. After a while I think they just couldn't be bothered to do anything about it. They're old friends and the food and drink were plentiful and the weather filthy.'

'So do you think it might have shocked them into behaving better, giving more time to their families?' Lorna asked.

'It did shock them,' Clara said, 'but none of them wanted to admit it, so they just had another drink and made jokes about it.' She threw a cautious look at Lorna. 'The house became an interest, too. Ivan and Adrian seemed to think Stephen should have a share in it, I don't know the law but...'

'That's just what I was afraid of,' Lorna said desperately. 'Do you think he wants something to do with it? Will he contact his lawyer and see what rights he has? If Fergus had died a few months earlier, before the divorce, I'm sure I'd have had to add it to my assets and share it out.'

'I don't know how the law works in such cases. His mind kept wandering, and Adrian was drunk most of the time. Only Ivan seemed to make sense. I talked to him about his voluntary work and said that it must help him with his own young daughters and that made him go quite quiet.' Jane said, 'And I wondered, as I'd often seen fathers of boys… and sometimes mothers, at the school where I worked, too busy making money to have proper time for their own families. I did ask him about it and it made him quite thoughtful.'

'Rosalind finds it hard that he never seems to be there for their daughters. He has an older daughter, Polly, from his first marriage and she's always been very difficult, especially when he married Rosalind. Perhaps feeling discarded, Polly went all out to make her life hell, so perhaps he can't face going through adolescence again with his own children, and finds it easier to cope with other people's,' Lorna said, not going into the fact he also seemed to have developed a penchant for social workers.

'I'm sure these men were charming once but they're quite a handful now. Well, Adrian and Stephen are. I think that being here has given Ivan time to think things over. I don't mind saying that I'm afraid if Gloria takes Adrian back again in the state he's in, she's is in for a very difficult time indeed.'

'I'm terrified it will kill her.' It was a relief talking to people who seemed so concerned about them, and had seen their husbands first-hand and understood. 'She works at all sorts of things to pay the bills and though we are all still young and reasonably fit, taking care of an alcoholic husband, especially one that seems determined to destroy himself, is very hard to take.'

'You don't have to take it.' Jane said firmly. 'If the three of them have chosen to live this destructive life, all but abandon their wives and children, perhaps they should be left to get on with it. Tough love, that's often the only way to deal with it. The more you make excuses and cover up for them, the less favours you do them, and the worse the situation becomes.'

'It is hard though.' Lorna frowned. Adrian could still seduce Gloria with his charm and contrition, swearing undying love after such events, invoking her sympathy when he was injured.

'I see it as a boat in a storm.' Jane helped herself to a large dollop of homemade marmalade. 'Sometimes the only way to save the innocent people – especially children, in all this, is to jettison the destructive ones.'

'If you'll excuse me saying this, Lorna,' Clara said, in the tone of voice that implied she would say it anyway, 'I think your three husbands are very selfish. Their talk was all about the women they'd had sex with – though I did wonder if that wasn't just wishful thinking – and the times they got drunk, just as if they were adolescents. I suspect,' she paused while she poured boiling water over fresh coffee, releasing the rich aroma into the room, 'that they are all going through some sort of life crises.'

Her words thrust painfully into her. Clara was only enforcing what she already knew. It may not be their fault that the three of them had careered off the rails like that, but they had, and if they refused to get help, or change their behaviour, their wives must let them go. Toss them overboard.

'I know that my marriage is really over and I don't want to see Stephen again,' Lorna gulped down her coffee. 'I want to leave as soon as possible.'

'You'll have plenty of warning, you can hear the water thudding through the pipes in the bathroom he uses,' Jane said. 'It's probably best if you hurry back to London and your new life, come back here again after they've gone.'

Clara said, 'Enjoy your lives with your children. After all, this situation is mucking up their lives too, and they don't want to lose both parents, with their mothers getting ill from the stress of it all.'

The kitchen door opened with a jerk and Gloria came in. She looked pale and strained but better than she had the night before. Jane and Clara fussed round her and Clara put in an egg to boil for her. Gloria sat down beside Lorna. She seemed quiet, yet somehow stoic. Lorna steeled herself for Gloria insisting that they go to fetch Adrian from hospital before driving him back to London. Gloria took a few fortifying gulps of coffee then, looking firmly at her, said; 'When are you leaving for London, Lorna? I'd like to come with you.'

'And Adrian?' Lorna saw the pain in Gloria's eyes.

'He can stay in hospital. I've decided,' she paused, as if the words wounded her, 'that I will put Justin first.'

Lorna looked at Gloria with surprise and admiration. There was a new determination in her eyes and in the set of her jaw. 'You really mean it this time, don't you, Glory?'

'I take it then that the men will stay?' Jane broke in.

'We'll get Rosalind to pick them up. I'll ring her now.' Gloria left her half-eaten egg and went to use the phone hidden behind the bread bin. Even though it was early, Rosalind answered at once and Gloria explained the situation. After listening a moment, she said, 'Well, they'll have to stay here then. Lorna and I are leaving almost at once, when we've finished breakfast.'

'So she won't come?' Lorna asked as Gloria sat down again.

'She says she's met a man at a party she went to on Christmas Eve and doesn't want to leave London in case he rings her.' Gloria giggled. 'Reminds me of the old days when we were all young together. Heavens, do you think we've got to jump through all those dating hoops again?' she grimaced.

'Talking of which, what about that party over at Mulberry Farm?' Clara said, before Lorna could comment on this surprising news. 'Sonia was insistent that you all come. I don't think she realises that you are not staying here.'

'No, I told Nathan I'm going back to London this morning.' Lorna said, and then was covered in confusion in case one of them asked her when she'd told him, or Gloria, with her radar eyes, got her to admit he'd found her in the library dressed to kill.

'I would have liked to have gone and seen Nathan, and...' Gloria caught Lorna's expression, 'see the pictures of Ravenscourt for the brochure if they're ready, but I think it's better we go back to London as soon as possible. Justin is at home and some of his friends stayed over. I'd like to be with them. I'll catch up with Nathan later.'

CHAPTER TWENTY-FOUR
Easier Said Than Done

Gloria hurried through her breakfast, frantic to leave Ravenscourt before Ivan and Stephen surfaced. Both of them had given her a bad time last night over leaving Adrian here. 'He nearly killed himself,' Stephen had accused her, as if she had purposely set a trap to dispose of him, or any one of them.

She'd been so exhausted last night she'd fallen into bed and been asleep at once. But she'd woken early and lain there in the cold room in a strange bed away from home, replaying Justin's expression when Ivan had rung her to tell her of Adrian's accident. Lying there, with the thin grey light poking through the curtains, she realised that this was crunch time. The choice was stark before her; it was the end or she would lose Justin to Ellie's family, who sounded so normal and cosy, just the sort of atmosphere that Justin craved.

Hearing noises above – the flush of a loo, the water banging in the pipes – made the two women squeak like frightened rabbits and head for the car. They crept across the drive, fearful that the crunch of gravel under their feet would alert the men. A glint of sun caught something on the ground and Lorna bent down to examine it. 'Sonia's watch,' she exclaimed, picking it up. 'So it was true,' she muttered.

'Do come on, they might see us.' Gloria was panicky now. Her panic increased when Lorna turned back to the house, a glitter of gold in her hand.

'Sonia lost her watch; I'll just give it to Clara.' She was blushing. She dashed back into the kitchen and then came out again making for the car, not looking at Gloria.

They were so keen to get away before they were caught that Gloria didn't remark upon it until they were safely out of the drive and well up the lane towards London.

'What do you mean, Sonia's lost her watch?' she turned to her.

Lorna became flustered, 'Oh... she lost her watch, don't you remember her telling us at the hospital? Or were you still with Adrian? It must have dropped off last time she was here, lucky I saw it glinting on the drive like that.' Gloria knew her too well. She was trying to make it sound unimportant but was failing, there was more to it and she was keeping it from her.

'Very lucky.' Gloria watched her, wondering why she was so agitated over such a simple thing. 'Did Sonia and Nathan come round last night then, to look for it?' She asked, wondering why Lorna looked so guilty, as if she'd stolen it or something.

'No. It was just luck I found it, though it may not work after being outside in the wet and cold all night.'

She was about to question her further when Lorna exclaimed cheerfully, 'We've escaped. Clara and Jane seemed to have really enjoyed this adventure and are rather sad it's coming to an end.'

'But it's been a turning point for us too hasn't it?' Lorna turned to look at her. There was a slight air of suppressed excitement about her, Gloria noticed. Was that because they'd got away before the men appeared… or something else she was determined to keep to herself?

'It has, and I hope for the men too,' Lorna said. 'A new year and a new chapter in our lives. She blushed, and said hurriedly, 'I've accepted my marriage is over and a new life beckons.' She laughed.

'Brave girl,' Gloria meant it, but why was Lorna blushing? Had she met someone else already? She was about to ask when Lorna said, 'So, apart from Adrian falling down the stairs, did your day go well? Did you like Justin's girlfriend?'

'It was a lovely day, and Ellie is perfect. They seem mad about each other, but it's early days; they've only just met.' Seeing Adrian lying there in pain, with his arm strapped up and needing so much help with everyday things had wrenched her heart and if she hadn't been tortured by Justin's face and his misery and fear when he heard about his father's accident, she'd have taken him home and cared for him… until the next time. Perhaps the doctors would insist he go into rehab. She didn't know how it worked, she supposed they couldn't force him, unless he was violent and a danger to the public. But hard though she found it, she would leave him there in hospital and he would have to make his own decisions.

'I'm so glad Glory... young love.' Lorna sighed, and then went on as if she were shaking the memory from her. 'I expect the two remaining men will want to leave Ravenscourt as soon as they can. It's icy upstairs away from the fires, and of course they are put out at night and the cold seeps in everywhere,' Lorna said. 'I'd forgotten that teeth-numbing cold when undressing; even baring one's bottom to go to the loo is an act of endurance.'

'I know,' Gloria giggled. 'But what about Sonia's party this evening? I'm sure they'll want to go to that.'

'That's up to them. If Rosalind's too occupied to pick them up they'll have to take a train back tomorrow. I expect Adrian will be kept in hospital, or the social services will find somewhere for him to go. You have told him and them that you are no longer going to be responsible for him, haven't you?'

She hadn't. Well, not really. She was going to telephone the hospital when she got home and tell someone there. Her first and most pressing thought was to get back to Justin and make it clear that she was going to put him first, get his father looked after by someone else, people with experience of alcoholism who'd know what to do instead of her scooping him up each time, crying over him, begging him to get help which he didn't think he needed. It was time to leave him with the experts.

'I'll ring the hospital when I get back, I expect they'll keep him until after the holiday and they'll know where to send him,' she said vaguely. She didn't want to admit that she was afraid to face him, and tell him her intention to leave him to the medical staff. Seeing his face and the pain he was in would melt her heart and before she knew it she'd have bundled him back home to continue the whole sorry saga all over again. There was only one way to save him and that was the hard way, leave him to face his future on his own. Only then might he face up to his addiction and get professional help.

'But you haven't told him?' Lorna said bossily.

'Not exactly, the truth is we ... well, *I*, am so used to being needed, rather like Jane and Clara. It's going to take time to fill that void. At least you have a grandchild coming,' she said enviously.

'I know what you mean, Glory,' Lorna threw her a sympathetic glance, 'but we have each other, we'll get through it.'

'I suppose so.' She chewed the skin on the side of her thumbnail. 'Anyway,' she turned to her, smiling, determined not to torture herself with it, 'we've got Flora's baby to look forward to and you being a Granny. Can you imagine that? No one will believe it, you're more like an elder sister.'

'It's a bitter sweet situation though, isn't it?' Lorna said. 'You should have seen my sister's reaction when Flora told her.' She laughed, 'Poor Felicity, she somehow turned it into being her fault for not supporting me more over Stephen's debacle.'

Sounds familiar,' Gloria laughed. 'How our lives have changed since last Christmas, I wonder where we'll all be next year and how it will all pan out.'

CHAPTER TWENTY-FIVE
All's Fair In Love And War

Lorna dropped Gloria home, and though Gloria half-heartedly asked if she wanted to come in, she declined, knowing that her friend just wanted to be with Justin and to try and come to grips with her decision to leave Adrian in the care of the experts.

'Good luck,' she kissed her. 'Ring the hospital now, before the day runs away with you,' she said, wondering if now Gloria were home she would weaken over her decision taken at Ravenscourt and dash down and bring him back.

Her own house was in darkness. The curtains were still drawn, the remnants of supper scattered on the table, and half the lunch plates from yesterday littered the worktops in the kitchen. The dishwasher had washed one load and waited to be emptied and refilled. She and Gloria had talked about 'being needed', but who wanted to be needed to clear up after one's adult children?

Flora appeared, pale and yawning, in a long T-shirt and an apricot coloured pashmina. 'Hi Mum,' she curled up in a chair and regarded her. 'I feel so sick and I'm so tired, and Katie wants me to go over to her place and...'

'I'd much rather go out with my cousin than see to all this,' Lorna snapped, yearning to crawl into her own bed and think over all that had happened during her over night stay at Ravenscourt.

'We meant to do more, but we got watching this film on television, then we went to bed,' Flora half uncurled herself as if to appear to be making an effort to help, then thinking better of it, curled up again. 'So is Adrian dead?'

'No, just drunk with a broken arm.'

'I'd leave him if it were me,' Flora said. 'Like Dad, he's gone disgusting. Perhaps men are only nice until they're sixty, if they live that long,' she said morosely, sixty being a long way from twenty.

'She's left him in the care of the hospital. Rosalind apparently met someone at a party, I don't know the details, but she might prefer him to Ivan. And your father left me before I could leave him.' Lorna took out the clean plates from the dishwasher, stacking them rather noisily back in the cupboard.

'So you're all on the pull again?' Flora said incredulously. 'Boyfriends, Mum? You do know about … you know, sexual diseases and things? Apparently there's a big rise in old people getting them.' She sounded disgusted as if 'old' people shouldn't be getting up to such things.

A sudden flush seeped through her as she thought of the passionate kiss she'd shared with Nathan.

Seeing her confusion, Flora said kindly, 'You needn't have sex if you don't want to Mum. I mean… well…' she looked embarrassed.

'You think I'm past it? I'm only in my early forties!' Lorna felt an annoying pang of desire as she thought of Nathan.

'No.' Flora said, in a tone that meant 'yes'. 'Just that the men will be too old or too arthritic or need Viagra, then they'll have heart attacks.'

'It doesn't bear thinking about. I'll take up art, or travelling instead.' She thought of Nathan and his lean muscular body and those lips; she'd never get that again. If she wanted a sex life she'd have to make do with inferior men. She was plagued suddenly by lurid pictures of elderly men with their kit off. She'd been so used to Stephen she'd never thought anything of it. Besides, she'd loved him, loved his body. And what about her with her kit off? Perhaps she better sign up to a gym. Oh, it was all too embarrassing to contemplate.

'Ben hasn't rung me.' Flora went on. 'He promised he would but you are the only person on the answer phone, saying you were staying over. Oh, and Aunt Felicity, who wants you to ring her as soon as you come in.'

'She'll have to wait.' The last thing she needed was Felicity in full steam firing off about unmarried mothers and the sanctity of marriage. She sat down beside Flora.

'Ben's place is with his wife,' she said gently. 'Try and imagine how hard it is for her, longing for a baby, trying all sorts of intrusive, and probably painful, procedures, and still not getting pregnant. Then Ben goes with another woman and she gets pregnant straight away.'

'I know all that,' Flora squirmed uncomfortably, 'but it's happened and he has some responsibility towards me and this child.'

'He does and I'm sure he'll honour you must give them this time to try to sort this out.' Lorna sighed. Life was such a mess. 'Marcus here?'

Flora shrugged, 's'pose so. Why wouldn't he be?'

'He might have gone to a party or something.'

'So was Dad all right?' Flora tried to sound nonchalant, but she could sense her pain.

'Fine, I hardly talked to him.'

'But you were all together at Ravenscourt, weren't you?'

'Yes, but not alone. We did have a moment to discuss things, and it's clear that our marriage is over, darling. We're divorced, after all, and there's no going back. But perhaps one day we'll be friends again.' Stephen had hardly behaved as if he wanted to be her friend but she wanted to offer some comfort to Flora.

Marcus appeared, announcing that he was just off to meet up with his mates. Flora eventually got dressed, and wandered off to Katie's, leaving Lorna feeling discarded, and alone.

Later in the afternoon Gloria rang. 'I've got to go back to the hospital to talk to the doctor about Adrian. Jane and Clara can't, as they are not his next of kin. I'll persuade them to keep him in while they come up with a solution. I thought I'd go to Nathan's party while I was down there. Sonia suggested I stay the night at Mulberry Farm, so that's where I am should you need me.'

'But I thought you wanted to be with Justin,' Lorna bleated feebly.

'I do, but when I got back I found that he's spending the night with Ellie's family, so I'll only be home alone. I'm a bit upset about it as I imagined he'd be here, and I can't help thinking he made the plan because I'd dashed off to Ravenscourt the minute I heard about his father. It had been such a good day, everyone so happy together and then... well you know how it is.'

'Don't beat yourself up over this, Glory,' Lorna said sympathetically. 'You had Ellie for the day and it's only natural she'd ask him to her home. 'You're right, I'm overreacting as usual,' she laughed, before sounding more serious. 'I'm dreading this meeting with Adrian and the doctors. Do you think they'll insist he comes home and gets treatment here, in London?'

'I don't know how it works, but be strong, Glory, for both Adrian and Justin's sakes. You can't go back to how things were.'

'I know. It's a relief I've got the party to look forward to, I'll let you know how it goes, bye.'

'Bye, good luck,' Lorna said, annoyed with herself for feeling jealous that Gloria, warm ,voluptuous Gloria yearning for support to go through her decision to leave Adrian, was spending the evening, and indeed the night, with Nathan at Mulberry Farm.

CHAPTER TWENTY-SIX
Tough Decisions

If only Lorna had come with her, but she couldn't expect her to come this way again to bail out Adrian. This was something she must do alone.

She hadn't told Justin she was going to see his father today either, and she felt bad about it, though he knew she'd left Adrian to be looked after by the hospital system, and that he was safe – as long as he stayed there. He and Ellie were so happy together that she couldn't bear to spoil it, especially at such an early stage. So she'd told him that, as he was away with Ellie's family for the night, she was going down to Mulberry Farm for a party and would be back the following day.

She parked at the hospital and went straight in, not allowing herself to conjure up any negative thoughts. She was shown into a side room where Adrian was sitting, rather morosely, in a wheelchair. He looked up when she came in.

'Good, you're here, can we go home now?'

He looked beaten, sitting there with his right arm strapped up, his face badly shaved and pale. Her heart went out to him, but she mustn't weaken, for all their sakes.

She sat down on the only other chair in the room, her stomach cramping with anxiety. 'How's your arm?'

'It aches and it's damned inconvenient. It will be ages before it mends, apparently.'

'I'm sorry.' She thought how difficult this was, but she remembered Jane at Ravenscourt talking about tough love. This was the only way to save him. She said, 'I want you to stay here, or go somewhere where they can help you overcome your drinking. We … you can't go on like this, next time it could kill you.'

'Not that old thing again, Gloria. I'm fine, or I will be when this damn arm mends. Help me get dressed, then we'll be on our way.' He tried to struggle up.

'No, I'm sorry, Adrian, this is the hardest thing I've ever had to do, but I'm going to ask the medical staff here to find you somewhere safe to go and have treatment for your alcoholism. If you stick to it, I'm sure it won't be long before you'll be allowed out.'

She didn't know what she'd do then, but she'd face it when it came.

'You're a hard-hearted woman, Gloria,' he said, but his voice had no fire.

'I've got to be, to save you,' she said, and got up to leave the room. 'I'll be back to tell you what's been decided,' she said, before she closed the door.

She was near tears and felt it beyond her to fight any more. To her surprise and relief, the medical staff were very sympathetic, and she was further heartened when his sister, Joanna, telephone her on her mobile to ask for an update on his condition.

'There's a good place up here, and I'd be close to him and could visit him. I don't mind saying I'd be glad of his company, I'm finding it very lonely without Hugh and both the girls living down South,' she said. 'Shall I come down and fetch him? I'm very happy to.'

'Oh, Joanna, that's an awful lot of ask of you,' Gloria said, overcome with relief. Joanna was so capable. She and Adrian had once been close, before her husband became so disabled and Adrian became a drunk.

'I know how hard it's been for you and I haven't been able to be much help, with Hugh being so ill, but I'd like to do it, it will give me something to do… I miss not having someone to look after.'

Gloria couldn't believe how well it had all worked out. Even Adrian looked happier when she explained the plans to him, and when she left him to go to Mulberry Farm, she kissed him. 'Do your best to kick the habit,' she said, 'so that one day we might be together again as a family. Justin's got a new girlfriend, a sweet girl called Ellie.' She told him about her, yearning for the old days when he'd have made her feel welcome instead of his behaviour scaring her away.

'And you don't want me to ruin it,' he said sadly. He sighed, not looking at her. 'I know it's been hard for you, Gloria, and I'm surprised you put up with it so long, but I was upset the way you dumped me at Ravenscourt for Christmas, that was a bit harsh.' He faced her, his expression grim, his voice now bordering on belligerence 'Christmas is meant to be spent as a family, and the others, Rosalind and Lorna… though I understand Lorna, she and Stephen are divorced - but just leaving us there? I suppose you all egged each other on. You find us too old now I imagine.' He sounded bitter.

She struggled not to weaken and agree to take him home. 'I'm sorry,' she said, 'but your behaviour made us all take drastic action, I hope you'll all realise how desperate we are to keep our families together.'

'Funny way of doing it,' he said, waving her away with his good arm. 'I hope Joanna will arrive soon and take me away from here.'

CHAPTER TWENTY-SEVEN
A Difficult Meeting

It was almost a week after Christmas, and the fridge was still half-full of delicious leftovers, mostly courtesy of Nathan. The New Year loomed, such a year of change ahead. Lorna wished she felt up to the challenge of it.

Flora and Ben sat together in her living room. He'd turned up, rather reluctantly Lorna thought, after Flora eventually got hold of him and demanded he come round to see her.

Flora had gone all huffy and childish when Ben appeared, asking why he hadn't come before and where had he been, since apart from ringing her on Christmas day, he had not bothered to contact her at all.

Lorna had seen this exchange, and how Ben seemed to retreat into himself, scraping back his sparse hair in agitation, muttering words of explanation. She said, rather tersely, 'Flora, give Ben a chance to explain. This is a very difficult situation, especially for Tess, and you must be more patient.'

'I only asked why it had taken him so long to contact me, it's not as if he'd been on the moon.' Flora snapped, curling up on the sofa and glowering at them all.

'I'll get some coffee,' Lorna said, thinking it best to leave them together to sort things out, and escaped to the kitchen. She fiddled about setting up a tray, putting a few of her Christmas spicy cupcakes on a plate, in case Ben needed fortifying, and making a carafe of strong coffee and a mug of peppermint tea for Flora. She went back into the living room, a cheerful smile pinned onto her face.

Although she'd known Ben was coming, Flora had made no effort with her appearance at all; she slumped in grey jogging pants and a huge, much-washed jersey, which had started out in life a strong pink and was now a dull flesh colour. Her stomach was quite rounded now; no wonder Felicity had noticed the change in her. Her hair was scraped back untidily in a rubber band. She had no make-up on and her face was pallid and puffy. Lorna felt disappointed in her, thinking that if she hoped to keep Ben she ought to at least make more of an effort with her appearance. Besides, she thought it a sort of arrogance to feel someone was not worth making an effort for.

Ben just looked like himself, this plain sparrow of a man, bewildered at having one woman in his life, let alone two, and one pregnant.

It was obvious the two had been arguing. Ben looked miserable and Flora grumpy. They sat opposite each other in an apparent stalemate. Hoping to break the mood, Lorna asked Ben if he'd had a good Christmas.

'Yes he has, he's been with Tess.' Flora snapped.

'She is his wife, darling,' Lorna said firmly. 'And you have got to see this from her viewpoint. She was longing for a baby and suddenly you come along and get pregnant immediately. It must be very hard for her.'

Ben seemed to diminish in misery before her eyes, which irritated her. She wished he had not become involved with Flora, involved with the whole family and now a baby was on its way. She held her tongue; it was hard for him too. Perhaps Christmas with Tess had made him realise the mistake he'd made, perhaps he regretted his time with Flora and wanted to finish with her and go back to his wife. But the baby would always be there as a symbol of his infidelity, even the barrier between them rekindling their marriage.

'It's hard for me, feeling so fat and tired.' Flora snapped back.

Ben squirmed in his chair, his eyes swivelling, fearful of making contact with anyone.

'It shouldn't have happened and for that I'm sorry,' he mumbled. He turned to Lorna, his face flushed with embarrassment. 'We were told that my sperm were weak and Tess is... irregular so I didn't think it would happen. I know I shouldn't have been with Flora and...' He took a deep breath and faced Lorna squarely. 'I shouldn't have had sex with Flora and I'm sorry. She's a lovely person and so kind and...' he struggled for more words to describe her, while Flora sighed heavily, her arms firmly crossed over her chest as if to hold herself together.

'You said you loved me, you couldn't help it,' she said, near tears.

Lorna was exhausted. There was enough on her plate; it was overflowing and running down the sides. Here were two adults – three, if you counted the spirit of Tess – caught up in a very grown up situation. Couldn't they cope with this appalling problem themselves? She was only here as a moderator to stop murder. She said wearily,

'Whatever the reason, it has happened, and we must decide what to do for the best. The only innocent party, and the most vulnerable one, is the coming baby and that is the responsibility of you both as the parents.'

Both of them seemed stunned by her words, perhaps realising for the first time the enormity of the situation. Neither spoke; neither looked at each other.

'So, Ben, what do you think is the best move in this?' Lorna threw him a tight smile of encouragement, wishing he were more assertive.

Ben squirmed some more. 'I ... well, we haven't decided. Tess might… we could share it.' He looked desperate.

'No, we can't, it's mine. I'm not going through all this crap to give it away.' Flora scowled. Lorna saw a flashback of her aged three, clinging to a doll, a doll she'd never much liked, refusing to share, or even to show it to her cousin Katie.

Ben broke in. 'I want to stay with Tess, we…' he glanced guiltily at Flora, 'we've been through so much and we know each other so well.'

'So you'll leave me and the baby to cope alone?' Flora howled at him, as he cowered in his chair.

'N… no, I won't. The baby is my responsibility and I will see to that, be a good father to it, but we can't live together, can we, Flora? We never really have and I don't think we could, do you?'

Lorna wondered if Ben loved Tess, or if love was just a luxury, an unobtainable Holy Grail, glimpsed now and then in a relationship, but quickly smothered by the problems of everyday living. Being comfortable in a relationship as, despite all this, he and Tess seemed to be, was no doubt the easiest thing for a smooth life, though it may not be very exciting. Perhaps sometimes couples confused a lack of excitement, especially in their sex lives, with lack of love, treating it as a major fault in an otherwise sustainable relationship.

Ben sat there staring into space, Flora furiously picked at her nails and Lorna, feeling she'd said her bit, decided she would leave them alone to sort it out themselves. Saying that they were out of fresh milk and bread, she left them and went shopping. She'd barely left the house when Gloria texted her, saying she was in the High Street and asking if they could meet up for a drink or lunch. She agreed, relieved to be able to escape the scene going on with the parents of her grandchild in her living room.

Gloria looked wonderful, bubbling with energy and relief, as she explained the arrangements she had made for Adrian to go to Scotland under the care of his sister.

'I hated leaving him, he was quite upset about being left at Ravenscourt for Christmas, but he's relieved Joanna is taking him to live with her, they've always been close. She lives in a quite secluded place and it will be quite an effort for him to find some booze and find a gutter to lie in,' she said. 'But I must tell you about the pictures of Ravenscourt, they are beautiful, do it great justice.'

'Good, I hope to see them,' Lorna said, wishing she'd been there too.

'Also,' Gloria wouldn't meet her eye,' Nathan's looking for somewhere to move all his business and everything and I thought …'

'Oh, Glory,' her heart sank, she remembered that Rosalind had mentioned it, 'I hope you didn't suggest Ravenscourt.' Had Gloria been up to her bossy head girl tactics again? 'I wish everyone would stop making plans for my house. Please just leave Ravenscourt alone, and I'll decide what to do with it.'

CHAPTER TWENTY-EIGHT
A Dubious Offer

Lorna, Gloria and Rosalind met for a catch up gossip together in a café off Sloane Square. It was teatime, the lights outside glowing in the velvety dark. It was the end of the second week of the New Year and the first time they'd all three spent time together since the Christmas that had changed their lives.

Lorna had gone to a dinner party with friends on New Year's Eve and as midnight stuck and they all toasted in the New Year she wondered what it would bring. As they raised their glasses to the New Year, she heard the 'ping' of her mobile and discreetly glancing at it saw a message from Nathan. 'Happy New Year, Lorna, meet up soon. X' Her heart soared, filling her with hope. She wondered how he was celebrating it and sent one back, 'Happy New Year too, hope it's a good one. X'

Rosalind was positively sparkling. No doubt, Lorna thought gloomily, fired up with a sizzling love affair with the man she'd met over Christmas. She braced herself to hear all about it.

It was Gloria, who said, 'you look wonderful Ros, so tell us all, what's he like?'

Rosalind blushed and looked down at her hands twisting the handle of her bag in her lap. 'You... won't believe it,' she said cautiously, as if she hardly believed it herself, 'but it's... Ivan... he's come back.'

'Ivan... you mean *Ivan*?' Gloria said with surprise, 'but I thought you'd met someone else at a party at Christmas?'

'I did and he was very attractive, asked me out too, but Ivan came home unexpectedly and heard me talking to him on the phone,' she giggled. 'You should have seen his face, it gave him a fright and I think it made him realise I was not going to sit about and wait for him to deign to come home whenever it suited him.'

'So you didn't go out with the new man?' Gloria asked.

'No.' She turned to Lorna. 'It's all thanks to you and Ravenscourt, really. Being there without us shocked him into realising that our marriage is in trouble. We were alone in the house – the girls were out with friends – and we just talked, talked as we haven't for ages. He's promised to give up his charity work, at least for the moment, and give more time to us.'

'Oh, Ros, I'm so glad' Lorna said, 'and you look pleased about it too.'

'I am, I've always loved him, but these last years have been so difficult. I felt so abandoned, as if he was bored with me ... like when my father left me when I was a teenager. I wanted to leave him but then, as you know Lorna, you don't leave just a person but a whole lifestyle too. He's back. I hope he is, anyway, the man I loved, so thank you... and Ravenscourt, for your part in it.'

Lorna shrugged. 'I did nothing, it's just luck I have Ravenscourt and luck our plan worked out, though I'm sorry about Adrian,' she said to Gloria.

'It worked out a bit for me, too,' Gloria said, 'as I told you, Adrian has gone with his sister, Joanna, to Scotland. She will see he keeps to his regime with the rehab sessions. I've sent all his clothes on,' she said determinedly, as if she'd closed that door on her life and was ready to open another.

'You've done well, Glory, you've made the right decision. Let's hope he does stick it out.' Lorna laid her hand over hers, thinking that now Justin had gone back to Uni she must be lonely. 'We must think of new things to do with our lives.'

'I have,' Gloria smiled at her. 'Nathan wants a base in London so I'm having him as a lodger. I have four bedrooms and two are empty so I suggested he stay with me while he sorts himself out.'

'Oh… I see.' Lorna struggled to hide her consternation at this piece of news. Had something gone on with Nathan the night she'd stayed at Mulberry Farm?

Gloria eyed her sharply, 'I'm stony broke and having him there will bring in some cash, you should do it too, Lorna, have a lodger, might help pay towards Ravenscourt.'

'Oh, I…I don't know, I don't really want a stranger in the house and anyway I'd need a whole stack of lodgers to pay for Ravenscourt,' Lorna said, going on to ask about Justin and Ellie to steer her away from talking about Nathan.

The restaurant was buzzing with people having tea, cosy in the warm. Lorna bit into a tiny pistachio macaroon, savouring the burst of creamy filling. Flora had gone back to Oxford already and Marcus had gone to stay with friends in Scotland, 'to celebrate New Year as it should be' and was still there. Stephen was with Odile. Gloria and Rosalind appeared buoyant and enthusiastic with life, and Nathan had sent her a New Year text suggesting they meet up. Perhaps the New Year held more than she thought, for the joy she should be feeling at the arrival of a new member of the family was muffled under layers of painful complications.

According to Flora, the marriage could be over, which was terrible for Tess. But Flora didn't want to marry him, though she expected his support.

'I'm too young to be stuck at home, like you were with Dad,' she'd announced defiantly, as if daring Lorna to lecture her on her responsibility to give a stable home to the baby, which she probably naively thought could be tucked away somewhere like a doll and taken out when she wanted to play with it. Lorna bit her tongue and said nothing, reminding herself that Flora must make her own decisions – saying anything now would only antagonise her.

'So this year you'll be a granny,' Gloria said, as if she guessed Lorna's feelings. 'Something to look forward to.'

'It should be, but as you know, it's fraught with difficulties,' Lorna filled them in about the situation.

'So you don't think they'll marry?'

'No, or live together apparently, though things might change when the baby is born. I doubt Flora's flat mates will want to share with a crying baby. As we know, nothing in the world changes you quite as much as the birth of your first child. But by then Ben might have gone back to his wife, if she'll have him, or not want to be with Flora and the baby. Or she might ditch him, find someone else, go back to Jamie, who knows?' Lorna sighed.

'What a mess,' Rosalind frowned. 'Let's hope when the baby is actually born they'll see sense, but I hope they won't dump it on you, Lorna. You don't want to be stuck back in the nursery again.'

'No, I don't, I'll help of course, but not full time.'

The waiter arrived with another pot of tea and when he'd gone, Rosalind turned to Gloria. 'So, tell us about the party on Boxing Day at Mulberry Farm. Ivan has told me nothing – well you know what men are like, so let's have all the gory details.'

'It was fun, wonderful food of course,' Gloria enthused, going on to describe the décor in the house and the other guests.

'So what about Nathan? Did he not have any sexy, free men friends for you?' Rosalind giggled.

'One or two, but I talked mostly to him.' Gloria said, picking up her tea and drinking it slowly as it was so hot.

'So what did you talk about?' Rosalind teased Gloria, 'his food?'

'A bit, but,' Gloria faced Lorna, putting her cup down carefully in front of her. 'Actually he talked about you.'

'Me. Whatever for?' She shrank with embarrassment. He'd joked about her appearing like a pantomime dame, amused the whole county with his description of what she wore in bed.

'Nothing much, just asked if you had a man in your life, I think he was confused by the men staying at Ravenscourt, wanted to know who fitted with whom.' Gloria regarded her intently, noticing her discomfort.

'So what did you say?' Had Gloria gone on about her plan – real or imagined – for him to buy Ravenscourt and he was sussing her out to check if she had a man in her life who'd decide the fate of Ravenscourt, or even pay for its restoration?

Rosalind laughed, 'I suppose it was a bit odd seeing the men and finding out they were at Ravenscourt for Christmas on their own,' she said.

'He didn't know that when he first saw them, remember we were all there... I think he wondered if you might be having another go at your marriage.'

'So what did you tell him?' Lorna asked, feeling uncomfortable about being discussed, wondering how much Gloria had embellished her situation. She had a momentary vision of that kiss, why had he kissed her if he thought she had gone back to her marriage? No doubt it was just an impulsive gesture, taken without thought.

'Just that you were divorced and had no one else at the moment. What did you think I was going to say?' Gloria demanded, watching her as if she guessed there was something she was keeping from her.

'I hope you didn't go on about Ravenscourt,' Lorna said bleakly. 'My sister and brother-in-law are showing interest in it as well. Felicity has plans for a spiritual retreat.'

'From what you've told us about Fergus, he'd turn in his grave at that,' Rosalind laughed.

Lorna smiled but kept her eyes on Gloria 'I've got to get estimates on how much it needs spending on it and what is urgent, and if it's worth doing and how much it will cost, so just leave me to it, please, Gloria.'

'O.K, if that's what you want, I'm only trying to be helpful,' Gloria said defensively, her head down searching in her bag for something.

'That's what I'm afraid of,' Lorna said to herself.

❊ ❊ ❊

Lorna was half way home on the bus when her mobile rang. It was Nathan.

'Happy New Year again Lorna and thanks for your greetings too. I meant to get in touch before but I've been snowed under getting the brochure together and various things, how are you?'

'F…fine, hope all's well with you.' How strange he'd rung just after she'd left Gloria and Rosalind. Had Gloria rung or texted him?

'Yes, lots of decisions to make, New Year and all,' he said. 'How about you?'

'The same…. I'm going to be a granny; my daughter's having a baby.' She blurted, wondering what he'd think of that.

'A granny? You're far too young, when did she get married?'

'She didn't… she hasn't.'

'One of those. Well, I hope it all works out. I want to show you the pictures of Ravenscourt, I'm thrilled with them. Have you any plans to come down this way?"

'I must come down soon, and decide how best to deal with the house. Everyone seems to have ideas – some more far-fetched than others – but I'll get it surveyed first, go from there.'

'Good thinking. If you need any advice about who to ask I might be able to help you, you've only to ask.'

'Thanks, I'll bear it in mind,' she said, wishing she didn't always feel that Ravenscourt loomed over any relationship that might develop between them.

'Well, lovely to talk to you. Lorna, Beth's just come in with various designs for the brochure. Pity you aren't here to help me choose, but let me know when you next come down, I'm stuck here for a while.'

It would be Beth disturbing our conversation, she thought bitterly. 'I will, but I'm not sure quite when,' she said, wishing she sounded warmer towards him but the thought of Beth hovering around him no doubt with her clip board, curbed her feelings. Telephone calls were so impersonal, if only they were together, she'd be able to judge his feelings better then.

CHAPTER TWENTY-NINE
An Unwelcome Visitor

It was a filthy day in January, the grey, winter sky leaning hard down on them, squeezing rain over everywhere. Lorna set off, with a heavy heart, for Ravenscourt.

Jonathan, her brother-in-law, had recommend a surveyor and his report made shocking reading. Ravenscourt needed immediate attention if it were to be saved and reading through the estimate Lorna was forced to accept what she'd known all along, that the cost was miles out of her reach. Apart from the considerable structural damage, it needed to be rewired and the plumbing, hot water system and boiler were years past their sell-by date. It would have to be sold, if possible, before it succumbed to the ravages of winter. Facing up to it hurt deeply, but it had to be done, and it wasn't as if she'd been expecting such a present. She'd do her best by it and try to find someone who would love it and have the funds to restore it back to its original beauty, not rip it to pieces and turn it into some soulless monstrosity.

She couldn't bring herself to tell Gloria and Rosalind just yet and have Gloria bombarding her with ideas to save it, each one probably more outrageous than the next but she had to tell

Clara, and a couple of capable estate agents (who were hopefully not enamoured with Sonia) that she was coming.

Her car squelched up the drive, water running down in snaking rivulets on either side of her. She glimpsed the house through the curtain of rain. There it stood, stoic in the grey veil of teeming water. Her heart lurched and the image and the feel of Nathan's kiss took over her senses. She stopped the car close to the house, and sat for a moment to compose herself. Clara was watching for her at the scullery window and rushed out with a large umbrella to lead her into the kitchen.

'What a day, it makes Ravenscourt look at its worst,' Lorna said. The house appeared bleak and sad, waiting for her as if to entomb her in its gloom. 'I wouldn't buy it if I saw it today.'

'The sun may come out and someone who knows the house already won't mind,' Clara said brightly, bustling about putting on the kettle and pushing a plate of newly baked brownies in her direction. 'You must feel the cold after sitting so long in a warm car. The draughts here are dreadful, as you no doubt remember from when you spent the night here. Would you like coffee or tea? We've a little time before the agent comes.' Clara glanced at the wooden clock on the wall. 'He said he'd be here at eleven.'

Lorna consulted her notes. 'So, Philip Carson from Carson's is coming this morning and Angela Walsh from Kingdon and Pearson, this afternoon.' Clara had rung her with the names of those she considered – after discreet enquiries; she emphasised the word 'discreet' – the two best agents for the area. Lorna had looked them up on the Internet and found that they had quite a few large properties in the county on the market already. The houses she had seen advertised had large modern kitchens with smart alcoves to eat in, and sleek cupboards and work tops. This poor shabby kitchen with its narrow cupboards and the wooden draining boards either side of the old sink, seemed very dated indeed.

Clara, usually so full of conversation, appeared subdued. Having bustled about with coffee and milk she then set to, wiping all conceivable surfaces down with a damp cloth, although everywhere looked as clean as was possible for somewhere that needed a complete make-over.

'It looks good, you must have worked very hard,' Lorna tried to reassure her, supposing that Clara was afraid that the estate agent would think the place uncared for, and think badly of her because of it.

'It's the best I can do,' Clara said, with another swipe at the sink.

'What is it then?' She was surprised at Clara's agitation. 'Is something wrong?' Had something happened that she had not told her? Was Philip Carson a sex maniac, or Angela Walsh a kleptomaniac? When she'd first broached the subject with her, Clara had seemed to imply that there was not a reliable estate agent in the whole district. Or, and the thought made her blush, did she know about her and Nathan? Heard him joking about it with Gloria?

'Nothing… it's just sad the house must go and Fergus is gone.' Clara said lamely, not meeting her gaze.

'Your cottage is well hidden and not too close to the house, so whoever buys it shouldn't intrude.' That must be what was worrying her. The study where Nathan had seduced her was quite a way from the kitchen and the thick walls would cut out any sounds, so unless Nathan had mentioned it, she couldn't know about it. Her guilt was making her anxious, that was all. 'You even have your own bit of drive,' she went on, hoping to soothe Clara's anxiety.

'Yes, I'm glad about that,' Clara said. Then, hearing a car drawing up outside, she said, 'That must be Philip Carson now.' She darted to the door, snatching up the dripping umbrella from its stand on the way.

Poor Clara, this must be more difficult for her than she'd thought. Ravenscourt was like her home and held so many memories of Fergus. It would be hard for her to see it go. She suspected that Gloria had probably talked to her about *her* idea of Nathan buying it, but it was hardly surprising that she was nervous that a new owner would ruin the house and intrude on her settled life.

A car door slammed and a man's voice answered Clara's greeting. In a moment he was in the kitchen, divesting himself of his coat. He came towards her with his hand outstretched. 'Ah, Mrs Sanderson, Philip Carson.'

She had not expected someone quite so young. He was pleasant looking in a fresh, boyish sort of way, his brown hair short and tidy. He was dressed in a suit and tie, as neat as if he had been cut out of a fashion magazine. He turned down Clara's offer of coffee and bounced about the room, Tigger-like, eyes everywhere, saying how cosy it all was and how the room reminded him of his grandmother's kitchen.

'Sad it's such a bad day, I'll leave looking outside until last.' He smiled. 'It certainly is a big house and as soon as the spring comes, buyers will be out in droves looking for a country house.'

Lorna showed him round, explaining that today she just needed a valuation. Clara seemed reluctant to come with them, though she did at least answer his questions about the ancient heating and the water system.

It was almost lunchtime when Philip left, assuring Lorna he would send her his valuation as soon as he'd worked it out, saying, 'It's a lovely house but sadly in very bad condition,' as its epitaph. 'I'm starving, did you get some lunch in, or shall we go to the nearest pub before the next agent comes?'

'Oh, I…um' Clara wrung her hands, not looking at her.

'It doesn't matter if you didn't get anything in, we'll just go to the pub and get some soup or something. Angela's not coming until three, we've plenty of time.' It would be good to get into the bustling cosiness of a pub. The house felt bleak and unloved – rather as she did.

'We've been asked out to lunch,' Clara said in a rush, 'I'm sorry. They found out and insisted that we go.' She regarded Lorna defiantly.

'Who? Gloria and Rosalind?' Had they come down and were waiting for them in the pub? It seemed unlikely, they were not the sort to hide out somewhere, they would have come straight here to be in on it under the guise of supporting her.

'No, Sonia Harwood, she insisted on you going over for lunch. I said you would probably not have time, but …'

'But how does she know I'm here?' Lorna asked. 'I didn't want anyone to know, I haven't even told Gloria and Rosalind. I just wanted to get a couple of experts in and hear their verdict on my own so I can think about it without being bombarded by other people's opinions.'

'I'm sorry, Sonia is very hospitable and when she heard you were coming she insisted you came to lunch. She wanted to see you and, knowing how cold and damp this house is, warm you up. I did say you probably hadn't the time and just wanted to get advice from an agent.'

'I thought the name was familiar. Carson's belongs to one of Sonia's admirers,' Lorna remembered. 'I know everyone means well, but I wish they'd leave me alone,' she finished, feeling rather tired by it all.

'They are the best agents round here,' Clara bleated.

Lorna wondered if Nathan would be at this lunch. She remembered his call and how he'd asked her to let him know when she came down again, and she hadn't contacted him for the same reason that she hadn't told Gloria and Rosalind. It would be embarrassing when he heard she'd come here without telling him, but she couldn't help it, perhaps he would understand.

Seeing her expression, Clara said in her own defence, 'Sonia insisted you come to lunch. It was impossible to refuse her.'

'Well you should have at least asked me first if I wanted to go.'

'You wouldn't have gone then,' Clara said, her mouth tight.

'No, and I'm not going now. I'll ring them and say I haven't time. Please could I have their number?' She went towards the bread bin to use the telephone they'd hidden behind there over Christmas. There was the sound of another car arriving; the slam of the door, running feet, and a wet Nathan shot into the kitchen. He saw her hovering by the telephone, the receiver in her hand. He smiled.

'Hello Lorna, sorry to disturb your call, finish it and…'

'It's all right, it's too late. I was about to ring your mother and say I can't come to lunch.'

He frowned. 'Have you another date?'

It was all such a muddle. 'No, it doesn't matter,' she said wearily, knowing she'd have been pleased to see him in other circumstances, but not like this, lunching with his mother and all wrapped up with her anxiety over Ravenscourt.

'It's such a pig of a day and it's so good to see you. I've come to take you to Mulberry Farm for lunch. I promise I'll get you back here in plenty of time for the next agent.' The rain ran off his wax jacket and dripped from his hair and down his face. He had a slight air of defiance about him yet she could glimpse a touch of amusement in his eyes, and she blushed, certain he was laughing at her, remembering that flannel nightdress. 'It won't be ham, it's steak and kidney pie and my mother's pastry is the best.'

Her heart did a triple flip and she cursed it. Her body seemed to have gone soft, yielding as if all her bones had melted away. 'I… I can't come,' she said firmly.

'Of course you can. Everyone knows everyone else's business in the country so you mustn't blame Clara for spreading the word. Besides, I'd hoped you'd ring me and tell me you were coming here,' he said.

'This wasn't meant to be a social visit, I just need to get a valuation.'

'You've time for both if we leave now so you can have time to enjoy the pie,' he said, taking a few steps closer to her. Her body warmed, thinking he might touch her, even greet her with a kiss.

Clara had put on her coat and fetched Lorna's, which she handed to her. 'This is not fair. I feel as if I'm being high jacked,' Lorna grumbled, but she pulled on her coat and picked up her bag.

He laughed. 'No, 'course you're not. My mother has just invited you to lunch. She was so grateful you found her watch and wants to thank you personally.' His eyes shone with suppressed laughter and she felt infused with heat, relieved that Clara was busy shutting doors and checking the ancient boiler before leaving the house and wasn't watching them.

'Also I want to show you the pictures of Ravenscourt, I'd like your opinion. Your cakes have a star role, they were delicious and I'd like to include them on my list, if you're willing.' His smile was warm. She glanced away; he wouldn't slay her with charm. In fact, she thought, it might be best to keep their relationship strictly neutral while the fate of Ravenscourt (perhaps that of the cakes) was being decided.

'Thank you,' she said, hoping she sounded professional, 'I'll send you the list of our range, we're doing quite well, though we've had a slight drop in sales now Christmas is over and so many people have put themselves on diets, but we're working on some more healthy recipes with less fat and sugar.'

'Good idea, But I expect your sales will soon go up again when people get sick of lettuce and water, especially in the winter,' he said, taking her arm and shielding her from the rain as he led her to the car. He opened the door for her and she reluctantly got in.

When they were settled, with Clara in the back, and had started on their way he said quietly, 'I wish I'd known the reason you left your husbands at Ravenscourt for Christmas.' He glanced at her. 'Gloria told me all about the problems the three of you are going through with your marriages. I'm so sorry. I quite understand why you did it.'

She kept silent, not able to look at him in case he guessed the turmoil in her heart. He went on, 'Gloria said she'd always have fond memories for the house, as it changed your lives forever and gave you a chance to move on. I hope it had the same outlook for you, Lorna.' His voice was gentle but she could not look at him. The moment seemed too intimate and she was embarrassed with Clara sitting behind them. His kiss had given her strength, filled her body with warmth and hope, but perhaps she expected too much from it; she must just remember it as a wonderful memory.

'Yes, it cleared up some things,' she felt she had to say something.

'I must say,' Nathan said, with a broad smile, that of all the things Ravenscourt could be turned into, I never thought of it as a depository for dissolute husbands.'

'Don't mock,' His teasing grated on her. 'We were desperate not to lose our children, and they couldn't bear to see their fathers behaving as they were. It sounds mad, but it worked, Ivan is trying to be a better father and husband and Adrian is with his sister in Scotland, hopefully getting dried out, But I don't expect you to understand.'

'But I do,' he said, his voice softening now; his face touched with sorrow. 'I've been through divorce too and the breaking up of a family and its one of the most painful, destructive things. I'm sorry, it was a sick joke, forgive me.'

'I suppose everyone round here who doesn't know the true facts, think we are the wives from hell – especially those who met them at your mother's party,' she said.

'No,' he said, 'they don't, if anything, the men seemed reticent to talk about it. Only we know, don't we Clara,' he eyed her in the driving mirror as she sat silently in the back seat, 'and we won't tell anyone.'

'No, I wish I'd done the same to my husband, only he'd disappeared before I could,' Clara said darkly.

Nathan laughed. 'Nearly there, now,' he said, slowing down.

Lorna watched his hand changing gear. It was a nice hand, long-fingered, elegant and slightly damp from the rain. The gold wedding ring glinted on his finger. Did he still mourn the wife he'd lost; keep her memory safe by wearing it? She had got rid of hers immediately, feeling it mocked her for her failure.

For one mad moment she had the urge to slip her hand on top of his, but she restrained herself, clamping her hands between her knees to prevent such foolishness.

CHAPTER THIRTY
No Such Thing As A Free Lunch

A wave of shyness came over her as Nathan pulled up outside Mulberry Farm and parked close to the house. If only it was just her and Nathan in some cosy pub and she could share her anxieties about Ravenscourt with him without having to do battle with other people's views, or listen, she thought, to his mother's strident opinions.

He opened the door and she went into a large hall, which contained some pieces of good furniture, including a table with an extravagant floral display. She wondered if it was one of Beth's arrangements and hoped nothing would roll off and cause ructions as she walked past. It was warm and welcoming and there was a rich aroma of cooking, tempting her appetite. The trap bated by steak and kidney pie, she thought cynically, as Nathan took her coat and said how glad he was that she was here at last.

The front door opened again, throwing in a wet gust, and Nathan went to help Jane Purdy tackle her umbrella and close the front door.

Lorna half expected Gloria and Rosalind to jump out from behind somewhere, singing, 'Di da, here we are.' She pictured

Gloria beaming with goodness, having come up with a plan to turn Ravenscourt into a cooking school or something equally far-fetched with Nathan as the chief chef.

Trying to calm her awkwardness at being here she looked about her. Through two small arches cut into the wall in the centre of the house near the stairs she could see glimpses of other, expensively done-up rooms.

Nathan led them into the sitting room, which featured more beams, an inglenook fireplace and a host of photographs, many of an older man who, from the look of him, must be Nathan's late father.

'Lorna, it's good to see you again,' Sonia gushed, appearing from somewhere and kissing her effusively. She was wearing the raspberry pink cashmere, which looked very good on her, Lorna conceded, ridiculously pleased that Nathan had bought it for his mother and not for Beth, who, though not his wife, was surely close to him?

'Such a dispiriting time of the year, don't you think? So, having you here has cheered me up.' Sonia smiled delightedly at her. 'Oh, and I forgot, thank you so much for finding my watch. I was distraught when I realised I'd lost it. Desmond, my late husband, had it especially designed for me.'

There was a sudden silence in the room, and it seemed dreadfully hot with the log fire dancing in the ornate grate.

'Champagne?' Nathan smiled at her, it was an intimate smile, his eyes sparkling with humour. He leaned over her, steadying her glass with one hand, while re-filling it with the other, his fingers over hers as she clutched the stem of her glass, the warm proximity of him made her blush, remembering that kiss. She moved away quickly, glancing around the room to see if anyone had noticed her agitation…

Beth, with her familiar clipboard – perhaps she even took it to bed with her – came into the room, throwing her a rather fake smile, before accosting Nathan with some query. She hadn't seen Beth since her carefully constructed still life had collapsed before her, and her exaggerated fervour in interesting Nathan in whatever was on her clipboard, made Lorna suspect that she had still not forgiven her, or, and this was a foolish thought, that she wanted to stake her claim to him.

To her relief, Jane Purdy came and sat in a chair beside her, and asked her how things were.

'Adrian is living with his sister in Scotland and attending a rehab centre near her, so Gloria is getting on with her own life.' And mine as well, she thought, acidly, thinking of Gloria's new energised persona who, she feared, had turned her sights on to Nathan – not that she'd blame her – having him as a lodger in her not very large house where they would easily fall over each other, or … on top of each other.

'And Ivan?' Jane asked.

'I think he's done the best of the three. His time at Ravenscourt seemed to shock him out of his selfish behaviour and he's gone back to Rosalind, and has given up his charity work … for the moment anyway, realising at last that charity begins at home.'

'That's good news,' Jane said, 'and Rosalind's happy?'

'Yes, she is, she only really wanted him, but as he was when things were good between them, not as he'd become. She's giving him another chance and so far,' she crossed fingers and held them up, 'it seems to be working.'

'And you?' Jane regarded her kindly. 'How are you getting on?'

'Fine, thanks, going to be a granny soon, I can't believe it.' Lorna was not going to go into Marcus's latest theory that Stephen's fling with the sulky Odile had lost its fire. Even if he did dump her, there was bound to be a line of other sexy women willing to seduce an old man for a visa and outings to smart places.

'We must eat, or Lorna will be late back for the estate agent.' Nathan announced, opening the door of the room and leading them out.

Lorna reluctantly followed them to the dining room, fearing that once they were all seated round the table, they would start to peck at her like a group of chickens.

The steak and kidney pie was indeed delicious; golden, flaky pastry covering succulent meat in a rich, winey sauce. Despite her emotions raging through her, Lorna could not help but enjoy it. Nathan sat one side of her, and Beth on the other.

The conversation centred on the beef and the local farm where it came from. They discussed how the taste and texture of the meat depended upon the food the animal was fed on, then Sonia asked her what she thought of Philip Carson, the estate agent. 'He is a nice enough young man, but not a patch on Henry, his father,' Sonia started. 'He was so attentive . . .'

Nathan interrupted his mother impatiently, saying he was sure Lorna didn't want to talk about Ravenscourt. This surprised her, for she'd convinced herself – after hearing Gloria's idea that Nathan wanted the house – that he'd bought her here with the people most likely to benefit from him buying Ravenscourt to try and persuade her into selling it to him at a knock-down price.

'I must show you the proofs for my brochure before you go. They'll go out in August, in plenty of time for Christmas,' he said, his eyes lingering on hers, provoking the memory of his kiss. Determinedly, she turned her attention to her plate.

'Thank you, I'd like to see them, Gloria says they are wonderful.'

'They've come out very well, I think we managed to capture the best bits,' Beth said, and Lorna braced herself for her to start on about her skill at lighting and turning tired and sad old places into sumptuous palaces, but to her great relief she did not.

The lunch limped on; the pie was replaced with fresh fruit salad and cheese. Clara remarked how nice the cheeses looked, arranged on the olive wood cheese board. They talked of events happening in the district and gossip concerning various neighbours and Lorna felt more and more tense, feeling that Ravenscourt was the huge elephant looming among them threatening to charge upon them, though everyone seemed determined not to mention it.

When the meal was finished, Nathan suggested she come and see the brochure. She followed him into a room on the first floor. It was a very masculine room, with a large leather-topped desk by the window; two leather chairs, one in front of the desk, the other by the wall; and a smart filing cabinet made of dark wood with gilt handles. Various pictures were well arranged on the walls. Some were etchings of ancient cities, others seascapes. On the desk was a large photograph of a young man with a surfboard, grinning into the camera.

'This was my father's study, I still feel him here,' Nathan said, going over to the desk and opening a large file which enclosed the photographs.

'You must miss him. I miss my parents still,' Lorna said, looking down at the photographs.

She had to admit that Beth and the photographer had made a good job of them. The table, laden with food, looked wonderful in the hall in front of the elaborate fireplace and the glowing fire; the fine moulding on the ceiling edged the top of the picture just enough to add to the sumptuousness of it, but not enough to show the cracks and broken pieces.

The food display in the kitchen – the one that Beth had accused her of ruining – just homed in on the produce, leaving out the drab kitchen. Nathan pointed out her cakes.

'Look, pride of place. We must make a date to set that up. I have a smaller brochure around Easter and perhaps I could put them in that…baby Simnel cakes in pretty boxes: small, edible presents or just treats. Do you bake them yourself?'

He was standing close to her, turning the pages; she could feel the warmth of him.

'Yes, I bake some and Martha, whose shop it really is, bakes the rest with her sister. We have a shop in Wandsworth, and supply some to coffee shops around. We hope to go online one of these days.'

'Sounds good, well maybe we could set up a meeting. I'm going to be coming to London quite a bit in the next few weeks so we could make a date to meet at the shop?' He smiled and she waited for him to say he was going to lodge with Gloria, but he did not.

'Any time … I'm around.' Then, to change the subject, she said, 'Who's that good looking young man? He doesn't look like you, and yet he does.'

'That's my son, Kit,' he said easily. 'He's on his gap year in Tibet.'

His son? She knew so little about him. 'Interesting, how long is he there?'

'He's having a great time, he's a wonderful boy and I miss him, but then children have to spread their wings and leave the nest, don't they?' He smiled. 'He'll be back in the summer to go to university. He put it off for a year, having had enough of school.'

Clara came into the room. 'Excuse me, but we ought to get back, the next estate agent will be due soon. Jane is leaving too so she'll give us a lift, save you doing it Nathan, I'm sure you've got lots to do.'

'Oh … OK, that would be helpful, Clara, thank you.' He shut the folder.

Lorna wished she could stay here with him instead of going back to Ravenscourt and the estate agent and another gloomy verdict. She felt pleasantly sleepy after such a good lunch and she couldn't help feeling that she should be making more effort to find a way to keep the house, but short of winning the lottery – perhaps she should start doing it at once – there was surely no way she could raise the sort of money needed to save it.

CHAPTER THIRTY-ONE
An Unexpected Arrival

'I can't believe Ravenscourt is worth so much money.' Gloria stared at her in disbelief. 'Almost two million pounds! It can't be true; it needs so much doing to it. I'm sure the agents are only saying that so that they can get it on their books. Then, when it won't sell, they'll tell you some nonsense about houses like that having suddenly gone out of fashion and you must drop the price dramatically.'

'You should see the prices of the houses that are done up. I suppose if a developer buys it and does it up he will sell it on for far more, and there's quite a chunk of land with it too.' Lorna was surprised herself at the price quoted but both the agents she'd consulted over Ravenscourt had suggested virtually the same valuation. A sick feeling cramped her stomach. There was no guarantee Ravenscourt would sell in this financial climate and all the time it was deteriorating. If the winter took a turn for the worst, it could finish it off. Would she be compelled to watch it slowly disintegrating like a person dying of a disease? If only she could find a way of keeping it, but after seeing the survey, it would be impossible.

'I will always love it, as it played such a part in sorting out our lives.' Gloria poured Lorna some coffee, bringing it over to her at the table. She put it down beside the jewellery Lorna had brought round to sell alongside the cashmeres in an empty shop that Gloria and some others had hired for a month. She sat down opposite her.

'Ivan and Rosalind seem to be happy together, and the girls are behaving better, especially Chloe. I suppose it helps that Polly has gone travelling with some boyfriend, so is not popping round all the time causing havoc, but I'm sure Ravenscourt played a big part in making Ivan see sense. It certainly helped get Adrian into rehab, even though he had to break his arm on the stairs to do it.' She sipped her coffee, her eyes sad.

'Is he still there?' Lorna asked.

'As far as I know. Joanna will be very supportive and now she's a widow she can give her time to him, and it will help her get over her husband's death. And you, Lorna,' Gloria snapped out of her mood, saying encouragingly, 'It didn't actually solve your marriage problems but at least it clarified everything. Setting you free now to do what you want. I'm sure in time you'll find love again; you're still young and very attractive.' She smiled at her, a sort of bracing smile that did not lift Lorna's mood.

Had Nathan already moved in as a lodger? Was he part of the group who had hired the empty shop? He had not yet contacted her about buying some of her cakes and she wondered if he had only said it in gratitude for her lending him Ravenscourt for his brochure and because she was there at Mulberry Farm.

She would not ask Gloria who, with her sharp eyes, would surely winkle out her own confused feelings for him.

It was over a week since her kidnap to Mulberry Farm. They were in Gloria's kitchen overlooking the garden. The jewellery she'd made over the last few evenings lay on a tray among their coffee mugs and a miscellany of books, newspapers, a jar of beauty cream on its way upstairs and a parcel waiting to be posted.

Usually she enjoyed being with Gloria, but the arrival of Ravenscourt and Nathan in their lives was like a stone in a comfortable, well-worn shoe. She'd meant to just drop her jewellery and leave, but habits die hard and Gloria had been so pleased to see her that she'd felt annoyed with herself for her negative feelings towards her, and stayed.

She managed to keep Gloria busy by discussing Justin and his girlfriend, before getting back to Adrian. 'We have talked on the phone. He can't come back here to all the temptations, in fact he can never really come back to this house. We'd have to move if we got together again,' she said.

'Move?' Ravenscourt flashed into her mind. Any mention of selling or buying a house now filled her with anxiety. Felicity was still going on about their spiritual retreat and Gloria thought Nathan should have it, not that he'd mentioned it at all, anyway not to her, the owner. She was beginning to feel that the house was part of her, like another limb, but she must harden her heart and do what was best for it, and that meant selling to someone who could save it.

'Yes, apparently it's better to start somewhere fresh, away from one's old life, or that's one of the theories anyway.'

'So you are going to take him back?' She thought of Gloria's agony over the years; waiting up all night wondering where he was, crucifying herself with lurid accidents that had befallen him. And what about Justin with his new girlfriend? Surely she didn't want to risk losing him?

Gloria sighed, 'I don't know, not as he was, never, but it's hard being alone after being married so long isn't it? Well, you must know.' She touched her arm.

'Yes. I wish the old Stephen would come back to be a support with Flora and the baby, but I've come to accept... since Christmas and that night at Ravenscourt when he refused to come back... that it won't happen, and you'll come to feel that too, but it takes time, Glory.'

Gloria smiled, 'I must say, it's wonderful not having that day to day worry about Adrian. I felt like a warden or a nurse, always keeping an eye out.'

'Nurse and a purse, that's what Mum used to say,' Lorna finished her coffee.

'That's what I've been all these years to Adrian. A nurse and a purse, working like mad to pay the bills as his work decreased, and picking him up out of the gutter.'

'But you've stopped now. Remember, you are now going to live life for yourself and Justin. You deserve it,' she said firmly, hoping that Gloria wouldn't have a wobble and take Adrian back unless there was a miracle cure.

Gloria's face clouded. 'It's a bit like being joined at the hip to someone most of your life; once they have gone, you have to re-balance yourself. But I'm determined to start all sorts of new things. I'm thinking of doing a course in making herbal beauty products to sell online or at those fairs.'

'That's a good idea. I must make more of an effort with my cakes. Nathan hinted that he might take some, I must chase him up on that,' she said.

'He might pop by soon,' Gloria glanced at the clock on the wall, 'and then you can ask him yourself.'

'He's coming here … today?'

'He said he might … not to stay, though we might sort something out for later. He's looking for somewhere to move to with his business.'

'In London?'

'Probably not, the prices are astronomical and you get nothing for it, but he's looking all over the place. Also, he has things to do in London and it's a bore, especially in the winter, to have to keep going back to Sussex.' She didn't mention Ravenscourt, but she might as well have had it up in neon lights dancing from the walls.

'Well I must go. Thanks for the coffee and for taking my jewellery, let me know if you need help in the shop and I'll come over,' Lorna said hurriedly, getting up.

But before she could collect up her things the doorbell went and Gloria got up. 'Probably Nathan, I'll just let him in,' she said, leaving the room.

Lorna wasn't sure she could face seeing Nathan right now – Nathan and Gloria together, especially if Gloria was going to bring up Ravenscourt. Anyway, it was time she went; she'd promised Martha she'd experiment with a new kind of skinny muffin to tempt people hoping to stay thin.

Lorna could hear the low hum of their voices, too indistinct to make out any words as a clue to their conversation.

She jumped up smartly, the legs of her chair squeaking against the floor. Making more noise than she needed to, she began to clear the table of their mugs and a jug of milk, opening the dishwasher, hoping the noise would curb their ardour – if there was any, or Gloria urging Nathan to make an offer for Ravenscourt. Her mobile rang, scattering the notes of Debussy's *La Mer* over the room. At the same moment, Nathan and Gloria appeared, neither dishevelled as if they had been disturbed in a moment of abandon. Nathan smiled at her, took a few steps towards her and might even have kissed her if her mobile hadn't rung and he'd indicated that she answer it before she greeted him.

It was Flora, her voice raw with panic. 'Oh, Mum, help me, the baby is on its way and it's not meant to be born yet.'

Flora's anguish shocked her. Lorna stumbled, shot out her arm to save herself from falling and Nathan caught her. She clung to him with one arm while desperately trying to soothe Flora through her mobile clamped to her ear with her other hand. She found herself mouthing platitudes she did not believe; that everything would be all right, that it was a false alarm. Flora may have mistaken the pains for indigestion but she knew, with sickening intelligence, that the situation could be very serious indeed.

She must keep calm for Flora's sake, but Flora's fear transferred itself to her, adding to the anxieties that burdened her already, and it was Gloria who ended up taking the phone from her and sending down soothing messages.

'Your mother's on her way,' she said. 'Stay calm, that will be good for the baby, too. Don't worry, you're in the best place, they will know what to do. This may be terrifying for you, but it is every day stuff for them.'

Nathan gently untangled Lorna from him and sat her down on one of the chairs by the table, pulling up another chair so he could sit beside her, facing her. They were so close their knees touched, and he leant forward and took her hands. Quietly but firmly he tried to piece together what had happened, asking where Flora was, saying he would take her there at once.

'John Radcliffe hospital, I know it. She'll be fine, I'm sure. It is her first baby, they usually take ages, as you probably remember.' He smiled as if humouring her, stroking her hands as they ground together in her lap.

'She's only six months pregnant,' Lorna said, and his expression changed, eyes darting with pain, his lips clenched so tight the colour went from them. 'Let's get there, as soon as we can.' His voice was brusque and he jumped up, picking up her handbag that was under the table, fetching her coat from the hall and easing her into it. He gave off a sort of calmness and momentarily she felt soothed by it.

Once she had rung off, Gloria, who had lost so many babies herself, was less calm. 'Poor darling, I can't bear it for her. I could take you there if Nathan's busy. But it may be a false alarm and the contractions might stop, though she will probably have to stay in bed now until the end.'

Gloria meant well but her anxiety and grief at the memory of her own miscarriages increased Lorna's panic. Nathan, seeing her suffering, said, 'Lorna will be all right with me. We'll keep in touch, I'm sure everything will be fine.' He led her to the front door.

If only she had wings and could fly to her. Lorna pulled at his hand to go faster, not caring who came with her. She must get to her daughter as soon as possible. With a further word to Gloria, Nathan came out with her into the street. His car was outside and he opened the door and helped her in.

'We'll get there, try not to worry,' he said as he drove off.

The journey was a nightmare. Nathan drove fast, cutting expertly into the traffic, dashing through traffic lights just before they changed, but every time he did have to slow down or wait for some hold up, she wanted to scream. She prayed, made promises to fate or any God who was listening, to make everything all right and she would never ask for anything, ever again.

'They may be able to stop the baby coming. Or it may not be on the way at all and she is just having pains.' Nathan said. 'How old is she? Is there someone with her?'

Lorna told him the whole story, throwing out her fears about Ben and Tess and how she worried that they might somehow take the baby from them. Such foolish fears now, when there may not be a baby to take. Nathan did not interrupt her flow with questions but just listened, turning to her every so often to offer a word of support.

'Can it live born so early?' She implored him, going on before he could speak, 'I didn't want her to be pregnant this way, but it would be terrible to lose it.'

'The baby will always be there in your life, if it lives or not,' he said, and something about his voice made her look at him. She saw how tight his face had become; a muscle twitched with tension by his mouth. 'It will always be part of your lives, whatever happens.'

'Has something like this happened to you?' Why had she asked this? The words had formed themselves and slipped out before she could stop them.

'Yes,' his brief nod of acknowledgment was resigned; as though it was a burden he'd carried a long time. 'It broke up my marriage.'

'I'm so sorry.' Should she ask what had happened or would it be better to leave it as it was? But he went on,

'Helen, my ex-wife, and I lost a baby daughter, five Christmases ago. She didn't survive the birth and it broke our hearts.'

'Oh, Nathan, I'm so sorry,' Lorna put her hand on his as it gripped the steering wheel, the skin so tight she feared it would split. Gloria had mentioned he found Christmas difficult, now she knew why and she felt ashamed for making such a fuss about lending him Ravenscourt for his publicity shoot.

'I thought I'd got used to Lucy's death but suddenly, being confronted with the situation now with your daughter has brought it back. Grief is cruel, isn't it? Creeping up on you, tearing holes in you when you least expect it.' He turned briefly to her, his eyes tense with pain.

'If I'd known you'd been through this I wouldn't have let you drive me there,' she said violently.

'I'll be fine; you can't hide from such things. Look, we're here now.' He manoeuvred the car into a parking place and turned off the engine. 'Deep breath,' he said firmly, 'don't create dreadful situations in your imagination, worry about nothing until you have to. It may all be a false alarm.'

Now they'd arrived, Lorna felt leaden, unable to move. Flora needed her, yet she dreaded the grief she might find and her inadequacy in dealing with it. Then she remembered Stephen – why had she not thought of him before? Should she have told him? But how would he react? Turn up with the Pekinese woman? No, better to tell him when she knew more, it could, after all, be a false alarm.

For a moment she was fearful of leaving the intimacy of the car. Here she was safe, once she got out she must face up to whatever lay ahead, be strong, perhaps in the face of tragedy.

Nathan, sensing this, came round to her side of the car, opened the door and took her arm. He eased her out and led her into the hospital. It took a great effort not to lean on him, to put her arm round him and feel him close to her. Only a short time ago, she had driven Gloria to Adrian's bedside and how she hated hospitals, but this was worse, far worse, for this concerned her child, and she could not bear to think of her suffering.

Flora was in the delivery room with her 'partner', the nurse in the maternity wing told them. So Ben was there too. Flora had not mentioned him in her panic. She wondered if they'd been together when the pains had started.

'You must be her parents, she's doing well,' the nurse smiled. 'First grandchild?'

'N ... no ... yes ... I,' Lorna started, but Nathan said, 'Can her mother see her? I'll hang about, don't worry about me.' He gave Lorna a little push towards the closed door of the delivery room. 'Be strong and don't worry about me, I'll wait for as long as it takes ... oh, should I contact her father?'

'I ... I don't know.' She was afraid that Stephen, as he was now, might cause havoc. Would he turn up with that girl? That would upset Flora and she needed to stay calm, yet Flora was his daughter too and he would be grandfather to the child – if it survived. 'Yes, now we know she's in labour, perhaps he should be warned.'

'I'll ring Gloria for his number, has she got it?' Nathan asked her. She nodded, as the nurse said, 'see you later then, we'll let you know as soon as we have news.' She smiled broadly at Nathan as if she understood his squeamishness.

Lorna paused for a moment to watch him leave, feeling desolate without him. He turned back as though he knew she needed his strength and comfort, lifted his hand to his mouth and blew her a kiss. Then he turned the corner and was gone.

She was terrified at what she would find but she followed the nurse through some doors, put on a sterile gown, in a daze, before going into the delivery room.

The room was very bright, lights beaming down on Flora, whose face was clenched in pain, dripping with sweat. She was on the bed supported by pillows, her legs bent up. Ben sat miserably beside her. He was as white as a sheet, looking as if he would throw up at any moment. Flora caught sight of her and cried out, whether to Lorna, or in her pain, and in that moment the baby was born, slipping out into the midwife's outstretched hands.

The memory of that extraordinary feeling of bewilderment and wonder as a new being joined them, returned to Lorna, as if it were she who had just given birth. But this time she dared not look at the baby. She reached Flora, who was sobbing, and held her close.

'It's over now, darling, the pain is over.' She could be lying – the agony of grief if the child was stillborn would be far worse to bear than the pains of childbirth.

There was an air of calm efficiency in the room. Someone had taken the baby and was bending over it in a corner of the room. Then it cried, a tiny wail like a plaintive kitten, showing it was alive.

'A little girl,' someone said. 'You can hold her a minute, then we'll take her to be properly checked.' Wrapped in a towel, the baby was laid in Flora's arms.

Flora looked down at the tiny screwed-up face, her minuscule hands beating at the air. She held the child but seemed bemused by it. Ben too stared at it as if he was astonished by it. Lorna put her hand on the towel, feeling the tiny body though the material. She was so small, how could she possibly survive? Yet she seemed strong enough; large eyes staring, stick-like arms waving. None of us are ready for her, she thought. All the problems of her conception had not prepared them for dealing with a real, living thing, a person that would, as Nathan had said in the car, change their lives forever, whatever the outcome.

A minute later, the baby was whisked away to be cared for in the neo-natal intensive care unit.

'Oh, Mum,' Flora sank back, her face streaked with sweat and tears, 'I've never known such pain! It all came so fast. She's so tiny, what will I do?' She turned to Ben, perhaps hoping for some calm support from him, but he was too stunned to do more than grunt.

'She's lovely,' was all Lorna could say. A terrible dread had seized her heart. She wanted this child; she'd loved it at once, and could not bear to think she might not make it. She wanted to ask someone what her chances were, and yet she did not dare in case the news was bad. Stephen should be here. She ached for his support, the support she used to bank on. She must tell him that he had a granddaughter. The tears rose in her, such a special family occasion, but the joy would be taken from her as he was no longer there to share it. Marcus must know, and the rest of the family. Perhaps Felicity's hot line to God would come in useful now. She was about to say all this to Flora when she remembered that Nathan had come with her and was waiting for her. She felt relieved that it was him who was with her, and not Stephen in his new persona.

The midwife suggested that Lorna and Ben leave Flora so she could be tidied up. They could see her in the ward, and later Ben could go and see his daughter. He was visibly startled when the midwife, her black face creased in a smile, said 'his daughter', as if he had not taken in the events. Lorna kissed Flora, gently extracting herself from her clinging arms. 'You won't be long, darling, I'll see you in a minute,' she kissed her and tugging at Ben, led him out into the corridor.

'Let me get you a coffee, or something stronger,' she said when they'd left the room. 'It must be a shock for you both, her being born so early. We'll find a doctor and ask how she is. I'm sure you want to know.'

'I can't cope,' Ben bleated, coming to a halt, not noticing a patient being pushed on a trolley towards him, so Lorna had to pull him to one side so they could pass. 'We were just sitting there in this café talking and she had pains and water and now ...' his voice petered out.

'That's how it is,' Lorna said. 'Let's have a coffee, or perhaps a brandy, as we are both quite shocked – which is hardly surprising. Then we'll find someone to tell us how the baby is. We may have to wait while they thoroughly check her, but, small though she is, she did look strong.' She said this to comfort them both but she knew, from hearing stories of such events, that there were many things that could go wrong with premature babies, and the days ahead could be hazardous.

'I want Tess,' Ben said in desperation, 'I need her here to help me through this.'

CHAPTER THIRTY-TWO
On The Wrong Track

To her relief, Lorna saw Nathan coming in through the glass doors to the hospital. For a second before he saw her, his expression was unguarded, and she saw the strain etched there, and realised what this trip had cost him. His eyes were anxious as he reached her, his hand taking one of hers as he studied her face, bracing himself for bad news.

'The baby is alive. She's in the neo,-natal care unit as she's prem, but she's not a bad weight so the outlook is quite positive,' she said.

'I'm so glad, and Flora?'

'She's fine, well physically anyway. She's in a side room in the ward now and trying to sleep, but the whole thing was a terrible shock. I don't think she's realised that she is now responsible for another human being. But perhaps none of us realise it until we are faced with it. It's Ben who is not coping and perhaps I should hang around with him, but I told Flora I'd go home now and fetch some clothes and come back tomorrow and stay with her as long as it takes.'

'Ben? Oh the father. He'll come round to it, won't he?'

'He's called for his wife.' Lorna sighed, thinking painfully of Stephen. Families were meant to stick together in times of trouble, but he had broken the circle, and she could not forgive him for that.

'Ben is stunned by it and it seems he can't cope without her. Poor woman, it will be hard for her to get involved with his child, the child she wanted to carry herself.' A wave of exhaustion swept over her and she slumped down on a chair nearby. 'The complications of modern life are too much, I wish I could escape.'

'I know what you mean, and you've been through so much.' He sat down beside her, and took her hands in his. 'Can I get you a coffee or something stronger?'

'No thank you.' She tried to smile at him; he was being so kind. 'I'd like to go home if you don't mind. I've said goodbye to Flora, told her I'll be back tomorrow. Ben is with her and the baby is safely in special care. Though I long to stay, I think it important that the two of them are alone together to bond over this. If there are any dramatic changes I'll come back at once.'

'That's a good idea. You need rest too,' he said.

'I need to clear my head. I can't really believe I'm a grandmother,' she smiled wearily. 'It sounds so old.'

'You're hardly old.' His smile warmed her heart.

'Did you get hold of Stephen?' She asked, an ache in her heart.

'Gloria said she'd tell him, it's probably better coming from someone he knows,' he said.

How hard it was, not being able to share this with Stephen as he used to be. It was all too much; she covered her face in her hands and sobbed. The tiny girl wired up to life in an incubator was the next generation, a precious product of their marriage. She deserved the grandfather he used to be. Birth and death may bring families together, but they also exposed the broken relationships with painful clarity.

'It's all right, it's just the shock.' Nathan's mouth was against her ear, his arm round her shoulders, hugging her to him. She took a shuddering breath, kept her face hidden. How embarrassing was this? Almost as cringe-making as him seeing her in Clara's nightdress. She hoped she had a handkerchief in her bag, but she would have to reveal her face in all its ghastly, slobbering mess, while she searched for it. She felt the soft cool touch of linen against her face as Nathan said, 'here, take my handkerchief. Blow your nose and you'll feel better.'

'Thanks,' she mumbled, taking it and turning from him slightly so she could mop herself up without his scrutiny. She blew her nose. 'Sorry,' she said, still not looking at him. 'It has all been too much. I'll just go and wash my face.' She threw him a watery smile before she rushed to the Ladies.

She looked dreadful; blotchy and slug-eyed. She got some wads of paper towels, soaked them in cold water and pressed them to her face. After a few moments she looked slightly better. She tidied her hair and went out to find Nathan, and saw Ben and Tess standing at the reception. Ben looked pale and strained and Tess, her face stretched with tension, had her arm round him. She turned away, not wanting them to see her. Somehow they must resolve this drama between them. Poor Tess; what an ordeal for her.

Nathan joined her and put his arm round her shoulders.

'Sure you want to go?'

'Yes. That's Ben over there and his wife. It must be hell for her but I'll be intruding if I go over. Flora knows I'll be back tomorrow, and she needs to sleep. I'll be here really early. We're not allowed to be here at night anyway and it's almost that now.'

Nathan kept his arm round her as they walked to the car park. The air was sharp and cold and there was a slight mist of drizzle mingling with the dusk. 'I can see it's one hell of a mess but you've had enough for one day. Flora is well; the baby in good hands and now it is your turn to take care of yourself, or rather, perhaps you'll let me take care of you. Would you like dinner somewhere or home?'

'Home, please, but if you are hungry?' She turned to him gratefully. 'Thank you Nathan, for bringing me here and putting up with all this emotion, I really appreciate it, especially after ...' She paused, not wanting to wound him further by referring to his dead child. 'Thank you,' she smiled at him in the dark as they sped down the road.

There was silence for a moment then he said quietly, 'I would do anything for you, Lorna, if you would let me. This is hardly the place, or the time, but it may be the only opportunity I'll have of getting you all to myself,' he smiled, 'apart from that moment at Ravenscourt.' She could hear the amusement in his voice. 'I don't know what overcame me. I have to say you did

look a fright but a sexy fright and… well, there was something in
the air that night wasn't there?'

Before she could sort out her muddled emotions, he went
on, 'From the moment I first saw you …' he laughed, '… eating all my ham, I was drawn to you. And then you turned up
at Mulberry Farm with Gloria and Rosalind …' He paused, as
if waiting for her to say something, but she had not expected
this from him and tired and emotional after the day's events, she
stayed silent, not knowing how to react, he'd said he cared for her
and yet he was laughing at finding her in Clara's nightdress. Was
this a light hearted thing or…? He went on, 'and then there was
Ravenscourt.'

The word hung between them like a sword. What did he
mean? Was this the moment he would ask if he could buy it? She
couldn't cope with it, not now, not with all that had happened
today and her anxiety over the baby and Flora and how it would
all pan out. Her mind was half occupied with what she would
pack and how soon she would leave to drive back to the hospital,
she couldn't think of Ravenscourt now.

Nathan stopped the car, pulling into a lay-by. 'Sorry, silly
place and time to have started this, I just felt intimate with you,
the two of us together, alone in our tin bubble and I've known
this for a while, I can't get you out of my mind and I thought …
well, after that kiss that perhaps you … felt the same way, though
I admit you gave no sign of it.'

She could feel his gaze on her, and the increasing pressure of
his impatience for her answer, but she felt unable to respond, her

thoughts were so bound up with Flora and her tiny granddaughter, who as they sat here, could be fighting for her life.

'I don't know what to say. I'm so muddled with all that has happened to me over these last months. I'm not used to . . .' she paused, 'this sort of thing.' She finished lamely. 'I've been married so long, I've forgotten how to cope with it.'

Gloria wouldn't be sitting here, nervous as a nun, she'd have her arms round him by now, pulled him close to kiss him.

'I understand your feelings and I'm sorry to have started it just now, but Lorna, do you think there is a chance for us to get to know each other better? We share so much, don't we?' She imagined she detected a slight edge to his voice, which could have been nerves, or wanting to clinch a business deal to be done and dusted with no more delay.

They were so close in the dark warmth of the car. On one side of them was black, impenetrable undergrowth and on the other cars passed relentlessly on, the flash of their headlights picking them out as they whizzed by, reminding her of life outside and yet she felt no part of it, being here with him.

'At first I thought you were married to Beth, or anyway, with her,' she blurted, still feeling too vulnerable to unleash her true feelings for him.

'Beth,' he laughed, 'she's a great girl, been wonderful for the business, but that's all there is to it. I would so like you to be part of my life.'

She longed to say how much she wanted that. How she'd dreamt of it, but never thought it would happen. How when they'd kissed she'd meant it with every fibre of her body but had been too insecure to admit to it, in case it had meant nothing to him. He waited, watching but not touching her in the darkness. The tension in her mounted as she fought to find the right response, fearful that he would dismiss her declaration of love with some joke, some amusing remark that would belittle it. In her nervousness and tormented mind she killed the moment. Her voice came out like a rush of icy water dowsing a fire. 'And Ravenscourt?'

Brutally he started the car and shot out in the road, causing an oncoming car to blast its horn at him in panic.

She was mortified. She hadn't meant it to come out like that. She said, 'Gloria thinks it would be perfect for you. She said you wanted to move to a larger place and I … thought …' She stopped. She couldn't say anymore, couldn't bear to think that he was only saying these things to her because he wanted Ravenscourt. It obsessed her, had taken over her life and now it had destroyed it.

'Gloria is always full of ideas. Ravenscourt has nothing whatever to do with my feelings for you. But I'm sorry the emotion of today made me let down my guard. I apologise if I have embarrassed you by this, especially today.' His voice was hard, she felt as if he had slapped her. He had opened his heart to her and she'd responded by almost accusing him of trying to seduce her so he could get his hands on Ravenscourt. Or that is how he, with his painful pride, had interpreted it. He drove fast, his face tense, his eyes intent on the road ahead.

She was weary and shocked by the day's events; bruised by Stephen's betrayal, wishing he were here with her now, the man he used to be. If only Nathan had waited until she was more in control. She'd blown it and lost something important. She searched desperately for the right words to find it again. They were both too damaged from their past experiences and took offence too easily where none was intended.

'I didn't mean it like that,' she said at last. 'It's been a difficult day and ...'

'I know,' he said, 'and I was a fool to go on like that. Forget it, you're right. Ravenscourt is business and you know what they say about business and pleasure. I wouldn't want you to think I was trying to get it from you in any underhand way.' They drove miserably on until they reached her house. It was past ten o'clock and she felt she must offer him a meal, even a bed for the night, though he'd probably go to stay with Gloria, who, with her warm spirit, would surely comfort him.

'Please come in and have something to eat,' she said.

'No, thanks, I'd better get on.'

'I can't thank you enough for taking me to Flora,' she said. 'I feel ... I ... I'm sorry if I have upset you. I didn't mean to.' If only she had the strength to say she cared for him too, that she was inexperienced in the dating game after being so long married. With her loss of self-confidence and the anxieties of the day, she'd blundered in the wrong direction. Could he not understand that, and forgive her? It annoyed her now that he expected so much of her at this difficult time. She stayed silent, afraid of making things worse, too exhausted to struggle to make him understand.

He got out of the car and came round and opened the car door for her, standing back as if he were a just a chauffeur, a stranger to her.

'Good night, I hope all goes well for Flora and the baby.' He waited while she unlocked her front door. She longed to turn round and throw herself into his arms, but his coldness was like a barbed wire fence around him.

'Good night and thank you so much again,' she said, going into the empty house that should be singing with her husband and family cautiously celebrating the birth of this child, instead of being cold with desolation. She did not turn back to watch him leave.

CHAPTER THIRTY-THREE
Granny and Grandpa

She sat on the sofa in the living room with only a lamp on, the soft light and the darkness more fitting to her mood than full light, trying to process the magnitude of the day. She should try Marcus again. She fumbled for the phone and rang his mobile but there was still no answer. She debated leaving a text but thought that too cold. She yearned to talk to him, tell him the concerns for his … niece – so strange to think of him as an uncle. She'd try him again in the morning.

Gloria sent her a text saying that she'd told Stephen. He had her number, so why hadn't he contacted her to hear how Flora and the baby were? Was he so devoid of feeling he was unable to care? She'd texted Gloria with the news of the birth but she hadn't the energy now to speak to her. Also, she admitted to herself, she couldn't bear it if Gloria told her that Nathan was there, staying the night.

She was not going to contact Stephen, unable to cope with the thought of that girl, tucked up in bed beside him. The pain twisted in her. Even at this crucial time in their lives he had not contacted her. It was Nathan who'd been there, kind and supportive, even though it was so hard for him. He was grieving for his own lost child and in the turmoil of her mind, she had rejected him. It would be tough justice if he were in Gloria's arms.

She went upstairs to bed and lay there in the dark thinking about how her life had changed, praying for that tiny girl who had arrived too soon.

It was a painful, lonely night but eventually sheer exhaustion took her off into a troubled sleep. She woke early, the now-familiar sick feeling of dread squirming through her as the events of the day before thudded back to torment her. Flora had had her baby and she'd lost Nathan – not that she'd really ever had him – but she'd blown any chance she might have had with him by her crass response to his declaration of his feelings for her.

She hunched her pillows together and sat up against them, the empty side of the double bed, where Stephen ought to be, mocking her. She concentrated on the familiar objects in the room; portraits of the children done in Montmartre, some delicate porcelain figures left by her mother, a worn Steiff teddy bear much loved by three generations, but they brought her no comfort. Panic fluttered in her with fear and concern for the baby and Flora. She assumed, and hoped, that someone would have rung her if the baby's condition had deteriorated.

Nathan had all but said he loved her. It had cost him so much to admit it, and she'd not respected that. Unhappiness was a selfish emotion. Bound up in her own anguish she'd not noticed it in him, imagining him to be in control of his feelings and his life. True, she'd not known of his baby daughter's death, but now, as she recalled the times she'd been with him, his suffering had been there in his eyes and sometimes in his expression, and she had not taken it into account, forming her own opinion of him, without seeing the truth.

But overshadowing all of this was the premature birth of Flora's baby, her grandchild.

She crawled out of bed, feeling every inch an aged grandmother. It was almost six o'clock; she must get dressed and get ready to go back to Flora. First, she needed to talk to Marcus, but it was too early to wake him.

She checked her mobile to see if Stephen had left a message but there was nothing, only one from Rosalind promising prayers. Surely Stephen was concerned for Flora? She realised with a jolt that, she, his ex-wife, was the only person he could voice this to, and expect a consoling response. Odile didn't know Flora and would probably become jealous if his attention became diverted from her to his daughter. It seemed that Stephen had cut the lifeline that bound him to his family; the rhythms of births, marriages and deaths of their friends and family would always be in the background to haunt him.

She bathed and dressed, and made some coffee, flicking on the radio to fill the silence. She longed to ring the hospital, yet dreaded to find out whether the baby had made it through the night, fearful of facing up to it on her own, if she had not. The doctors had been reasonably optimistic about her chances, but there were many dangers ahead that could still snatch her away.

The telephone rang, making her jump and filling her with fear. She picked it up, and whispered 'Hello', her heart beating fit to burst. It was Gloria. 'How are things?' Her voice was strong, yet braced for bad news.

She burst into tears and Gloria, thinking that the baby might be dead, and maybe Flora too, told her to hold on, saying she'd be straight round. Before Lorna could control herself enough to tell her that as far as she knew everything was fine, Gloria had rung off and when she tried to ring her back, her telephone was switched on to answer phone. She left a message saying she hadn't heard anything and was leaving soon for Oxford, but ten minutes later Gloria was at the door.

'Oh Glory, I didn't mean you to rush round, but it's so good to see you. It's all been too much,' she blew her nose. 'The baby and Flora were all right when I left them. When do you think I can ring the hospital?'

'They would have rung you if anything terrible had happened.' Gloria said. She'd run round so fast she hadn't had time to put on her make-up. This she now did quickly in front of the hall mirror. 'What a fright for you, sweet of Nathan to take you though.' When she mentioned his name, Lorna saw her eyes glance imperceptibly upstairs, as if she expected him to appear half clothed in a towel, a lover after love.

Lorna guessed her thoughts. 'He's not here. It was so kind of him. He was wonderful, especially as he had been through a sad ordeal with his own little daughter. She was also born prematurely, but she didn't make it.'

Gloria regarded her with horror, 'I didn't know. I'd heard he'd had a difficult time in his marriage and it ended badly at Christmas time, so it's not his favourite time of the year. What happened?'

Lorna related the story, her heart aching with remorse at how badly she had treated him.

'Poor man, how dreadfully sad, no wonder he finds Christmas so hard. Where is he now?' Her eyes flickered over Lorna's face, searching out any hidden emotions. She couldn't keep anything from Gloria; she didn't feel up to it anyway, so shamefully, she confessed how she had blown it when he'd tried to tell her how much he cared for her, though she said nothing about that moment of abandonment in Ravenscourt. That would remain a secret, something she would pack safely away in the recesses of her mind, perhaps taking it out to mull over in the future when her body was long past lovemaking.

'Ravenscourt. If only I hadn't mentioned it, but it's such a major thing in my life. I never expected it and what with everyone telling me what to do with it, my sister and ... you, Glory, and Clara being worried it will go to some horrible person who'll somehow turf her out of her cottage – I've hardly grasped it's mine anyway,' she finished, desperately.

'Well, it is a major thing,' Gloria said. 'It's not every day you get left a huge and wonderful house let alone one that's on its last legs and needs urgent rescuing.'

'I must forget it now and ring Marcus, I couldn't get hold of him last night.' She dialled his number but still there was no answer. 'Tell me more about your call to Stephen, how did he take it?'

'It took me a little time to explain that it was a serious situation – for the baby anyway. He seemed more concerned about Flora, but it was a shock, as it was for all of us. I'm surprised he hasn't rung you, he's got your number hasn't he?'

'Yes,' Lorna said. 'It just shows how distanced he's become from the family.'

'Nathan told you he cares for you,' Gloria said, a little enviously. 'I've seen how he looks at you sometimes, and he often asked me casual questions about your marital state and all.' She paused. 'I have to admit, I fancy him like mad. I've only really got to know him this past year through the fairs. He's an amazing person, so attractive, but I'm not free yet from Adrian and any love affair I embark on would be for all the wrong reasons.'

'Perhaps we are chasing a fantasy and we can't cope with the commitment of the real thing,' Lorna said sadly. She'd been offered the real thing, and she'd mistaken it for a ruse by Nathan to get his hands on Ravenscourt.

Oh, Ravenscourt, what a poisonous chalice it had turned out to be, or perhaps, she had made it so. Dear Fergus, he should not have left the house to her. She did not deserve it.

Gloria, having not had time for breakfast before her dash here, made them both some toast and coffee. 'Everything always comes at once, but now concentrate on Flora and the baby. I can't get over the fact that you are a granny while you still could have another baby of your own!' she laughed. 'Crazy isn't it? But what fun we will all have with this little girl.'

The telephone rang again and both women stared at it in terror. Gloria picked it up and handed it to Lorna, putting her arm round her for support. It was Flora, ringing on Ben's mobile. Lorna's heart dropped when she heard her voice, dreading bad news, but Flora was upbeat. 'I've been to see her. She's so tiny, but they are pleased with her progress. Ben rang Dad, he said he ought to, as you already knew, and he rang his mother.'

'Oh, that's good of him. Gloria rang him to tell him you were in labour but it's good he knows she's here. I'm sure he'll ring you and come and see you,' she said, feeling guilty now that she hadn't spoken to him, though surely he could have rung her to ask how things had gone? 'How do you feel, darling? I'm so glad she's doing well.'

'Very sore, but OK. Will you come?' She sounded so young. Lorna remembered giving birth to Flora, the fear, the pain and the sudden joy when she was born, but then Stephen had been there, supporting her, sharing the whole, precious event with her. Resolutely she pushed the memories from her mind.

'I'm on my way. I'll stay down there until you come out, or need help at home. Where is home, by the way?' She thought of the flat Flora shared with three others, she'd been talking about finding something more suitable but the early birth had caught her out. 'We'll decide when I get there. I'll throw some stuff in a bag. Anything you want me to bring?'

There followed a list, most of which Lorna managed to dissuade her from having, since there was so little room in the ward she'd now been moved to. Just as she was about to ring off, Flora said, 'Can you ring Marcus? We're not allowed mobiles in the ward. I'm outside in the passage but I want to go back to bed. I've tried him but his mobile's off, forgot to charge it I suppose, or left it somewhere. And could you ring Dad too, see if he's coming to see us?'

'OK darling, see you soon, all my love.' She rang off. 'She wants me to ring Stephen but I can't ring him now, he'll be in bed with that girl,' she said to Gloria. 'He knows the baby's arrived, Ben rang him after her birth, he felt he should, and anyway Stephen could have rung me'.

'He's a grandfather now, that might cool her ardour,' Gloria said tartly. 'Foolish old men. I can see the same scenario happening with Justin and me; Adrian too incompetent with alcohol to be a reliable grandfather. God, if we'd known …' Her face creased with despair.

'Would we really have changed anything? We loved them and they loved us. For many years we were happy, then fate and circumstances turned them into impossible strangers. So many people never experience the happy times we once had.' Lorna was near tears yet again.

'But so many do, and stay happily together for a lifetime.' Gloria retorted. 'But I suppose you'd better ring Stephen. Get it over with, then he can't go for you saying you were too cruel not to tell him about your granddaughter. Then we can set off for Oxford. I'll come with you, I'd love to see Flora. Besides, you need some support, don't you?'

'But have you time?' How she'd welcome her company, but with all Gloria had to do, Lorna felt it was too much to make her feel she had to come.

'I have today. I've a meeting to arrange a charity lunch tomorrow afternoon and I'm going to see that shop we're using for the sales the day after but I'll take the Oxford Tube back. Now ring Stephen, then pack a bag and we'll go,' she said briskly, handing Lorna the telephone.

Feeling sicker by the minute, Lorna dialled his number. It rang five times and she almost put it down with relief, when it was picked up. A woman said, ''ello'.

'I want to speak to Stephen, it is his ex-wife and it is urgent,' she said sharply.

There was a quick intake of breath, and a mumbled something to Stephen. Then his voice, clipped and curt. 'Hello.'

'You heard from Ben yesterday that Flora's baby girl was born prematurely, making you a grandfather. She wants you to go and see her, or text her, perhaps, as mobiles are not allowed on the ward.' She sounded as if she was reading from an autocue.

'Is she all right, the baby … and Flora?' She could hear the panic in his voice.

Would he go down to see his daughter, taking that girl with him? This family crisis showed up his irresponsibility and defection in all its brutal light.

'She's in the John Radcliffe hospital. I'm going there in a minute with Gloria and will find out more then. If you want to see her I suggest you go there … alone.'

His voice was almost pleading now, 'When can I ring her?'

The tone of his voice melted her heart. He loved his daughter, despite his peculiar behaviour; somewhere inside him he still loved his children.

'I'll ring you, or she will when I get there. It's so sad that you've made it impossible for us to enjoy being grandparents together.' She put down the phone and dashed away her tears. Flora and that tiny girl were her priorities now.

Lorna packed a bag while Gloria found her a bed and breakfast on the Internet, then she said, 'Oh, Marcus, I suppose he's still asleep, but I must try and get hold of him again.' She rang his mobile.

'The baby's come early,' she said, when at last he answered. 'I tried to ring you yesterday and earlier today, so did Flora, but your mobile was turned off, and I wanted to tell you not text you.' She explained to him what had happened.

'Couldn't find my charger, but Jeez, so I'm an uncle, then,' he exclaimed, calling over to someone with him, 'Guess what? I'm an uncle.'

A new member of the family, Lorna thought, as she wondered what family Ben had apart from a mother who longed for a grandchild. Poor little girl, she'd landed herself in a complicated one. But that doesn't matter as long as she stays with us, she thought frantically. Please God, she whispered fervently under her breath, let her stay with us, be part of all the joys and all the imperfections of her family.

CHAPTER THIRTY-FOUR
Independence

Gloria sat at the table in Lorna's kitchen eating toast dripping with honey – comfort food in a crisis - and drinking black coffee, while Lorna dashed around getting ready to go to Flora. She'd offered to help and occasionally threw out comments, reminding her to pack a tooth brush and a book in case she had time on her hands and her mobile charger, but Lorna said she'd rather concentrate on her packing herself, she was only going to Oxford after all, not being cut off in some wilderness miles from anywhere.

The arrival of a new baby should be a happy occurrence, a celebration, but this birth was fraught with problems, the worst of which was that she was premature.

Poor Lorna, it had been one blow after another since Stephen went peculiar and left them. Now she was faced with this dreadful anxiety of a baby born too soon and the pain of having to face up to the fact that even that had not seemed to knock some sense into Stephen, or brought him home to be a support for them all.

Gloria thought of her own babies; four little ones she'd lost in the first three months of their existence. Then they'd had Justin and she'd been so close to losing him over Adrian's shaming behaviour. It had been so hard but she'd been right to ditch him to keep Justin close. She spoke to him occasionally and he'd seemed quite rational ... far away in Scotland, not slumped about at home.

She missed him even more now that Justin had gone back to Uni. The house seemed so quiet and the bed so cold and empty without Adrian's warm body snuffling there beside her at night. She must stop this nonsense; she'd done the right thing – thanks to Ravenscourt and their mad idea. She smiled as she thought of it; Ravenscourt had changed their lives.

Rosalind and Ivan seemed to have sorted out their differences, Ivan was trying to give more time to his family and as far as she knew, he hadn't bought any social workers home recently. Adrian, with the support of his sister was still in rehab, at least for the moment and Lorna ... Nathan loved Lorna.

She was stabbed with a pang of sorrow, envy even, but did she really want him? He was attractive, kind and fun but she'd sensed that pain in him and now she knew the cause of it; the loss of a child, the hardest pain to bear.

She was exhausted ... drained with the years of caring for Adrian. And what good had it done her? She was free now, independent, anyway for the moment, and she must savour it; use her freedom while it was here.

She wanted love; she wanted a loving sex life again but she wasn't ready for it yet. She'd married young, given so much and there were so many exciting things left to do without a man; travel, for example. Some of her friends lived abroad and she could visit them. They'd begged her to come and see them, but without Adrian, as they couldn't cope with his drinking. Now she could go while Justin was at Uni; flights were cheap if you shopped around. And she was going to learn how to make beauty products. She'd always been interested in the benefits of herbs and plants but coping with Adrian had curbed her time and energy to explore it. Now she would study them, see if it were possible to make some beauty creams and lotions and sell them at the fairs, or even further afield if they caught on, many people were now interested in using more natural products.

There was no shame in being a single woman today; in fact a lot of married women might envy them their freedom if they were grounded by the demands of increasingly difficult husbands. She laughed, joy rising in her, she'd enjoy this new independence. Perhaps she'd find love again one day, but she would not hang about waiting for it. She cleared up the breakfast things with a light heart. Having come to this conclusion, it really was quite a relief.

CHAPTER THIRTY-FIVE
The End Of The Affair

Their lives were taken over by baby Daisy; she was such a small person but she loomed so large in their lives and in their thoughts. Flora was soon discharged from hospital but stayed in Oxford to be near her, spending most of the day with her baby, feeding and caring for her as best she could. Lorna was amazed at the change in her, the drama queen, who exaggerated the smallest of life's trials; the petulant child who wanted things her own way. Flora had accepted and taken on this serious trial of motherhood with a courage and an energy that surprised her.

Lorna spent those first anxious days supporting Flora; Ben had to work, and visited each evening. Daisy was still in hospital. There had been a few setbacks; a flare of fever, and difficulties with her breathing, but she'd overcome them all, was getting stronger every day and would soon be allowed home. But where was home to be? In this tense time when no one dared ask if Daisy would survive and not be snatched away by some emergency, they'd not got round to thinking about that.

'She can't just tuck into Flora's bedroom like a hamster,' Gloria said, when she rang her. 'Remember babies need so much paraphernalia.'

'I'll talk to her.' Lorna found that she was too besotted and concerned about her tiny granddaughter to give her full attention to anything that did not feature her. She was also afraid to tempt fate by buying cots and prams and everything else a baby needed.

They spent a riotous day with Marcus. 'Let's hope she remains small and dainty with such a name,' he teased Flora. 'I'd have thought it better to have called her 'Cabbage' in case she grows to be round and fat.'

Flora swiped at him, but she was laughing, teasing Marcus back. He'd been afraid of his first sight of his niece, as if bits of her would snap off in his hands if he touched her.

Stephen had been to see the baby ... with the girl, though she'd remained outside. Lorna was relieved he'd come at a time when she wasn't there. Apparently he'd been overcome with tears at the baby's vulnerability. Lorna could not bear to question Flora about the meeting, tormented by the fact that they both worshipped and worried about this small girl alone. Instead of her, he would talk to the Pekinese woman about their grandchild, a girl who probably would not care, might even be jealous and demand a baby of her own. Perhaps as time went on, things would become easier between them, the two grandparents, but not yet, it was still too soon.

Back home for a few days, when all seemed calm, Lorna went out to supper with Gloria and Rosalind. She was longing to see them, to catch up on their lives and tell them about Daisy. She guessed they would want to talk about Ravenscourt. With the drama of Daisy's birth she had not even put it on the market. Now she must deal with it, swallow her pain, and indeed her guilt at having to sell Fergus's gift, as it was the only way to save it. Ravenscourt was a dream, just as Nathan had been.

'I'll contact an estate agent, one of my choice, for Ravenscourt at once, no point in prolonging it.' Lorna said, before Gloria and Rosalind could start on it. To keep her sanity, she did not allow herself to think about Nathan, or dream up various scenarios over the treasure she'd so foolishly thrown away. She must remain strong for Flora and for Daisy, who seemed to be thriving, and would soon be discharged into the care of her parents.

'Let's go down to the house once more.' Gloria said. 'I feel we owe it a debt, using it to get the men out of our hair over Christmas and changing our lives. Justin and Ellie are so in love, it's wonderful and it would never have happened if Adrian had been drunk all over the place. I feel like putting up a blue plaque,' she giggled, forming her fingers into a square. 'Ravenscourt, Depository for Difficult Husbands.'

Rosalind giggled. 'I can't believe the change in Ivan and the girls now he's realised his responsibilities as a father and husband. It helps that Polly's away too, he's so much more relaxed, and it's all thanks to Ravenscourt.'

'It's helped us all in its way,' Gloria said. 'Adrian seems to still be drying out and Justin and I – and possibly Ellie – are going to France to stay with my cousins in their chalet for Easter. We'll have given up the shop by then.'

'Let's drink to Ravenscourt, to Granny Lorna and Daisy.' Rosalind suggested, lifting her glass, her face glowing with the joy of living.

The highlight of Lorna's life was visiting Flora and Daisy, often staying a night or two at a pleasant B & B she'd found. At first, all attention had been on the progress of this tiny girl and Flora's recovery. Ben flitted in and out. When he arrived, Lorna always made an excuse and left them together. Once his mother came, a thin, whisper of a woman, who ignored everyone but the baby, cooing over her in a way that obviously irritated Flora, but, as she reminded her, she was Daisy's grandmother too and had as much right to love her as they did. This strange little family must make their own decisions, but now that Daisy was doing so well, Lorna thought she should be practical and offer to buy some baby equipment.

'I've been told of a good second hand baby shop, so I can buy her a cot and all that, or go to Peter Jones or Mothercare,' Lorna said. 'It's a granny thing to help out at the beginning, but of course you must choose,' she said quickly, before Flora told her not to fuss and that Daisy could happily sleep in a drawer or something. She bit back the real question she wanted to ask, which was 'where will you both live?' Flora had a couple of years more studying to do yet, and the flat she was in now was hardly a place to bring up a baby, especially one that needed extra care. It was like all student flats, a doss house with a succession of young people trooping through it, and would she live with Ben or on her own?

Flora looked at her, her clear eyes homing in on Lorna's face. 'We can come home for a little while, can't we? I don't want to go to Ben's mother,' she scowled.

'Of course you can come home while you get settled, there will always be a place here for you, Daisy and Marcus, but what about the future? Where will Ben fit in?' Despite her determination not to interfere, Lorna had to ask.

'He wants to be part of it,' Flora said. 'Of course he does. He's besotted with her, we all are. His mother lives miles away and fortunately his sister has just announced that she is pregnant and she's almost fifty,' she exaggerated.

'And Tess?' Lorna asked, wondering how this poor woman was coping.

Flora looked uncomfortable. 'She and Ben are still together and I suppose that when Daisy is bigger she'll visit their house, I don't know, but I think Ben's better with her than with me.'

'I expect you're right, darling,' Lorna said, thinking they would have to work it out for themselves; relationships came in all sorts of shapes and sizes.

'I'll find a flat or something until I've finished Uni and I can put Daisy in a crèche while I'm studying, we'll take it a step at a time, see what happens,' Flora said.

Life at home was busy when Flora and Daisy came, the nights often disturbed, and she felt exhausted. Gloria begged her to take them to Ravenscourt one more time before it was sold. She agreed she would, but always gave some vague date sometime in the future; when it was warmer, when Flora and Daisy had moved into the flat they'd found, until Gloria said if they didn't do it soon Ravenscourt would either be sold or have fallen down.

But events took over. To her surprise, a couple of weeks after it was put on the market (with a different estate agent to the ones sent by the Harwoods) the agent rang her to say that an offer, just over the asking price, had been made. There were quite a few large and better cared-for houses on the market, and though Ravenscourt had been viewed by a sizable amount of people, not much interest had been shown in it, and it was a good offer. She agreed it was, far more than she thought she would get for it, and yet she felt sad that she had to let it go. But it was to save it, she reminded herself, the only way to preserve it. So, after questioning the agent, she reluctantly accepted the offer.

The name of the buyer meant nothing to her. The agent thought it was a developer, which didn't surprise her, but he said that they loved the house and would restore it and not pull it down and fill the space with smaller houses, which clinched the deal for her. She put it all into the hands of a conveyancing lawyer to deal with. She would take the girls down before it went, but first she would go alone and say goodbye to Ravenscourt on her own.

It was ridiculous that she didn't have a key to the house. Each time Clara had been there to let her in, so she hadn't bothered to get one. She was wary about telling her she was coming in case she told the Harwoods and Nathan got to hear of it. She had not heard from him since the day of Daisy's birth and as time passed she'd convinced herself it was for the best that she'd had a lucky escape from being hurt again. But it would be madness to drive all that way and find that Clara was out or away with her daughter, and she could not get in. No doubt she could get a key from the estate agent, but they were ten miles further on and then she'd have to drop it back, it was too much of a hassle.

She rang Clara and said firmly, 'Will you be there tomorrow, Clara? If not, there must be somewhere you could leave the key for me. But please, you are to tell no one I am coming. I've lots to do here so I don't know exactly what time I will be there.' She hoped that sounding vague about when she'd arrive would deter Clara from telling anyone.

'I'll be here tomorrow,' Clara said.

The day was bright, hard brittle sunlight on the winter land. Ravenscourt looked better now in the sunlight, as though it held hope of a new life instead of one ending in decay. The sight of it tugged at her heart, but she had no choice but to let it go.

Clara welcomed her with the usual coffee and homemade biscuits, though she was quite subdued, no doubt chastened at the thought of Ravenscourt changing hands. She asked about Flora and the baby, and told her about the progress of her grandson. When they had exhausted that topic, she tentatively asked if Lorna knew who had bought the house.

'I saw quite a few of the people coming round and I wonder which one made the offer. I didn't know their names, so I won't be able to put a face to them,' she said.

'It's a company, some complicated name, I'll check later with the agent. He said he'd meet me here later this afternoon, we'll know more then. He promised they'd be sympathetic to the house, restore it rather than pull it down, and leave you in peace in your cottage.'

Clara got up and took her coffee cup to the sink. 'I'll leave you to potter around on your own, if you don't mind. I'm packing to go to Gina's at the weekend. Ring me if you need anything.' She left quickly, as if she couldn't bear to think that Ravenscourt had gone.

Lorna wandered from room to room. The windows had been cleaned, the greenery cut back and the sunlight poured in, touching each room, somehow softening the bad bits, adding a kind of magic. She peeped into Fergus's study; it was plain and clean. For a moment she allowed herself to remember that sudden flash of passion. The irony of it was that she'd thought it was just a game, a sudden impulse soon forgotten. How foolish and tragic were such misunderstandings. She shut the door on it. It would become just another secret to grow old with the house.

Going back into the hall, she saw a wrinkled piece of holly left from the shoot which had transformed the house into a Christmas wonderland. Dear Ravenscourt, it had set them free from their destructive marriages, given them a new life.

Fergus had loved this house, cared for it until he had become too infirm and too broke to continue; rather like their husbands had become unable to love and cherish their families any more. It was right that the house should be sold to someone who would love it in their turn and restore it again, pity that all their marriages could not be treated in the same way.

She went outside and wandered up the old lawn, thick with moss, until she reached the clump of trees and the stile. She climbed over and jumped down into the field that still belonged to the property, drinking in the view of the Downs; the sweep of green and the ancient trees. Nathan had found her here, lent her his jersey, taken her hand and led her back to the house. Her heart ached and impatiently she tried to shake off the thought of him. She was moving on, saying goodbye to Ravenscourt and Nathan – by proxy – before starting out again on a new life – a life that included Daisy, which lifted her heart.

She turned to go back to the house and there was Nathan at the edge of the field, watching her. She blinked; surely she was imagining it, a silly woman seeing things. He pounded across the field to her, too strong and vital to be a ghost. Clara must have disobeyed her and told him she was here. No doubt Sonia and Beth were here too, ready to do battle for Ravenscourt, forbid her to sell it to anyone but them, but it was too late. She scowled, could no one leave her alone; let her get on with her own life?

'You don't look pleased to see me,' Nathan reached her. 'Am I disturbing you?'

'Yes,' she said. 'I wanted to be alone here, drink in this wonderful view for the last time while it is still mine. I told Clara not to tell you I was coming, but I suppose she took no notice.'

'I told her, ordered her, to tell me if you came here again. I'm afraid she did what I asked.'

'Are Sonia and Beth here, too?' She asked, keeping her eyes on the sprawling land.

'No. Why should they be? It's just me. Me and you.'

He was so close she could have put out her hand and touched him yet she did not. He'd said that he cared for her, but those words were said at the height of supreme emotion; he must now be relieved that she'd turned him down. He'd wanted Ravenscourt, not her, but now someone else had snapped it up. She wondered if he knew that, she'd only just accepted the offer after all. Once he knew it had gone, he could stop this charade of pretending that he loved her.

'How is Flora? And the baby?' he asked.

'Fine, Daisy is doing well.'

'I'm so glad.'

She turned to him then and caught the pain in his eyes. Why do we make each other suffer so, she thought, when fate puts us through enough as it is?

'I came to say goodbye to Ravenscourt,' she said. 'I'll be down again; Gloria and Rosalind want to come for the last time.' She braced herself for his anger. 'I accepted an offer on it a couple of days ago. I came alone to say my own goodbye.'

His expression remained calm. 'Maybe that's a bit premature.'

'Oh, I know deals fall through. This one probably will when they have a survey, but I came all the same.'

'This one won't fall through.' He watched her but she would not look at him, as if she were afraid he'd see her feelings deep inside her. For a moment he concentrated on the landscape;

the gently undulating earth, the ancient trees offering their bare branches to the sun.

She said quietly, 'You seem very confident.'

'I am. I made it.'

She faced him, frowning. 'Made what?'

'The offer. I made the offer for Ravenscourt and you have accepted it.'

'That's not true,' she burst out. 'Oh, why do you torment me so? It's a business that's bought it. I can't remember the name off the top of my head, but it's not you, you don't have enough money. You told me you didn't; that you couldn't afford to pay to use the house to photograph your brochure.' She accused him before he could deny it.

He grabbed her hands, holding them tight in his own, determined now to have no more misunderstandings.

'Lorna, *you* have decided that I have no money. *You* have decided that I don't love you but swallowed my revulsion and kissed you, and later when you were most vulnerable after Daisy's birth, said I loved you so I could get my hands on Ravenscourt. Admit it.' He shook her hands impatiently. 'Both of us have been badly hurt and we're like two hedgehogs that can't get near each other because we're too prickly to trust each other's feelings. Why can't you accept that I love you? Even if you hadn't inherited Ravenscourt, I would still love you.'

She looked bewildered, as if she assumed this was some trick. Like him, she'd built a wall around her emotions, protecting them from further pain, but he was determined to knock them down.

'But Nathan, you said you had cash flow problems, you haven't …' she paused, looking embarrassed, 'well, you haven't made an offer you won't be able to honour, have you?'

'Of course not.' He sounded offended, then checked himself. He explained that he had said that he couldn't afford to pay the rent on a suitable venue for his brochure, which was true at the time, but that now he had rearranged his financial affairs and he had the funds. He said more gently.

'Lorna, *you*, and perhaps Gloria and Rosalind, have decided I have no money and perhaps my way of life confirms this. A man of my age living with his mother, cooking hams,' he laughed. 'I have a few Internet businesses of my own, with partners. I put them aside when my father became ill and I had to sort out his affairs. I told you that, but maybe you didn't take it in. My marriage broke up, I sold my flat in London, walked out of my job.'

'It sounds worse and worse,' she said.

He linked his arms round her waist, smiling at her. 'I need somewhere of my own to live and to run my business from, so I made the offer for Ravenscourt.'

She did not look convinced. 'My ex-husband's mind was changed by being given anti-depressants and I've lost trust in people. Inheriting Ravenscourt panicked me; I must sell it and you say you made the offer I've just accepted, but I'm sorry, it doesn't sound as if you have enough money to cover it.'

'I promise it's fine,' he smiled. 'I've just sold one of my Internet businesses for a fortune, a holiday letting thing, so I've plenty of money for Ravenscourt. I plan to expand and move my food business to it, get someone else to run it. Beth, perhaps,' he watched her.

'I see, so it all worked out for you in the end,' she said quietly.

'Not quite.' He stroked back her hair, which the wind had blown over her face. 'None of it will work unless I have you.' He held his hands out to her and she saw that his wedding ring was no longer on his finger 'I love you,' he said pulling her to him, 'I want it all, you and Ravenscourt, together.'

He saw the joy in her face, slight at first, as if she couldn't quite believe it. She said, 'But surely there are other women you'd rather be with.'

'Of course there are other women,' he said in exasperation, 'but I don't want other women. I want you, in that huge, pink nightdress and those long, black boots, they were a real turn on,' he laughed, kissing her.

At last they drew apart and, holding hands, they walked over the field and back through the trees. There was Ravenscourt, lit by the winter sun as if it were waiting patiently for the next phase in its history. Nathan put his arms round her, holding her close, 'We shall save Ravenscourt together,' he said, as he kissed her.

EPILOGUE

Christmas At Ravenscourt

A whole year had gone and what a year it had been starting with Daisy's birth then coming together with Nathan and the two of them saving Ravenscourt. Lorna stood outside the house now in the dark, the snow falling silently around her. She shut her eyes a moment and could feel the silence around her and the cold touch of the snow flakes on her face.

She'd come from Clara's cottage with Nathan's Christmas present; a cheerful Norfolk terrier. He loved dogs but Gloria told her he wouldn't have another one until he was settled somewhere. This was her surprise present for him. She'd chosen – or rather the puppy had chosen her – from a litter of a friend's dog. She'd decided to give him to Nathan today, Christmas Eve.

The lights from the windows of Ravenscourt glowed out in the dark. It was only teatime and soon the curtains would be drawn, locking in the magic of the house, the feeling that all the slumbering memories of the past years had been given new life.

She lingered a moment outside the massive front door flanked by two carriage lamps, lighting up the wreath hanging from the brass knocker. Lorna smiled. When she opened the front door this time, there'd be no film extras acting out 'happy' guests, no room concocted in the corner of a bleak warehouse, no glitzy paper hiding imagined presents.

She opened the door. The puppy pulled forward on his lead, barking an introduction. The hall was garlanded in fresh evergreen leaves with fruit, berries and gold painted walnuts threaded through them. A huge, sparkling tree stood by the stairs; logs glowed in the fireplace, the scent of apple wood mingled with the sweet smell of roasting ham. There were sounds of people laughing, of music. Fergus, she thought fondly, this is how you wanted it to be, I wish you were here to share it with us.

Kit, Nathan's son, ran by, closely followed by Marcus. She heard Gloria's infectious laugh coming from the drawing room. Marcus stopped and whirled round to face her.

'A puppy.' His face lit up, he called to Kit and then they were all there; Sonia, Gloria, Justin and Ellie, Rosalind with Ivan (happily back together), and their daughters, Adrian here with his sister for Christmas on one of his frequent visits back home, and Flora carrying Daisy, who shrieked with excitement when she saw the terrier, who nearly wagged his bottom off with delight at being the star of the show.

'What's happening?' Nathan came down the stairs; she smiled at him over the heads of the others.

'Just your Christmas present,' she said.

The others stood back and Nathan came into the hall. The little dog watched him with excitement. He put his arm round her as the puppy jumped up at him, licking his hand. Who would have thought so much could have happened in a year? She was so happy, complete again, surrounded by her children, her granddaughter, Nathan, the man she loved, and her best friends. This year, Christmas at Ravenscourt would be a triumph.

Letter from Mary

First of all, I want to say a huge thank you for choosing *Difficult Husbands*, I hope you enjoyed reading my novel just as much as I loved writing it.

If you did enjoy it, I would be forever grateful if you'd write a review. I'd love to hear what you think, and it can also help other readers discover one of my books for the first time.

Also, if you'd like to keep up-to-date with all my latest releases, just sign up here:

www.bookouture.com/mary-de-laszlo

Thank you so much for your support – until next time.

Mary

Printed in Great Britain
by Amazon.co.uk, Ltd.,
Marston Gate.